AVENGERS
OF THE
MOON

AVENGERS
OF THE
MOON

A CAPTAIN FUTURE NOVEL

ALLEN STEELE

TOR

A TOM DOHERTY ASSOCIATES BOOK · NEW YORK

AVENGERS OF THE MOON

Copyright © 2017 by Allen Steele

Illustration on p. 9 by Rob Caswell

Permission granted by The Huntington National Bank
for the Estate of Edmond Hamilton.

A Tor Book
Published by Tom Doherty Associates
175 Fifth Avenue
New York, NY 10010

www.tor-forge.com

Tor® is a registered trademark of Macmillan Publishing Group, LLC.

The Library of Congress Cataloging-in-Publication Data is available upon request.

ISBN 978-0-7653-8218-4 (hardcover)
ISBN 978-1-4668-8644-5 (e-book)

Our books may be purchased in bulk for promotional, educational, or business use. Please contact your local bookseller or the Macmillan Corporate and Premium Sales Department at 1-800-221-7945, extension 5442, or by e-mail at MacmillanSpecialMarkets@macmillan.com.

First Edition: April 2017

Printed in the United States of America

0 9 8 7 6 5 4 3 2 1

*For Edmond Hamilton—Captain Future's creator
and the father of space opera*

Contents

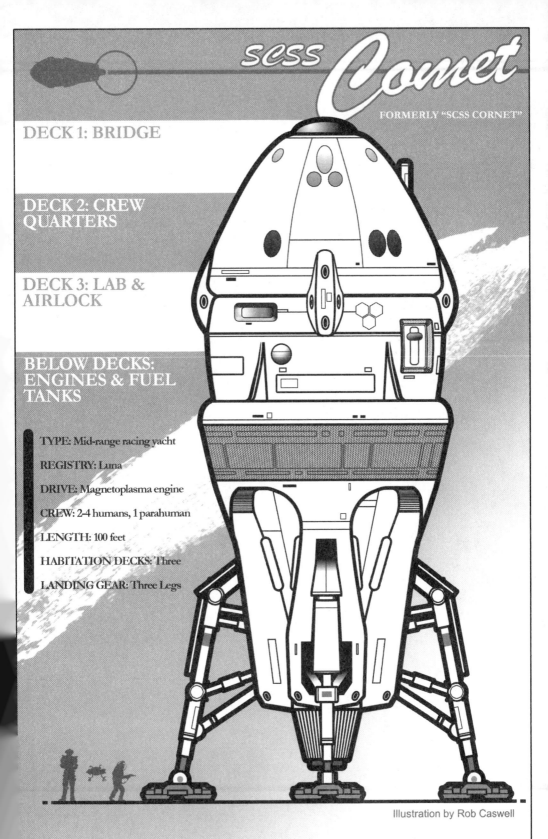

scss Comet

FORMERLY "SCSS CORNET"

DECK 1: BRIDGE

DECK 2: CREW QUARTERS

DECK 3: LAB & AIRLOCK

BELOW DECKS: ENGINES & FUEL TANKS

TYPE: Mid-range racing yacht

REGISTRY: Luna

DRIVE: Magnetoplasma engine

CREW: 2-4 humans, 1 parahuman

LENGTH: 100 feet

HABITATION DECKS: Three

LANDING GEAR: Three Legs

Illustration by Rob Caswell

AVENGERS
OF THE
MOON

PROLOGUE

The Solar Age

It was an age of miracles. It was an era of wonder. It was a time of new frontiers.

In the twenty-first century, humankind gradually came to the realization that its home world—crust depleted of nearly all usable resources, ice caps melted and coastal cities flooded, skies tinted a sickly reddish-orange hue at sunset from overdependence upon fossil fuels—could no longer support everyone, and therefore long-term survival lay in the colonization of space. Because the stars were too far away (at least for the time being) this left the other worlds of the solar system as the only places to go.

Gradually, tentatively, with small and reluctant baby steps that soon became a confident pace and finally a headlong sprint, the human race left Earth and went out into the void, exploring worlds previously visited only by unmanned rovers and flyby probes, transforming them into humanity's new home.

At first, few efforts were successful. The effort to terraform Mars into Earth's companion took longer than expected and eventually would have to draw upon the resources of the rest of the system. Venus has always been Hell in real life, and the catastrophic failure of the first expedition there reinforced the belief that it always will be. The moons of Jupiter and Saturn, along with the minor planets of the asteroid and Kuiper belts, possessed seemingly endless resources, but were cold and hostile places that could kill a careless person in seconds. For a time, it seemed that the solar system would never be anything more than a remote frontier populated only by the desperate and the crazy-brave, until it was realized that the answer didn't lie in trying to conquer these planets, but adapting to them.

And so humankind tinkered with its own genome and eventually created cousins who could live comfortably on these distant worlds. By the first years of the twenty-fourth century, the human race and its relatives had become a spacefaring species that inhabited more than one world.

It was a golden age. From the sky city of Venus to the desert settlements of Mars, from the craterhabs of the Moon to the underground burrows of Titan and Ganymede, from the mining stations of Ceres and Vesta to Pluto's prisons and Sedna's border outposts, there were politicians and poets, scientists and wanderers, dancers and soldiers, savants and holy fools, the powerful and the powerless, the wealthy and the destitute, those who fought the good fight and those whose intentions were selfish, if not downright evil.

It was a time of troubles. Wasn't it always?

It was all of these things and more . . . except there were no heroes.

Naturally, one had to be born.

PART ONE

Encounter at the Straight Wall

1

The Straight Wall is considered one of the great sights of explored space. Included in *100 Wonders of the Universe* as the Moon's sole entry, it's one of the only three planetary formations on the list visible from Earth, the other two being the Great Red Spot of Jupiter and Saturn's ring system. It's located in the southeast quadrant of Mare Nubium, in the lunar southern hemisphere just east of Birt Crater; a good telescope can find it on a cloudless night.

A sheer and unbroken row of bluffs about eight hundred feet tall, the Straight Wall runs southeast by northwest across the flat volcanic mare until it disappears over the horizon. Sixty-eight miles long and a mile and a half wide, it resembles a dark gray tidal wave suddenly suspended and petrified in place. If one stands at its base and looks up, it can even appear as if the Wall is about to fall forward, crushing everything beneath it.

Although its origins as a fault scarp are well understood by lunar geologists, some have claimed that the Wall is anything but a natural feature. It is instead, they say, an extraterrestrial artifact, an immense sculpture carved from native rock by visiting aliens for reasons that remain mysterious. The Sons of the Two Moons in particular hold this belief, but it goes back as far as the late twentieth century, when pseudoscience was but one of the many problems bedeviling the inhabitants of that dark time. This notion was discredited long before the first explorers set foot in the Mare Nubium at the dawn of the Solar Age, and it might have remained a lunatic theory—no pun intended—were it not for the discovery of the Deneb Petroglyphs.

The petroglyphs are a major reason why the Straight Wall is considered one of the Wonders of the Universe.

It took years for scientists and historians to get their way, but they finally persuaded the Solar Coalition Senate to pass a resolution declaring the site a System Monument, thereby enabling the Lunar Republic to take measures protecting the petroglyphs from souvenir collectors. The petroglyphs were treated with a chemical preservative and shielded behind a glass screen, then the entire site was enclosed by a pressurized dome erected against the cliffside. When the work was finished, it appeared that the western flank of the wall due east of Birt Crater had sprouted a semitransparent blister that glowed from within, making it brightly visible when the Moon entered its waning phases and the Wall cast a slowly lengthening shadow across the adjacent plain.

It was the dedication of the Straight Wall System Monument that drew Curt Newton. He'd visited the Wall a couple of times, and only two years earlier he'd spent a week hiking the entire length of its upper parapets, an ordeal he'd undertaken with no company except Grag as his quiet but indispensible sherpa. Yet the petroglyphs had fascinated him since childhood, and when the Brain finally gave him permission to leave Tycho, this was one of the first places he asked Simon and Otho to take him.

Curt was nine the first time he visited the Wall. Eleven years later, he came back again. Now he had returned once more.

Curt dropped the hopper at the edge of the landing field. He was still shutting down the engine nacelles when Otho turned to him. "All right, now listen," he said to the young man sitting beside him in the bubble cockpit. "There's going to be a crowd here, maybe more folks than you've seen before. So whatever you do—"

"Don't stare." Curt unsnapped his seat harness and stood up to squeeze past him. "Don't stare and don't talk to anyone."

"Not unless you have to. Let me handle the security detail. Is your tattoo still in place?"

Curt checked his left hand. The temporary (and fake) ID he'd let

Otho heat-transfer to the back of his hand was still there. Its code attested that his name was Rab Cain and that he was a freighter crewman from Earth, North American Province; Otho's tattoo stated that he was Vol Cotto, a native selenian, resident of Port Kepler. "What if I meet someone interesting?"

"Then it's okay to talk, but just enough not to be rude." Otho followed him into the aft compartment. Like Curt, he was already wearing his vacuum suit; all they needed to do was put on the rest of their gear from the suit rack. "You know the rules. Nothing about yourself. You have no name—"

"I have no home, and it's nobody's business who I am." Curt recited the edict from memory. It had been drilled into him from the very first time he'd been allowed to come up from beneath the crater. Obeying the rules was the only way the Brain let him journey out from Tycho Base; if he broke them, he'd spend the next three lunar days underground, an isolation that had become increasingly hard to stomach.

—We're serious about this, Curtis. You're still becoming acclimated to dealing with others on their own terms, and your safety depends on maintaining anonymity. No one must learn who you are . . . particularly now!

The Brain's voice coming through his Anni implant caused Curt to glance at the large ring on his left hand. He hadn't yet pulled on his gloves, so he could see the central jewel in its platinum setting. The diamond glowed with a light of its own, affirming that the Brain was connected to him via augmented neural-net interface.

—What do you mean by that, Simon? he thought. Why not, "particularly now"?

A reluctant pause, unusual for Simon Wright. —All will be explained. Just stay close to Otho and don't speak to—

"Sure," he said aloud. "Got it." He glanced at Otho, who was tapped into the conversation. He was expecting the sly wink the android often gave him when Simon lectured him. Yet Otho's face—stark white, hairless, and unblemished—was solemn. For some reason, his closest friend wasn't in a joking mood today.

They pulled on their gloves, airpacks, and helmets, and then depressurized the hopper, opened the side hatch, and stepped down the ladder to the landing pad. It was crowded with transports of all kinds, from short-range craft like their own to big lunar buses chartered from the big cities in Mare Tranquillitatis and Mare Imbrium to the north. The fanciest, though, was a limo that had touched down beside the blister itself, with a pressurized ramp leading to the monument's main airlock. Curt admired the ornate and utterly nonfunctional scrollwork around its landing gear, and the cherubs holding its lamps and communications array, and knew at once that it belonged to a wealthy individual. Exactly whom, he could not say, but apparently the dedication was being attended by some very rich and powerful people.

This impression was confirmed once he and Otho cycled through the airlock, removed their suits in the ready-room, and made their way through the security checkpoint. Lunar society had a class system of its own, and one way of telling who belonged to the upper crust was how they entered the blister. The elite didn't have to bother with the messy business of standing for five minutes in the scrubber while electrostatic brushes whisked away the regolith, or having to peel out of pressure suits. They walked straight into the dome through the enclosed gangways mated with taxis sent to collect them from their private transports; the rich never needed to put on or take off helmets, or put up with filthy decontamination procedures.

Past the main entrance was the monument's central atrium, a geodesic half-hemisphere of radioactive-filter lunaglass built against the lower bluffs of the Straight Wall, illuminated by light fixtures within the support rafters. The floor was crowded with visitors, both those who'd received invitations and the hoi polloi who'd somehow managed to get in. The former were dressed for the occasion: the men in frock coats, striped trousers, and mandarin collars, the women in sleek gowns with plunging necklines and thigh slits, their shoulders warmed by brocaded silk capes. Even the weighted ankle bracelets worn by those who weren't born and raised on the Moon were fancy; some were made of gold or silver, with elaborate designs inscribed upon them. The waiters came to them with champagne stems and canapé platters, pointedly ignoring those wearing functional yet unadorned bodysuits commonly found beneath a loony's vacuum gear. Clearly anyone dressed like that would've had to come in through the public airlock, and those weren't the people on the guest list. The Lunar Republic prided itself on its efforts at democratic inclusiveness, but the fact remained that, as always, the rich were different.

Curt didn't care. Standing against the curved lunaglass wall behind him, he quietly observed the crowd. Regardless of what the Brain had told him about staring, he couldn't help himself. Seldom had he seen so many people before, and never in such variety. Here were not only terrans and selenians such as himself, baseline Homo sapiens whose genomes remained unaltered, but also the cousins of humankind, *Homo cosmos*: red-skinned, raven-haired aresians of Mars, barrel-chested and thin-limbed; the ebony, platinum-haired aphrodites of Venus, elegantly slender, the women in particular possessing a haunting beauty; the pale and hairy jovians of the Galilean moons, taller and more muscular than anyone else, the men bearded and perpetually scowling. And here and there, scattered among them, individuals who superficially resembled terrans but whose clothing and manners revealed them to be kronians and tritons. There was even a pair of kuiperians, visitors from the outermost reaches of the system rarely seen this close to Earth, their features hidden by veils and cowls, shunned by everyone around them as the cannibals they were reputed to be.

Curt had seen inhabitants of the Solar Coalition worlds before, but never this many at once. He wanted very much to speak with a few, and his desire must have been obvious to Otho, for his companion stepped closer to him to speak softly in his ear.

"No," he murmured. "I know what you're thinking . . . and I'm sorry, but you can't."

—*It's much too dangerous,* the Brain added.

"What's so dangerous about talking to people?" Curt asked aloud, keeping his voice low. He tried to take a glass of champagne from a passing waiter, but the tuxedoed servant sidestepped him without so much as a glance; the drinks were not for riffraff like him. "C'mon, Simon . . . how am I supposed to learn more about them if you won't let me speak to some?"

—At any other time, my boy, I'd agree. But now isn't the time. The reason why members of all these different races are here is because most of them are representatives of the Coalition Senate or members of their staffs. Others are corporate executives, business representatives, plane-tary traders, and the like. President Carthew will be speaking, so secu-rity is tight. The last thing you want to do is draw attention to yourself.

"I hate to say it, but Simon's right," Otho said. "There's a reason why we're here . . . and I don't want to do anything that may put you at risk."

Curt gave him a sharp look. "What are you talking about? We came here to view the Deneb Petroglyphs."

"And we will, but—"

—There is something else as well. Something that is very important to you.

Curt knew better than to argue with either Simon or Otho. Indeed, it often seemed that the only member of his family with whom he was ever able to win a fight was Grag. All the same, though, he was puz-zled, and a bit irritated as well. But he kept his mouth shut as he and Otho slowly made their way through the atrium, slipping between knots of people as they headed toward the front of the room. Curt did his best to avoid colliding with anyone, but this was the first time he'd been in a crowd this size; he jostled a couple of elbows and stepped on someone's foot, and by the time they reached the temporary stage set in front of the Wall, several people had hissed curses at him and Otho.

Several rows of chairs were roped off for the VIPs. A security officer in the dark blue uniform of the Interplanetary Police Force wordlessly waved them away from the seating area, so they found a place off to the side where they could still view the podium and—more impor-tant, so far as Curt was concerned—the petroglyphs.

The Deneb Petroglyphs were considered the most mysterious object in the solar system. No one had even suspected their existence until men ventured into this region of the Moon in the mid-twenty-first century, and in the 250 years that had passed since then, none who'd studied them had learned more about their meaning or origins than that which had been deduced shortly after their discovery.

First, the petroglyphs were old, very old. One hundred feet tall by seventy feet in length, carved into a smooth, semirectangular slab of lunar basalt by some form of focused energy; the presence of overlaying surface erosion caused by tectonic movements and micrometeorite impacts led selenologists and archeologists to determine an approximate age of one million years, give or take a millennium or two. This meant that the aliens who'd made them had passed through the solar system during the Pleistocene, when humankind was little more than a few Homo erectus tribes that still hadn't made their way out of Africa.

Second, the aliens who'd come here had provided a clue about the place from which they came. At the very top of the slab, in the petroglyphs' first horizontal row, was a cruciform with a pair of long, crooked arms. The nine dots at its center and along the arms helped identify it as the constellation Cygnus; the largest dot, located at the head of the cruciform and surrounded by radiating lines, was the star Deneb. Because a long horizontal line led straight to the next figure in the top row—eight small dots in a halo of unevenly spaced concentric circles surrounding a large central dot, with the sixth dot surrounded by a small circle, obviously an ideograph for Earth's solar system—it was determined that this indicated that the aliens had come from Deneb . . . quite a journey, considering that the star system is estimated to be about 870 parsecs from Earth.

Third: of the dots represented within the figure of Earth's solar system, two apparently had some significance, for they were surrounded by crosshatches. These were the third and fourth dots: Earth and Mars. But while the petroglyphs themselves attested to the fact that the aliens had visited Earth's moon, whether they'd ever actually visited Earth or Mars was still a matter of debate, for no other extraterrestrial artifacts had ever been found on either of those worlds.

And fourth, the Denebian explorers—whom the Sons of the Two Moons reverently called the Old Ones—were humanlike yet not completely humanoid. Assuming that the figures in the petroglyphs represented themselves, they had been bipedal, with four limbs and a triangular head on an ovoid thorax. They also displayed a wide range of motion. The petroglyphs showed rows of tiny figures in a vast and bewildering array of poses that some called "the Dancing Denebs." They walked, squatted, pranced, raised their left arms and legs, raised their right arms and legs, stood on their hands . . . and no one who'd studied them had any idea what these gestures meant, nor figured out the meaning of the geometric shapes—circles, squares, triangles, hemispheres, lines slanting both left and right—that periodically interrupted their performance.

For two and a half centuries, the Deneb Petroglyphs had been the object of attention of scientists, historians, scholars, poets, and crackpots. Stacks of books, treatises, and monographs had been written about them, each a determined effort to divine their meaning, yet no one had ever come close to devising a definitive and inarguable solution to the enigma they posed. The petroglyphs were a riddle without an answer . . . or at least one that was clearly true.

Otho and Curt stood before the petroglyphs, for the moment ignoring the sounds and sights of the reception as they gazed upon the mysterious pictographs. Then Otho quietly chuckled.

"Well, I don't know about you," he said, "but I'd say the answer is obvious."

Curt raised an eyebrow. "It is?"

"Oh, certainly." Otho pointed to the petroglyphs. "The writing is on the Wall."

"Yes, it is." Curt slowly nodded. "I only wish I knew what it means. Perhaps—"

"You don't know? It's pretty plain to me . . . the writing is on the Wall."

"Of course it is. People have been studying this for years, but no one's yet been able to translate the language. With no Rosetta stone, deciphering it is very nearly impossible."

"They don't need to, because"—a significant pause, then Otho spoke slowly—"the writing . . . is . . . on . . . the Wall!"

"I know the writing's on the Wall!" Curt was becoming annoyed; Otho wasn't usually this obtuse. "But no one knows what it means."

Otho smiled but said nothing. When Curt continued to glare at him, his smile faded and he shook his head. "We need to work on your sense of humor," he muttered as he turned away.

"What?"

—*Never mind him,* the Brain said. *He never knows when the writing is on the Wall.*

Bewildered, Curt was about to respond when he heard a faint whirring from somewhere close overhead. He turned his head about and looked up to see a small surveillance drone hovering just a few feet above him and Otho. As he watched, it descended a few inches, its lens reflecting a distorted mirror image of himself gazing up at it.

"Don't pay attention to it." Otho's voice was low and no longer playful. "Just go back to looking at the petroglyphs."

"All right." Curt reluctantly turned away. "Simon, do you think it—?"

Otho made an urgent shushing noise and Curt immediately shut up. When he glanced down at his left hand, though, he noticed that his ring had gone dark. The Brain had gone off-line, silencing his Anni interface as he did so.

Meanwhile, the drone continued to study Curt and Otho.

11

Joan Randall, inspector third class of the Interplanetary Police Force, Section Four (Intelligence), was at the VIP entrance when Ezra Gurney's voice came over her Anni.

—*Busy over there, kid?*

—*What do you think?* Joan watched from beside the entrance arch as the IPF corporal under her supervision motioned for a middle-aged woman who'd just come through the connecting tunnel from the landing field to insert her hand into the identity scanner. The lady scowled at the indignity but obediently stuck her hand beneath the plate. It read the tattoo on the back of her palm while the arch searched her for weapons. Having ascertained—within reason—that the old matron wasn't a Starry Messenger terrorist, the corporal waved her through.

—*If you're not, I could use your help.*

Joan glanced down the tunnel. About a dozen or so other people were waiting their turn at the checkpoint.—*They're still coming in, Chief. I don't want to leave Mario by himself.*

—*Look, I know you got your hands full, but y'think you could check out a couple of guys for me? They kinda pushed their way through the crowd to get near the podium, and something 'bout 'em gives me the willies.*

Joan smiled. She always got a kick out of the way Ezra spoke, the Dixie slang and aphorisms that had been imported to the Moon long ago to become the native language of the loonies. —*Would you care to be more specific? 'Gives me the willies' doesn't tell me much.*

—*Their Annis went dead as soon as my drone dropped down to check 'em out. I call that a bad sign.*

—*That's suspicious behavior?* Joan wasn't getting what Ezra meant. Nearly everyone here was probably linked to the neural net, and people logged in and out all the time. Sure, a cop was supposed to develop a nose for trouble, but still . . .

—*Yes, missy, it is.* Ezra's voice, dry and reedy from a lifetime of off-duty whiskey and cigars, became a little tougher. —*What I want you to do is mosey over there and speak with those two gents, and make sure they're just a couple of good ol' boys we're not gonna have to worry about. Now hop.*

—*Okay, Chief.* Joan knew better than to argue further. Ezra Gurney might be her mentor in the IPF and even something of a father figure, but first and foremost he was her superior officer in Section Four. She'd never seen a frog in real life, but she well understood that she was supposed to emulate one if Marshal Gurney told her to. So she told Mario to hold things down until she came back, then began picking her way through the crowd toward the stage.

As always, appreciative eyes traveled over her as she made her way through the atrium. On her, the blue dress uniform of an IPF officer, with its epaulets, lariat, and comet insignia, was as elegant as many of the glamorous outfits worn by the wealthy young women attending the ceremony. With straight black hair cut at the neckline, solemn brown eyes, and a trim figure that moved with an athletic yet sensual grace, Joan was one of the most beautiful females there, yet she had no desire to sip wine and make small talk with a wealthy bachelor. When she was on the job, duty came first . . . and she was a woman who was almost always on the job and preferred it that way.

Ezra hadn't been specific about which two people near the stage he wanted her to investigate, but it wasn't hard to figure out whom he'd meant. Beneath the drone were two men. One was thin and bald, with narrow eyes and the snow-white skin of an albino—not unusual for native-born loonies, for whom melanin deficiency was a common genetic defect. His companion had his back turned to her as she approached. He was tall as a loony but more muscular, with longish red hair that looked as if it had been cut with gardening shears. Both wore gray bodysuits, which indicated that neither were dignitaries but instead were average citizens who'd somehow managed to wrangle a couple of the passes that the organizers had grudgingly released to the general public.

The albino gazed past his friend's shoulder as Joan approached. Spotting her, he quietly said something she didn't catch but which she figured out anyway: *Heads up, cop's coming.* The other character turned about just as Joan reached them, and she found herself being regarded by cool gray eyes.

"Hello, Officer. May I help you?" His voice was softer than she'd expected, and lacked any sort of accent she might have been able to immediately identify, loony or otherwise. His face had the helmet tan of someone who'd spent a lot of time in a vacuum suit, and was handsome in a mannish-boy sort of way. Joan figured that he was about her age, perhaps two or three years younger. Rather good-looking, too, but that was only a passing thought she quickly pushed aside.

"Just curious about why you're so close to the stage." Joan tilted her head toward the floater. "A colleague noticed you here. He asked me to come over and see why you and your friend made such an effort to get near the podium."

"I'm sorry. We weren't aware that we broke any rules by getting this close." A rueful shrug. "It's my fault. I'm fascinated by the petroglyphs, and just wanted to get a better look at them."

As he spoke, his gaze traveled down her body. Joan was accustomed to this; she was aware of her beauty and the sort of response it provoked in some men. Still, it was surprising that someone so handsome would also be so rude, and she was grateful for the distraction of Ezra's voice.

—*Scanner says he's telling the truth.* Ezra would be using the drone's biometric instruments to monitor any changes in skin temperature or respiration that might indicate a lie. —*But I'm still just a l'il bit suspicious, if y'know what I mean.*

"No need to apologize," Joan said with a neutral smile. "I don't think anyone can see these things and not wonder what they mean. For this event, though, we'd prefer it if anyone who isn't an invited guest to refrain from getting any closer than these seats." She gestured toward the nearby row of chairs. "Security reasons. I'm sure you understand."

"We do," the albino said, "and thank you for informing us. My friend and I will be only too happy to cooperate."

Joan was about to acknowledge him with another smile when Ezra snapped in her inner ear. —*Whoa! Something's off here! I'm getting almost no readings from this fella! If this guy was any colder, he'd be in a mortuary!*

There was no way she could respond without the two men hearing, so she remained quiet. But Ezra was right. The more closely she studied the albino, though, the more peculiar he became. His eye color wasn't the pale pink typical of albinos, but rather a lovely shade of green. He had no eyebrows or eyelashes, and his face was free of blemishes and wrinkles. He could have been a mannequin come to life.

—*Maybe the drone's not finding him,* Joan replied.

—*Suppose it's possible. Maybe there are too many people around for it to lock onto his vitals. Still, I'd like to know who these guys are.*

"If you don't mind," she said aloud, "I'd like to see your ID's, please." She kept her tone light as she reached for her scanner with her left hand, but nonetheless she let her right hand fall casually to where her holstered pistol was strapped against her thigh.

The pale man hesitated, but his companion didn't. "Not at all," he said, stepping forward to raise his left hand. "Here . . . see?"

Joan looked down, and for the first time noticed the large ring on the middle finger of his hand. It was an unusual piece of jewelry, a multifaceted diamond in a platinum setting. As she watched, a holographic image slowly rose from the diamond: a miniature, three-dimensional model of the solar system, with the eight major planets in their respective positions around the sun.

"You like this?" the red-haired man asked. Intrigued by the projection, Joan nodded. "A friend of mine named Simon gave it to me some time ago," he went on, "and he claims the sidereal motions of the planets are accurate. Now watch . . ."

A slight movement with his hand and the planets began to revolve around the sun, Mercury moving the fastest, Neptune the slowest.

"See?" the red-haired man said quietly, his voice a pleasant purr. "Perfect synchronization. If you watch for a while, you can actually see their respective apogees and perigees. Look, I can make them move just a little faster—"

—Joan, don't watch!

She heard Ezra, but it seemed as if he were calling her from a distant place. Besides, where was the harm in admiring the ring? "See how Mars is now in aphelion as opposed to Earth?" the red-haired man asked. "And notice how long it takes Saturn to catch up with Jupiter even though their orbits are adjacent." Fascinated, she slowly nodded. "Here, let me make it go just a little faster—"

—Damn it, Randall, don't—!

By then, Marshal Gurney's voice was a little more than a whisper. The tiny solar system had grown to fill her view, Mercury, Venus, Earth, Mars, Jupiter, Saturn, Uranus, and Neptune all moving in perfect harmony about the Sun. Watching this display from a godlike height, Joan felt herself relaxing, soothed by the sound of the red-haired stranger's voice. Nothing mattered except the planets, nothing but—

"Joan!" Ezra snapped, and slapped her face.

All of a sudden, she found herself standing against the back wall of the atrium, her left cheek stinging from the impact of a calloused male hand.

Astonished, she blinked against the tears that welled in the corners of her eyes. Marshal Gurney stood before her, his mouth trembling in anger beneath his white handlebar mustache. She stared at him in bewilderment, with utterly no recollection of how she'd come to be here. Just a second ago, wasn't she . . . ?

"What . . . Ezra, how—?"

"Hush." A little more calmly, Ezra lowered his voice. "Keep it down. The speeches have started."

The ceiling lights had dimmed, and when she gazed past him, she saw that a spotlight was casting a luminescent circle on the podium. The crowd standing between them and the stage was applauding the woman who'd just walked onstage; Joan recognized her as the new director of the Straight Wall System Monument. Just now, though, this was the least of her concerns.

"What happened, Chief?" she whispered. "How did I get here?"

"Slickest bit of hypnosis I've seen this side of the Interplanetary Circus." Despite his irritation, Ezra shook his head in wonder. "I saw the whole thing. First he got you gawkin' at that gimmick ring of his, and once he had you pulled in, he told you to never mind anything else, just turn around and walk away. And damned if that ain't exactly what you did."

"What?" Joan stared at him. "Where is he now?"

"Right where you left him, the sneaky son of a—"

Curling a hand around her holstered pistol, Joan started forward, intending to barge through the crowd and apprehend both the red-haired man and his weird companion. But Ezra stepped in front of her and planted his hands on her shoulders.

"No, not now," he said quietly. "We're certain neither of 'em are armed, and I put a coupla guys on 'em to make sure they don't cause any trouble. Whoever they are, they ain't getting very far . . . but we can't let them interrupt the dedication ceremony if we can help it."

Joan felt a surge of helpless fury, but Ezra was right. Making an arrest here and now would only unnecessarily create a scene. So she nodded, let go of her weapon, and contented herself with gritting her teeth as the director finished her opening remarks.

"And now," she said, "please allow me to introduce the person most responsible for persuading the Senate to allocate the funds to build this lovely new monument . . . the senator of the Lunar Republic, the honorable Victor Corvo."

///

The man who walked onstage was tall and slender, obviously earth-born and not a native selenian, with thick, dark hair turning gray at his temples and receding at his forehead. Victor Corvo had glowering, deep-set eyes in an otherwise handsome face, and there was little about him that suggested a ward healer who'd achieved his position by shaking hands and kissing babies. Nonetheless, somewhere along the line he'd learned enough about the acquisition of political power to become the Moon's junior representative to the Coalition Senate, and one of those lessons had obviously been how to address an audience.

"Thank you for that lovely introduction, Dr. Chase," Corvo said once the applause had subsided and the director had stepped away from the podium. "You flatter me greatly by stating that I'm the person responsible for the construction of this monument. All I did was what a politician usually does . . . accept bribes and share them with my colleagues."

Loud and sustained laughter from the crowd, peppered with howls of mock-outrage from other Senate members. A rueful grin crossed Corvo's face as his narrow shoulders rose and fell in a self-deprecating *who-me?* shrug. It would have been a lot funnier if his joke had been reflected in his eyes. But they remained humorless; this was a gag created by one of his speechwriters, dutifully recited as a way of warming up the audience.

All the same, Curt laughed and clapped his hands along with everyone else. When he glanced over at Otho, though, he saw that his face remained stolid, his hands at his sides. He regarded the senator with an expression that was cold and malevolent. In fact, Curt couldn't remember seeing him quite this way before.

"Hey, at least he's got a sense of humor," Curt whispered. "I thought you like that sort of thing."

Otho regarded him coldly. "You think he's funny?" he asked quietly.

"Well, yeah, kinda . . ."

The android returned his attention to the podium. "Just listen . . . and study this man."

Curt wanted to ask why, but kept his mouth shut. In the past few minutes, he'd become aware of a couple of men wearing ordinary business suits unobtrusively taking up positions near the place where he and Otho stood. Too late, he'd realized that he'd gone too far by using the hypnosis trick Simon had taught him several years ago to get rid of the IPF officer who'd asked to see their ID's. She'd obediently wandered away without pressing the issue—necessary, since Curt's instincts told him that she'd picked up something wrong about Otho, and their tats probably wouldn't have survived close scrutiny—but his actions had apparently raised the suspicions of the presidential security team . . . and that, no doubt, was what the two men were.

Now there were cops all around them, and even though the Brain had gone silent and Otho wasn't saying much either, Curt knew he had to be careful what he said and did the rest of the time they were here. So he continued to watch Senator Corvo, and hoped that they'd get out of there without any problems.

"The Deneb Petroglyphs represents one of the greatest unsolved mysteries of history," Corvo said, barely glancing at the text scrolling across the podium surface. "It's a puzzle that has consumed generations of scientists, and while many theories have been made as to their meaning, no certain interpretation has ever been accomplished."

He gestured to the rock face behind him. "With the establishment of this monument, we're taking measures to preserve the petroglyphs for many years to come, thereby enabling researchers such as the current team from the Planetary Institute, Dr. Philip Winters and Dr. Cole Norton, to examine these etchings in a safe and comfortable environment.

It will also allow members of the public to visit the site and view the petroglyphs without damaging them. The modest fees that they'll pay for the privilege of visiting the monument will be used for its upkeep and maintenance, and in time the Institute hopes to be able to use some of the money to endow modest grants for visiting scholars."

More applause. Curt clapped along with everyone else, but he noticed that Otho did not. He continued to stare at the senator, his expression still menacing. Curt hoped that the security guys weren't noticing this. At least the drone had disappeared. Without it hovering above them, the security team wouldn't have a clear look at Otho's face.

"I'm very proud to have been part of the effort to erect this monument," Corvo continued, "but the fact remains that it could not have been accomplished without support from the top floor of Government Tower. Without further ado, I'd like to present the true hero of the moment . . . my friend and ally, the president of the Solar Coalition, James Carthew."

The applause was even stronger as Corvo stepped away from the podium to extend his hands to a stocky figure with a goatee who'd just walked onstage. The Brain insisted that Curt pay attention to current affairs, so he knew that President Carthew didn't often leave the executive suite of Government Tower in New York. Indeed, he was occasionally accused by members of the opposing political party of secretly disliking travel beyond Earth. So the fact that he'd come all the way to the Moon for a dedication ceremony was a testament to the senator's political clout. Carthew and Corvo were, indeed, political allies, and it was often speculated that, once Carthew stepped down, he'd throw his support behind Corvo if the senator decided to run for higher office.

Yet Otho continued to glare at Corvo, his hands remaining still at his sides. As the president walked across the stage, Curt moved closer to his friend. "What's your problem?" he whispered.

Otho turned to look Curt straight in the eye. In a whisper that only Curt could hear, he said, "Victor Corvo is the man who murdered your parents."

IV

Curt's first thought was that Otho was kidding, yet nothing in his expression suggested that this was a joke, even a bad one. As Curt realized this, the rest of the world suddenly vanished, leaving only three people: Otho, himself, and the man Otho claimed was responsible for the deaths of his mother and father.

"It can't be true. You must be . . ." His words caught in his throat as a dry whisper.

—He's not mistaken, Curtis. The Brain spoke up again. *He's telling the truth. Victor Corvo killed Roger and Elaine Newton. I was there. I saw it happen.*

"Long before he became a senator," Otho said softly, presciently answering Curt's next question. "When you were still a baby, while I was still in my bioclast, Victor Corvo and his men came to Tycho and killed first your father, then your mother." He paused. "They were your parents, but in a sense they were mine, too."

Curt barely heard him. His gaze was locked on the man shaking hands with President Carthew. For as long as he could remember, he'd been told that his parents had been murdered in cold blood by intruders who'd found the hidden laboratory beneath Tycho. But . . .

"You've always told me Grag killed the people who murdered my parents," he whispered.

The Brain said nothing. He'd gone silent again, Curt realized, as a precaution against having his Anni tapped by the floater that was still hovering nearby. "That's correct," Otho replied, "but they were just the ones who actually pulled the trigger. The person who gave them the order"—he nodded toward the stage—"is standing right there."

Curt gave his friend a sidelong glance. Again, no sign that Otho was pulling his leg. Instead, the android met his gaze with slanted green eyes that remained uncommonly serious. He silently nodded. He was speaking the truth. Senator Victor Corvo was the man who'd ended the lives of Roger and Elaine Newton.

It was as if his heart had been replaced by a cast-iron machine, black and merciless, pumping cold anger instead of blood. Carthew had taken Corvo's place at the podium, and as he politely waited for the applause to subside, the senator left the stage, walking down a short flight of steps to the VIP seating section, where a vacant chair awaited him in the front row. Corvo took his seat there, only a dozen or so yards from where Curt was standing.

He could reach Corvo in just a second. If he kicked off his ankle weights, in one jump he could clear the red velvet rope separating him from the VIP seats and land next to the senator. Grab him, pull him to his feet, turn him around so his back was braced against Curt's chest, wrap his left arm around Corvo's shoulders, grasp his head with his right hand and twist hard. *Snap!* and that would be it . . .

He'd just taken a step toward the rope, though, when Otho grabbed his arm. *"No!"* he hissed. "That's not why we're here."

Curt tried to shake off his hand, but couldn't. He'd never been able to match Otho's strength. Curt was mere flesh, bone, and blood, after all, while his friend was a dozen different kinds of pseudo-organic material; he was more than human, and unique because of that. "Then why—?"

"Later." Otho glanced past him. "We need to leave . . . calmly, please, but immediately nonetheless."

Curt didn't have to follow Otho's gaze to know what he meant. In the past few moments, they'd further aroused the attention of the IPF presidential security detail. Until then, they might have been only mildly suspicious, even after Curt had used hypnotic suggestion to make the inspector who'd come over to question him and Otho go away. But if the drone hadn't detected the involuntary changes in skin temperature indicating a violent mood swing when Senator Corvo appeared onstage, then the two cops who'd replaced the inspector couldn't have missed his impulsive attempt to charge the senator.

"All right," Curt whispered, "let's go."

Otho nodded, then the two of them turned to begin making their way back through the crowd. Everyone was listening to President Carthew as he extolled the virtues of the new monument; they paid little attention to the two men who politely shouldered a path through them as they headed for the rear of the dome. Curt expected a firm hand on his shoulder, a murmured command to halt, yet nothing of the sort occurred. By the time they reached the monument entrance and the public airlock that lay just beyond, he'd figured that the IPF was content to let him and Otho leave just as long as they did so in peace.

That was not to be. Someone was waiting for them just outside the airlock ready-room: an older IPF officer with a handlebar mustache and glacial-blue eyes, and the lovely young woman who'd confronted them earlier.

V

"Howdy, gents," Ezra said as he stepped between the suspects and the ready-room. "I'm wondering if you'd be so kind as to have a l'il chat with us."

Joan hung back as ordered, quietly giving Ezra backup. The two officers tailing the suspects stopped at the edge of the crowd, each folding their arms across their chests. The two men who'd just left the crowd were now boxed in; there was no way they would be allowed to leave until Marshal Gurney questioned them.

Joan unfastened her holster flap and tucked her right thumb in the belt so that her hand was only an inch from her particle beam pistol. The trick that the red-haired man had pulled on her had been deeply embarrassing, and she knew that Ezra wasn't going to forget it anytime soon. So she wasn't about to let herself get fooled again.

"Of course." This time it wasn't the hairless albino who spoke first, but the man whose tattoo had identified him as Rab Cain. He stepped forward to stand beside his companion. "How may we help you, sir?"

"Well, for starters, you can explain why you felt it necessary to mesmerize my fellow officer when she attempted to question you and your buddy."

"Mesmerize? I don't . . . oh, that!" Cain's face broke into a grin. He raised his left hand, showing off the ring Joan had seen earlier. "I'm sorry, really. I sometimes forget that this can have sort of a funny effect on people. See, if you look closely—"

"Knock it off," Ezra snarled. "I'm not falling for that." Cain shrugged and started to drop his hand, but Ezra grabbed his wrist. "Let's see your tat," he said, turning it over to expose his ID. "Inspector Randall, check the other guy's."

"No need to get rough." The albino calmly pulled back the cuff of his sleeve to let Joan examine his identification. She didn't have a scanner, so instead she focused on the tattoo, squinting her eyes slightly to activate her Anni.

—*Anni, run identification and status check, please. IPF authorization JR26-4.*

—*Certainly, Inspector Randall,* Anni replied, using the grandmotherly version of her voice that Joan preferred. A translucent rectangle formed around the tattoo and a row of tiny digits appeared at the bottom of the coronal screen. —*Identified as Vol Cotto. Resident of Port Kepler, Lunar Republic. Occupation: freelance astronavigator. No IPF record.*

"Anything wrong, Officer?" Cotto asked, the soul of innocence.

Joan didn't reply, but instead looked over at Ezra. Her boss had just finished checking Rab Cain's ID. His gaze met Joan's; neither of them spoke, but the glance they exchanged said everything that needed to be said. Both men had valid identification, neither had any entries in the IPF database of known criminals . . . and neither she nor Ezra was buying it. The old marshal had taught his protégé that police work often involved gut instinct, and her guts were now telling her that Rab Cain and Vol Cotto weren't as innocuous as they were pretending to be.

"You're leaving in a hurry." Ezra released Cain's wrist but continued to stare him straight in the eye. "Any particular reason why?"

"Not really." An indifferent shrug and a smile. "You've heard one boring politician, you've heard them all. And Carthew could put anyone to sleep."

"Yeah, uh-huh." Ezra didn't smile back at him. "Y'know, son, we were watching you from over there, and it appeared you had some kinda . . . shall we say, *adverse reaction* when you saw him. In fact, I'd say you rather dislike our president."

"No, not at all." Rab shook his head. "I have nothing at all against the president—"

"You told me that you voted against him," Cotto said, interrupting him.

It sounded to Joan like Cotto was giving Cain a verbal nudge. "Oh yeah, well, sometimes I disagree with his policies," Cain quickly added. "But still . . . no, I don't have anything against him."

"Is there a reason for you to detain us?" Cotto asked.

Joan and Ezra looked at each other. Ezra cocked his head to one side, and then he and Joan moved away.

"We got nothin' on 'em, kiddo," Ezra murmured, "but I still think they stink."

"I'm with you, Chief," Joan replied, her voice just as low. "You want to detain them? We can hold them for twenty-four hours without charges."

"What would that get us?" Ezra shook his head. "If they're with Starry Messenger, then they've probably covered their tracks. Putting 'em on ice will just tip off their people that we're on to them. No, we're gonna cut 'em loose, but . . ."

"But what?"

"Let you know in a sec." Ezra returned to the suspects. "You can go," he said to them, stepping away from the ready-room hatch. "Just a routine check. Many apologies for any inconvenience."

"Yeah, sure. No problem." Cotto gave Joan and Ezra a cold look as he sauntered past.

"No problem at all. Good day, Officer." Cain turned away from Ezra, but didn't immediately follow Cotto to the ready-room. Instead, he paused before Joan.

"A pleasure to meet you, Inspector Randall," he said, just quietly enough for only the two of them to hear. "Many apologies for pulling that trick on you. It was mean."

Then, before Joan could stop him, Cain bent forward in a formal bow, took her hand, and lifting it to his lips, tenderly kissed it.

Joan was so surprised that, when she opened her mouth to object, nothing came out. Men had kissed her before, of course, or at least tried to; she was an attractive woman, accustomed to advances of all kinds. But this was different: not a fumbling grope or a lewd pass, but a gallant, romantic, and respectful gesture. No one had ever kissed her this way before. His lips barely brushed the back of her hand. All the same, though, this was no way to treat an officer of the law.

"Cut it out!" she snapped and jerked her hand away.

Now it was Cain's turn to be embarrassed. Face turning nearly as red as his hair, he hastily straightened up. "Sorry," he whispered. "Didn't mean to offend."

Without another word, he turned to enter the ready-room, ignoring both her angry glare and Ezra's gape-mouthed astonishment. Even Cotto seemed to be taken aback. The only people to make a sound were the two IPF officers standing nearby, but their snickers quickly died when Ezra cast a scowl in their direction. Cotto closed the hatch behind them, leaving the lawmen behind.

"Well . . . umm . . ." Joan struggled to recover.

"Slick, ain't he?" Ezra watched through the hatch window for a moment as Cain and Cotto retrieved their pressure suits from the wall racks, and then he turned away. "Okay, I got a job for you. I want to know where they're going."

"Track them via lunasat?"

"Uh-uh. I want eyes on 'em. Requisition a patrol hopper—come to think of it, take mine, it's all set to go—and follow 'em to wherever they came from. Be careful not to let yourself be seen, but make sure they never leave your sight, and report back to me as soon as you've got something. Understood?"

"Yes, sir." Joan gave him a quick salute, then hurried off to the secondary airlock being used for official IPF business. She'd have to work fast if she was going to suit up and get the hopper off the ground in time to catch up with Cain.

Twice already, the red-haired stranger had embarrassed her. Joan determined to find out where he was going, and when she did, she'd make him sorry for treating her as he had.

At least this was what she told herself.

VI

"I do believe we are being followed."

Curt had taken off from the Straight Wall only a minute earlier when Otho spoke up. Sitting in the copilot seat, Otho had been keeping an eye on the center console radar screen while Curt took the hopper up to cruise altitude 1,500 feet above Mare Nubium while performing the southerly turn that would put them on course for Tycho.

Keeping a steady hand on the stick, Curt glanced at the screen. Just as Otho said, a small blip below and behind them was forming a nearly identical ground track. Whoever was flying the other craft was evidently trying not to be noticed, staying at the edge of radar range while maintaining an altitude of only seven hundred feet. It would have to climb a bit once they entered the southern highlands, but for now the pilot was hugging the flatlands of the lunar mare.

"I'm afraid you're right," Curt said. "Any chance this could be a coincidence? Might just be someone else flying home the same way."

Otho shook his head, and Simon answered for both of them. *"You know the answer to that as well as I do, lad."*

This time, Curt heard Simon's voice through the comlink instead of his Anni. It was the voice of an elderly sage, someone who'd lived many years and had acquired the wisdom of experience. As usual, the Brain was right. So far as Curt knew, there were no settlements, stations, or mining facilities within a hundred miles of Tycho Base. In fact, the Straight Wall System Monument was the closest inhabited

area of any kind. Aside from the fact that it was one of the Moon's largest impact craters, Tycho was a rather uninteresting place, remote
from most of the locales humankind had chosen to inhabit. No one
ever came down there.

"Someone's following us home," he said quietly.

"Really? You think?" Otho's dry comment came with an irate scowl.
"Maybe it's your girlfriend wanting another kiss. Smooth move, Captain
Future."

Curt's face turned warm. "Don't call me that."

"Captain Future. Wizard of science. Man of tomorrow."

"I'm warning you . . . knock it off."

"I agree," Simon said. *"This is no time for sarcasm, Otho. He made a
mistake, and now we'll just have to deal with it. Any ideas, Curtis?"*

Pushing aside his annoyance, Curt forced himself to work the problem. Tycho was just a little more than four hundred miles south by
southwest of the Straight Wall; at their present ground speed, they'd
be there in a little less than an hour. Any deviations from their present
course would probably be considered suspicious, and dropping altitude
wouldn't do much good either. The nearest settlement on their flight
path was the South Pole lunar ice facility at Cabeus; flying unnecessarily close to the ground wouldn't deceive another pilot who was already
at the same low altitude.

Fortunately, the hopper was equipped with something he and
Simon had recently invented in their spare time. Curt had been looking
for a chance to try it out; this looked like an excellent opportunity.
"Simon, put me through to Grag."

A moment passed, then a voice, deep and metronomic, came over
the comlink. *"Grag here. How may I help you, Curt?"*

"Go to the hangar control station and stand by. When I give the
word, elevate the hopper landing pad, but don't open the hangar door
until I tell you. This is going to be a fast touchdown, so you need to be
ready. Understand?"

"Understood."

"Don't screw it up, rivet brain," Otho added. "We're counting on you." He caught the sour look Curt gave him and shrugged. "Just a friendly reminder, that's all."

"Just keep an eye on the scope," Curt replied, "and let me know if the hopper changes altitude, speed, or course in any way." He smiled. "And warm up the fantome generator. Time to give it a test."

VII

From the bubble cockpit of the IPF hopper, Joan watched the small, unblinking spot of light that was the civilian craft she'd trailed from the Straight Wall. It was an older hopper, the sort commonly used by prospectors in more remote areas of the Moon. The fact that it wasn't heading in the direction of any major settlements led her to speculate whether the two suspects might, indeed, be nothing more than a pair of miners returning to camp.

Yes, they might be only a couple of troublemakers . . . but she didn't think so. Something about them was more interesting than that.

A few hundred feet below, the highlands of the Moon's southern hemisphere stretched out before her as a wilderness of sharp-peaked hills broken here and there by impact craters. Even in the middle of the lunar day, darkness lay deep within their shadows. This part of the lunar countryside didn't have the comforting serenity of a mare, but rather a more chaotic landscape that had never welcomed visitors. If her quarry weren't a pair of rockhounds, Joan reflected, they must have one hell of a reason for being here.

She carefully maintained radio silence—it was always possible that her signal could be intercepted, despite comlink encryption—and flew close to the ground in an effort to keep from being spotted. Staying in visual range meant that she might be picked up on radar, but that was a risk she'd have to accept. Joan could only hope that Cain would mistake her hopper for a water tanker on its way to Cabeus.

She had been following the other vehicle for almost an hour when the light above her slowly began to descend. As it did, it grew a little brighter, and Joan realized that it was slowing down as well. The hopper was coming in for a landing. Looking down, she saw the outer wall of a giant crater looming upon the horizon, the terrain surrounding it sprayed with rays of material ejected by some great primordial impact.

Joan didn't have to check the console map before her to know where they were: Tycho Crater, almost fifty-three miles in diameter, one of the most prominent features of the lunar nearside. The hopper was descending upon it, spiraling downward as it made its primary approach for touchdown.

Joan pushed the stick gently forward, cutting her own altitude in hopes that she wouldn't be spotted. Aware that she might lose track of Cain's hopper once it entered the crater's vast interior, she didn't reduce her velocity, though, but continued to approach Tycho at the same speed. Never once did she let herself look away from the distant spot of light. Which was why, at just the moment that she got close enough to make out its rotary engine nacelles and tripod landing gear, the hopper did the impossible:

It vanished.

One instant, it was there. The next, it was gone.

At first she thought it was only an optical illusion. Perhaps the craft had momentarily turned in such a way that it didn't reflect the sunlight. When it failed to reappear, she glanced at her radar. To her astonishment, its blip had disappeared as well.

"What the hell?" Joan's mouth fell open as she looked first at the scope, then out the cockpit, then at the scope again. The hopper had still been a couple of hundred feet or more above the crater when it disappeared, so that wasn't an explanation. And even if it was capable of going into stealth mode, it should have remained visible to the naked eye. Perhaps the hopper was somehow able to become invisible . . . but she'd never heard of any technology that could do *both*.

The crater wall was coming up fast. Joan pulled back on the stick and throttled up the engines, and the hopper soared up and over the rim. Now she was looking straight down into the crater; it yawned before her as a vast pit, its terraced walls twelve thousand feet deep, so far across that its opposite side disappeared over the horizon. The jagged tooth of the central mountain peak towered from the center, and although the inner walls cast long shadows across the rocky floor, she had a clear view of everything below the approximate point where the hopper had vanished. There was nothing down there . . .

No. Not quite.

Something glimmered on the crater floor about halfway between the eastern walls and the central peak.

Joan couldn't make out what it was, but it wasn't moving, and it appeared to be a little too big to be a hopper that had just landed.

Joan considered breaking radio silence and calling back to report what had just happened, but she cringed at the thought of admitting to Ezra that she'd lost her quarry. She could hear him already when she told him that Rab Cain's hopper had disappeared like a desert mirage: *I don't believe in phantoms, Inspector. And the IPF never loses its man!*

No, she wouldn't report in until she'd checked every possible clue. So she pulled back on the throttle, twisted the stick down and to starboard, and commenced the right turn that would bring her in for a landing.

The hopper touched down about a hundred yards from what appeared to be an abandoned base: a mooncrete dome resembling an igloo, surrounded by smaller drumlike prefabs. No vehicles of any sort, though, and no signs of life. The windows were dark, and a dish antenna lay upon the ground where it had fallen.

Joan studied the settlement through the cockpit as she zipped up the front of her vacuum suit before going aft to put on her gloves, helmet, and lifepack. While she cycled through the airlock, she buckled her gun belt around her waist. This place was probably what it appeared to be, a ghost hab—there were several like it on the Moon, relics from the first decades of lunar colonization—but Ezra had drilled into her the fact that most IPF casualties occurred when officers failed to take precautions. *Always prepare for the unlikely and you'll never get caught with your britches down.* Joan smiled as she tucked her pistol back into her holster. Ezra was probably the only man she knew who could say that and not have it come off as sexual innuendo.

Nonetheless, as Joan slowly walked across the crater to the base, it was clear that no one was here. When she got near, she saw the reason why: one side of the dome was collapsed, with a massive hole at the center of the wreckage. Walking closer, she peered through the shattered mooncrete at the blackened inner walls and twisted ceiling supports visible within. It appeared as if there had been a fire, one bad enough to reach the oxygen tanks of the life support system. The explosion had done the rest.

No telling how long ago this happened, but myriad bootprints on the gray regolith all around the site attested that it was quite some time ago. The bodies of the dead had since been removed, and the hab was visited many times after that, most likely by scavengers. Joan switched on her helmet lamp and let its beam travel across the ruined interior. No, nothing usable remained. All the furniture and fixtures were gone, and gaping holes in the interior walls showed where even the electrical wiring had been ripped out.

Joan walked around the base, inspecting the adjacent buildings. An empty flivver shed, a greenhouse with all its windows either broken or carried away, a power center with an open hatch and drag marks leading across the ground to a blackened spot where a small craft had once landed, evidence to the fate of the base's nuclear reactor. Vacant stilts resting at skewed angles showed where the solar array formerly stood. The water tanks, of course, were long vanished.

For how long had this place been deserted? She could check the IPF database later to see if there was any record of what had once been here, but only if she was curious. Nothing here gave her a clue where Cain's hopper had gone. Indeed, the more she thought about it, the more she suspected that he might have pulled a clever move. He'd only pretended to be landing, but as soon as he'd gone invisible—or at least seemed to; she still wasn't convinced he'd done just that—he'd changed direction and flown away from the crater altogether, leading her to foolishly believe that he'd touched down.

"Randall, you idiot," she muttered to herself. "He foxed you, but good." Which was a pity, really. After the way Cain kissed her hand back at the reception, she might have been interested in him . . .

No. Not professional. Not professional at all.

There was nothing left to do but report to Ezra, admit what had happened, and receive further instructions. Letting out her breath in a disgusted sigh, Joan turned and began trudging back to the hopper, unaware that hidden eyes observed her from within the ruins she'd left behind.

VIII

Fifty feet beneath the ruins of his parents' laboratory—the part visible from the lunar surface, that is—Curt Newton watched as Inspector Randall walked away.

She appeared just a few feet before him as a life-size image within a projection cast against the wall of a large, circular room. The ceiling lights had been dimmed, so it appeared as if he was standing before a floor-to-ceiling window, with the crater floor just outside. The image captured by holocams concealed within the ruined hab was so realistic that Curt could have sworn, with just a few bounding steps, he could step through the window, walk up beside the young woman, and give her a tap on the shoulder.

He wished he could. If he'd had any choice in the matter, he would have.

"She's cute, I'll give her that." Otho's voice came from the darkness behind him. "But she's not for you."

"I'm afraid he's right." From nearby came Simon Wright's voice, the same he'd heard earlier but with a mild electronic burr of a vocoder beneath it. "I know how you'd very much like to meet a young lady, my boy, but—"

"I'm not your boy," Curt muttered under his breath.

"—what you did was dangerous. You and Otho were supposed to go there without being noticed, just two more members of the public. Instead, you got the IPF's attention. And if it isn't bad enough that you attracted the tiger's notice, you stepped on its paw, too."

"I didn't step on anyone, Brain. I just kissed her hand, that's all." Curt tried not to sound annoyed, but he couldn't help himself.

"Curt—" Otho sighed. "Screen off. Lights up."

The image vanished and the ceiling lights came to life. They revealed a round room nearly thirty feet in diameter, its curved windowless walls lined with sliding doors leading to adjacent rooms and passageways. Crowded against the walls between the doors were the consoles and workbenches of a well-equipped laboratory devoted to a number of different disciplines: cybernetics, biotechnology, astrophysics, and xenobiology, among others. At the center of the room, just a few feet from where Curt stood, was a long central table, its chemical-stained surface fashioned from a polished slab of lunar basalt.

Directly above the table, in the center of the ceiling twelve feet above the floor, was a large round window comprised of multiple panes of lunaglass two inches thick. The window was presently closed from the outside by pie-wedge shutters fashioned to resemble a half-buried boulder. When open, the window became a skylight allowing the inhabitants to view the Moon's eternal night sky . . . along with Earth, which perpetually hung in sight from the crater floor.

The shutters were closed, hastily shut when Curt had come in for the emergency touchdown. Otho was seated at the table, legs stretched out before him as he watched his friend with curious green eyes. Yet even the android's gaze wasn't as strange as that of the lab's other occupant.

Resting upon the table was a saucer-shaped contrivance about two feet in diameter. Resembling a Chinese wok placed upside down over a serving platter, it had rotary ductfans evenly arranged around its outer circumference. Two small optical scanners that strangely resembled eyes protruded upon elastic stalks from a hemispheric bulge at the wok's center; other lenses were inset around the bulge. Two multijointed arms, each with its own three-finger manipulator claw, were mounted on either side of the upper shell.

In whole, the machine resembled a drone. It was far more than that.

"It was a mistake, Curtis." Simon's voice came from a speaker just below the eyestalks. The fans softly whirred and the machine rose from the table. "I realize that you meant no harm, but Otho and I spent years trying to teach you the necessity of avoiding attention. And now, at just the moment when you needed to be as unnoticeable as possible—"

"Okay, all right. I understand . . . I blew it!" Turning away from the place where the holo had been projected, Curt threw up his hands in frustration. "I kissed her hand. Big deal. It's not like I tried to . . . to . . ." He stopped to glare at the machine floating toward him. "What would you know about that, anyway?"

Simon halted in midair, eyestalks twisting around to study him. "That's rather insensitive, don't you think?"

Curt started to retort before he realized what Simon had just said. Embarrassed, he looked down at the floor. For just a moment, he'd forgotten that, deep within the machine, lay a cell filled with warm broth of oxygenated nutrients that biochemically resembled blood. Suspended within it was a human brain. Dozens of hair-thin wires led from its major lobes and the severed stalk of its spinal cord to the central functions of the machine surrounding it, thus enabling it to see and hear along with the limited ability to move and touch.

This was all that remained of Dr. Simon Wright, once one of the system's foremost cyberneticists, now a disembodied brain existing in the eerie afterlife that had followed his body's death from a rare and inoperable form of cancer. Upon his demise, Elaine Newton had overseen the experimental procedure, conducted in this very room by a robosurgeon programmed by her and her husband, that had transplanted the brain of Roger Newton's mentor from his dying body to the specially adapted cyborg form that now kept him alive.

That was nearly twenty years ago, when Curt was still an infant. He'd never known Simon Wright as anything except the Brain, a nickname he and Otho had given him when they were both still young enough not to realize how callous it could be. Simon didn't seem to mind, but on occasion he was obliged to remind his best friends' son that he had once walked like a man.

"Sorry, Simon," he said. "I forgot again, didn't I?"

"Yes, but I forgive you." One of the more interesting features of Simon Wright's neural interface with his cyborg form was his ability to subtly manipulate the vocoder that gave voice to his thoughts, allowing him to express emotions as well as words. So while the vocoder had a slight buzz—Roger had still been trying to fix this imperfection at the time of his death—Simon's voice sounded exactly the way it had when it was formed by a human larynx.

Otho cleared his throat. "Look, I know what you did was out of impulse. I might have done the same, if I didn't give ladies the creeps." He paused. "Come to think of it, who taught you to kiss a girl like that?"

Curt shrugged. "I saw it in an old movie. Something from the early twentieth century . . . I forget which one." He grinned. "Like it? I thought it was kinda classy."

"'Kinda classy'?" Otho raised a hairless eyebrow. "Did you get that from the same movie?"

"She'll remember it, that's for certain." Fans whirring softly, Simon floated across the room until he reached the elevated pedestal, upon which he rested to recharge himself. "What's done is done. Crater sensors indicate that her hopper has just lifted off, so apparently your ruse fooled her."

"Couldn't have pulled it off without you and Grag. Speaking of whom . . ." Curt turned toward an open door leading to a nearby passageway. "Hey, Grag? Are you going to come in here?"

"Right away, Curt."

Heavy footsteps, muffled only slightly by the threadbare carpet, came stamping down the hall. A few seconds later, an enormous figure walked into the lab: a robot, seven feet tall and constructed of dark gray titanium. While its body was designed to emulate the human form, any resemblance to a living person ended there; its limbs were cylindrical, its chest a solid and featureless mass, its hands knob-jointed and menacingly large. The robot's face resembled an inverted shovel blade, with a broad forehead and a receding chin; there was no visible mouth, for its voice came from a speaker hidden beneath the chin, and a nose was unnecessary.

The eyes were strange: oval and unblinking, with red lenses that softly glowed from within; they seemed to express emotions that the rest of its face was unable to convey. The robot always looked as if it was regarding the world with wide-eyed wonder, like an oversize child perpetually amazed by everything going on around it.

A representative from the Grag Corporation might have been surprised to find what had been made of one of its Series 320-A robots. That line was manufactured by the Grag factory in Youngstown, Ohio, principally as industrial construction equipment, with the 320-A performing the role of supervisor. This particular 'bot was no mere automaton, though, but something unique and unexpected.

"Nice work, getting the hangar doors open and shut in time." Curt smiled as Grag marched toward them. "I imagine you had to disengage the automatic controls and go manual."

"Yes, that's what I did." Grag halted a few feet from the table, massive arms dangling at its sides. "Once I disabled the motion-detection sensors and the servos, I was able to open the doors myself and close them again as soon as your hopper was on the landing pad and lowered into the hangar."

"Yeah, well . . ." Otho crossed his legs and arms, assuming an unimpressed pose. "Don't pat yourself on the back too much. You didn't repressurize the hangar once we were down. Curt and I had to put on our gear again to climb out, and then we had to cycle through the airlock just to come in."

Grag's impassive face turned toward him. "I neglected nothing. If I had done as you said, there's a chance the individual pursuing you might have seen the dust plume being vented through the hangar exhaust port when the regolith scrubbers came on. That would have indicated the presence of an underground facility. I made what I considered to be the prudent choice. I apologize for the inconvenience."

"He got you there," Curt said, running a hand through his hair as he gave Otho an amused wink.

"And if she'd discovered the hangar doors?" Simon asked. "Or the stairs leading down to the airlock?"

"That's easy. She would have met me, and I would have broken her neck."

Curt's eyes widened, and Otho scowled. "You're heartless, Tin Man."

"And you don't have a brain, Scarecrow." As always, Grag's voice lacked any emotive quality.

Despite what Grag had said about Inspector Randall, Curt tried not to smile. This sort of exchange had been going on since he was a kid. Both beings had never determined which of them was the better creation, but at least they agreed on one thing: they were superior to humans, and therefore it fell to them to help Simon Wright raise and protect the orphaned child of the two people who'd been murdered here.

"Oh no you don't," Curt said. "We're not going to kill anyone who finds this place, and that most especially includes IPF cops. I'm just glad the fantome works, because—"

He stopped, gazing down at the floor as he contemplated that which he had learned only a couple of hours ago. "What troubles you, Curtis?" Simon asked.

Curt didn't answer him. Instead, he looked at Otho. "If you will, find out everything you can about where Senator Corvo lives."

"I can answer that," the Brain said. "When he's on Earth and the Coalition Senate is in session, he has a small apartment in New York about three blocks from Government Tower. But when the Senate is in recess—as it is now—he lives in a crater estate on Mare Tranquillitatis, not far from the Apollo 11 memorial."

"Then he should presently be on the Moon?"

"Yes, most likely he is . . . particularly since he's hosting President Carthew during his state visit."

"Good. Find out all you can about Corvo's residence. Particularly about ways to get in." He turned to Otho again. "While he's doing that, I'd like for you and Grag to disassemble the fantome generator from the hopper and transfer it to the *Comet*."

Otho sat up a little straighter. "The *Comet*? Why?"

"The hopper doesn't have the range to get to Mare Tranquillitatis and back without refueling. The *Comet* does. If necessary, rig a separate generator to give it adequate power to cloak the entire ship. But I want it done soon."

"Sure, but why . . . ?" Otho began.

Curt didn't respond, but instead walked toward an unmarked door on the other side of the main room. "I'll be resting in my quarters, if you don't mind."

"Curtis, what do you have in mind?" Simon's voice was quietly insistent. "I think we have the right to know."

Curt stopped. He turned to look first at the Brain, then at Grag, and finally at Otho.

"You know what I'm going to do," he said. "I'm going to kill Victor Corvo."

IX

Alone in his quarters, Curt stripped off his bodysuit and stepped into the bathroom shower. He gave himself the luxury of five minutes under the scalding spray, but while the water relaxed his muscles it couldn't ease his mind.

Toweling off, he put on a robe, then carefully selected an outfit from his closet and laid it out on his bed: a dark, close-fitting tunic and trousers, faux-leather knee boots, a utility belt with an attached sidearm holster. Clothes that could be worn beneath space gear but were more durable than a bodysuit. The pistol he intended to use was in another room, waiting for his hand on this day.

He didn't immediately get dressed, but instead spent a half hour in tai chi and karate exercises, working out in the middle of the large, rock-walled room that had once been his parents' bedroom; he didn't move into it from the smaller room where he'd lived as a child until his eighteenth birthday a couple of years ago, when Simon had finally given him permission to do so. He sought to put his thoughts aside as he physically prepared for the task ahead, but even so it seemed as if a hundred thoughts were going through his mind, and Corvo was at the center of every one of them.

He wondered where the rage he felt came from. He had no memories of his parents, other than a vague sense of emotional warmth when he thought of his mother. They were killed when he was still an infant; in a sense, the only family he'd ever really known was a cyborg, an android, and a robot. Nonetheless, he'd been raised knowing that Roger and Elaine Newton were murdered in cold blood and that there were still forces extant who'd extinguish his own life if they knew that he'd survived. And now those forces had a name and a face.

Every time Curt reconsidered, even for a moment, the vow he'd made to the others—*I'm going to kill Victor Corvo*—he found himself remembering the senator's smug, self-assured face. If Simon and Otho were correct—and they must be; they'd witnessed everything that had happened here twenty years ago—then Corvo had not only gotten away with murder, but had even risen to a high place in society.

But why hadn't he been told any of this until now?

Curt had just finished his workout and was resting on his bed when there was a knock at the door. Otho walked in, datapad in hand. "Sorry to bother you. Were you napping?" Curt shook his head. "Just wanted to let you know that Grag and I successfully disconnected the generator from the hopper, and Grag is now installing it in the *Comet*." He held out the pad. "Here's the status report if you want to see it. We should be ready to go in a few hours."

Sitting up, Curt took the pad from him. He gave it only a cursory glance, though, before putting it aside. "Sit down. I want to talk to you."

"Figured you might." Otho took the chair at the small, cluttered desk on the other side of the room. "What's on your mind? As if I can't guess."

"Why didn't you, Grag, and the Brain tell me about Corvo until now?" Curt sat cross-legged on the bed, resting his forearms on his knees. "Why did you make me wait all my life to tell me the truth about how my parents died?"

"We did tell you the truth . . . just not all of it." Otho shook his head. "Remember that while I may have been present, I was an adult in form only. I'd been decanted only a couple of months earlier, so I still had the mind of a child. Grag wasn't much better"—a disgusted upward flicker of his catlike eyes—"and probably never will be. So, really, Simon knows better than anyone else here what happened that day. You're going to have to ask him—"

"I'm asking you."

Otho nodded, understanding that which Curt was leaving unsaid.

For all of his incorporeal strangeness, Simon Wright had always been a paternal figure to them both. He'd taken Roger Newton's place as Curt's father, and by extension Otho's as well. And although Otho had matured much more quickly than Curt due to the accelerated education his bionic mind had received, nonetheless the Brain remained his mentor. So while they both respected and obeyed Simon, they were also aware that, like any parent, he didn't always tell them everything. The Brain had his secrets, and this was one of them.

"Long ago," Otho went on, "Simon and I agreed to wait until you were old enough not only to understand what happened, but also to decide for yourself what action you wanted to take. Victor Corvo escaped justice that day. Since then, he has become a powerful individual, even more than he was. If he'd known that any of use—even you, only a baby—were still alive, he could have effortlessly destroyed us all. So it would have done no good to have you hungering for revenge at the same time that we were trying to remain hidden."

Curt was quiet for a moment, gazing down at the woven bedspread that he absently tugged at with his fingers. "You could have taken me back to Earth . . ."

"No. You were dead. In fact, all four of you—Simon, your father, your mother, and you yourself—had been declared dead even before you arrived here. If you'd shown up on Earth, with or without the rest of us, it would have raised questions that Corvo couldn't allow to be answered. Again, he would have stopped at nothing to have you killed, even though you were only a baby. As to my fate . . ." Otho shrugged. "If I were allowed to live, then I probably would've had my mind scrubbed so that I'd become nothing more than a stupid slave. Or worse, the prototype of a stupid slave."

"What do you mean?" Curt shook his head. "I don't understand."

"No, of course not . . . because you haven't been told everything. But when you said you wanted to attend the dedication ceremony at the Straight Wall and the Brain found out that Corvo would be in attendance, he and I realized that an opportunity had come for you to see your parents' killer, not as a face on a screen but in the flesh."

"And now, you're going to let me go out and kill him?"

Otho didn't respond at once. Instead he gazed at the mirror above Curt's dresser, as if assessing himself and his place in things. "We all lost something the day your parents were killed," he said at last. "I lost my creators. Simon lost the only chance he had to become a living person again, albeit an artificial one like myself. Even Grag, dumb as it is, gained not only intelligence but even emotions because Elaine saw potential in it and raised its sapience to human levels." He looked at Curt askance. "Don't let it know I said that, okay?"

"So that's what you want me to do? Avenge my parents?"

"We're going to let you decide for yourself what you want to do. But Curt . . ." Otho paused. "You need to understand that you're not just talking about taking revenge. You're also contemplating the assassination of a member of the Solar Coalition Senate, the elected representative of the Lunar Republic. If you fail, you'll die, and if you're successful, there's nothing any of us can do to protect you. You'll become a hunted man, and the IPF won't rest until you're either in custody or dead."

"I understand." Even as he said this, though, Curt felt the weight of Otho's words. Like it or not, the android was correct. Curt was planning the most heinous of crimes. Once committed, there would be no turning back from his deeds . . . and the rest of his life would probably be measured in seconds.

Otho silently regarded him for a few moments. "Before you commit yourself, perhaps you should hear everything, from the beginning. And not just from me, either."

Curt nodded and raised his left hand. "Brain, would you come to my room, please?" he asked, speaking to his ring as he'd done for most of his life. It wasn't necessary for him to communicate with Simon this way, but he'd inherited the ring from his late father; it had been a gift to Roger from Elaine, who'd used it to keep in touch with her husband when Anni nodes weren't always accessible. Curt had worn it almost constantly ever since the Brain gave it to him on his eighteenth birthday, and in one major way it was superior to an Anni, which could be intercepted by anyone capable of hacking into an individual's neural-net system.

A minute passed, then the door slid open again and the Brain floated into the room. "Yes, Curt?" he asked, his eyestalks twitching in his direction. "You have a question?"

"What happened the day my parents were killed? I mean, what really happened?" Curt glanced at Otho. "He's told me a little, but he said that you're the only one who knows everything."

"It's time, Simon," Otho said quietly. "He's ready."

"Very well, I agree. But first"—Simon moved backward, his props reversing to carry him into the main room—"let's get you some dinner. This will take a while to explain, and you haven't had anything to eat since—"

"No, Simon." Curt's tone was quietly insistent. "I want to hear it now."

The Brain hesitated, and then moved forward into the bedroom again. "All right," he said, purring past Curt and Otho to make a soft landing on the desk. "Let's go back to the beginning . . ."

PART TWO
Twenty Years Before

1

"I know we have some disagreements," Victor Corvo told Roger Newton, "but I'm sure you'll eventually see things my way."

They stood together on the jetty beneath Roger's condominium tier and waited for the water taxi. Beyond the banked walls of the New Montauk oceanarcology, the sun was beginning to set. Across the fourteen floors of the horseshoe-shaped artificial island, the lights of condos, restaurants, and nightclubs were starting to come on, reflecting off the placid waters of the enclosed lagoon. An evening breeze, scented with salt, came in fresh and cool from the Long Island Sound. Amid the elms and maples of the nearby municipal park, English sparrows were chirping farewell to another day as, in the courtyard of an outdoor café, a four-piece string ensemble warmed up by rehearsing a few bars of Mozart's "A Little Night Music."

A pleasant evening, Roger thought. It would get better once Victor was gone. Or then again, maybe not.

"I wouldn't count on it," he replied, but then he caught the look on Corvo's face and carefully amended himself. "I'll keep what you've said in mind, though. The otho project wasn't intended for what you have in mind, but I agree there's potential for . . . other uses."

"And profitable ones at that." Corvo watched as a small catamaran slowly approached the jetty, its pilot keeping at harbor speed as he steered past the pleasure boats moored around them. "Medical applications are fine, Roger, and I appreciate that the major reason you and Elaine are doing this is to save Dr. Wright's life. But your androids—"

"I prefer the term othos."

"Sure you do." A patronizing smile. "But don't be surprised if the public calls 'em androids. It's an old term, and one they understand better than"—Corvo peered upward as if trying to drag a difficult term down from the sun-streaked twilight clouds—"'orthogenetic transhuman organism.' That's what it means, yes? Whatever you call it, if you're successful, there's going to be money to be made from your work. A *lot* of money."

"And a lot of potential for abuse, too."

"Not your problem or mine." Corvo gazed down at the water lapping against the jetty boardwalk; this was, Roger reflected, one of those rare moments when Victor actually appeared to . . . well, *think*, for lack of a better word. "I appreciate your ethical considerations, Rog," he went on, using a nickname that Roger secretly detested, "but I can't eat ethics. I've already invested considerable sums of money into your work, with more in escrow. I expect a return on my investment."

"You'll get it, Vic," Roger said, retaliating with Corvo's own despised nickname and ignoring the scowl he received for doing so. "You're not wasting your money, and I promise that you'll see a healthy return. But as I've said all along, sometimes the best profit can't be measured by a bank statement, but by the gift you'll have bestowed on the human race—"

"Save it for your Nobel acceptance speech." Corvo impatiently waved him off. "I want money, not a boon to mankind." He shot Roger a knowing look and added, "And since I'll be controlling ownership of the patent, you can bet I'll get it . . . no matter what it takes."

"I'm sure you will." The chill that went down Roger's spine didn't come from the fading of the sun. He'd always known that Victor was interested only in amassing wealth. Corvo was a millionaire with aspirations of becoming a billionaire, but that hadn't bothered Roger and Elaine when they'd approached him in search of the enormous capital they needed to accomplish their goals. Yet it wasn't until this afternoon, when Corvo had come out to New Montauk for a private meeting at the lab, that Roger had truly realized that Corvo wasn't just greedy, but unprincipled as well.

Dangerously unprincipled.

The water taxi bleated its horn as it drew close to the jetty. The pilot cut his engine to coast the rest of the way in. A dockhand extended a boat hook to grab hold of the gunnel. As Corvo bent to pick up the attaché case at his feet, the pilot stepped out of the wheelhouse to help him aboard. "You headed for Port LaGuardia spaceport, mister?" the pilot asked. Corvo nodded, and the pilot reached for his case. "Right this way . . . I'll take that."

"No, you won't." Corvo yanked the case away, and the pilot got the idea and backed off. Corvo turned to Roger again. "We'll have another meeting when I get back from Mars, with you and your wife both. I expect she'll be able to attend this time."

"I'm sure she will," Roger said. "Curt was being a little bit of a problem today. He needed his mother."

"Yeah, of course." Again, the humorless smile. "Y'know, that's another job androids could do . . . function as babysitters."

"You're quite right," Roger said. "If you study history, you find many children had nannies who were slaves."

Corvo either didn't catch the bland sarcasm or simply wasn't offended. "I'll be in touch," he said, turning to carefully step aboard the boat. "Keep me posted on how things work out."

Roger stood on the jetty and watched as the water taxi pulled away, slowly growling its way across the lagoon to the opening in the ocean-arc walls. He allowed a polite interval for the taxi to recede before he started walking back down the jetty. As he did, he raised his left hand. The large jeweled ring he wore on his hand was Elaine's gift to him last Christmas after doctors told him that he wasn't a suitable candidate for nanosurgical Anni implants, so the ring was her solution.

"Anni, call Elaine, please," he said.

A few moments later, he heard his wife's voice in his ear. —*How did it go?*

"Not well. Not well at all. Call Simon and ask if he's feeling up to coming over this evening. We need to discuss something."

11

Roger and Elaine Newton lived on the top floor of the East Tier. From the fourteenth floor, the view from their condo balcony included the Long Island Archipelago. Beyond New Montauk's seawall could be seen other oceanarcs floating atop the flooded remains of the Hamptons. The view was one of the reasons why Roger paid for the privilege of living in New Montauk's highest residential level. Elaine protested the expense when they moved here from upstate New York, but she had to admit that the ocean breeze coming in over the wall was an added bonus. And now, Roger appreciated something else about the place: an added measure of privacy that came from having nothing above their balcony but open sky.

He was sitting outside when the doorbell rang. "Can you get that, sweetheart?" he called, barely looking away from the pad open before him on the patio table. "It's probably the pizza I ordered."

Elaine was in the living room, gently rocking Curt in her arms. "All right, I'll get it," she replied, then gently laid the baby in his wicker bassinet before walking over to the front door.

Curt barely stirred, for which Roger was grateful. A couple of weeks earlier, he'd received the neck injections that had introduced Anni nanites to his cranium; fortunately, Curt hadn't inherited his father's resistance to neurological nanosurgery. Nonetheless, while the hair-fine neural network gradually developed within the lobes of his brain, the slightest motion of his head was likely to spark a headache. The fact that he was sleeping soundly was an indication that his Anni was nearly complete. Of course, the fact that Elaine had just finished breast-feeding him probably helped a bit as well.

Simon Wright was on the other side of the door, sitting in the gyro-chair that lately had become his sole means of mobility, an oxygen line running from his nose to a tank on the back. He said nothing as Elaine stepped aside to let him in, but waited while she carried out the pretense of accepting a pizza from a deliveryman and paying for it. Simon lived on the East Tier's ocean level, just a quick elevator ride from the Newtons'. When they started to become suspicious of Victor Corvo's motives, they'd worked out protocols for visiting each other's condos without attracting notice. It was entirely possible that he might have arranged for electronic surveillance of their apartments as well as their workplace; the less he knew what they were saying behind his back, the better.

"I take it the meeting didn't go well," Simon said as he rolled out on the terrace.

"No . . . no, it didn't." Roger waited another moment while his wife made sure that the baby was sleeping soundly, then she followed Simon out onto the balcony, sliding shut the glass door behind her. "In fact, I'd say we're in worse shape than we were before."

"We should have never brought him in as a partner." Elaine crossed the balcony to take a seat next to her husband. Small and petite, with long chestnut hair and soulful gray eyes, she was a contrast to the tall, blond athlete whom she'd married. "I didn't like him from the start, and—"

"We've been through this before." Roger was tired of reiterating arguments they'd had already. "We needed a higher level of R-and-D funding than we could've received from government or university grants, and Victor was recommended to me."

"Don't . . . blame yourself." Simon's voice was an asthmatic wheeze. He was noticeably pale, his skin nearly as white as what remained of his hair; Roger wondered at the effort it must have taken for him just to get in his chair and leave his condo. "I heard that . . . Corvo was a venture capitalist who . . . was willing to invest in technology. I figured that he might . . . put us over the top and that's why I . . . suggested that we go to him." A scowl beneath the nose clip of his oxygen line. "Didn't know he . . . had other ambitions."

"Look, it's both our faults." Roger leaned back in his chair. "We knew a long time ago that his interest in artificial life isn't the same as ours. We want to create replacement bodies, he wants to make a slave race. But we figured that we could gamble a little by making a Faustian bargain with him, then go public with the medical applications—hopefully with you as the living example—while taking measures to make sure that Victor doesn't get his way."

A taut smile appeared on Simon's face. "I'm hoping you're . . . on the right track. Starting to run . . . out of time here."

"Don't worry, Simon." Elaine reached forward to gently grasp the back of his hand. "I've nearly finished the redesign for the cerebral-support unit. Even if your body gives out before the otho is ready, we'll be able to sustain your brain indefinitely . . . even give you a certain measure of mobility."

Simon nodded gratefully. This had been the plan all along, even before Corvo had become involved. The objective of Roger and Elaine's research, which they'd been doing ever since they met at the University of Chicago where Roger Newton had been Simon Wright's brightest student, was the development of a fully functional artificial human to whom a person's consciousness could be transferred upon the death of his natural body. A kind of immortality, really. When Simon became terminally ill, with no possible cure, it was agreed that he would become the willing test subject for the first orthogenic transhuman organism.

They feared that Simon might die before the otho was ready, so Elaine had turned some of her attention to a side project, the development of a cyborg whose form Simon would temporarily occupy. Cerebral support units had lately been introduced to preserve human brains after the death of the body, but they were little more than wetware interfaces; the minds sealed within them could do nothing more than see what was going on around them and answer questions. For Elaine, this was a form of living death, but for Simon there was potential for something far greater. As a preliminary stage toward a new life as an otho, he was going to test their work by first becoming a cyborg.

Elaine looked at Roger again. "So what did Victor say to you today that's making you hit the panic button?"

"He . . . didn't tell you already?" Simon asked.

"No. I wanted to wait until we were all here together." Roger slowly let out his breath. "Victor sees a potential military application in this . . . namely, replacement bodies for soldiers killed in combat. His idea is to have othos on standby in medical facilities not far from the battlefield. When a soldier is mortally wounded, he or she would be brought to the facility and have his mind scanned into the new body and—"

"I don't see the problem with that." Elaine shook her head. "I mean, we don't have wars very often anymore, but when we do, they're bloody as hell. It's just as important to save the life of a soldier as it is to save a civilian."

"It is, but that's not Victor's idea. He doesn't want to simply save a soldier's life, but to do it quickly enough so that he or she can be sent straight back into combat. No attrition rate . . . just send in the same troops again and again and again."

Simon stared at him. "Horrifying."

"At the very least, highly unethical." Elaine idly watched the lights of boats moving in and out of the lagoon. "It's bad enough that he sees potential in creating a slave race. This would mean creating cannon fodder as well, with soldiers condemned to die over and over again."

"Not just that," Roger said, "but othos will be superior in many ways to humans. Carbon-fiber skeleton, infrared night vision, auditory channels more sensitive to higher frequencies . . ." He reached for the pitcher of ice water he'd set out on the table. "No country wouldn't consider possessing that kind of capability. If they could replace troops as fast as they were killed, they'd never lose a war . . ."

". . . because the wars would never end," Elaine finished.

Roger nodded as he poured a glass of water and offered it to Simon. "But Victor doesn't see this. All he sees is the money he'd get from military contracts."

"You mean . . . how much money we'd earn . . . don't you?" Simon shook his head at the offered glass.

"That's the interesting part." Roger took the water back and had a sip. "All during our conversation, he kept referring to the company with the singular 'I'—'I'll approach the contractors,' 'I'll own the patents,' and so forth. As if the three of us don't exist."

"Perhaps we don't." Elaine's voice was so soft as to be nearly a whisper. "Not so far as his plans for the future are concerned."

"You don't think . . . he'd go that far . . . do you?" Simon asked.

Roger didn't answer at once. Resting the glass on the table, he folded his hands together and silently regarded them for a few moments. "I hate to say it," he said at last, "but I think he would. He knows he can't count on you being around very much longer, but as for Elaine and me . . ." He shook his head. "There've been rumors that Victor has some . . . well, let's call them what they are: criminal associations. People in the underworld he's called on in the past to do dirty work for him."

"I've heard the same thing," Elaine said. "He's been seen with former members of Starry Messenger, for instance."

"If it becomes convenient for us to disappear," Roger said, "then I have little doubt that he'd have no qualms about arranging for us to mysteriously vanish." He looked through the balcony windows at the bassinet. "Curt, too."

No one spoke for a minute. The three of them gazed at one another, realizing the danger they were in. "So what . . . do we do?" Simon asked. "Abandon the project?"

There was no mistaking the quiver in his voice at the prospect of having to face death when an alternative was so close at hand. Roger smiled and shook his head. "No, we're not going to do that . . . not while we have a choice."

"And that is?"

"We disappear . . . but under our terms." He turned in his chair to gaze toward the east. "And there's where we'll go."

While they'd been speaking, the Moon had risen over the Atlantic, three-quarters full and shining brightly upon the dark waters. Roger pointed to it. "I've been looking around, and I've found a perfect site. An energy research lab in the Tycho crater that was abandoned half finished when the company that owned it went bankrupt. It has both surface and underground facilities, and—"

"What are you saying?" Elaine asked. "That we pack up and move to the Moon?" Roger nodded. "And, of course, Victor will never find out."

"Not if we work fast, he won't." Pushing back his chair, Roger stood up from the table. "His private shuttle lifted off from LaGuardia just a couple of hours after our meeting. By now, he should be boarding the next beamship for Mars." He began pacing back and forth across the balcony. "Another interesting rumor about Victor . . . he's got an aresian mistress whom he's recently made pregnant. He doesn't intend to marry her, but he's also afraid that if he dumps her, she'll use her pregnancy to take him for everything he's worth. So—"

"What does that have . . . to do with us?" Simon asked.

"I checked the schedule for return flights from Mars. There's none for the next nine months. Victor's outbound flight is the last one for the current launch window. After that, Mars's orbit takes it on the opposite side of the Sun from Earth, and so nothing will be launched from Mars to Earth during that time. This gives us a window of opportunity."

"To do what? Run away to the Moon and disappear?" A skeptical look from Elaine. "He'll just track us down."

"No, he won't." Roger walked behind her and gently laid his hands on her shoulders. "Not if he thinks we're dead."

///

Roger Newton was the scion of a wealthy North American States family that traced its British lineage back to Sir Isaac Newton's family. While he and Elaine had done well from the biotech patents developed by the small research company they'd started with Simon Wright, it wasn't necessary for them to live off their work; his family already had a sizable estate. So when Roger decided a few years earlier that he needed a hobby as a diversion from his research into artificial life, there was enough money in the bank for him to buy a new toy: a spaceship.

The craft he'd purchased was a secondhand racing yacht, the kind used for competition regattas. Christened the *Cornet* by its original owners, it was a hundred feet long and shaped like an elongated teardrop, with a round bombardier window at its broad bow and the exhaust bell of its magnetoplasma main engine at its tapered stern. Ducted maneuvering thrusters along the titanium-alloy hull allowed for precision steering, while recessed rungs enabled it to be coupled to a beamsail for interplanetary travel.

Although the *Cornet* had tripod landing gear, it was meant for emergencies only. The yacht was principally designed for races in which a small fleet of spacecraft would launch from Earth's orbit, fly at top speed to the Moon or a near-Earth asteroid, circle it, then race back home to aerobrake in the upper atmosphere before returning to the starting point, where the winner would be determined by minimum elapsed time. So the *Cornet* seldom touched down on a planetary surface; when it did, it was usually the Moon, where the little craft would make a tail-first landing at a spaceport maintenance field. Its engine, while powerful enough for racing, didn't have sufficient thrust to achieve Earth escape velocity.

The *Cornet* could be operated by a single individual. Indeed, shortly after purchasing the craft, Roger took the mandatory flight instruction courses and earned his spacecraft master pilot's license. Although regatta rules normally called for a crew of four, a safety precaution that serious competitors considered a nuisance, Roger came to realize that he enjoyed the fact that the ship had accommodations for four. He'd twice entered the *Cornet* in lunar races, with Elaine as first mate and experienced spacers as crew, and both times he'd come in near the end of the pack. That was enough to convince him that he preferred leisurely weekend jaunts around near-Earth space to the white-knuckle challenge of trying to beat another ship to the finish line. He kept the *Cornet* but quietly decided that, from now on, it would only be used for the occasional pleasure cruise with family and friends.

Six months after the furtive meeting at Roger and Elaine's condo, the Newton family and Simon Wright disembarked from the Ecuador skytower at Station Aztec, the doughnut-shaped geosynchronous habitat that marked the endpoint of space elevator ascents from the South American Federation. It was unusual for Roger and Elaine to take the long way to orbit; they usually preferred catching a commercial shuttle from New York or Boston. Curt was still too young for high-g liftoffs, though, and Simon had become too frail, so this time they'd taken the elevator to Aztec, where Roger already reserved a skiff to transport them the rest of the way to the *Cornet*'s slip at the Highgate anchorage.

Those who spotted them getting off the elevator would later report a curious thing; along with nine-month-old Curt, Roger, Elaine, and Simon were accompanied by what appeared to be a large, saucer-shaped drone, one capable of carrying two nylon duffel bags in the station's low gravity. Robots were not uncommon on Aztec, but no one had ever seen one quite like this. When an IPF customs agent questioned them about it, Elaine told him it was the prototype of an all-purpose service drone she and her husband were testing. People watched the machine carrying their bags through the station's low-g corridors and told each other that they'd like to see something like that come on the market; a flying 'bot with claw manipulators could be useful around the house. No one had the faintest suspicion it could be anything else.

An hour later, the skiff hard-docked with the *Cornet*, which was moored at the same anchorage as other regatta yachts. At Roger's request, Highgate personnel had already pressurized the fuel tanks with argon. While Elaine began warming up the engine's magnetic superconductors and ion cyclotron and Simon stowed the drone, Roger put on his vacuum suit and went out through the airlock. The ostensible purpose of his spacewalk was a routine preflight inspection, but while he was on the side of the *Cornet* facing away from the rest of the anchorage, he strapped a large, foil-wrapped bundle to the hull near the stern. He took a moment to switch on an attached radio receiver and conduct a quick test with Simon, and then returned to the airlock. No one saw what he did.

Once he'd removed his suit and stowed it away, Roger pulled himself to the command deck, where Elaine and Simon were already strapped in. No longer asleep, baby Curt watched in fascination from his mother's arms as his father filed a flight plan with Highgate traffic control. Just a simple, two-day jaunt to the Moon and back, no landing intended, return destination the same as the departure point.

It was identical to nearly every trip Roger and Elaine had taken with the *Cornet* since they'd retired from regatta racing. The traffic control officer filed the flight plan, relayed a copy to lunar trafco at Port Copernicus, and bade the pilot a pleasant trip. A few minutes later, the yacht detached its mooring lines and slowly backed out of its slip along the docking spar. Once it was far enough away from the station, the little teardrop-shaped craft performed a ninety-degree starboard turn and fired its main engine. Within seconds, it vanished from sight.

This was the last time anyone saw the *Cornet*.

IV

Lunar night lay heavy upon Tycho.

Earth was three-quarters full above the rim, but shed little more than tepid light; the towering crater walls and central peak flung a carpet of shadows across the rock-strewn floor. Even at the construction site on the crater's east side, the spotlights had been extinguished, the robots temporarily stilled.

The dozen Grag 'bots who'd been constantly working day and night for the last five months had done so without direct human supervision. Nothing except machines had set foot in the crater since the half-finished energy research lab was purchased a month earlier by an obscure New York biotech firm. The robots were leased from a lunar construction company and brought to this place by the same unmanned hoppers that had carried in construction equipment and pallets of building materials. A Grag 320-A had overseen the refurbishment of the abandoned site, making sure the other robots accurately and efficiently carried out instructions transmitted from Earth.

With no need for shift changes or union-mandated rest breaks, the robots—no two of which were exactly alike, each designed for specialized tasks—had tirelessly labored for 3,367 hours, 29 minutes, and 18 seconds before the Grag 320-A received, via a long-baseline antenna buried just beneath the lunar regolith, a brief message from a spacecraft in low orbit above the Moon. Following orders, the supervisor robot ordered all the other Grags to cease work at once and shut down the tripod-mounted spotlights.

The boss 'bot now stood at the edge of the construction site, its eyes emitting a soft red glow as it peered at the sky above the crater's eastern rim. Watching. Waiting.

Less than ten minutes after the 'bot received the transmission, a bright spot of light hurtled into view above the crater rim.

It was moving fast and low. On Earth, it might have been mistaken for a large meteor entering the upper atmosphere, save for the fact that it was fewer than five hundred feet above the ground. As it streaked over the crater walls, the fireball flared even more brightly, creating a false dawn on the crater floor far below. At the same time, it abruptly slowed down, braking as it commenced a quick descent into the vast crater.

As backwash from the fireball revealed the teardrop-shaped spacecraft behind it, the Grag 320-A watching its descent sent a signal to machinery deep below the crater floor. A hundred yards from where it was standing, long thin bars of light forming a luminescent H suddenly appeared upon the ground. They quickly expanded, becoming two mammoth doors cleverly disguised to resemble the surrounding terrain, opening to reveal an illuminated landing platform just below.

In the silence of the lunar night, the small yacht came in for touchdown. Flanges opened upon its aft fuselage to allow its multijointed landing tripod to unfold into position. As its pads made contact with the platform, the spacecraft's engine shut down.

The *Cornet* had reached its destination.

Visible only by the platform's landing beacons and the soft illumination of the yacht's bow and side portholes, the platform began to slowly descend into a large hangar hidden beneath the crater floor. The moment the *Cornet* disappeared from sight, the doors began to close again. The Grag 320-A watched the doors until they were completely shut; no light escaped to betray the hangar's existence.

The robot continued to observe the sky above Tycho. Several minutes went by, then another spot of light appeared. This one was much farther up, though, and moving much more slowly: the engine exhaust of a spacecraft in low orbit, searching the lunar badlands thousands of feet below. The robot watched as the craft passed over Tycho; it did not slow down or change course, and in less than a minute it passed over the horizon to the west and disappeared.

Inside the cockpit, Roger Newton had just reconfigured the pilot's seat from a horizontal to vertical position and was unbuckling the harness when a blandly mechanistic voice came through his headset. *"Search craft sighted above Tycho,"* the Grag 320-A reported. *"It has moved on. No indication of having noticed the base or your presence."*

Roger smiled. "Thank you. Remain on station and report any unusual activity." He turned to Elaine, whose seat was still reclined in landing position. "Good news from the consruction team supervisor. It spotted a search and rescue craft, but apparently it wasn't following us. Still searching for wreckage, I guess."

Elaine nodded, not returning the smile but nonetheless quietly relieved. "So we're dead," she murmured. Looking down at the sleeping child in her arms, she added, "Such a tragedy. At least it was quick . . . you probably never felt a thing."

"With luck, that's what everyone will assume." Roger reached over to touch the controls for his wife's seat. With a soft whirr it slowly tilted upward, allowing her to place her feet on a deck that, until now, had been an aft bulkhead. "I packed enough phosphorous into the limpet charge to simulate a catastrophic engine failure. If anyone on the ground or in orbit actually saw what happened—"

"They'll think the main engine . . . blew just as you were throttling up . . . for the perigee burn to return to Earth." Behind them, Simon had already lowered the passenger seat. "You're lucky . . . I'm already a dying man," he wheezed. "You would've scared . . . ten years off my life with . . . that dive you made."

"Sorry. Couldn't be helped." Roger stood up and arched his back, sighing a little as he felt the vertebrae of his lower spine crack. It had been years since the last time he'd visited the Moon; it felt good to get back in its lower gravity. "We got here without being detected. That's what matters."

After he'd jettisoned the bomb strapped to the *Cornet*'s hull and sent the radio signal that ignited it, Roger had thrown the stick forward and fired the engine, putting the yacht into a dangerous power-dive that had shed 1,500 feet in seconds. A tricky maneuver, and dangerous as hell; he'd put the lives of his wife, child, and mentor at risk, not to mention his own. But if it worked, as he believed it would, any lunar traffic control officers observing the small yacht on radar after it transmitted a Mayday would believe that its engine had suffered—as accident reports tended to call such things—"a major malfunction" that obliterated the small craft and its passengers. Such accidents were uncommon, but not impossible. Magnetoplasma engines customarily sustained temperatures of nearly two million degrees Kelvin; if the magnetic fields that confined them to the reactor vessel failed, the result would be catastrophic.

Which is what happened to the *Cornet*, or so Roger wanted everyone to believe. There would be many people at home who'd be shocked and saddened by the tragedy. Neither he nor Elaine had any living parents or siblings, but they each had relatives and close friends who were probably just now getting the news. There was nothing that could be done about this, though, at least for the time being.

But if Victor Corvo was fooled, too, then it would be worth it.

Roger climbed down the ladder from the control room to the middeck. Pausing in the galley, he opened a wall locker between the curtained bunks to collect ankle weights. He strapped on a pair and left two more on the galley table for Elaine and Simon—Roger smiled as he wondered how long it would take Curt to adapt to one-sixth g; this would be interesting to observe—then continued climbing down to the third level where the ready-room and airlock lay. He didn't need to suit up again. A glance at the indicator panel beside the outer hatch as he stepped into the airlock told him that positive pressure lay outside the ship. Roger turned the recessed wheel to undog the hatch, then grasped the lock lever and pushed it down. A faint hiss of escaping air, then he shoved the hatch open.

The *Cornet* stood on its tail within an underground shaft resembling a twentieth-century ICBM silo, except that it was big enough to also accommodate a lunar hopper that had its own elevator platform and doors. The shaft had been originally intended to contain instruments for the energy research that the lab's original owners had planned to conduct before they ran out of money; Roger and Simon had redesigned it to hide the *Cornet* and the base's short-range transport.

Roger heard the whirr of immense fans winding down, and his nose picked up the faint burned-gunpowder aroma of moondust. The hangar computer had automatically decontaminated the shaft during the pressurization procedure. As expected, the gangway had also been extended. It led straight from the *Cornet* to a door high in the hangar's curving wall.

Roger stepped out on the enclosed catwalk and looked up at the vessel. The fast little ship had gotten them there safely, but it would be a long time before he'd fly it again. It was officially destroyed, after all . . . yet it wasn't the only regatta yacht out there. Peering at the ship's name christened on the hull beside the hatch, it occurred to him that it wouldn't take much to change the *r* and *n* to an *m*. Perhaps if the *Cornet* became the *Comet* . . .

The door slid open on the other end of the catwalk, and he turned to see the supervisor robot standing there. "Good evening, Dr. Newton," it said, lowering its bulbous head slightly to regard Roger with unblinking red eyes. "I hope your trip went well."

"It did, umm—"

"You may call me Grag."

Roger raised an eyebrow. Most robots, when asked to identify themselves, usually rattled off a serial number, then offered their owner or operator the option of picking a name for them. This one had not only made the choice itself, but had apparently selected the name of its manufacturer as its own. Interesting . . .

Roger turned to see his wife standing in the airlock, Curt riding in a papoose sling upon her back. "Where's Simon?" he asked.

"Coming." Then she dropped her voice. "He's having trouble, Roger. I think the trip took more out of him than he wants to admit . . . particularly the last part."

Roger nodded. It was nothing less than a miracle that Simon had remained alive this long. The last hour or so must have been an ordeal.

"Go on ahead of us," he said quietly. "I'll take care of him." She nodded and walked across the gangway, squeezing past the giant robot that stood on the other side. "Come here, Grag," Roger said. "I need your help."

"As you wish, Dr. Newton." As Grag stepped onto the gangway, the padded soles of its massive feet making a solid thud with each step, Elaine gave Roger a significant look. She'd overheard the conversation he'd had with Grag and noticed the same thing he had: this particular robot had not only chosen a name for itself, but it was also that of its creator. An indication of emerging sentience? Something worth investigating . . . later.

"Simon?" Roger called out as he reentered the ship, Grag right behind him. Hearing no answer, he moved quickly across the readyroom and up the ladder.

He found Simon in the middeck galley, clutching the folded frame of a dining table chair and struggling to hold himself up. The old man was breathing hard; his skin was sallow, his forehead lightly beaded with sweat. He apparently knew where he was, because he raised his head to stare at Roger as he scrambled the rest of the way up the ladder, but when he tried to speak, all that came out was a dry whisper.

"Roger . . . sorry, I . . ."

Simon's legs gave way beneath him. Even in the Moon's lower gravity, they no longer had the strength to support him. Roger caught his old professor as he fell; he gently lowered him to the floor and tore open the collar of his shirt in an effort to help him breathe better.

"Grag! Find the med kit! I need the oxygen mask!" Roger didn't look to see whether the robot was complying, but instead raised his ring to his mouth. "Elaine!" he snapped, praying that the base's Anni node was active. "Get up here! Simon's having a seizure!"

It was soon clear that Simon Wright was beyond their ability to save him. He lost consciousness by the time Grag located the oxygen mask. When Elaine returned to the ship, she found her husband huddled above the old man, cradling his head in his lap.

"Roger . . . ," she whispered.

"Go to the lab, make sure the suspension tank has been installed."

Roger's voice was breaking, his eyes moist. "Take the drone with you. Grag and I will carry him in when you tell me you're ready."

"All right, but . . . are you sure we can do this? I mean, we've just arrived."

"We have to try, don't we? Hurry."

V

The empty beaker on the lab bench weighed no more than a tenth of an ounce in lunar gravity, but it might just as well have been ten pounds. The three fingers of the drone's right manipulator fumbled with the receptacle, their rubberized tips seeking a firm grip on the glass surface. The robot hand finally grasped the beaker and lifted it from the bench, but then the drone swung about too fast on its ductfans and the beaker slipped out of its grasp.

"Damn it!" Simon snapped.

Roger darted forward and grabbed the beaker before it shattered on the floor. "No, no, you're doing fine," he said patiently, straightening up to return it to the bench. "At least you didn't break anything this time. You just need to learn how to coordinate your lateral movements with your—"

"I know what I have to do." Simon Wright's voice came from the speaker grill on the drone's body . . . on *Simon's* body, Roger silently reminded himself. A short burst of fuzz that had mystified both of them until they realized that this was an approximation of a sigh as delivered by a vocoder instead of a pair of lungs. "It's just . . . oh hell, son, I never figured it would be so hard to get used to this."

"Neither did I. Maybe we should have." Roger took a seat on a nearby stool. "But look . . . Curt took his first steps just the other day, right? So it's taken a little more than ten months for him to get to that point, and that's even after living at one-sixth g for the last four. You're having to relearn many of the same basic motor skills, and seventy-eight years of prior experience doesn't mean much when you've got manipulators for hands and props for legs."

"Perhaps, but . . ." Simon's eyestalks shifted from Roger toward the two long metal caskets set side by side in the middle of the laboratory floor. "I'm still missing him . . . the old me, I mean."

The two caskets, white and featureless, dully reflected the earthlight coming in through the lunaglass window in the ceiling high above. Connected to each other by cables, both were large enough for a person to lie supine. And indeed, each contained a body: one dead, the other in the process of being born.

The casket on the left was a modified version of the standard-issue suspension cell, the type commonly used in hospital emergency rooms to keep a dying person alive until he or she could either receive proper medical treatment or, if the condition was hopelessly terminal, euthanasia. This one contained Simon Wright's body . . . or rather, his original body. It had been hastily placed there during the coronary seizure he'd suffered four months ago immediately after the *Cornet* touched down in Tycho Crater. As they'd already planned, Roger and Elaine allowed their old friend to pass away, but as soon as his heart stopped beating in the cell, they wheeled in the robosurgeon that, along with the rest of their equipment, they'd had shipped to the hidden lab for exactly this purpose.

Over the course of the next fourteen hours, the robosurgeon, under Elaine's supervision, had opened Simon's skull, carefully removed his brain, and placed it inside the self-contained life-support cell of the drone they'd brought with them on the *Cornet* . . . or rather, the *Comet*, as it was now called. Before leaving Earth, Elaine had spent months designing and building the machine as an intermediate step toward Simon Wright's second life, with the ultimate goal of having him be able to assist her and Roger in the final steps of creating his replacement body. Two and a half hours later, Simon returned to consciousness as a cyborg, inhabiting an artificial body both radically different from yet far more useful than the form in which he'd been born.

That was just the first phase of the experiment.

The other casket was a bioclast, an apparatus specifically designed to build a full-size human body from scratch. Within this artificial womb, the individual Roger and Elaine had affectionately christened Otho—it occurred to them that the acronym derived from his scientific designation was as good a name as any—was being created.

Androids had usually been conceived as robots in human form, but the only part of Otho that was mechanical in nature was his carbon-fiber skeleton; the rest was a composite of low-stiffness polymers more resilient than human flesh. Suspended in a viscous goo of programmable nanites and organic compounds, a body was slowly being formed from the inside out. The blueprint for this new body was the old one; over the past four months, Simon Wright's body had been slowly and methodically scanned at the molecular level by lasers, which then relayed their information to the bioclast. The second casket then used this information to gradually fashion the artificial replacement for the original, drawing upon biochemicals contained in a collection of attached tanks for the material needed to construct the new body, while also integrating the subtle improvements that would make the new body superior to the first one.

This was how Roger and Elaine intended to give Simon a second chance at life. His present existence was only meant to be a temporary measure, one that would sustain his brain—the one part of him that couldn't be flawlessly duplicated—until his new body was ready. Once this was done, his brain would be scanned via high-resolution magnetic resonance imaging into Otho, and Simon Wright would return to the world of the living, this time in a body stronger and more adaptable than his original.

"I'm not sure why I even bother." Simon's ductfans tilted slightly and he floated over to the two caskets. "By the time Otho's ready, I'll have figured out how to pick up that beaker without breaking it. All that work for nothing . . ."

"No. Not for nothing." Roger folded his arms together. "You need to keep the motor skills active, or you'll have an even tougher time adapting to your new body—to Otho—once you've been transplanted. And we also want to see if the cyborg form will work as well, as an option for . . . well, people who might want to have it instead."

"I can't imagine why." Simon paused. "Well, maybe I can. I now have 360-degree peripheral vision, with no blind spots except directly beneath me. Ability to see in ultraviolet and infrared frequencies, too." His manipulators moved up and down, giving him a crablike appearance. "Claws instead of hands, if I could just learn how to make them work. Aerial mobility, limited only by power supply and gravity—"

"You'd have a short range on Earth," Roger admitted, "but here or on Mars, those fans work just fine. But it's not just that. You don't need to sleep, eat, or drink. You can directly access communications and data networks. You can even interface directly with the *Comet* if we retrofit the guidance system with a portal." He shrugged. "I can name a few people who'd give a lot to have those things."

"And I can name one person who'd like to enjoy a good meal again."

"You will. Just be—"

"I'm not sure I'd count on that," Elaine said.

She entered the main room from the stairway pushing Curt's stroller. Although he'd delighted his parents just days earlier by taking his first steps, his mother still insisted on wheeling him about the lab. From his stroller, the child beamed and waved his tiny arms at the sight of his father.

As always, Roger grinned when he saw his son. "There he is!" he exclaimed, coming down off his stool to kneel on the floor. "The Man in the Moon!" He threw open his arms, and the baby burbled and shrieked with infantile glee. "Let me see you come to Daddy!"

"Maybe a little later," Elaine said wearily. "We just got through walking around the solarium, and I think he's ready for a bottle and a nap."

At least once every twenty-four hours or so, they made a point of leaving the underground warren and going up to the part of the lab visible from the crater floor. The dome wasn't used for very much except as a surface entrance and a storage area, but it also had a solarium where they could do a little sunbathing behind the filtered lunaglass.

Lately, it had also become Curt's playroom. Elaine didn't want her child growing up with a molelike existence, so they went up there every Earth day for exercise. And while Roger and Elaine were careful not to let Curt walk too fast, lest his staggering baby steps in one-sixth gravity cause him to bounce off the ceiling, they were also mindful that he'd eventually have to return to Earth, and therefore needed to maintain proper muscle tone if he wasn't going to be the weakling that many native loonies were.

"Of course," he said, reluctantly dropping his arms. "Lunch and a nap is always good, too."

Elaine relented a little. She picked up Curt from the stroller and carried him over to his father. As Roger took his son into his arms, Simon lost patience. "What do you mean?" he demanded, his eyestalks twisting in Elaine's direction. "Is there something you're not telling me?"

Elaine didn't look at him. She rarely did anymore. Although she'd helped design the cyborg and had supervised the transfer of Simon's brain into it, she'd come to regret her role in the creation of something she now regarded as horrific. Although she was careful never to say so, hearing her old friend's voice coming from something that looked rather like a flying crab gave her the creeps. Which made what she had to tell him all that much harder to say.

"I downloaded the status report from the bioclast this morning," Elaine said, "and we're still having trouble with subcutaneous formation. For some reason or another, the bioclast is having trouble replicating certain epidermal functions."

"Which ones?" Roger asked, gently bouncing Curt in his arms.

"Follicle growth and melatonin infusion. Strangely, we're finding melatonin in the optic centers at the irises, but nowhere else. Otho will have your eyes, Simon . . ."

"But the rest of me will be pale and hairless." Simon made a slight bobbing motion that might have been a shrug. Seeing this, Roger was again intrigued by how Simon's subconscious movements were manifested by the cyborg. "So I'll be a little cold and should stay out of the sun. I can live with that."

"Yes, but there's something else as well." Still not looking directly at him, Elaine walked over to the refrigerator where she kept bottles of baby formula. She didn't open it at once, though, but paused with her hand on its door. "The neural pathways are developing at a higher rate than anticipated. Otho's brain is becoming . . . mature."

Roger stopped playing with Curt, gave her a sharp look. "Mature? He isn't completely formed yet. How can—?"

"I don't know either." Elaine shook her head. "The fact remains, though, that neuron synaptic development is occurring ten to twelve percent faster than the rest of his body. This isn't the same sort of brain we have, remember, but rather an organic silicon matrix. We designed his neural pathways to be more efficient, so—"

"His brain is growing faster," Roger finished.

"Correct. By the time he's ready to come out of the bioclast, he'll have the learning aptitude of an adult male. Not the same intelligence, of course, but we'll be able to educate him more quickly than . . . well, Curt." She paused. "If we choose to do so, that is."

None of them said anything for a few moments. Each knew what this portended. When it was still considered likely that Otho would be born an empty vessel, no one had any trouble replacing his mind with Simon's. But if he was destined to become a conscious individual, it would be ethically questionable to erase what amounted to a developed, receptive brain to make room for someone else's.

"You can't be serious," Simon said at last. "We can't come this far just to let that get in the way."

"I don't see how we have a choice," Roger said. Curt was beginning to get cranky; hungry and tired, he was starting to whimper just a bit. Elaine opened the refrigerator and pulled out a nipple bottle. "If we proceed with this as we planned, eventually we'll have to produce the results . . . and when that happens, all hell will break loose."

When Roger came up with the idea of faking their deaths and relocating to the seclusion of Tycho Crater, it had never been meant to be a permanent solution. Once Otho was fully formed and Simon's mind was transformed to the new body, the four of them would emerge from hiding, perhaps holding a press conference where they would go public with their accomplishment. Granted, it was possible that they might face criminal prosecution for perpetrating a hoax, but this way they'd be assured that Victor Corvo couldn't assert ownership of their work for his own purposes—namely, the creation of a race of androids to be used as slaves or disposable soldiers.

If, however, Roger and Elaine Newton produced an artificial being that once had a conscious mind of its own before it was replaced with that of a dead man, the scientific community would learn this as soon as they examined the data. And they would doubtless be repelled, just as the public would once they learned about this as well. And if Roger and Elaine's work were morally compromised, their efforts would be in vain. At the very least, it would give Corvo an opportunity to push them aside while he claimed it for himself.

"We can't do this," Roger said. "Not the way things are working out."

"Oh no." Simon's voice gained an edge they'd never heard before; even Elaine looked at him as he drifted closer. "Oh no you don't. I don't give a damn about your fine sense of propriety. Don't you dare leave me in this . . . in this . . ."

"Otho doesn't have to be the end result." Roger gestured at the bio-clast. "This could be just the first version, the one we learn with. We can do this again, and the next time—"

A soft chime from his ring interrupted him. A second later, Grag's voice came through.

"I'm sorry to intrude," the robot said from his habitual post on the lunar surface, *"but a spacecraft is approaching the crater. It appears to be coming in for a landing."*

Roger and Elaine glanced at each other, eyes wide with surprise. Simon was the first to react. "Can you make out a registration number on the hull?"

"Just a moment, please. It's not close enough yet." Several seconds went by, during which no one in the lab said anything or even dared breathe. Then Grag's voice returned. *"Yes, I can see the registration number. It is MRC-7611-F."* Another pause, then: *"I've checked the SolCol spacecraft registration records. The registration number matches that of a lunar shuttle belonging to the Corvo Company."*

"Victor." Elaine's voice was a fearful whisper. "He's found us."

VI

Three figures in vacuum suits emerged from the shuttle airlock and climbed down the ladder. As they marched the short distance to the dome, two things became apparent.

First: the person in the middle was their leader, and even before they reached the dome, there was no doubt who he was. No one but Victor Corvo could walk on the Moon like he owned the place.

Second: the two figures with him, a man and woman, were both armed. They wore particle-beam pistols on their suit belts, and when they cycled through the airlock, Roger noticed that the holster flaps were unbuttoned.

"Tell your people to put away their guns," he said as they entered the solarium.

"Hello, Roger, Elaine. Nice to see you again." Victor cradled his helmet beneath his left arm; in his right hand was an airtight attaché case that he placed at his feet. "For a couple of dead people, you're looking well."

Roger didn't return the smile. "The guns, Victor . . . I want them gone."

"Ummm . . ." Victor pretended to think it over a moment. "No, I think not. You don't trust me, but I have even less reason to trust you. After all, you're the ones who tried to cheat me with this rather elaborate charade. That being the case, I think it would be foolish to believe I could safely walk in here unarmed. So the guns stay, along with my bodyguards."

There was no expression on the face of the hard-eyed young man standing on Victor's left, or on that of the pretty but vaguely repellant young woman standing on his right. They'd removed their helmets, too, but left them in the airlock, keeping their hands free. Their right hands lingered near their holstered guns, and each wore gunsight monocles in their right eyes. Professionals.

For the first time, Roger regretted not bringing any weapons to the Moon. He'd spent millions on state-of-the-art scientific and medical equipment, including some that was unique and built to custom specification . . . and just then, he would have traded all of it for a PBP of his own. The only protection he and Elaine had was Grag, whom he'd instructed to join them in the dome. But while the giant robot was intelligent—even more than before, now that Elaine had upgraded his quantum AI to allow for non-Asimovian judgment and independent decision making—he'd never before been asked to guard the lives of the people who'd recently acquired him. Roger could only hope that his presence was intimidating enough to give Corvo's thugs second thoughts about drawing their guns.

"Very well," Roger said. "So you've found us—"

"And now you want me to leave? Without even asking how I figured out the four of you are still alive?"

"Three," Elaine said. "Simon died right after we got here."

Which was true enough. There was no point in mentioning that Simon Wright had been resurrected in cyborg form. He'd remained below to watch over Curt, and had strict orders from Elaine not to open the airtight door of the shaft leading underground until told to do so. Simon was observing them via a pinhole camera hidden in the ceiling and had a subaudible comlink with Grag; this gave Roger a small measure of confidence.

"Sorry to hear that," Corvo said without a trace of sympathy. "And your baby? Curt, is it?"

"In our quarters. I'd appreciate if you kept your voice down . . . he's asleep."

Roger had to refrain from smiling when she said that. Corvo could have yelled at the top of his lungs and Curt wouldn't have heard him in his bedroom twelve feet beneath the dome. Elaine had told Victor this to subtly reinforce the impression that the dome was all there was to the lab. With luck, he and his people would leave without becoming the wiser.

There was something in the way the woman standing beside Corvo smirked, though, which gave him little hope of that.

"I'll try to keep it in mind." Corvo grunted as he bent over in his heavy suit to place the helmet on the bare floor. "Anyway . . . I'll give you credit for ingenuity. You played it very well, making it seem like your ship blew up while on a vacation jaunt. Even the fact that no wreckage was found didn't raise anyone's suspicions. Every expert I spoke to told me that, when magnetoplasma engines go boom at high thrust, there's generally nothing left but dust. So it fooled me—"

"Thanks," Roger said dryly.

"—but just for a little while. There was something about the whole thing that was just too . . . y'know, convenient. Particularly since you'd expressed reluctance about some of the possible uses I've envisioned for your work. So even before I returned from Mars, I put my security team to work on tracking you down, with the assumption that you weren't really dead but had simply gone into hiding somewhere. And lo and behold—"

"They found what you were looking for."

"Yes, they did, by closely examining your company finances. First, they noticed that, shortly after I left for my Martian holiday, quite a large amount of money was transferred from your corporate account to a second one you'd established under another name. While specific information about that account was supposed to be inaccessible by anyone except the two of you, you had the misfortune of opening it at a New York bank where I have quite a bit of influence."

Elaine closed her eyes. "Damn," she muttered.

Roger said nothing, but his wife had voiced his own reaction. His family fortune was accessible through a trust fund he'd established under another name, which he'd been able to continue using even after he and Elaine were legally pronounced dead. Lately, Simon had been given access to the same funds. But the three of them needed more money than that to continue their research, and although Roger thought he'd been sly about diverting funds from one account to another, apparently he hadn't been sly enough.

"Yes," Victor continued, "I'm afraid you were a bit negligent. Once we learned that you'd transferred most of your company's assets to a hidden account, it became apparent what you'd been planning to do . . . particularly since that money was going toward the purchase of equipment that you already had in New Montauk. But the real tip-off was the leasing of construction robots here on the Moon. All my people had to do was access the rental company's records to find out where those robots had been sent and . . . well, here we are."

Roger had to bite his lower lip to keep from swearing out loud. He'd taken pains to cover their trail, going so far as to erase the memories of the robots before they were returned; Grag, they'd purchased outright after he and Elaine decided that it would be useful to have an intelligent 'bot to handle routine tasks. In hindsight, though, he should have known that someone like Victor might suspect subterfuge and would use his resources to follow up on his suspicions.

"So you've found us," he said. "What do you intend to do now?"

"Yes. What indeed?" Victor cocked his head a bit to squint inquisitively at them through one eye. "Let me ask you something . . . how much progress have you made the last few months? If my money has been well spent, then I can forgive a lot of things. We might even be able to start over with a clean slate."

"Not very far," Elaine said before Roger could come up with a plausible lie of his own. "I'm afraid the otho project has been something of a dead end. We lost Simon before we were able to preserve his brain, and even if we hadn't, our attempts to develop an artificial body failed."

"The best we were able to do was devise a higher order of cybernetic intelligence, using this robot as our test subject." Roger turned to Grag. "Say hello to Mr. Corvo, Grag."

"Hello, Mr. Corvo," Grag replied. "I'm Grag."

Corvo stared at the robot for a moment, then slowly let out his breath. "I'm very disappointed in you, Roger," he said, shaking his head. "I thought you were smarter than this. All that money I invested, just so the two of you could play house. You never even intended to produce an android, did you?"

It was all Roger could do to keep from smiling. If Victor believed that he and Elaine had done nothing worse than embezzle investment capitol, then they'd won. Corvo would go away, and even if he later sued them, at least he'd be out of their hair. By the time they were ready to go to court, Otho would be born . . . and even if he, Elaine, and Simon hadn't met their primary objective of developing a replacement body for recently deceased individuals, at least they would have produced a fully functional artificial person.

"I'm sorry, Victor," he said. "I hope we can make it up to you."

"I'm sure you can." Corvo stepped back and pointed to him and Elaine. "Get rid of them."

VII

It was through the camera concealed in the ready-room ceiling that Simon Wright saw everything that happened next.

On a viewscreen of the underground lab's surface monitor console, he watched helplessly as the bodyguards accompanying Victor Corvo snatched their guns from their holsters. In a moment, their weapons were leveled at the Newtons.

"*No!*" Roger shouted and flung up his hands, but before he could do anything more, the male bodyguard squeezed the trigger. A ruby particle beam lanced from the barrel of his gun; it went straight into Roger's chest and came out through his back. Even as it burned a tiny hole through the dome wall behind him, Roger collapsed to the floor.

In the same instant, Elaine screamed and tried to dive behind a stanchion. The woman who murdered her was laughing as she tracked Elaine with the barrel of her gun. She fired before Elaine could take cover. Elaine fell in midstep, the beam slicing through her neck. Nearly beheaded, she hit the floor a few feet from her husband.

The second particle beam burned another hole in the wall, but the slow, hissing decompression posed no danger to either Roger or Elaine. Both were dead in seconds. Roger lived just long enough to make a feeble attempt to reach out for Elaine, then life left his body and he laid still.

Simon stared at the scene for a long moment, not quite comprehending what he'd just witnessed. Then horror and disbelief were swept away by cold fury, and he yelled:

"Grag . . . *kill them!*"

The robot was already in motion. A titanium monster with burning red eyes, it stamped forward with arms raised. The woman was the closest of the three; she managed to get off a shot that grazed the robot's right bicep before his arm swept forward. Simon heard bones snap like dry wood as Grag swatted the killer across the room. Her eyes were still open as her body collapsed just a few feet from that of her victim.

Grag was advancing on the other bodyguard when Victor knelt beside the attaché case he'd brought in. As Simon watched, he opened the case. Inside was a metal cylinder rigged to an electronic device. Victor pushed a button, then leaped for the open airlock behind him.

"Grag, get out of there!" Simon snapped. "Corvo just set a bomb!"

The airlock hatch swung shut, and Corvo disappeared from sight. By then, the second killer was another corpse on the floor, his skull crushed by a single blow. Grag started to follow Corvo, but halted when he heard Simon's voice. The robot looked down at the bomb just a few steps away, and started to move toward it.

"*I will attempt to disarm it,*" Grag said, as calmly as if he were discussing a routine housekeeping task.

"No! Don't even try! We don't know how much time you have! Get back down here now!"

Grag stopped. A moment of hesitation, just long enough to make Simon Wright realize, in an oddly detached moment of appreciation, that the robot's intelligence exceeded normal cybernetic parameters; it was capable of questioning and even disagreeing with its orders. Then it lurched out of sight, leaving the camera range in the direction of the vertical tunnel leading to the underground lab. Simon slapped the button that unlocked the egress hatch from the inside, and hoped that Grag would remember to seal it shut behind him.

For several seconds, Simon Wright regarded the bodies that laid on the floor. He cared nothing for the dead killers; it was Roger and Elaine who held his attention.

In those seconds, he remembered them as they'd been. As students who'd met each other in the same place and time they'd met him, in his lecture hall at MIT. As colleagues who'd often come to his house for dinner, and with whom he'd decided to form a partnership to develop the first otho. As close friends who'd determined not to let death take their mentor—only, in the end, to have it take them instead, even as they sought to protect him as if he were a member of their own family.

Victor had obviously been planning their liquidation all along, with the bomb to wipe out all trace of their murder. No one would know what he did; so far as everyone else was concerned, Roger and Elaine Newton had perished several months earlier, and now there was no chance that the killers themselves would ever talk.

But Simon knew. And while he was no longer what most people would consider human, nonetheless he still retained human emotions. And just now, what he felt was rage.

"I'll avenge you," he swore to Roger and Elaine. "However long it takes, I promise, I'll . . ."

From somewhere far above, a hollow boom that shook the walls. A brilliant flash on the screen, then the image went dark, followed by silence from the world above.

VIII

"You've seen their graves, of course," Simon said. "I'm there, too. Grag took your parents out there a couple of days later and buried them. A couple of weeks later, after Otho came out of the bioclast, I had him do the same for me."

Sitting on the end of his bed, Curt slowly nodded. He'd visited the little graveyard at the western end of the crater many times. Three mounds, each with their own small marker, as fresh as the day they'd been dug. Six feet below were pressurized shipping containers holding the remains of Roger Newton, Elaine Newton, and Simon Wright. But he had only hazy, impressionistic recollections of his parents, and none at all of Simon when he was still a man; his feelings for them were abstract, largely based on what he'd heard.

And now he knew that he hadn't been told everything.

He looked over at Otho. "When did you know? I mean, the whole story of what happened to my parents, not just the partial version."

"When I was five." Otho was leaning back in his chair, arms folded across his chest. "You're almost a year older than me, but that's only in biological terms. I came out of the bioclast a full-grown adult physiologically similar to Simon's original human form, but with a brain many times more developed than yours—"

"I'm surprised that you didn't scan yourself into him," Curt said to Simon, interrupting Otho.

"Even if I wanted to, I couldn't," the Brain replied, his eyestalks twisting from Otho to Curt. "I couldn't have performed the transfer procedure on myself, and it was too complicated to trust to Grag." His voice became bitter. "But it wasn't what they wanted. Perhaps if we'd had a little more time together, I might have changed their minds, but . . ."

His voice trailed off, and Otho continued, "After it became apparent that I was going to . . . well, be my own man, so to speak, Simon put me on an accelerated learning pattern, much the same heuristic method with which you'd program an AI. When I was intelligent enough to join him and Grag as your teachers, he took me aside and told me the whole story."

"And swore you to silence." Curt's voice was accusatory.

Otho closed his eyes and let out a quiet sigh. "Curt, it had to be done. We needed to keep you hidden until the time was right, when you were old enough to not only understand what happened, but also be able to do something about it."

"And meanwhile, the man who killed my parents not only escaped justice, but prospered."

"I hate to admit this," said the Brain, "but yes, that's what happened. Victor Corvo got away with murder. Because Grag killed his bodyguards, there were no witnesses other than it and me, and because the explosion left nothing of your parents' killers that could be identified, it was assumed by those who discovered the site later that they were settlers who'd been killed in some kind of accident. The IPF investigated the scene and removed the remains, but Corvo was never linked to anything."

"Sure," Curt said. "He just got richer and richer, and eventually went into politics and became a senator."

"An old story, I'm afraid. Many crooks have discovered that politics is better than crime . . . you can accomplish much the same thing, and if you're careful enough you'll never be caught or spend a day in jail."

Curt slowly let out his breath. "He got everything he wanted, and I got . . . well, a life alone, without my father and mother."

He didn't look at either Otho or Simon as he said this, but Otho's green eyes narrowed in anger. "That's not true, Curt, and you know it. Simon, Grag, and I have been your family. Perhaps we didn't raise you as well as your parents might have, but you haven't lacked for companionship."

Curt snorted, and Otho lapsed into an uncomfortable silence. They both knew the truth: Curt had spent the first ten years of his life in this underground laboratory, rarely seeing anyone else except for the three beings who'd raised him. He didn't even know that Otho was an android until he was eight years old, or that Simon had once been something else other than a machine that talked and flew about the room. It had been many years before his guardians allowed him to even leave Tycho, and then only under the strictest supervision.

Lately, this lack of normal human relations—of ordinary friendships, really—had come to chafe at him. The reception at the Straight Wall had been a disaster. He didn't even know how to talk to a girl without making a fool out of himself.

"We've done as best as we could," Simon said. "I'm sorry you don't agree, but considering the alternative . . . well, you could be grateful for still being alive. More to the point, though, Victor didn't get what he wanted either." His eyestalks moved toward Otho. "His ultimate objective was to have your father and mother create a slave race, an army of creatures who would've looked like Otho but lacked minds and souls of their own."

"I'm the only one of my kind," Otho said quietly. "All things considered, I'm rather glad that I am."

"So Corvo is still out there," Simon continued, "and now that you know the truth about him and what he did to your parents, the decision falls to you. Do you want to avenge your father and mother, Roger and Elaine, knowing what the consequences may be?"

Curt didn't answer at once. He continued to gaze away from Simon and Otho, his mind's eye opening again to the past. This time, though, the memory was something he himself could recall. A day from his childhood, one not quite like any other . . .

IX

When Curt was a child, he'd play in the tunnels that connected the main lab with its adjacent rooms. He had no playmates except Grag and Otho, and while they were willing to keep him company, neither of them were the right size to be good companions for an eight-year-old boy. He had an active imagination, though. Tycho's data library had a bottomless supply of books, vids, and games, and the Brain had encouraged him to download them whenever he was bored. As a result, Curt had a rich fantasy life, a world filled with people only he could see and hear, in which he was a hero.

In this world, he was Captain Future.

He was a laughing, red-haired adventurer, a corsair with sword in hand, roaming the corridors of mysterious castles in search of villains to slay and princesses to rescue. Stacked storage containers became guards to be surprised and overcome, and ceiling light panels were disintegrator beams that needed to be avoided. He obediently stayed out of the hydroponics room where the base's food crops and aerobic algae was cultivated, and likewise avoided the hangar and airlock, but otherwise the rest of the base was his.

Curt took his name from *Captain Blood*, an old Errol Flynn pirate movie from the twentieth century that he loved, but also from something the Brain often told him: he had a destiny that, one day in the future, would be fulfilled. Anyone watching him play would have seen a little boy in baggy shorts and shirts made from adult clothing cut to child size, running back and forth seemingly at random, waving his arms and yelling at people who weren't there. Grag or Otho tried to join in, but they couldn't keep up with the story going on in Curt's mind, so after a while they left him alone, and Captain Future had his adventures all by himself.

One day, that changed.

Curt was stalking the invisible alien who'd abducted the colonists of Pluto's companion Charon when the Brain's voice came through the headset he always wore:

"Curtis, go to Storeroom Three, please. You're needed there."

Curt sighed, his shoulders slumping. While Simon Wright didn't seem to mind the nickname Otho had recently given him, he never tolerated disobedience. When the Brain told the boy to drop what he was doing and go somewhere, there was no argument.

"Coming, sir," he mumbled. In his hand was a discarded broom handle, which he imagined to be a magic sword he'd found in a forest on Earth, the distant world he could see through the ceiling window but which he'd never visited. One day, the Brain told him, he might go there—but only if his body became strong enough to withstand its higher gravity, which Simon assured him would crush him to the ground unless he worked out for at least two hours every sol.

Fortunately, playtime was considered a form of exercise, and the Brain was happy to give Captain Future a chance to save the universe when Curt was done with his lessons. Which was why it was a little unfair to be summoned to one of the storerooms. It held supplies that Otho purchased during occasional trips to distant settlements, and Curt had seen Grag removing spare machine parts and cartons of freeze-dried food from there just a few hours earlier. He'd told Curt that he was consolidating their supplies; perhaps the robot wanted his help.

When he arrived, the door was closed and the robot was nowhere to be seen. Curt didn't hesitate; he opened the door and stepped in. The room was dark, but when he called for the lights, they didn't come on.

Annoyed, the boy stepped farther into the storeroom, his right hand searching for the wall switch. He had just begun to grope for it, though, when the door slammed shut behind him . . . and before he could turn, a pair of hands laid themselves upon his shoulders and shoved him forward.

"Hey!" Caught off balance, Curt went sprawling on his hands and knees across the polished mooncrete floor. "What . . . who did that?"

No answer. In the darkness, the boy picked himself off the floor. "Lights on!" he snapped, but the ceiling panels remained dead. "Lights!" he repeated. No response . . . except for the soft rustle of cloth, followed an instant later by a rough hand against his chest that shoved him backward.

Again, Curt fell to the floor. The back of his head connected with the mooncrete. Amid the flash of pain he saw a brief sprinkling of stars, and again he cried out. "What's going on? Otho, is that—?"

Directly above him, a single ceiling panel came to life, causing him to wince and raise a hand against the glare. From seemingly nowhere, there came a voice he'd never heard before:

"Defend yourself!"

Something was tossed into the light; it struck the floor with a metallic rattle. An aluminum staff, three feet long and solid.

"Pick it up and defend yourself, Captain Future!"

The voice had a mocking edge to it. Curt crawled to his feet, but he didn't lay a hand on the staff. "What's going on here? Why are you . . . ?"

A figure stepped into the light: a full-grown man, dressed head to toe in loose black garments. Not even his eyes were revealed; opaque goggles concealed the one part of his face that wasn't hidden by a cowl. In his gloved hands was another rod identical to the one on the floor.

"Otho?" Curt peered at the figure. His build was the same as the android's, but . . . "Otho, is that you?"

The figure didn't reply. Instead, he swung his rod in a broad, one-handed arc that would have hit the side of Curt's head had he not ducked in time. Curt squawked in surprise, and the rod traveled back to strike him in the ankle, just hard enough to hurt.

"In this room, you have no friends." The disembodied voice was neither amused nor menacing; it simply stated a fact. "Today, you're no longer a child. If you truly want to be a hero, then pick up the rod and defend yourself!"

The figure stood before him, his rod held before him in both hands. Waiting, but not for much longer. It was Otho, of that much Curt was certain . . . but suddenly, Otho was no longer his best friend, but someone else entirely. An enemy.

Curt reached forward and picked up the rod. And twenty years later, he gazed at the man who'd disguised himself that day to become his lifelong instructor in the martial arts, and the hovering cyborg who'd set him on a course for revenge, and slowly nodded.

"Yes, I do," he said, answering the question Simon had asked a few moments earlier. "Now let's go kill Victor Corvo."

PART THREE
The Senator of the Lunar Republic

1

At the southern edge of the Mare Tranquillitatis, just above the lunar equator, lay three small impact craters: Aldrin, Collins, and Armstrong. Named after the three Americans of the first expedition to land men on the Moon, they were located in the Apollo System Monument. But while hundreds of people every day made the pilgrimage to the Apollo 11 landing site, where the footprints of the first men to walk on the Moon lay preserved beneath a lunaglass dome, only an invited handful visited Armstrong Crater just thirty miles away.

Armstrong Crater was the official residence of Senator Victor Corvo. One of the first things Corvo did upon taking office was to push through a bill allowing Senate members to purchase small parcels of government property as private residences so long as the Coalition was properly compensated. Although conservationists protested and the press criticized the bill as a particularly self-serving piece of legislation, Corvo had enough political clout to trample the resistance, and in the end, the senator got what he wanted: his own little island in the Sea of Tranquillity.

Corvo was the sort of man who always got what he wanted. A life devoted to accumulating wealth and power tends to have that result. So it wasn't a surprise that the senator lived better than even his current houseguest, the president of the Solar Coalition.

Joan Randall considered these things as she slowly drove a three-wheel flivver around the crater, a last-minute inspection before calling it a day. The flivver bounced on its massive balloon tires as it trundled across the pitted gray regolith. Floodlights illuminated the crater's outer wall; between them stood elevated mirrors that reflected sunlight toward a skylight in the regolith-covered dome that made Armstrong the largest privately owned craterhab on the Moon.

Through the cab's lunaglass canopy, Joan observed the presence of IPF officers in moonsuits every few hundred feet around the outer wall, particle-beam rifles cradled in their arms. She'd already passed the crater's main entrance, where a security checkpoint had been set up at the end of the ramp leading down to the underground garage. On the other side of the crater, an antimissile laser emplacement had been set up along with a radar dish that monitored the sky.

When Joan and Ezra met with the senator's staff to set up the presidential visit, they were told, with just a hint of condescension, that their precautions would be redundant: Corvo had his own security team, the best money could buy. The senator liked his privacy. But Joan and Ezra weren't satisfied, and neither was their boss, Halk Anders, the commandant of the Interplanetary Police Force. *I don't care if Corvo has the entire Lunar Republic Army on his side*, Anders had said. *Our job is to protect the president, and damned if that's not what we're going to do.*

Joan glanced at her helmet's heads-up display: 2209 GMT. Carthew and Corvo were probably having an after-dinner nightcap, if she recalled the schedule correctly. But once they'd had their drinks, the two men would be in bed and things could let up a little . . .

That's what bothered her. She had a feeling that this was the wrong time to relax.

The incident earlier that day at the Straight Wall had been on her mind ever since. True, neither Rab Cain nor his companion had done anything for which she or Ezra could have legally detained them. Cain had even been rather charming, in an eccentric sort of way. Nonetheless, Joan scowled at the memory of the kiss he'd given the back of her hand. She'd received nothing but snide remarks about that from her colleagues, and the fact that he'd managed to elude her over Tycho hadn't helped either.

And Ezra . . . Ezra Gurney had been particularly unforgiving. *Dammit, girl*, he'd snarled, *an IPF officer in pursuit of a suspect never gives up!* Nor was he about to accept her explanation that Cain's craft had simply disappeared. So far as the old marshal was concerned, there must have been some logical reason for this, the most likely being incompetence by his protégé, who'd suddenly become a little less promising.

There was something about the whole affair that was just wrong. The more Joan thought about it, the more she wondered whether Cain's reaction to the men speaking at the dedication had been directed at President Carthew, as she and Ezra previously believed . . . or at Senator Corvo instead.

In any case, her shift was nearly over. She needed to get some sleep. Yet Joan had a sneaking suspicion that her work wasn't done. It might still be the middle of the lunar day, but she couldn't help but feel that a long night lay ahead.

11

With those thoughts in mind, Joan turned the flivver in the direction of the garage ramp. Had she not done so, she might have caught a glimpse of something peculiar: a brief flare low in the sky to the southwest, like that of a spacecraft's engine exhaust except with no visible source. The flare was there for only a couple of seconds, though, before it vanished behind a range of hills a little more than a mile from the crater.

Curt landed the *Comet* as close to Armstrong Crater as he dared. Although the little ship was cloaked by its fantome field, he was well aware that its exhaust flare could still be seen by the naked eye . . . and this time, he wouldn't have crater walls to hide behind while he made his descent. So he chose a narrow valley nestled between a couple of nearby hills and hoped that none of the guards he presumed to be standing watch outside the crater would notice the flare as he brought the *Comet* in for touchdown.

"I'm not picking up any unusual chatter," the Brain said from behind him as Curt shut down the engines. "I think we're in the clear."

Curt nodded as he levered his seat into an upright position and unbuckled the harness. Simon was fully interfaced with the *Comet*; in a pinch, he could even take over the controls and fly the ship home by himself, although no one hoped it would come to that. "Good to hear," Curt said as he stood up. "Okay . . . Otho, you're with me."

Otho said nothing as he unsnapped his own harness and stood up, but Curt could see the reluctance on his friend's face. Otho remained silent, though, as they climbed down to the middeck. Curt paused long enough to open a locker and pull out a padded equipment bag. Slinging it over his shoulder, he continued down the ladder to the airlock deck, leaving the Brain behind.

Grag was waiting for them. The robot had already started pulling moonwalk gear from the suit lockers. "The lifepacks have been fully pressurized, Curt," it said. "Would you like some assistance putting on your gear?"

"No thanks." Curt carefully placed the bag on the floor and reached for his vacuum suit. "You can help Otho, though."

"Nope. No way." Otho shot Grag a warning look as the robot's enormous eyes turned toward him.

"Then come with us," Curt said. "We may need you."

Otho snorted at this, but continued to keep his own counsel as he reached for his suit. Curt knew what was bothering him, but decided to leave it alone. They'd argued about this enough already. The time for debating motives and consequences was over; now was the time for strategy and tactics.

It took only a few minutes for Curt and Otho to don their gear, but before he put on his helmet, Curt opened the bag he'd brought down from the galley locker. First he pulled out a utility belt lined with battery packs, a gun holster on its right side. Once he'd buckled the belt around his waist, he reached into the bag and pulled out his plasmar, a handmade pistol that superficially resembled a PBP except for its flared, musketlike barrel. He attached one end of an elastic power cable to the butt, snapped the other end into a battery pack, then shoved the gun into the specially made holster and closed the flap.

The third and last item to come from the bag was a flat metal disk about the size of a saucer, mounted on a chest halter, a small digital display on its side. Otho helped Curt pull the halter over his suit and watched as he connected another power cable from his belt.

"When was the last time you tested that thing?" he asked.

"A few weeks ago." Curt met Otho's dubious gaze with a smile. "Brain and I got it up to ten minutes."

"Yeah, okay, but you'll still be as blind as a bat."

"How would you know bats are blind? You ever met one?"

"There are no bats on the Moon," Grag said, "but I would like to see one."

"Open up your head sometime," Otho muttered. "I'll bet you'll find a few up there."

"I don't understand. Why would there be—?"

"Knock it off, both of you." Curt was fed up with the bickering. "Let's get to work."

He put on his helmet and twisted it tight. He didn't immediately switch on the comlink, but instead made a silent gesture toward the airlock. Without another word, Grag opened the inside hatch and stepped into the small compartment. Once the three of them were inside, Curt and Otho pressurized their suits and tested the comlink while Grag depressurized the airlock.

A rope ladder slung from the bottom of the outer hatch got them to the ground. Curt had switched off the fantome field shortly after landing to preserve the batteries; the *Comet* rose above them as an ellipsoid shining in the sunlight. "Brain, are you with us?" he asked, looking up at the lighted cockpit windows high above.

I'm here, Curtis, Simon replied. *"I've interfaced with Grag, so I can see everything he sees."*

Curt turned to Grag. The robot—or rather Simon, temporarily assuming control of Grag's actions—raised a hand to give him a brief wave. Curt didn't respond, but instead looked around the landing site. About a hundred yards away lay the low hills they'd landed behind.

"All right, then," he said, pointing to the nearest hill. "Thataway . . ."

It took only a few minutes for the three of them to hike up the sandy slope. As they neared the top of the ridge, Curt gestured for Otho and Grag to go down on hands and knees. They crawled the last few feet to the ridgeline and found a boulder to hide behind, and it was from this vantage point that they gazed down on Armstrong Crater.

Even from there, they could see that the place was well guarded. Vehicles prowled the perimeter, and tiny figures who were no doubt armed guards stood in a broad circle around the reflector mirrors. At the end of the road leading to the crater, a checkpoint had been set up near a ramp leading under the crater, with three more men waiting to inspect any vehicles that might arrive. As Curt, Otho, Grag, and the Brain watched, a hopper took off from a nearby landing field to make a low pass over the dome. Curt was afraid for a moment that it might expand its sweep to the nearby hills, but apparently its pilot didn't think that was necessary.

And it probably wasn't. Nothing could get within a mile of the craterhab without being spotted.

"This is going to be tricky," Otho said. "Even with a fantome field."

"If I've got the field hiding me, I can slip in." Curt hesitated. "The problem is getting close enough."

The disk he wore on his suit was a portable fantome generator. After he and Simon had developed the light-deflection device for use aboard the *Comet* and their hopper, they'd decided to make a smaller version for personal use. It had taken years of work and countless tests, but they'd finally succeeded in devising the means by which an individual could vanish from sight. Light rays and even radar would be bent around a person wearing a fantome device, giving them the appearance of invisibility.

There were a couple of drawbacks, though.

First, because the generator was enormously power hungry, the invisibility effect was good for only a few minutes. As he'd told Otho earlier, Curt had lately managed to stretch the duration to ten minutes; what he didn't admit was that he'd used up every battery pack on his belt doing so, leaving his plasma gun good for only a few shots.

Second, the undesirable effect of having the fantome deflect light was that a person standing within the field became temporarily blind. Since light rays couldn't penetrate the field, the retinas of the eyes had nothing to work with; the effect was akin to being surrounded by a bubble of darkness.

When the generator was used aboard a craft, the pilot was able to use a number of tricks to compensate. As long as the onboard computers still functioned, for instance, it was still possible to navigate via three-dimensional topo maps. So when Curt used the fantome to avoid being tracked by the hopper that had followed him and Otho from the Straight Wall, he'd switched off the generator as soon as his craft was out of visual range, using crater walls to hide his own hopper while he made a successful landing at Tycho Base.

This time, though . . .

"There's no way you're going to be able to get close to the crater before the field gives out," Otho said. "Look how spread out the guards are. Even if you sneak past them, you'd still have to make it through the checkpoints they've set up at all the entrances."

"If I hurry," Curt said, "I might be able to do it."

"Get from here to the crater in ten minutes or less?" Simon asked, his voice a thin rasp in Curt's helmet. *"I sincerely doubt that. Besides, even if you could, there's always a chance someone might spot your footprints as you make them."*

"Then I'll stay clear of the guards . . ."

"Sure, you could do that . . . *if* you could see 'em." Otho looked at him askance. "But you'll be blind all the way in. Even if we tried to guide you, there's a lot we can't see from here. What if your foot hits a rock and you go sprawling? You'll raise a dust cloud when you hit the ground, and that might raise someone's attention."

Curt opened his mouth, then closed it again. Otho was right, whether he liked it or not. The fantome field would be just as much an impediment as it would be an advantage. It wouldn't last the time it would take for him to cross the distance, and even if it did, the fact that he couldn't see practically guaranteed an accident that would lead to his discovery and arrest. And the last thing any of them wanted was to have Victor Corvo become aware that the son of Roger and Elaine Newton still lived.

"Perhaps you can ride in on that truck," Grag said.

Curt looked over at the robot. "What's that? Come again?"

"Look there." Grag pointed downhill behind them, away from Armstrong and toward the packed-dirt road that connected it with Collins and Aldrin craters. "A vehicle is approaching."

Shading his eyes with a raised hand, Curt twisted about on his hands and knees to peer in the direction the robot indicated. In the far distance, almost on the horizon, a tiny silver-gray fantail of regolith caught the sunlight as it was kicked up by a set of wheels. Although it was still far away, Curt knew that Grag was right. The vehicle was a tandem-trailer truck, the sort used to haul supplies from one lunar settlement to another.

This one was probably coming from Aldrin or Collins; it could be carrying food, water, machine parts, toilet paper, anything. What mattered was that it was on its way to Armstrong, and it was making good time.

"Okay, so it's a truck." Otho was unimpressed. "What's he supposed to do? Go down there and thumb a ride?"

" 'Thumb a ride'?" Grag's impassive face turned toward Otho. "I'm not familiar with this expression."

"Maybe not, but I am . . . and that's not a bad idea." Curt grinned. "Listen, here's what I'm thinking . . ."

III

"Here it comes, Curt," Grag said.

"How far away?"

"One hundred yards and closing. Approximate land speed thirty-five knots."

"Understood." Curt adjusted his grip on Grag's shoulders. He was standing behind the robot, positioned so that its massive shadow fell across him. This wouldn't have hidden him if he was visible, but they were hoping that it would cover his footprints. All he had to do was make sure that he didn't lose contact with Grag, or he wouldn't be able to know which way to go.

"Captain Future, do you copy?"

Otho's voice coming through his helmet phones gave him cause to grit his teeth. He wished dearly that the Brain hadn't insisted on everyone using call signs on the comlink, or that he hadn't picked this particular one for him. An added measure of security, sure, but he was feeling childish enough already.

"Affirmative, *Comet,*" Curt replied. "Report situation."

Otho's voice was a calm, reassuring presence in the darkness surrounding him. *"The truck is a two-car tractor-trailer rig. Can't tell yet if there's anyplace for you to climb aboard. It hasn't slowed down yet."*

"Has it seen me? Seen Grag, I mean."

"No, it's not slowing down." Otho hissed under his breath. *"Hey, buckethead, raise your hands! Let the driver know you want it to stop!"*

"Affirmative," Grag said. "And please don't call me buckethead."

"Yeah, okay, spoonface."

Curt felt the robot shift beneath his hands. He'd adjusted the fantome generator to emit its narrowest possible field, concealing him but not Grag. They'd considered having him ride piggyback atop the robot, but realized that the generator might cause Grag to become partially invisible as well. So he'd have to depend on Grag being his guide . . . his "Seeing Eye dog," as Simon called it, an archaic term he didn't bother to explain.

"The truck's getting closer," Simon said, observing everything through Grag's eyes, *"but it's not slowing down."*

Curt glanced up at the one thing he could see, his helmet's luminescent heads-up display. Nine minutes left before the field faded, and there were no other vehicles on the road leading to the crater. In Earth time, the hour was getting late; this truck was probably carrying the last shipment of the day. If this didn't work, he'd have to wait until tomorrow to try again, and he didn't want to give Otho a chance to talk him out of what he meant to do. He had to take a chance, so . . .

"Grag, walk out into the road."

"Are you crazy?" Otho's shout was startling in the darkness. *"That damn thing is just a couple of hundred feet away. It—"*

"Grag, do as I say! Raise your hands and walk out into the road!"

"Yes, Curt." Apparently the danger wasn't sufficient to cause Grag's self-preservation programming to kick in, because Curt felt the robot march forward. This time, Curt was ready for the movement. Holding on tight, he matched the robot's gait as Grag trudged into the road before them. It came to a sudden halt and made a one-quarter turn to the right, and Curt did the same, using his hands to make sure that he was still behind the robot.

He knew that they were now facing the oncoming truck from dead center in the middle of the road.

Curt braced himself, waiting for the impact. He had the sudden thought that he may have pushed his luck a little too far this time. Over the years, while Simon and Otho had trained his body and mind for the task that lay head, he'd occasionally taken risks that horrified his guardians. He'd never been reckless, though, and each time he'd managed to get away with nothing more than bruises, sprains, or small cuts. Nonetheless, he always knew that the day would come when he—

"The truck is stopping," Grag said.

"*Confirmed. The truck is coming to a halt, with just a dozen feet to spare.*" Otho slowly let out his breath.

"Affirmative." Curt became aware of his own heartbeat. "Curt . . . Captain Future out."

Otho went silent, as did the Brain. From now until he reached the crater interior, he was observing radio silence with everyone except Grag, lest their comlink transmissions be intercepted by the IPF.

"Grag," Curt said, "patch me into your main band, please. And put your responses to me in text mode."

A glowing word appeared across the inside of his faceplate—**Affirmative**—followed by a soft click. In the same instant, a new voice came through the darkness:

"*. . . the hell are you doing here?*"

"I am lost," Grag replied.

"*Lost?*" Another voice, also male, more amused than the first. "*I didn't think it was possible for you guys to get lost. Where are you from?*"

"Zero degrees, forty-one minutes, fifteen seconds north, twenty-three degrees, twenty-five minutes, forty-five seconds east."

A sigh. "*In plain English, dummy, not coordinates . . . where are you from? I mean, where was the last place you were before you got lost?*"

"The Apollo System Monument. I am a maintenance robot there. A visitor gave me the instruction to get lost. I complied and now I am here."

The sound of braying laughter over the comlink. Curt had to keep from laughing himself. Grag was playing its role well: the stereotypical dumb robot, misinterpreting an innocuous remark as a literal command.

"*Yeah, all right . . . no wonder you're lost.*" A chuckle from a voice that was no longer angry. "*Tell you what . . . climb aboard and we'll give you a lift to our destination. Once we're there, I'll have someone call the park and have them come out and pick you up. Okay?*"

"Thank you," Grag said. "That would be suitable."

Curt felt the robot march forward again. He followed it closely, still holding onto its shoulders with both hands. He hoped that the robot was keeping itself between him and the driver's line of sight, for he had no idea whether Grag's shadow was still hiding his footprints, but no one said anything so apparently the trick was working. After about ten steps, Grag turned to the right. Five more steps, and they turned to the right again. Two more steps, and they came to a sudden halt. Again, Grag spoke to him in silent text only Curt could see:

I am standing next to the left rear side of the tractor behind the cab. There is a ladder directly in front of me. It appears to lead to a small cargo rack on the roof. If you climb down and take two steps forward, you will be able to reach up and grasp the lowest rungs of the ladder.

Curt didn't respond as he let go of Grag. Feeling his way with outstretched hands, he carefully stepped out from behind the robot. One step, two step, three . . . the palms of his hands came in contact with a vertical metal surface. He slowly moved his hands upward, and they found a U-shaped ladder rung at chest level, with another one a foot below it and yet another above.

—*Hey, what's taking you so long? We ain't got all day . . . c'mon!*

"Is this ladder the means by which you want me to climb on?" Grag asked.

Another laugh, this time unkind. *"Man, you* are *stupid. Yes, that's the way we want you to climb up here. Now get a move on."*

Curt grasped the ladder rungs and began blindly making his way up the tractor's side. Grag was obviously stalling for time, giving him a chance to climb aboard. He tried to pick up the pace as much as he could, but finding the rungs was harder than he'd expected, and he'd climbed only a couple of feet when a vibration against his hands told him that the robot was scaling the ladder just behind him. He hoped that the driver wouldn't get impatient and start the vehicle again before they reached the top.

He'd left eight or nine rungs beneath him when the vertical surface suddenly turned horizontal and he found what he took to be a small rail just a few inches high. On hands and knees, Curt clambered over the railing and felt his way along a flat surface interspaced with tie-down rings.

You are on the roof. Move one foot to your right and lie flat on your stomach. This way, you will not be seen from either the cab or the ground if your field generator fails.

Curt did as he was told, and a moment later he felt Grag heavily sit down beside him. *"You all right back there?"* the driver asked. *"Okay, here we go."*

Without waiting for a response, the tractor-trailer rig began moving again. Although it had twelve oversize tires on independent suspension, Curt felt the massive vehicle bounce every time it rolled across a rock or micrometeor pit. He found a couple of tie-down rings and clung to them, hoping that the driver didn't take his time. The readout on his faceplate told him that he had a little less than three minutes left until he became visible again . . . and this was only an estimate.

About a minute later, the truck came to a halt.

We have reached the checkpoint. A sentry is approaching the vehicle.

"You're behind schedule." A new voice, undoubtedly the guard's. *"We saw you stop down the road . . . what's going on?"*

"Picked up a hitchhiker. Some robot misplaced by the park. We found it and told it we'd find a way for it to get home."

"Really?" A pause. *"Hey, dummy . . . how'd you get all the way out here?"*

The sentry is looking up here, but he is not climbing the ladder.

"I was told to get lost," Grag replied. *"I did my best to follow my instructions."*

More laughter, and Curt found himself becoming embarrassed for Grag. Simon had told him that his mother had always been impressed by the extraordinary feat of consciousness the robot had somehow achieved, an unexpected emergence of sentience unusual for a robot with a low-level artificial intelligence. She'd expanded upon this, adjusting Grag's programming parameters to further allow it to make decisions and choices of its own. Even so, if Grag was truly developing an emotional life as well as an intellectual one, it was an unprecedented leap forward in the evolution of machine intelligence. So while

Grag wasn't quite as intelligent as a human, it deserved respect all the same. Pretending to be an idiot was beneath its dignity.

"*Yeah, all right . . . take it in,*" the guard said. "*Go.*"

The truck began moving again, and Curt let out his breath in relief.

We have entered the ramp leading to the underground vehicle entrance. The truck will shortly enter the airlock decontamination chamber.

Curt said nothing, but continued to watch the heads-up display. He had less than a minute left when the truck came to a halt. A dull vibration from below and behind him told him that the entrance's airtight double doors had closed. An instant later, he felt something like enormous wings beating against his back; those would be electromagnetic scrubbers removing moondust from the truck and everything on it.

The scrubbers had just finished their cycle when the darkness suddenly went away. He was visible again.

IV

Otho waited until he saw the truck disappear within the crater, then he rose from where he crouched behind the boulder and began making his way back down the hill, his boots sliding against the loose gray regolith. Returning to the *Comet,* he climbed up the rope ladder to the airlock, pausing to pull it up behind him before shutting the outer hatch.

He cycled through the airlock, but didn't remove his suit in the ready-room. He took off his helmet and gloves and stowed them in the suit locker, then climbed up the ladder to the flight deck.

Simon was there, hovering above the pilot's chair. He didn't say anything when Otho came in, but instead moved aside to let the android have a seat. Otho sat down heavily, slumping forward to rest his elbows on his knees and gaze down at the floor.

"Grag reports they've reached the decontamination facility," Simon said at last. "Curt has become visible, but no one has spotted him . . . at least not yet."

Otho nodded but didn't reply. A moment passed, then he raised his eyes to fix Simon with an angry, unblinking stare.

"You know as well as I do," he said slowly, "that this is more about your revenge than his. And I swear to you, if he doesn't come back from this, I will rip your drone apart and leave you blind, deaf, and speechless for the rest of your life."

The Brain said nothing, but his eyestalks twitched.

V

Curt knew the fantome field had failed the instant his vision cleared and he found himself able to see the roof of the truck. He squinted against the abrupt glare from the ceiling panels, but he'd barely closed his eyes when the truck suddenly began moving forward. Through narrowed eyelids, he saw the vehicle airlock's massive inner doors slide open. The decontamination procedure was finished, and now the vehicle was entering the garage.

Lying facedown on the roof rack, Curt remained motionless. He hoped there were no security cameras, or if there were, they weren't positioned so that they could make out the tops of the vehicles entering the garage. He felt the truck roll across a long stretch of mooncrete floor until it finally swung to the right and came to a halt.

They had arrived. Now came the tricky part: not getting caught.

"Grag," he said, speaking softly even though his voice was muffled by his helmet, "climb down before the drivers get out. Hurry."

The robot stood up from where it had been sitting beside him and moved across the roof platform toward the ladder. Turning his head within his helmet, Curt watched as Grag went to the ladder and, grasping its top rungs, began climbing down. Its head had just disappeared from sight when he heard the cab hatches opening and slamming shut, followed a moment later by voices just audible through his helmet:

"Hey! Who told you to get down from there?"

"We have arrived," Grag replied. "I thought it was appropriate to disembark."

"You thought it was . . . oh, geez! Who taught you how to talk like that?"

"Aw, let it go, man. Some of these guys speak better than we do, even if they're dumb as rocks."

"Yeah, I guess. Okay, dummy, follow us. We'll take you up to the office and see if we can find a serial number on you."

"If you don't mind, I prefer to wait here until my owners come for me."

"What? No, wait . . . stop! Don't go over—"

"Assuming standby mode until registered owners issue new orders."

"No! Don't stop! Walk forward! Hey, are you listening? Walk . . . forward. Don't . . . stop . . ."

"Oh, that's just excellent. Now it's stuck here!"

A disgusted sigh and a muttered curse, followed by the dull clang of something soft, like a boot sole striking metal. "Stupid 'bot. Okay, might as well leave it. Damn thing's too big to move, so at least it's not going anywhere on its own. We'll just have to tell someone in the security office what we've found and let them handle it."

"Yeah . . . okay by me. C'mon, I'll buy you a drink."

Curt heard footsteps walking away from the truck. The faint squeal of an elevator door sliding open, then closing again. Then silence.

The garage is empty. There is no one in sight.

"Thanks. Any cameras?"

None that I can see.

Curt slowly sat up, his limbs stiff and sore from the rough ride. The truck had been pulled into a parking bay beside a loading dock to await the arrival of workmen who'd come later to open its trailer. Looking over the side, he saw Grag standing beside a ceiling support column, arms at its sides. The robot seemed inert and nonfunctional, but then its head abruptly turned on its thick neck and its luminous red eyes peered up at him.

"Nicely played," Curt said as he stood up. "You can go vocal now."

"Thank you," Grag replied, just loud enough to be heard through Curt's helmet. "Sometimes it's an advantage to have one's intelligence underestimated."

"Never by me, old friend." Curt scrambled down the ladder, and then paused to remove his helmet and look around. As Grag said, the garage was vacant. A few other vehicles were parked nearby, including a three-wheel flivver with IPF markings. A quick glance within its open dome confirmed that it had two seats: perfect for a getaway.

Curt walked over to the flivver. Grag unfroze and started to follow him, but Curt pointed back to where the robot had been standing. "No, stay where you are. You're in the perfect place. Don't let anyone move you, but be ready to grab that flivver and make a run for it."

"Understood." Grag obediently returned to his previous position. "Where are you going?"

"Up there." Walking behind the parked vehicle, Curt put down his helmet and began to climb out of his vacuum suit. "Topside, I mean. Observe radio silence with me, but get in touch with Simon and Otho if something goes wrong. When I'm done, I'll make my way back to this place. You're going to stay here and be ready to leave in a hurry."

"Understood. Good luck."

"Thanks." Curt folded the vacuum suit as small as he could and hid it along with his helmet, lifepack, gloves, and boots behind the flivver. The utility belt with his holstered gun went around his waist, but he left the fantome generator behind. He'd need the remaining reserve charge in his belt batteries for the plasmar; besides, becoming invisible again wouldn't help him very much if he couldn't see where he was going and wouldn't have Grag to guide him.

An elevator stood nearby, probably the same one he'd heard the two drivers board. It might take him straight to the crater floor, but it might also take him somewhere where he'd likely be spotted. Curt looked around again. There were probably service tunnels he could use that would accomplish the same thing . . .

Yes, on the wall over there: a white arrow within a red border, EXIT stenciled beneath it. Approaching the sign, Curt saw that it pointed down a short passageway to an airtight door. The door wasn't locked; behind it was a narrow corridor stretching away into the distance, its ceiling lined with insulated conduits. Curt quietly shut the door and started jogging down the corridor.

Most of Armstrong's infrastructure lay beneath the crater floor, a labyrinth of electrical and data networks, water tanks, sewage reclamation systems, and emergency radiation shelters, all connected by service corridors for servants and maintenance personnel. Fortunately, maps had been helpfully posted at major junctions, so Curt never became completely lost. Nonetheless, he got turned around a couple of times before he found what he was searching for, a lunasteel stairwell leading up to the surface.

He was only halfway to the first landing, though, when he heard a loud bang of a door slamming open somewhere above, followed an instant later by the sound of something running downstairs. Not the footfalls of a human, though, but rather the softer and more rapid steps of a small, four-legged creature.

Looking up through the metalwork of the stairs, he barely caught a glimpse of an animal frantically running down toward him. A small dog, its legs taking the steps three or four risers at a time, more of a controlled plummet than a run. It had almost reached the landing above him when the door crashed open again.

"Down there! After him!"

Curt turned to jump back down the stairs. He landed with bent knees as quietly as he could and ducked into the shadowed stairwell beneath the metal risers. Planting his back against the wall, he pulled the gun from its holster; a flick of his thumb adjusted the plasmar to its lowest setting. The dog and the two men pursuing it were nearly on top of him. He held his breath and waited.

Through the gridwork risers above his head, Curt watched the dog sail the rest of the way down the stairs. Off-white with tan markings and wide brown eyes, it was, Curt saw, a moonpup: a Jack Russell–beagle mix, specifically bred to live on the Moon. The dog landed on the mooncrete floor and tore off down the corridor. In one-sixth lunar gravity, the moonpup's escape was more of a series of bouncing leaps than a sprint. Tongue lolling from its mouth, it bounded down the way Curt had just come; it either didn't notice the human hiding beneath the stairs or didn't care.

Seconds later, two men came down the stairs after the dog, a terran and an aphrodite. Both wore the uniforms of IPF officers, and neither looked particularly amused.

"That way!" the terran shouted as they reached the bottom of the stairs. "There goes the little bastard!"

"I swear, when we catch him, he's going right out the airlock!" his partner snarled. Then both disappeared down the corridor.

Curt let out his breath, but didn't holster his gun again. Probably a household pet fleeing from some canine misdemeanor. For a moment, he'd been tempted to stun the two men chasing the dog. He couldn't afford to do so, but he wished the moonpup the best of luck and hoped its pursuers weren't serious about throwing it out an airlock.

Curt continued climbing the stairs, and this time reached the top landing without further interruption. He found an ordinary swinging door, one easily opened by a fleeing dog, and on the other side . . . darkness and silence, broken only by a soft chirping sound. Curt paused beside the half-open door and listened carefully for a few seconds, then eased himself into the night beyond.

Armstrong Crater had been transformed into an immense terrarium, an enclosed and self-sustaining biosphere replicating life on Earth. Specifically, a plantation in the Deep South of Old America, circa the mid-nineteenth century. Darkness lay deep upon groves of magnolia, sycamore, and weeping willow, while crickets and bullfrogs chorused amid shallow ponds fed by meandering creeks. Gravel footpaths led among manicured lawns and well-tended gardens; the air was warm and fragrant with honeysuckle and roses.

Pausing to take all this in, Curt wondered at the effort and expense it must have cost to build this place. Victor Corvo was rich even before he'd murdered Roger and Elaine Newton; since then, his wealth must have exploded. A new career in politics had given him the ability to create an oasis amid the lunar desolation, but this was a paradise as corrupt as the past it emulated. Corvo had wanted to create a slave race; he didn't get his wish, but he could always dream . . .

The stairwell emerged from an underground service entrance disguised to look like a woodshed. Creeping around its side, Curt saw the stately plantation house at the crater center. Its architect had designed it to resemble the mansions of old Alabama. Two stories tall, with a columned portico above the front door and open porches along the sides, its whitewashed walls were ghostly luminescent in the earthlight reflected through the dome aperture high above. Lights gleamed within the ground-floor windows, and above a piped-in recording of a tender Italian guitar—Morricone's "Il Tramonto"—he heard voices: two men standing on a porch, engaged in quiet conversation.

They were little more than silhouettes, but he had little doubt who they were. One of them, at least.

The house was only about sixty feet away. He could reach it in seconds if he ran. Curt resisted the temptation to do so, though, and instead studied the mansion from behind the woodshed. He expected to spot bodyguards—IPF officers, perhaps—patrolling the lawn; to his surprise, there were none. Maybe the IPF considered the defense cordon outside the crater to be adequate, but it was still peculiar to find no one protecting President Carthew *inside* the crater . . .

Unless they'd been distracted by something. And then he remembered the moonpup, and the two men who'd run past him in pursuit of it.

Had this been staged to lure away the bodyguards? And if so, then why?

Curt turned his gaze away from the mansion, and carefully peered into the darkened grounds surrounding the mansion. He searched for movement, or a shadow that shouldn't be there . . .

And he found it.

VI

"I'm so sorry about this, Mr. President," Victor Corvo said. "I didn't think he would—"

"It's all right, Senator." James Carthew chuckled, albeit ruefully, as he grimaced at the sour-smelling urine stain spreading across the front of his shirt. "Quite all right. Puppies can be rambunctious even under the best circumstances . . . and that one was more active than most, wasn't he?"

"He was, indeed," Corvo said, and privately reflected that there was more truth in this than President Carthew would ever know.

At least in the few minutes he had left to live.

For the past eight weeks, ever since the nameless moonpup was weaned from its mother, it had been trained for just this moment: to panic the instant it was placed in the arms of anyone resembling the president of the Solar Coalition, the person to whom he was ostensibly being given as a gift. The face mask worn by his trainer, along with pinches, slaps, and rewards for proper responses, had rehearsed the little mutt for its small but significant role, and it had reacted just the way it was supposed to, by peeing on the president, knocking the drink from his hand and nipping him for good measure, then leaping from his arms and running off the porch and away from the house.

Corvo had yelled for the two IPF officers who'd accompanied him and the president out onto the porch to catch the dog, and they'd obediently taken off in pursuit. But the moonpup had been trained to head straight for the nearby entrance to the crater's subservice levels, the door of which had been conveniently left unlocked and slightly ajar. The security officers had chased the dog downstairs, and once one of Corvo's servants had picked up the fallen mint julep glass and gone back into the house to replace it with a fresh drink and, against Carthew's wishes to do so himself, fetch a clean shirt, the two men were alone—if only for a few precious minutes—on the porch.

Somewhere out there in the darkness, hidden by magnolias and the night, a killer was lying in wait for this moment. All he needed now was a clear shot . . .

"Come over and have a seat, Mr. President." Corvo extended a hand toward the two rocking chairs they'd been sitting in just before another one of his servants had brought out the moonpup. "We were having such a good chat before all that, and I'd hate for the night to end on such a—"

The screen door leading out to the porch swung open with the elastic sound of an unoiled spring, and a woman's voice behind them said, "Is everything all right?"

Randall. It was that damn IPF inspector, Joan Randall.

Corvo was becoming very sick of her. Ever since she was introduced to him as one of the leaders of Carthew's security team, Randall had been much too efficient for comfort. If the senator only had to deal with her superior, things would have gone much more smoothly. Ezra Gurney was a familiar type, an old flatfoot who could be lulled by an outward appearance of peace and calm. Not so for his assistant. Ever since an unforeseen incident at the dedication ceremony—apparently the IPF had questioned a couple of suspicious individuals—Randall had been on edge, and now she was apparently sleeping with one eye open.

"Nothing to be concerned about," Corvo said. "I tried to present the president with a puppy from the litter our moonpup had a few weeks ago, and the little cur—"

"Not his fault, Victor. Or yours either." Carthew carefully lowered himself into the rocking chair. A large man, he never moved fast. "Just an accident. Once your people find him and bring him back, I'm sure we'll be friends."

"Once our people find him?" Joan stepped the rest of the way out onto the porch, and Corvo now saw that she'd hastily thrown her uniform jacket over a short nightshirt that revealed more than she probably realized. "Mr. President, are you saying your bodyguards took off to catch a runaway dog?"

"Oh, be reasonable, Agent Randall," Corvo said, giving his voice a condescending tone. "There's no danger here. Your agents aren't necessary just now, and they—"

Randall was no longer listening. She blinked a couple of times to activate her Anni. "All stations, attention. Attention, all stations. Orange alert. Backup officers, report to the senator's residence immediately."

"Agent Randall, stand down." Corvo couldn't allow her to take control of the situation. "This is my home, and the president and I don't need your protection."

Randall ignored him. Turning away from the two men, she gazed out over the landscaped lawns surrounding the house. "Marshal Gurney, you're needed at—"

Suddenly, she stopped and stared at something she'd glimpsed in the darkness. In the next second, she hurled herself across the balcony. Before Corvo could react, she shoved him aside. She then grabbed the back of the president's rocking chair and, with an adrenaline-fueled shove, toppled Carthew to the porch floor.

"Gun!" she yelled. *"Gun . . . everyone down!"*

VII

Curt might have missed spotting the assassin if the gun had been camouflaged as well as the man. The man was dressed head to foot in black, and thus blended in with the darkness that surrounded the mansion, but he hadn't taken care to do the same thing with the sniper rifle he carried. So as the assassin, unaware that someone nearby suspected his existence, raised his weapon from behind the ornamental hedge he was using for cover and took aim at the porch, the rifle's long silver barrel caught the earthlight coming in through the ceiling, revealing his presence to another intruder hiding behind the nearby shed.

The killer was about forty feet away, maybe a little more. Seeing the rifle slowly moving to track the figures on the porch, Curt knew that it was only a matter of seconds before the assassin squeezed the trigger and a deadly particle beam lanced out to catch . . . who? Corvo, Carthew? Both?

It didn't matter. He knew what had to be done.

Stepping out from behind the shed, Curt aimed the plasmar straight at the assassin. "Hold it!" he yelled. "Drop your gun!"

Startled, the killer whipped around to point his rifle in his general direction, and Curt fired.

The plasma gun—or plasmar, as the Brain dubbed it—was a unique weapon. To the best of their knowledge, no one else had ever built a working model like the one he and Simon had cobbled together in Tycho Base's workshop, utilizing discarded pieces of old lab equipment and the particle-beam pistols used by Roger and Elaine Newton's killers. They had been forced to do so because, while it was necessary for Curt to arm himself, neither he nor Otho could legally acquire a PBP without presenting valid ID's, the acquisition of which would have exposed their existence, nor could Curt bring himself to carry one of the guns used to murder his parents. So he and the Brain had done better, and devised a weapon more versatile than a common particle-beam pistol.

Curt squeezed the trigger, and a nearly—but not quite—invisible stream of pulsed energy erupted from the gun's flared muzzle. Comprised of compact toroids of electrical plasma, the stream appeared as a series of translucent hoops vaguely resembling smoke rings that spread apart as they moved away from the gun. The charge they carried could be moderated, and Curt had flicked the selector switch just above the trigger from *kill,* its strongest setting, to *stun,* its lowest. So the plasma toroids should have knocked the assassin off his feet and paralyzed him for a few minutes, long enough for Curt to disarm him.

But it had been a mistake to order the assassin to halt. All that had accomplished was to warn him that someone had him in his sights and give him a chance to react. The killer dropped flat behind the hedge before the plasma bursts hit him; tiny leaves were ripped from the bush and it trembled as if caught in a windstorm, but the assassin had already rolled away. Scrambling to his feet, he fired a random shot at the shed before launching himself toward a willow tree a few yards away.

From the house, Curt heard a woman shout something. He had no time to pay attention, though. The assassin had missed, but nonetheless the particle beam he'd fired came close enough to bore a hole through the side of the shed. There was a faint odor of scorched wood as he dropped to one knee and fired twice at the fleeing figure. But the plasma bursts missed by several feet, and Curt's next shots did little more than drive splinters from the tree behind which the killer had managed to take cover.

Curt started to take aim again when a shrill beep from the gun delivered more bad news. He glanced down at the pulsing red diode just above the grip and swore under his breath. The gun was running low and would need at least thirty seconds to fully recharge before it could be fired again. As he'd feared, the fantome generator had drained the battery packs; this was a drawback he and the Brain hadn't yet been able to resolve.

The assassin wasn't aware of this, though. All he knew was that he'd been fired upon by someone with the spookiest weapon he'd ever seen, and now that he'd been discovered, there was no chance he'd accomplish his objective. Curt looked up again to see the killer bolt out from behind the tree and sprint across the lawn, doubtless heading for whatever airlock he'd used to enter the craterhab.

Shoving the plasmar back in its holster, Curt bent down and quickly unsnapped his ankle weights. Then he took off running after the assassin. No longer encumbered, his bounds carried him six feet or more at a time, nearly twice as fast as the killer was running. Although he'd spent most of his life in lunar gravity, Simon and Otho had never permitted him to let muscles atrophy the way loony immigrants often did. Two hours of each twenty-four-hour sol had been devoted to strenuous exercise; even on Earth, Curt would have been considered to be in superior physical condition.

The assassin hadn't reached the edge of the lawn when Curt caught up with him. He squawked as Curt grabbed the back of his shoulders with both hands and pitched him to the ground, but didn't let go of his rifle as he rolled across the grass and sprang back to his feet. Curt had just enough time to realize that the tall, skinny figure before him was probably an aresian before the killer raised his rifle and fired.

Curt dodged to the left and the shot went wild. Fortunately, both combatants were deep enough within the crater that its walls absorbed the random energy shots without compromising the dome's atmospheric integrity. Still in motion, Curt pivoted on the toes of his left foot, bent to one side, and swept his right leg around in a broad kick. His booted foot knocked the rifle from the killer's hands. Before the assassin could recover it, Curt regained his stance and, feinting with his upraised right arm, hurled his left fist forward.

An hour of each exercise period was spent with Otho in martial arts training. When it became too easy to overcome his android friend, he sometimes sparred with Grag instead, often with Simon interfaced with the robot's higher AI functions to double the speed of its reflexes. The assassin was combat-trained, too, but it didn't do him much good; he'd barely ducked the punch when the rigid palm of Curt's right hand slammed into the side of his neck, causing him to stagger and fall.

Curt rammed his foot down on his chest. There was an agonized *hummpphh!* from the other side of the full-face mask the killer wore and he curled inward to clutch at himself. Curt reached down and yanked him to his feet, and when the assassin made a feeble attempt to hit him, he swatted his hand aside and threw his fist into his solar plexus.

"Who are you?" Curt demanded.

"G-g-go . . . go to . . ."

Curt didn't wait for the rest. Still clutching the front of the assassin's skinsuit, he ripped the mask from his head. As he'd figured, the face that glared back at him had the red hue of a native aresian. He swung his hand across that face in a backhanded slap that rocked the killer's head on his neck.

"Who are you?" he shouted again. "Who sent you?"

"Sons of the Two—"

The killer stamped down hard on the instep of Curt's right foot. It caught him completely off guard, and before Curt could recover, the killer tore free from his grasp. The aresian went straight for the rifle he'd dropped moments earlier, and Curt looked up just in time to see its barrel move toward him. At this range, the killer couldn't possibly miss.

"For Ul Quorn!" the killer snarled.

Curt was just beginning to think the viscous smile on the killer's face was the last thing he'd see when blood spurted from the side of the aresian's head.

The killer fell like a child's discarded puppet, and from somewhere close by a voice shouted, "Don't move, amigo!"

Curt did as he was told. Keeping his hands in plain sight, careful not to take a single step, he slowly turned his head in the direction the voice had come from. About ten yards away stood the gray-haired marshal who'd confronted him and Otho at the Straight Wall, a PBP braced in both hands and aimed straight at him.

"I'm not moving," Curt said.

"Good." The old lawman nodded. "Now looky here . . . I want you to use your left hand and, with two fingers only, pull the gun from your holster and drop it on the ground in front of you. And make it slow, son . . . I got an itchy trigger finger."

"Marshal, with all due respect . . . I'm willing to cooperate, but my pistol is attached to my belt by a power cord." Curt moved his right hip ever so slightly to let the marshal see his plasmar. "If I try to do as you say, it'll only fall to my side. I assure you, though, it's harmless . . . its batteries are dead."

The IPF officer peered at the gun without lowering his own. "Okay, then . . . just fold your hands on your head and keep 'em there."

Curt obeyed, but as he did, he covertly twisted the ring on his left hand so that its face was turned toward the marshal when he folded his hands together on top of his head. Time to get some help.

—Brain, are you there? he asked, tapping his ring with his thumb to activate it.

A few moments passed, then Simon's voice came through the ring's Anni interface.

—I'm here, my boy, and I'm aware of your situation. Otho and I have been monitoring the IPF bands ever since they went on alert a couple of minutes ago. You're in trouble.

Curt had to restrain himself from laughing out loud. What a revelation. Past the marshal, he could see several figures running toward them from the mansion. As they got closer, one of them appeared to be the young woman—Officer Randall, if he remembered her name correctly—whom he'd also met earlier. Oddly, he found himself pleased to see her again.

—What should I do?

—Cooperate, but only to an extent. Do not reveal your true name, where you're from, or the reason why you're here.

—That's not much cooperation.

—Let me handle this. I may be able to get you out of this, but only if you do as I say.

—*All right.* Another thought occurred to him. —*Where's Grag?*
Have they caught him, too?

A short pause. —*Grag has its own problems just now. Its are ...*
slightly more amusing. Now, here's what I want you to do ...

VIII

Grag had remained exactly where Curt had left it, a motionless autom-aton standing against the wall in the garage. Since its Anni interface with Curt wasn't currently active, it had little idea of what was going on elsewhere in the craterhab. So Grag's first intimation that something was amiss came with the faint sound of a dog barking from somewhere nearby.

Turning its head, Grag allowed its auditory sensors to trace the sound to its source. This was the door behind which Curt had dis-appeared just a short time ago. The door was closed, but nonetheless it could hear a dog barking just behind it. The dog sounded afraid; fur-thermore, it was scratching anxiously at the metal, as if desperately try-ing to get through it.

Among the many traits that had manifested themselves in Grag's mind during the period of its life that it'd come to regard as the Great Awakening were two emotions: curiosity and empathy. But Curt had ordered it to stay where it was until further instruction. Grag weighed these things against each other for a very long time—approximately .756 of a second—before deciding in favor of satisfying its emotional needs.

Walking away from the wall, it approached the door and pushed the button that opened it. In that instant, a small dog dashed through the door and ran straight into Grag's legs. Stunned by the impact, the dog fell back on its haunches, then stared up at the robot with what appeared to be brown-eyed astonishment.

"Hello," said Grag. "Who are you?"

The moonpup responded by nervously squirting urine on Grag's feet. Then it turned its head as voices came from farther down the narrow corridor behind it. "*Eek!*" it yelped, and took cover behind Grag's legs.

"Eek is as good a name as any, I suppose." Grag bent over to very carefully pick up the moonpup. "I am Grag. Pleased to make your acquaintance."

The moonpup trembled as Grag gently scooped it up from the floor, but seemed to realize that this big, man-shaped machine meant it no harm. It curled up tight against the robot's massive chest and had just begun to pant with relief when two men came into sight down the corridor.

"There it is!" one of them, a squat terran with a black beard, yelled. "The 'bot caught him!"

"Yeah, hey, willya look at that?" His companion, a tall aphrodite, laughed unpleasantly. "Nice catch, robby!"

The fact that both wore the blue dress uniforms of the Interplanetary Police Force had no special significance for Grag. So far as it was concerned, the IPF was just one more group whom the denizens of Tycho had done their best to avoid over the years. No one had ever instructed Grag to obey them at all times. So it silently watched as they came closer, and made no effort to hand over the moonpup to them.

"Okay, you can give me the dog now." The terran IPF officer reached forward to take the moonpup from Grag.

Grag stepped back, wrapping its hands a little more securely around Eek. "No. I'm sorry, but I will not."

Startled, the terran stared at the robot. "'I'm sorry, but I will not'?" He looked at his colleague. "Didja hear that? The 'bot just talked back to me."

"Uh-huh. I heard." The aphrodite stepped forward, but didn't reach for Eek. "Okay, robby, gimme the mutt. That's an order."

"Many apologies, but I will not. Nor am I obligated to follow your orders."

"Really? Don't think so, huh?" The aphrodite glared at Grag.

"Awright, 'bot, get this straight. We're officers of the Interplanetary Police Force, on assignment as escorts for the president of the Solar Coalition, James Carthew. The dog you found is supposed to be a gift to the president from Senator Victor Corvo, the guy who lives here. The dog ran away. You found it. Now hand it over."

"If the dog ran away from President Carthew," Grag said, "then this indicates that he doesn't want to be given to the president. Furthermore, if Senator Corvo is giving up the dog, then it's clear that he no longer wishes to possess him. The dog is therefore unclaimed, in which case it's my right to adopt him as my own. That is what I'm doing now, and giving him the name Eek."

"Didja hear what he said?" the terran officer blustered, pointing a finger at Eek. "He's a cop, and he's just given you an order! Give him the dog!"

"I'm sorry, gentlemen, but you do not have legal authority in this matter. You may go now."

The two lawmen regarded Grag with slack-jawed astonishment. Neither could believe that a robot would act in anything other than a subservient manner.

"Oh, for the luvva . . ." The aphrodite reached forward to yank Eek away.

Grag broke his nose. When his partner reacted by pulling out his PBP, Grag broke first the gun, then his nose as well. The robot did all this in less than three seconds and with one hand, keeping Eek securely clasped against its chest the entire time.

Grag decided that playing the dumb, lost robot no longer served a purpose, so it began marching down the corridor, leaving behind two bleeding, cursing goons. But before Grag left them, it got in touch with the *Comet*, letting Otho know what had just happened.

"*You moron!*" Otho responded. "*You did that just to save a puppy?*"

"It's a very nice puppy," Grag replied.

"*But . . . oh, never mind.*" There was a hint of exasperation in Otho's voice. "*Just find Curt. He needs you right now.*"

IX

"Hello, Inspector Randall. A pleasure to see you again."

Curt didn't have to lie about that, at least. Even with sleep-tousled hair and a gun in hand, the woman he'd met earlier was the most beautiful he'd ever seen. That she looked as if she'd just fallen out of bed made her even more attractive. It took an effort to keep his gaze above her neck; her angry eyes were less inviting than her long, bare legs.

"My eyes are up here, not on my knees." She glared back at him, red-faced and unsmiling. "Ezra, can I shoot him? Please?"

"Not until after I've questioned him." Marshal Gurney also had his gun trained on him. "So your name is Rab Cain?" Curt nodded and the old lawman shook his head. "Wrong answer. Ain't no one by that name in the SolCol database of registered citizens . . . we checked. I'd say it's a good bet it's a fake identity. Who are you, really?"

Before Curt could respond, bright light burst all around them, instantly transforming night into day. Someone had apparently reoriented the craterhab's solar mirrors, allowing them to reflect the sun through the ceiling skylight. Everyone squinted and some cursed in surprise, but while most people instinctively covered their eyes with their hands, Curt kept his folded on top of his head. Almost a half-dozen guns were pointed at him just then; he didn't want to become a corpse just because of a misunderstanding.

When his vision cleared, he saw two more people approaching from the mansion. Victor Corvo and James Carthew, escorted by two more

IPF officers. Marshal Gurney's mouth twisted beneath his mustache when he saw them, then he lowered his gun.

"Senator Corvo, Mr. President . . . you shouldn't be here. The premises are under lockdown, and we need to have you—"

"The emergency is over, Ezra," Carthew replied, "and I'm not inclined to cower in the basement." He marched past Ezra Gurney—Curt now knew the marshal's full name—and didn't stop until he reached the body lying prone on the lawn. "Is this him, Joan? Is this fellow the reason why you knocked me down?"

"No, he's not, Mr. President," Agent Randall said, and now Curt knew her first name as well. Apparently the president liked to be on a first-name basis with his security team. Such a lovely name, and appropriate, too; he was reminded of Joan of Arc. "This is the individual I spotted from the porch," she continued, gesturing at Curt with her gun. "I spotted him when he stepped out from behind the toolshed—"

"To open fire on the man who was aiming at you, Mr. President." Curt kept his voice calm and unhurried, just as the Brain instructed. "Joan . . . Agent Randall, I mean . . . couldn't see him because he was camouflaged and hiding behind a bush, but I saw him clearly from where I was standing." He looked at Joan. "I'm sorry, Inspector, but there was no time to warn you. If I hadn't fired first, he might have hit the president."

"Or me," Corvo added.

Curt didn't say anything. He wasn't about to defend Victor Corvo, not even with words.

"Is this true?" Carthew asked Joan. "Was this gentleman aiming away from the house when you saw him?"

Joan hesitated. "Yes, he was, Mr. President," she said, reluctantly but truthfully. "When I looked up again, he'd exchanged fire with the deceased and was pursuing him across the lawn."

"I'd just arrived on the scene when I saw both of them." Gurney lowered his gun, although he kept it unholstered and ready to point at Curt again. "I chased both suspects on foot until this one"—he nodded toward Curt—"caught up with the other guy. They knocked each other around a bit, then the shooter got hold of his gun again and tried to shoot this young buck. That's when I stepped in."

"And I greatly appreciate it, Marshal Gurney." Curt cast him a grateful smile. "I only wish we could've taken the assassin alive to question him further about what he'd said just before you shot him, but—"

"You still haven't answered his question." Joan had lowered neither her gun nor her guard. "Who are you?"

"You can call me Captain Future."

She stared at him. "Whaaaa—?"

"That's the stupidest damn thing I've ever heard," Ezra muttered.

Curt felt his face becoming warm. It seemed as if everyone surrounding him—the other IPF officers, Victor Corvo, even President Carthew—were grinning in agreement with Ezra Gurney, with one or two on the verge of breaking up. He cursed Simon for telling him to say this, but it was too late to take it back. And with Corvo present, he had no choice; the last thing he could do was reveal his real name.

"I know it sounds—" He stopped himself. "I use that name for a reason." He turned to Carthew. "I'm what you might call a freelance troubleshooter, Mr. President . . . a paladin, if you will. I have a proper name, of course, but I prefer to keep it a secret in order to protect myself and my loved ones."

"Your . . . 'loved ones'?" Ezra's eyes flickered upward in disbelief. The other IPF agents quietly snickered.

"Companions, that is." Curt was beginning to think that repeating everything Simon told him to say verbatim was probably a bad idea.

Joan slowly nodded. She seemed tentatively willing to accept what he had to say, at least until she heard more. "So what brings you here, Captain Future?"

"Some time ago, I became aware that someone might mean the president harm while he was making a state visit to the Moon. Little more than a rumor, but credible enough to take seriously. I didn't know exactly who was responsible, but the trail led me to today's dedication ceremony at the Straight Wall—"

"This is where Marshal Gurney and I first saw him," Joan said, speaking to the president. "He and another person were there, standing near the stage. They were acting in a suspicious manner, and Ezra and I briefly questioned them."

"One of my companions," Curt said. "He's not here, but as I'm sure you've already discovered, his identity is also false, for the same reason mine is." He forced a smile. "I apologize, Agent Randall, for being less than forthcoming . . . but really, would you have released me if I'd told you that I prefer the name Captain Future?"

"I would've called for a straitjacket," Ezra said quietly.

"So what were you doing at the ceremony, anyway?" Corvo had been quiet during all this, but now he stepped forward, hands clasped behind his back. "If you knew an assassin was stalking the president, why didn't you inform Marshal Gurney and Inspector Randall when they questioned you?"

"Because there's no profit in that." Curt avoided looking at Corvo as he spoke, and hoped there was nothing in his voice to betray the animosity he felt for him. "This is my business. When I take someone down I expect professional compensation. How would I receive that if I blabbed my best lead to the first IPF officer who questioned me?"

"And when you disappeared over Tycho?" Joan asked. "How did you make that happen?"

"Pardon me?" Curt pretended to be baffled. He shook his head slightly. "I don't understand what you're saying. My associate and I flew over Tycho on our way home after the ceremony, but we didn't disappear." He gave Joan a querulous look. "Why, were you following us?"

Joan's face darkened. She glared at him but didn't say anything.

—*Very good, Curtis. It appears that they're willing to believe you.*

Simon had been quietly eavesdropping the entire time, using Curt's ring to monitor the conversation. He'd told Curt that he'd step in and help him through the conversation if he ran into trouble with the cover story Simon had concocted, but this was the first time the Brain had spoken up.

Curt took this as a positive indication that everything was going smoothly. Indeed, he noticed a certain look Joan and Ezra exchanged, along with the quiet nod the marshal gave his junior officer. "You can put your hands down," Ezra said. "Just keep 'em away from your iron."

He squinted at Curt's gun. "What is that, anyway? Never seen a piece quite like that."

"I call it a plasmar. It's my own invention." Curt slowly lowered his hands from his head, surreptitiously twisting the ring's band so that the jeweled setting still faced the people standing around him. "Thank you. My arms were getting tired."

"A troubleshooter, huh?" Ezra holstered his gun, and gestured for Joan and his other men to do the same. "Well, Cap'n Future, I appreciate what you've done this evening, particularly since you've made up for the failure of my security team." Another meaningful look was traded between him and Joan; this time she bit her lip and turned red. "But we really don't have need of adventurers, so it would probably be best if—"

He stopped all of a sudden, and the faraway look that appeared on his face told Curt that he was listening to something over his Anni. Then he focused on Curt again. "Did you come here with a robot?"

—Grag has located you. It's just entered the crater floor through the same entrance you used. The president's security team is going on alert again. You need to let Marshal Gurney know that it belongs to you.

As Simon spoke, the two IPF officers who'd followed Joan turned and began to trot away, heading toward the shed. Looking in the direction they were running toward, Curt saw Grag marching slowly toward him. The robot appeared to be holding something in its arms, but he couldn't see what it was.

"Yes, that's my robot," Curt said. "It helped me to enter the crater through the garage, and I left it down there. I assure you, it's harmless."

"How did you do that?" Joan asked.

"I hid on top of a truck that made a delivery just a little while ago. My robot stopped it on the road and I climbed aboard while the drivers were distracted." There was no point in hiding this, although he was careful not to mention the fantome generator. Like his true name, that was something he needed to keep secret.

Ezra scowled. "I've received a report that your 'bot attacked two of my men and broke their noses."

Curt heard a small, canine yip. He watched as Grag paused to bend over and release the object in its arms. To his surprise, it appeared to be the same moonpup he'd seen being chased by two men. The last time he'd seen them, they were running down the corridor, heading in the general direction of where he'd left Grag.

"Did you lose a moonpup just a little while ago?" he asked, and Joan reluctantly nodded. "That's probably the same one. Looks like my companion found him. If it attacked your men, then it was probably protecting the dog, although it may have overstepped its—"

"Two of our officers left their posts to chase a dog?" Ezra stared at him in disbelief.

Joan sighed. "Afraid so. They were on duty when a puppy the senator was attempting to give the president bit him and ran away."

"I don't think he likes me very much." President Carthew glared at the moonpup as it happily scampered around Grag's feet, barking with delight at its new friend and protector. "If your robot wants him, he can keep him."

"I'll happily give him to you as a gift," Corvo said to Curt. "With compliments for saving the president's life." There was little warmth in his voice as he said this.

"Thank you, Senator," Curt said, his own voice just as cool. He held up a hand for Grag to stop, and the robot halted at once. No sense in having it come closer if it was making Carthew's security detail nervous, especially when they were just beginning to trust him.

"Those idiots left the president's side to chase a puppy?" Ezra was incredulous. He turned to Joan. "I apologize . . . this ain't your fault at all. Tell those damn fool bodyguards to turn in their badges. They're fired." He shook his head in disgust. "Morons. Can't even trust 'em to take care of a puppy."

"Perhaps we owe you a greater debt than we thought." President Carthew walked over to Curt and extended his hand. "Thank you, sir. I appreciate the service you've done."

—Now is your chance! Take it!

"Thank you, Mr. President. It's an honor." As Curt stepped forward to accept the president's handshake, he dropped his voice to a whisper.

"May I meet with you in private, sir? It concerns something you ought to know about Senator Corvo."

Carthew hesitated. From the corner of his eye, Curt saw that Joan was listening. Judging from her expression, she'd heard everything. Carthew studied him for a moment, as if taking his measure, then slowly nodded.

"Yes . . . yes, we can do that," he said softly, then turned to Joan. "Would you find us a place where we may have some privacy, Joan? I think I'd like to have a word alone with . . . Captain Future."

The library of Corvo's mansion was a large room whose walls were lined with oak bookcases that looked real enough until someone actually tried to take a book off the shelves; the cases were nothing more than lenticular holograms, and there probably wasn't a real book in the room. But the brass table lamps, polished basalt-tile floor, crystal chandelier, and carved cherubim holding up the ceiling gave the library an air of Old South gentility, which the senator clearly wished to cultivate. He was fascinated with the plantation culture of the nineteenth century, and didn't mind its association with a time when wealthy men owned other human beings.

Because the library was located on the ground floor just off the entrance hall, it was the closest place Joan could find for Curt to privately meet with President Carthew. Corvo himself invited them to use it before excusing himself to take care of household matters. It was kind of the senator to provide them with this room, but before anyone went in, Joan nonetheless had the security team sweep the library with an anti-surveillance scanner make sure that it hadn't been wired for sound.

Once Joan was satisfied that the room hadn't been bugged, she led everyone in, then quietly excused herself. Ezra posted a man outside the door and another on the other side of French windows opening onto the porch before accompanying Curt and the president into the library. Once he'd closed the door behind him, he stood off to one side. Curt noticed that his eyes never strayed from him, and that his right hand stayed close to his pistol.

"Now then, Captain Future," President Carthew said, "what is it that you'd like to discuss with me?"

Curt smiled, trying to make the president relax. "First, Mr. President, I apologize for not revealing my true name. Captain Future is . . . well, it's not my first choice for a pseudonym, but my associates seem to believe it's appropriate."

"I could honestly care less what you call yourself." Carthew's voice became stern. He was not a man who enjoyed having his time wasted. "I appreciate the fact that you risked your life to save mine, but like Marshal Gurney here, I'm not sure I entirely accept your story that you're a . . . a troubleshooter who just happened to stumble upon the fact that someone intended to assassinate me."

"Nor should you, because it's not true. Not completely, anyway."

—*Careful, my boy! Ezra can still arrest you and charge you with being an accessory!*

Curt refrained from nodding or giving any other sign that he'd heard the Brain. It was fortunate that Joan had neglected to have her security team scan him as well as the room; otherwise they would have discovered his ring. And just now, he was glad to have Simon telling him how to respond.

"I told you this," Curt replied, "only because the senator was present and I don't want him to know the truth. The fact of the matter is that, while I am indeed pursuing a criminal, I wasn't expecting to find an assassin here. The person I'm hunting is Victor Corvo himself."

Carthew didn't respond at once. He glanced at Ezra Gurney, who said nothing but continued to study Curt. Then he turned to him again. "Go on."

Curt took a deep breath, but before he could speak, there was a soft knock at the door. It opened and Joan came in, this time in uniform; she had obviously gone upstairs to change into something less revealing than her nightshirt. She said nothing to either Curt or the president as she walked over to stand beside Ezra. Carthew gave Curt an encouraging nod, and he started again.

"My name is Curt Newton, Mr. President. My parents were Roger and Elaine Newton, a pair of scientists from New York Province, North

146 · **ALLEN STEELE**

America, and when I was an infant, they . . ." Curt suddenly found his throat becoming tight. "They were murdered by Corvo."

President Carthew's eyebrows rose a fraction of an inch, yet there were no indications of shock or disbelief. "Please continue. I'm listening."

Over the next few minutes, Curt told the president the story of his parents' murder, both what he'd known since he was a child and the details he'd learned only earlier today. Carthew listened quietly, as did Ezra and Joan. No one else in the room spoke until he was done, and when he was finished, all three were silent for a few moments. Then the president cleared his throat.

"I see," he said. "And so you've come here to . . . ?"

"To bring Victor Corvo to justice." Curt decided to omit one detail: his intent to kill Corvo. He'd been fortunate enough so far not to find himself in a jail cell, but such an admission would have pushed his luck past the breaking point.

"So finding the assassin—" Joan began.

"A stroke of luck, but one that I'm glad happened." Curt paused. "However, isn't it curious that he should be here?"

"Yes, it is." Her eyes narrowed. "And I'm still wondering if you had anything to do with him."

"I'm willing to take our friend at his word that he doesn't know the assassin." Folding his arms across his chest, Carthew shook his head. "It's unfortunate that Ezra shot him. If he hadn't, we might have learned who sent him."

"I did, sir," Curt said. "I managed to . . . um, interrogate him just before he broke away and retrieved his gun. He indicated that he belonged to the Sons of the Two Moons, and just before Marshal Gurney fired, he shouted, 'For Ul Quorn' . . . whoever that may be."

Carthew's gaze became sharp. "He said *what*?"

"Ul Quorn?" Ezra asked. "Are you sure?"

"Yes, I'm sure that's what he said." Now it was Curt's turn to be baffled. "I know who the Sons of the Two Moons are—they're a cult who worship the Denebians as some sort of alien gods—but I've never heard of Ul Quorn. Who is he?"

"An aresian," Joan said, "or at least so we've been told. Some say that he may be half terran as well. In any case, he's a gangster on Mars, the leader of its largest criminal syndicate. It's also believed that he may be tied to the Sons of the Two Moons, and may be their leader as well."

"Sometimes he's known as the Magician of Mars," Ezra added, "because he makes his enemies disappear without a trace. But that's not all." He turned to Carthew. "Mr. President, this is classified IPF info. Are you sure we oughta be talkin' 'bout this?"

Carthew thought it over for a moment. "Yes . . . yes, I think we should. Particularly if this young man knows something we don't." He turned to Curt again. "Within certain government circles, it's been rumored for a while now that there may be some sort of link between Senator Corvo and Ul Quorn. No one has yet been able to gather substantiating evidence, but . . . well, it's something I've asked Section Four to investigate."

"We haven't come up with anything," Ezra said, "but that's not surprising. People on Mars know better than to mess with the Magician. They say the deserts are filled with folks who've talked about Ul Quorn, and our efforts to infiltrate the Sons of the Two Moons . . ."

"Those agents haven't returned," Joan finished for him. "He's up to something, that's for certain. What, we don't know."

"So why would Ul Quorn have someone attempt to kill you?" Curt asked the president.

"That's an excellent question," Carthew replied. "Ever since Corvo came into office six years ago, he's done his best to politically align himself with me. I've never really trusted him, but he's been hard to ignore, especially since he's used his influence to muster votes in the Senate in support of some of my initiatives. And he's done other things to gain favor with me. The invitation to give the dedication speech is just the latest example." He frowned, then added, "It appears, though, he may have an ulterior motive, such as luring me within range of an assassin's rifle."

"But how would he benefit from having you killed? He's not next in the line of succession, is he?"

"No, he isn't." The president shook his head. "Vice President Medusa

Jal would take over." He thought about it a moment, absently brushing his mustache with a fingertip. "But Medusa is politically weak, while Corvo has been gathering supporters for years. If I was out of the way and she became president, it's possible Corvo could persuade the Senate to pass a vote of no confidence in her and install him as president pro tem."

"But wouldn't there have to be some sort of crisis for that to happen?" Ezra asked.

"You're right." The president nodded, his expression pensive as he gazed at the carpeted floor. "Under the constitution, there would have to be a 'grave and imminent threat' to the Coalition for the Senate to remove a sitting president and replace him with a senator they've elected . . . but I have no idea what that might be."

"Perhaps the answer isn't here, Mr. President," Curt said. "Perhaps it's elsewhere . . . such as Mars."

"Why Mars?"

"The assassin is an aresian who seems to have been with the Sons of the Two Moons. Ul Quorn apparently has some sort of ties to Victor Corvo. I'd say everything points to Mars as being the locale for some sort of conspiracy against you, sir."

"You may be right." President Carthew looked at him quizzically. "Do you have a suggestion?"

"Yes, sir, I do. Let me and my associates travel to Mars and try to find out what's going on." Curt gestured toward Joan. "Agent Randall said that the IPF hasn't been able to successfully penetrate the Sons. But if someone they don't know—a total stranger who doesn't belong to the IPF—were to infiltrate, perhaps he'd have more success."

"That's a very high risk."

"Yes, it is, Mr. President," Ezra said. "For you as well." His eyes were coldly suspicious as they turned to Curt. "We don't know for certain if he is who he says he is. For all we know, he could be in cahoots with Corvo or even Ul Quorn. Sending him out on his own, with no assurances that he'd act solely on behalf of—"

"I'll go with him," Joan said.

Everyone stopped to stare at her. Back straight, arms at her sides,

Joan Randall exuded confidence. "I'll go with him," she repeated, speaking to Ezra and President Carthew as if Curt weren't there. "That way, the IPF can keep an eye on him. I'll keep in touch with Section Four while in transit, and get in touch with the IPF station on Mars once I've arrived."

"And what if you run into trouble?" Ezra asked.

"I can handle myself, Chief. You should know that by now." Joan looked at Curt. "And if you're who you say you are, then you'll need the IPF to bring Ul Quorn, and perhaps Corvo, to justice."

President Carthew didn't reply at once. He looked at Ezra, searching for some sign of approval. Ezra said nothing for a moment, then he reluctantly nodded. "Very well, then," Carthew said, and turned to Curt again. "On presidential authority, I'm deputizing you as a temporary undercover agent of the Interplanetary Police Force."

"Thank you, Mr. President." Curt felt an electric current run down his back as he grasped Carthew's outstretched hand. "I'll do my best not to let you down."

"I'm sure you won't, son." Carthew smiled. "Because of the sensitive nature of your assignment, I'm giving you a designated code name, to be used for all future communications with my office and the IPF. I assume you already know what your nom de guerre will be."

Curt nodded, hoping that his feelings weren't obvious. Like it or not, he'd become Captain Future.

XI

Their conversation concluded, the four people who'd met in the library left the room. By then, the darkness of artificial night had returned to the craterhab; the outside mirrors had been reoriented so that earthlight was no longer reflected into Armstrong Crater. So none of them was surprised to learn from a tuxedoed butler waiting in the hall that Senator Corvo had already retired. The hour was late, after all, and it had been an eventful evening.

The butler closed the library door behind them, and after a moment the lights went out by themselves. For a few minutes, the only sounds came from outside, where Ezra Gurney was escorting President Carthew upstairs to bed while Joan was in the mansion with Curt. Soon the room was dark and quiet, and apparently deserted.

Then, at the center of the room, very close to the spot where the four of them had stood, a thin, luminescent line appeared in the basalt-tile floor.

The line stretched, with two more like it appearing at right angles at either end. A moment later, the lines expanded in width, becoming a trapdoor artfully concealed by the patterns of the surrounding tiles. The door silently opened on recessed hinges, revealing a vertical space just three feet wide but almost seven feet deep. The spy hole was large enough to hide someone standing beneath the seemingly solid floor; there, they could listen to what was being said, undetected by the equipment meant to ferret out electronic forms of surveillance. An old-fashioned form of eavesdropping, but effective all the same.

The figure who'd been the silent fifth party to the conversation that had just ensued climbed up the recessed ladder from the spy hole. He dropped the hatch back in place, then walked over to the desk, switched on a lamp, and took a seat in its overstuffed leather armchair.

Alone in the library, Victor Corvo pondered the conversation he'd just overheard.

Eyes shut, hands calmly folded together in his lap, he displayed no outward sign that his mind was in turmoil over what he'd just learned. Yet it wasn't President Carthew's distrust of him that surprised him so much as the other revelation: that Roger and Elaine Newton's son still lived, and that after all these years he was seeking revenge for the murders of his parents.

Very well, then: so be it.

The senator knew that his plans would obviously have to be changed, but there was no reason why they would have to be canceled entirely. The IPF couldn't act against him without evidence. With the assassin dead—for this, at least, he was grateful to Marshal Gurney—there was nothing to link Corvo to the attempt on the president's life. Carthew could be as suspicious as he liked, but there was nothing he could legally do to have Corvo arrested and removed from office.

And as for Curt Newton . . . although Corvo's eyes remained shut, a meditative smile appeared. Ul Quorn could take care of the Newton kid. Of that, he had little doubt.

"Captain Future." Corvo quietly snorted with distain. "You don't have much of a future, do you?"

PART FOUR
The Photon Express

1

"*Comet* to *Brackett*," Curt said. "On final approach, requesting permission for rendezvous and docking."

A moment passed, then a woman's voice came through his headset. "*Brackett* to *Comet. Affirmative, your fee has been received and processed. Permission granted. Rendezvous on the port side of cargo frame and dock in Berth Four.*"

"Thank you, *Brackett*." Curt tapped the mike wand to mute it, then wrapped his left hand around the stick and rested his right on the center control panel. "Systems check."

"All green. You're good to go." Otho was in the right-hand seat. He'd just finished running down the last few items on the checklist and was now watching Curt as he piloted the *Comet* for orbital rendezvous and docking with the beamship that lay ahead.

Curt inched the stick forward, at the same time touching the recessed studs for the reaction-control thrusters along the *Comet*'s hull. There was a soft rumble as the thrusters fired; through the rounded panes of the forward porthole, the *Brackett* slowly turned on the long skeletal truss of its main spar.

"Everything all right, Joan?" he asked, not taking his eyes off the controls as he addressed her over his shoulder.

"Fine." Joan was strapped into one of the passenger seats behind the pilot and copilot chairs. "No reason to keep asking. I was fine ten minutes ago, and ten minutes before that."

Curt didn't respond at once. His attention was focused on the immense spacecraft only a few hundred feet away. The *Brackett* dwarfed not only the *Comet*, but also every other spacecraft nestled within the cradles running down the length of its spar. Over six hundred feet in length, it was tethered by carbon-nanotube mooring cables to the enormous furled mass of its beamsail. *Brackett*'s crew modules were a small cluster of pressurized cylinders at the bow, and its only engine was the fusion stack at the stern meant solely for emergencies. Everything else was the sail and the row of ships being ferried across the gulf of space.

A pair of red and blue beacons had begun to flash at either end of a large, cradlelike berth attached about halfway down the spar. Apparently this was Berth Four, their slot aboard the interplanetary ferry. Curt pulled the stick a little to the left and fired the thrusters again, and the *Comet* began to glide toward it.

"Just checking," Curt went on, remembering that he'd left Joan hanging. "You've been a little—"

He cut himself short, not wanting to offend her. "He means you've been a little tense ever since we took off," Otho finished, glancing back at her. "I assure you, you couldn't be safer."

"I know that," Joan said coolly, but her poise said otherwise: back stiff, arms folded tightly across her chest, legs touching one another at the knees and ankles. She wore the dark blue bodysuit of an IPF officer, PBP holstered at her side. Although she demonstrated the easy grace of someone accustomed to zero-g, ever since she'd come aboard the *Comet* on the Moon a few hours ago, she'd behaved as if she was there against her will.

Perhaps it wasn't her fault. Curt absently considered this as he guided his little ship closer to the giant vessel. It may have been the strangeness of finding a craft that could turn invisible, its crew an intelligent robot, an artificial human, and a disembodied brain. Curt had to admit that he probably had the weirdest ship in space. If Inspector Randall didn't already think that he was the most bizarre individual she'd ever met, she was probably well on the way to suspecting so.

Maybe he should have left her behind. Too late for that now.

Curt refocused his attention on the controls and his docking maneuvers with the beamship. Once the sail was unfurled to its full diameter extent, the *Brackett* would enter an invisible yet powerful stream of photons collected by a nearby sunsat and projected by a 100-gigawatt laser in Lagrange-point orbit 930,000 miles from Earth. This beamed-energy propulsion system, comprising what the designers fancifully called the "photon railway," would boost the *Brackett* to cruise velocity. At Mars's current position relative to Earth and the Moon, this meant that the beamship would reach Mars in just three days, with another laser in orbit around the red planet braking it during primary approach.

The *Comet* had never before traveled so far from Tycho. Curt's previous travels to other planets had been aboard commercial spaceliners. As a racing yacht, the *Comet* simply wasn't designed for interplanetary flight. Even with its high impulse-per-second magnetoplasma engine, it would have exhausted its fuel supply before it was a quarter of the way to Mars, not to mention the fact that its life support system was limited to no more than a week for three people. But since Curt—or rather, Captain Future—had been deputized as a special agent of the Interplanetary Police Force by no less than President Carthew, it had been an easy matter for Joan to arrange for the *Comet* to be assigned a berth aboard the *Brackett*, even if it meant having a small freighter bumped from the manifest at the last minute.

Under Curt's steady hand, the *Comet* coasted in above Berth Four. Maneuvering thrusters silently fired along its hull, and the little teardrop-shaped craft gradually descended into the opened bars of the docking cradle. There was a slight thump; through the porthole, he saw ferry crewmen in vacuum suits glide toward the cradle. Dangling from the spar at the end of their tethers, they attached electrical cables and lines for air and water recirculation systems, then one of them moved from bar to bar along the clawlike cradle arms, locking down the joists that would keep the *Comet* in place until the Brackett reached its destination.

"*Comet, you are secure.*" Again, the captain's voice came through his headset. "*Stand by for departure in T-minus thirty-eight minutes.*"

"Thank you, *Brackett*. *Comet* out." Curt clicked off the com, then pulled back on the lever that reoriented his seat to launch-and-landing position. "All right, everyone . . . break out the cards and the chessboard, because we've got nothing else to do for the next three days."

"Except clean up after Grag's dog," Otho added unhappily as he lowered his own seat.

"I think it was very sweet of it to take in the little fella." Joan was fumbling with her seat harness. Like nearly everything else in the *Comet,* its design was over twenty years old; never before had she put on something like it, and she was still getting used to it. "Not what I . . . oh, c'mon . . . not what I'd expect from a robot."

"Grag is not your usual robot." Curt switched off the major systems aboard ship not needed for life support or communications. "I'm not even sure it likes to be called 'it.'"

"This is true," Simon added. "Lately Grag has been requesting that the word 'he' be applied as a personal pronoun." The Brain had just ascended through the manhole from the middeck where he, Grag, and Eek had spent the flight up from the Moon. "I've argued that, as a robot, gender-specific words aren't really suitable, but . . . oh, please allow me, Inspector Randall."

Simon floated toward her, pushed along by the impellors on either side of his saucerlike carapace. Joan shrank back in her seat as his claws reached down to her harness's six-point buckle; there was no way to tell whether the Brain's eyestalks noticed the barely disguised expression of horror that appeared on her face, but nevertheless Simon delicately unclasped the buckle for her.

"There you are, my dear," he said, moving away again. "All set now?"

"Y-yes, I . . . I think so." Eyes wide with revulsion, the young woman held tightly onto the armrest of her chair until Simon moved away, then hastily pushed herself out of her seat and over to the forward window. She did so ostensibly to look at the *Brackett,* but it was all too obvious that she wanted to put as much distance between herself and the Brain as she could in the tight confines of the flight deck.

Curt tried not to notice her nearness, yet again he wondered whether it had been a good idea to bring her aboard the *Comet*. She'd accepted Grag easily enough, although she was still surprised by a robot that was not only capable of independent thought but was also developing emotions. However, she remained suspicious of Otho, even more so now that she'd become aware that he wasn't a human being—at least not in the normal sense—but rather an android, the very same one created by Roger and Elaine Newton. And as for Simon Wright, it was clear that, so far as she was concerned, he was an abomination, a dead man whose living brain remained ghoulishly preserved and active within a bizarre cybernetic form.

The moment Joan met the rest of Curt's family, when she'd traveled with him and Grag from Armstrong crater to the nearby valley where the *Comet* stood, decloaked and visible in the lunar sunlight, he realized something he'd long since taken for granted: Otho, Grag, and Simon were stranger companions than most people had. He'd never thought there was anything unusual about growing up with an android, a robot, and a cyborg, but Joan's reactions to them reminded him otherwise.

And there was also Joan herself.

Not including his mother, whom he remembered barely at all, Curt could count the number of females he'd met in his life on one hand and still have a finger or two left over. The years he'd spent hiding beneath Tycho Crater had not prepared him for the full range of normal human contact, and meeting members of the opposite gender was one of those things with which he'd had little experience.

It was times like this when he regretted his upbringing. He'd never before had a female passenger aboard the *Comet,* particularly not one as attractive as Joan Randall. He very much wanted her to like him, at least just a little, but his interactions with the opposite sex were limited to a few random encounters . . . except for one notable incident from his teenage years that he preferred not to think about. So he didn't know what to do, and worse, everything he *did* do seemed to be wrong.

Curt deliberately fixed his gaze on the instruments, all too aware of the young woman hovering just inches away. He knew that, if he moved

just a little bit by accident—or even deliberately, if he cared to do so—
he'd brush up against her, perhaps without her noticing it. From the
corner of his eye, he saw Otho carefully observing him; his expression
was neutral but his green eyes were sharp and watchful. There was no
question that Curt would behave like a gentleman, even if he hadn't
already been inclined to do so. But still . . .

This was a woman.

His mouth was dry and his heart was pounding, his hands were
greasy with sweat and his skin felt like it was itching in a dozen places
at once. There was an uncomfortable sensation in the pit of his stomach; it seemed as if he was picking up a subtle fragrance from her, one
that he wanted to wrap around himself and—

"They're all coming in now," Joan said.

"What? Excuse me?" Startled, Curt jerked slightly in his seat.

"Looks like they're bringing the last ship." Joan nodded toward the
window. "A big lunar freighter just finished mooring on the other side
of the spine. We should be launching soon."

"Oh. Okay."

Joan looked down at him. He glanced away, but not fast enough. She
studied him for a a few moments, then pushed herself away from the
porthole.

"When you speak to me," she said, her voice quiet and yet remon-
strative, "I'd appreciate it if you looked at my face, not everything
below my neck."

Curt's face suddenly felt a little too warm for comfort. He couldn't
look at her. "I—"

"If no one objects, I think I'll go below and help Grag make Eek
comfortable." She paused. "Permission to leave the bridge, Captain?"

Curt didn't know whether she was addressing him by his status as
the *Comet*'s captain or by his nom de guerre. "Yes, sure, that's fine—"

"Thank you." Joan performed a graceful somersault, kicked off the
ceiling, and propelled herself headfirst down the manhole, carefully
avoiding making any contact with the Brain as she went past.

Curt watched her go. He let out his breath once she'd disappeared and was about to return his attention to the console when he caught a look from Otho.

"This was a mistake," he murmured.

Otho didn't reply. He only shook his head and, with a faintly amused smile, looked away.

11

A little less than an hour later, the *Leigh Brackett* gently coasted within range of the photonic laser thruster positioned at L-1 between Earth and the Sun. Powered by sunlight focused through an immense lens one and a half miles in diameter, a stream of photons shot forward like bullets of light, striking the mirror-bright surface of the beamship's seven hundred–foot polymer sail. Slowly at first, then gradually moving faster, the *Brackett* began to sail forth into interplanetary space, leaving Earth and the Moon behind as it let out on the long, shallow arc of its trajectory to Mars.

Inside the *Comet*, its passengers felt the slow yet persistent return of gravity as the beamship entered the outbound thrust phase of its journey. There was no need to strap in again, yet everyone was cautious about planting their feet against the deck as the ship caught the photon beam, lest they find themselves falling—albeit in slow motion—to the floor. The only person aboard who didn't have any difficulty was Simon; he continued to move about as freely as ever, his impellors whirring softly. But while Eek seemed to like having his paws on a stable surface again, the little dog was vexed to discover that he couldn't follow Grag from deck to deck as he'd learned to do in freefall.

"I don't see why you had to bring him along." Otho scowled at the moonpup as he lounged at the dining table in the middeck wardroom. The *Brackett* had broken lunar orbit several hours earlier, and now the *Comet*'s crew was relaxing after a pasta dinner Grag had prepared in the galley. "He's just going to get in the way."

Grag bent over to place a small bowl of freeze-dried kibble in front of Eek. The dog's tail happily wagged as he devoured his food, a parting gift from his former owners. "If I had left him behind, the two men chasing him might have put him out through the airlock," the robot said, kneeling beside its pet to stroke his fur with surprising tenderness. "And we didn't have time to return to Tycho. Besides, there would be no one there to take care of him while we're gone."

"Really," Joan said. "How interesting."

Otho closed his eyes. Although she already knew, from what Curt had told President Carthew, that they secretly resided beneath the ruins of Roger and Elaine Newton's lab, she was still unaware of a number of details, such as exactly how many people lived there. Grag had let this little piece of information slip. It might be trivial, but a sharp IPF inspector like Joan Randall might find anything useful, no matter how inconsequential it might seem.

She seemed to sense Otho's unease, because she put down her coffee mug and gazed at him from across the table. "Oh, c'mon. I already get that it's just the three of you—"

"The four of us. You're leaving out someone." He didn't have to ask whom she was neglecting; Joan apparently considered Simon to be less human than him or even Grag.

"Whatever . . . and I'm willing to trust you that Curt didn't go there to kill Carthew. So you don't have anything to hide from me anymore, do you?"

She was baiting him, of course, but Otho wasn't about to fall for it. There was no reason why she needed to learn that Curt's objective really had been to take out Victor Corvo. Plotting to kill a senator was nearly as bad as plotting to kill a president; she could easily put him under arrest as soon as the *Brackett* reached Port Deimos.

"No, not really," Otho replied. "I'm just not certain how much you need to know about us."

Joan toyed with her mug as she quietly watched Grag play with Eek. Curt had returned to the flight deck to stand watch; he'd said little during the meal, a curtain of embarrassed silence hanging between him and Joan. Simon had gone down to the airlock deck and hooked himself up to a charger pedestal, the closest he came to sleep. Now it was just her, Otho, and Grag, with Eek as an easily distracted bystander to what amounted to after-dinner conversation.

"Look, I'm not asking as a cop," she said. "I'm asking as someone who's just curious."

"About us?" Grag said. "Or about him?"

Joan looked around to see herself reflected in the lenses of the robot's unblinking red eyes. She was still getting used to the fact that Grag was capable of posing questions of its own. "Him. As I understand it, the two of you raised him—"

"The *three* of us." Otho's eyes narrowed. "Inspector Randall, let's get one thing straight . . . Simon might not appear human anymore, but he knew Curt long before either Grag or I came along. Simon was with Roger and Elaine when they came to the Moon, even though he died almost as soon as they got there. So maybe he looks a bit strange, but in many ways he's just as much Curt's father as Roger was. Maybe even more."

"And yours as well, as I understand."

Folding his arms across his chest, Otho sat back in his chair. "Yes and no. I consider Roger and Elaine to be my parents, albeit not in a biological sense, so in a way I'm Curt's half brother. But I've never forgotten the fact that I was originally meant to be Simon's replacement body. If my brain had been less efficient in its development, or if Roger and Elaine had lived long enough to find an ethical way of overwriting my emerging intelligence, it would be him who'd now be sitting here, not me."

"And this doesn't bother you?"

Otho shrugged. "Not really. The way I look at it, I'm like a child who was dropped on their doorstep, with Simon becoming a sort of foster parent. Would you ask an orphan if he resents the stepfather who adopted him or the boy who was raised as a younger sibling?"

"My apologies. I didn't mean any offense. It's just that he's . . . rather weird, isn't he?"

"Simon? Or Curt?"

All four of you, if you must ask, she thought, but kept it to herself.

"Curt's a bit odd, too, now that you mention it." Glancing at the open ceiling hatch, she lowered her voice. "I picked up on that when we first met and—"

"He kissed your hand?" Otho grinned. "I hope you'll forgive him for that. I'm afraid he hasn't . . . well, had a lot of experience with women. Aside from the usual casual contacts, he's met very few."

"Really? And how many would that be?"

"Four," Grag said, with the precision of memory that only a robot can provide.

"Not to mention the first to whom he's ever had any attraction," Otho quietly added, and snapped his fingers. "No, wait . . . there was that young girl he met when we visited Venus."

"True, but it didn't go anywhere," Grag said. "Simon made him break it off before it became serious. I'll hasten to add, though, that Curt is well educated in human sexuality. Simon's lectures in biology have included a dissertation on reproductive practices that featured visual demonstrations of—"

"Fine. I understand." Joan's face turned red, but something the robot said prompted another question. "So you're saying that the Brain . . . Dr. Wright, I mean—"

"He doesn't have a problem with being called the Brain," Otho said. "I gave him that nickname when Curt and I were young and it stuck."

"Like Captain Future," Grag added, "although I'm not sure Curt likes it."

"Then he's lived in isolation all his life," Joan said.

"Not true." Otho shook his head. "When he was about ten, we started taking him out regularly on excursions, first to the Moon, then to other places in the inner system. Once we altered this ship's registry and changed its name from the *Cornet* to the *Comet,* we were able to go anywhere without people recognizing this craft as Roger Newton's yacht. And when we've gone farther than near-Earth asteroids, Simon, Curt, and I have booked passage aboard commercial spaceliners, with the Brain posing as an ordinary drone. So we've not only visited Mars, Venus, and a couple of lunar cities, but we've also been to Earth a couple of times—"

"Very educational trips," Simon said. "Curtis learned much from them."

Joan looked around to see the Brain ascending through the manhole from the airlock deck. Apparently his recharge period had come to an end. This time, she made a conscious effort to hide her emotions. It was easier to pretend that he was simply a highly advanced 'bot much like Grag and not think about the fact that there was a living human brain behind the telescoping stalks of his eyes.

"We've done our best to raise Curt while at the same time keeping him hidden from Victor Corvo," Simon continued, gliding over to the table where Joan and Otho were seated. Eek growled and shrank back from him, and Grag responded by nestling the little dog in its lap and scratching him behind the ears. "It hasn't been easy. Otho has helped tremendously by escorting him to places where Grag and I would have stood out, but even so, opportunities to meet other people have largely been limited to brief exchanges in public places."

"So he's pretty naive when it comes to human behavior," Joan said.

"I wouldn't necessarily say that."

"No, she's right." Otho nodded in reluctant agreement. "I've done my best to acclimate Curt to the human race—not just terrans, but also aresians, aphrodites, jovians, and all the others—but there was only so much I could. After all, I'm an android."

"Well, I'd say you're as good as a human being," Joan said.

Her remark was meant as a compliment, but Otho's eyes narrowed. "And I'd say I'm *better* than a human being and don't you forget it. If you want to patronize someone, try buckethead over there."

"And I'm better than either of you," Grag said, its voice low as not to startle Eek.

Otho glared at it. "Hey, anytime you want to—"

"Quiet, both of you," the Brain said, his tinny voice taking on an edge. Grag and Otho obediently became silent, and Simon's eyestalks turned about to face Joan. "Curtis is a very knowledgeable person. I've done my best to give him a superior education and improve his mind, while both Otho and Grag have worked hard to train his body. If there are any deficiencies in the way we've raised him, they're not important. Not for the task at hand, at least."

"Which is?" Despite her instinctive revulsion, Joan gazed straight at Simon, focusing on the two visual receptors aimed at her. She'd told Curt to look her in the eye when he spoke to her; time to follow her own advice when it came to Simon.

"Bringing Victor Corvo to justice, of course."

"Well, then . . ." Joan pushed back her chair and stood up from the table. "You're going to have to work harder, because right now he's got some problems he needs to overcome if he's ever going to fit in with the human race."

"And I trust you'll help us?" Otho asked. "Particularly with . . . that is, what we were talking about just a few minutes ago."

He spoke tactfully, not looking at Simon. Joan hid her expression by carrying her mug over to the recycler and shoving it in. "That's above my pay grade, gentlemen," she said, resuming the coolly detached tone of a law officer. "Not my job."

The circular walls of the *Comet*'s middeck were lined with small, closet-size staterooms, four in all. Joan went to the one Curt had assigned to her before they'd lifted off from the Moon. She slid shut its pocket door, then unfolded the hammock from the wall. In a little while, she needed to send a message to Ezra, let him know what she'd learned.

But not just yet.

Joan slowly let out her breath and allowed herself to fall into the hammock's webbing. "Only the fifth woman he's ever met," she whispered to herself. "Well . . . that explains much, doesn't it?"

///

The *Leigh Brackett* raced through the everlasting night. Its boost phase complete, the ship was now in the unpowered cruise phase of its journey, coasting until it turned about to receive the deceleration beam of the Mars photon laser. Down the long spine of its main spar, a half-dozen smaller vessels clung to it like parasites, drawing power, water, and air from its forward tanks. It had been nearly two full sols since the beamship had departed from lunar orbit, and already it was more than twenty-five million miles from the Moon. Earth was a bright, blue-tinted star at its stern, and even the Sun had diminished slightly in size.

Within the ships being ferried to Mars, things were quiet. As was customary for outbound voyages, their crews had adjusted the internal chronometers to match those of Mars's Central Meridian. So just as it was the wee hours of the morning in Galilei on the Chryse Planitia, so it was within the *Blake Freight 209* and the *Princess of Mars,* the *Zephyr* and the *Dirty Old Man,* the *Smiling Baron* and the *Comet.*

On the *Comet*'s middeck, the doors were closed to the staterooms where Curt, Otho, and Joan slept. Outside, Grag sat alone at the table, silent and strapped down, an electrical conduit leading from a small port on the left side of its midriff to a bulkhead outlet. The robot wasn't asleep, but neither was it fully awake, having powered itself down for a six-hour recharge and internal maintenance period. On the other side of the room, Eek was curled up on a makeshift dog's nest made from a discarded suit liner tucked into a wall web, his paws twitching as he chased a cat in his dreams. The lights were dim, and the only sound was the low hum and hiss of the life support systems.

Up on the flight deck, Simon Wright hovered above the pilot's chair. Having already recharged his cyborg form, the Brain occupied his solitary time as he often did when Curt and Otho were asleep, with games. Tonight he was playing chess with the *Comet*'s computer net, trying again to outwit the ship by pitting its faster calculation rate against his knowledge of the winning moves of classic tournaments. So Simon was working a Kasparov gambit from the late twentieth century when trouble came to the *Comet*.

Sixty feet up the central spar, an outer hatch silently opened in the *Brackett*'s main hull, revealing a solitary figure within its airlock. Holding onto a door rail, the vacuum-suited figure leaned out of the hatch, reaching for the ladder that ran the length of the spar. This was dangerous, but the man in the vacuum suit possessed the kind of fanaticism that makes a person fearless.

Like his former companion who'd recently lost his life in Armstrong Crater, he belonged to the Sons of the Two Moons. He had also participated in the attempted assassination of President Carthew. Once a servant in Corvo's household, he'd provided access to the craterhab for the president's would-be killer. But he'd done more than that. When the attempt occurred, he was hiding in a closet near the front porch, ready to fulfill his part of the mission if the assassination succeeded.

The attempt had failed, but that meant the second conspirator was in the perfect position for another mission. He'd come aboard the ferry as a passenger and had patiently waited until this point in the journey, when the *Brackett* was midway between Earth and Mars. The crew was asleep except for a duty officer on the bridge, and the passenger had disabled the circuit in the airlock control panel that would alert the control room that it was being used. So the time had come for him to do that which Ul Quorn had commanded.

Ul Quorn's follower grasped the ladder with first one hand, then another. He pulled himself forward from the airlock and onto the ladder. Then, making a conscious effort not to look either up or down as he clung to the ladder, he groped for the nylon rope coiled at his suit's utility belt. A small two-wheel truck, the sort commonly used for EVA safety tethers, was attached to the end of the rope. He clipped it to the ladder's right leg and made sure that it moved freely.

The passenger reached back into the airlock to retrieve the crowbar-like multitool he'd taken from the engineering locker. He'd need it for the job ahead. Then, leaving the hatch open so that he could quickly return to the airlock, he began making his way down the ladder.

Heading for the *Comet*.

IV

—*Curtis . . . ? Curt, wake up, please.*

The voice was the Brain's, but in Curt's dreaming mind it came not from his Anni but the pilot's console of a different ship. An asteroid freighter also called the *Comet,* the kind used to haul ore to and from the Belt. Joan was there, but she was different, too: her hair was blond and much longer, tied back in a braid, while her face was tattooed with butterfly wings around her eyes. She was in the copilot's seat, and she turned to him to say—

—*Curt? Please wake up.*

The dream evaporated, and his eyes opened to darkness. In the sallow amber glow of the cabin's night-light, he saw his unencumbered hands floating above his chest. Freed from the restraints of the hammock, they'd floated upward in zero-g. It was a sight he never completely got used to, even after all the years he'd spent in space.

"Okay, okay, I'm awake." He yawned. "What d'ya want, Brain?"

—*I'm sorry to disturb you, but we may have an emergency. We've just lost our external air feed from the* Brackett, *and it appears we're about to lose power as well.*

As Simon spoke, the night-light flickered and went dark. A moment passed, then the light came back on.

—*I've restored electrical power from our batteries, and the ship is now on its internal life support system. But this shouldn't be happening.*

"No, it shouldn't." Curt unwrapped himself from the hammock's cocoon and reached for the bodysuit and boots he'd secured with stiktabs to the cabin wall after getting undressed for bed. "Have you contacted the *Brackett*'s bridge? Maybe they're doing some sort of maintenance or repair work."

—I've just spoken with their watch officer, and he denies any knowledge of this. Routine maintenance wouldn't be undertaken while the Brackett *is in flight, and there haven't been any emergencies.* Comet's *log confirms that the AI hasn't received any instructions to that effect from the* Brackett. *And we've just lost the water feed, too.*

Tumbling backward in freefall, Curt hastily pulled on his bodysuit. He started to put on his boots, but then thought better of it. If something was disconnecting the *Brackett* from the *Comet*—or someone, rather, if it wasn't being done automatically by the beamship itself—then they must be doing it manually from outside the *Comet*. Which meant that he'd have to go spacewalking to stop them.

"Wake up the others," he said, zipping up the front of his bodysuit as he reached for the door handle. "I'm going to have to go out."

Otho emerged from his cabin just seconds after he did, and Grag had already disconnected itself from the charger and was letting the cable reel itself back into the bulkhead. No sign of Joan, though; her cabin door was closed, and there was no sound of movement from the other side.

"The hell's going on?" Otho pulled up the suspenders of a pair of cargo pants he'd put on with a sleeveless T-shirt. "How come we lost power and air?"

"Someone's trying to sabotage the ship from outside." Curt pushed himself across the wardroom toward the manhole. "Go up and give Simon a hand. Grag, you're with me. I'm going out to check."

"Let me do that. I've had more EVA experience than you. I should—"

"Just do as I say." Curt wasn't inclined to stop and argue even though Otho was right. Seconds counted if someone was messing with the *Comet*. This was his ship, and he was responsible for the safety of its passengers.

"You heard him. Go up top and help the Brain." Grag had magnetized the soles of its feet and was stamping across the deck, following Curt to the manhole. "I'll help him suit up."

Curt didn't wait to see if Otho obeyed, but instead ducked down the manhole. He'd just emerged into the third deck when he found what had happened to Joan. She wasn't asleep, as he'd thought, but instead had beaten him down to the ready-room, where she was already unstrapping her vacuum suit from the rack.

"What do you think you're doing?" Curt caught himself with a ceiling handrail and twisted around until he was right-side up again.

"Getting ready for a spacewalk, what does it look like?" Floating in midair, Joan unfastened the suit's front and began to thrust her long legs into the thick garment. "I tapped into the Brain's Anni and heard what he said to you. If someone out there is committing an act of sabotage, it's my duty to take care of it."

"My ship, my problem." Curt pushed off from the ceiling, and sailed across the compartment toward her. "You're staying here. I'm going out."

"That's not necessary, I . . . hey, watch the hands!" Joan tried to jerk away as he grabbed hold of her forearm. "I'm a law officer and this is my job!" she snapped, doing her best to twist out of his grip. "And I don't appreciate—!"

"Grag, restrain her, please." Before she could fight him off, Curt shoved her across the ready-room.

"Yes, Curt." The robot had just come down the ladder; it caught Joan in its hands and pulled her tight against its chest. "I'm sorry, Inspector Randall. Please don't struggle. You may hurt yourself."

Joan fought to pull out of Grag's grasp, but the robot was too strong and too quick for her. "Curt, this is stupid!" she yelled at him. "I know you're trying to be gallant or something, but . . . *damn it, tell your 'bot to let me go!*"

Curt ignored her as he unracked his own suit. It took just a few minutes for him to put it on; one of the things that had been drilled into him since childhood was how to prepare for a spacewalk as quickly as possible. Still, he was slowed down just a little bit by not having Grag help him, so he'd just put on his gloves when the Brain spoke to him again, this time through his headset.

"Curt, Otho has just spotted someone outside the ship. He's tethered

to an access ladder on the Brackett's *spar, and it appears that he's now trying to release the berth's cradle bars."*

A chill swept down Curt's back. He now knew exactly what the saboteur meant to accomplish. If the man outside could jettison the *Comet* from the ferry—and once the little racing yacht was detached from the cradle, all that would take was a good, hard shove—he would effectively doom its crew. Although the little ship had enough fuel to reach Mars on its own, at this distance it would take nearly a month to get there. And without replenishment from the *Brackett*, the *Comet* had only enough air and water to keep him, Otho, and Joan alive for no more than a week.

There were many legends among spacefarers about crews who'd suffered similar fates. They usually ended with the crew members drawing straws to see who would take a one-way cycle through the airlock. The Brain and Grag would survive, but . . . Curt shook his head. If it came to that, he and Otho would sacrifice themselves for Joan, although he doubted that the *Comet* would have enough consumables to support her.

Curt snapped his utility belt with its holstered plasmar around his waist, checked the gun to make sure it was connected and fully charged, then switched it to its highest power. This time, he wasn't going to fool around with trying to take someone alive. They were plainly dealing with a killer.

"If I get in trouble," he said to Grag, "come out to help me at once."

"Curt, let me—" Joan began.

"Forget it." Curt checked his suit to make sure everything was closed. "If anyone is going to survive this—" He stopped himself as he reached for his helmet. "Grag, let her go once I cycle through, but keep an eye on her. Make sure she stays inside."

"Understood, Curt." The robot continued to hold Joan tight against its chest.

Curt nodded, then entered the airlock. Shutting the inner door, he put on his helmet and pressurized his suit, then started to touch the buttons that would commence the depressurization procedure before thinking better of it. No, that would take too long; the saboteur could have the *Comet* uncoupled by the time he opened the outer hatch. There was a faster alternative. It was dangerous, but . . .

"Simon, Otho, I'm going for emergency blowout," he said. "Stand by for my order."

A pause, then Otho's voice came through the comlink: *"Affirmative, Curt. Standing by. Be careful."*

Curt said nothing, but smiled as he found the tetherhook on the fuselage beside the outer hatch and clipped his safety line to it. Otho wasn't going to try to talk him out of this; he knew what was at stake. Turning his body parallel to the deck, Curt planted his boots firmly on either side of the hatchway and took a firm grasp of the handrail to his right and left.

"Blow the hatch," he said.

A sudden bang, then a roaring windstorm erupted around him. His helmet immediately frosted over, blocking his view with a patina of grainy white, but Curt didn't let go of the rail to wipe the faceplate clear. His body was being buffeted as if it were caught in a miniature hurricane; he had to strain to keep from being hurled through the open outer hatch.

Then, as quickly as it had begun, it was over. Only a couple of seconds passed before all the air in the small compartment rushed out into the void. In the abrupt silence that followed, Curt released his grip on the handrails and ran a gauntleted hand across his faceplate. The hatchway gaped open before him, the metal skeleton of *Brackett*'s spar just beyond.

The explosive decompression must have rocked the entire ship. No doubt the saboteur felt it. Curt cautiously pulled himself to the open hatch and peered outside. At first, he saw no one . . . but then he turned his head and there he was, about twenty feet away, a slender figure in a vacuum suit.

He'd already disconnected the air, water, and electrical cables leading from the *Brackett* to the *Comet*; they dangled nearby like decapitated snakes caught within a shimmering cloud of ice particles. Now he was using a long metal implement that Curt recognized as a multitool to pry open the cradle holding the *Comet* within its berth. Two of the cradle's scimitar-shaped bars had been released already. The sabo-teur had braced his legs between the spar and its ladder to gain the necessary leverage; he had fit the sharp end of the multitool between the cradle bar and the *Comet*'s hull and was preparing to pry it open.

Curt couldn't tell whether the other man had noticed him or not, but it didn't matter. Removing the plasmar from his holster, he pushed himself the rest of the way out the airlock and, grasping the gun with both hands, aimed straight at the saboteur. This time, he didn't give any warning, but simply fired.

The saboteur must have spotted him at the same instant, though, because Curt's finger had barely tightened on the trigger when the other man abruptly turned away, twisting himself so that he was shielded by the spar. The plasma toroids were invisible in a hard vacuum, with none of the smoke-ring effect that showed when the gun was fired in an atmosphere. The ladder trembled as the pulses hit it but effectively deflected the shot.

Curt swore as he reached for the ladder, intending to duck around it and get a clear shot. The saboteur had other plans. Before Curt fully realized what was happening, the man came around from behind the spar, kicked off it, and with the multitool raised above his shoulders, threw himself at Curt.

There was no time for Curt to aim and fire again before his enemy sailed into him. The multitool swung about in a wide arc that would shatter his faceplate if it connected. Dropping his gun, Curt ducked beneath the bar and scrabbled with his hands for the front of the other man's suit. He meant to yank loose the air hose running from the life-pack to the lower left side of the suit, a sure way of stopping an assail-ant in hand-to-hand space combat, but the saboteur slapped his hands away and swung the multitool again.

Once more, he missed Curt's helmet, but this time the multitool found a different target: Curt's lifeline. The multitool couldn't sever the nylon cord, but the cutting edge at its tip came down with sufficient force to sever the lifeline's connection to Curt's utility belt.

All at once, Curt found himself floating free from the *Comet*. How-ever, the severing of his umbilical also gave him just enough distance to retrieve his gun, now twisting at the end of its cable. As he started to tumble away, Curt snagged the plasmar and took aim at his foe.

In desperation, the saboteur raised the multitool as if to hurl it at Curt. He never got the chance; the plasma beam disintegrated his helmet.

Curt barely caught a glimpse of the red cloud that silently exploded where his enemy's head had been. In zero-g, the recoil from the beam striking another object at close range was as effective as if he'd been kicked. Before he realized what was happening, Curt found himself tumbling head over heels away from the *Comet*.

Stretching out his left hand, he made a desperate attempt to grab hold of the spar ladder, but he wasn't quick enough. The ladder was beyond reach, and in the next instant the beamship rushed past him and away.

Helplessly flailing his arms, Curt fell into the void.

V

Joan saw everything. Clutching a ceiling rail, she'd watched through the wardroom porthole as Curt engaged the saboteur in single combat outside the ship. Although she'd put on a headset and patched into Curt's comlink frequency, she dared not say anything that might distract him, and through the earpiece she heard nothing but his labored breath and the occasional grunt. The fight was in silence, with no words exchanged between the combatants.

When the saboteur's multitool parted Curt's lifeline, Joan immediately recognized the danger Curt would put himself in if he fired his gun at close range. Before she could warn him, though, he retrieved his weapon and fired at his enemy. The plasma toroids were invisible in a vacuum, but the effect was devastating . . . to both men. The saboteur was killed instantly and Curt was thrown clear of both the *Comet* and the *Brackett*.

"Curt's off the line!" she yelled.

"I know!" Otho shouted back from the flight deck above. "Grag, go out and get him!"

"Affirmative." Grag was still on the third deck, guarding the airlock to prevent Joan from suiting up and going out to help Curt. More than ever, she wished the stupid 'bot would learn to ignore its masters every once in a while.

"Grag, no! Cancel that order!" Shoving herself away from the porthole, she put herself between the robot and the airlock.

"You heard him." Grag responded. "If he gets in trouble, I'm to go out there and—"

"You'll only get lost out there, too!" She tapped her headset mike. "Curt, can you hear me?"

"Affirmative . . . affirmative, I hear you." Curt's voice was strained, his breath coming in fast gasps. *"I'm . . . I've been thrown off. My line . . ."*

"We know." Joan scrambled hand over hand along the rail to the ceiling manhole and hastily pulled herself through it. "Calm down, okay? Everything's going to be all right. We're coming to get you—"

"Oh no, we're not." The Brain was hovering beside Otho, who'd taken over the pilot's chair. One of his eyestalks moved in Joan's direction while the other remained turned toward the forward window. "We can't detach ourselves, Inspector. The *Brackett* has to do that for us, and they wouldn't do that because it would only put everyone aboard this ship—everyone who draws breath, that is—in mortal danger."

"Then we'll get 'em to turn around and retrieve Curt!" Otho reached for the com panel.

"They won't do this either." Simon's voice was maddeningly calm. "You know that. The *Brackett* is traveling too fast to decelerate on its own, and its engines are only meant for orbital maneuvers."

Joan understood. Without an active proton beam to provide propulsion, the *Brackett* would be in the same position the *Comet* would have been if the saboteur had succeeded. The ferry was traveling too fast to stop on its own, and it couldn't turn around to retrieve someone who'd fallen overboard.

"You can't . . . you mean you can't get to me?" Curt asked.

Too late, Joan realized that the comlink had been active the entire time. Curt had heard everything they'd said, including the Brain's cool assessment of the situation. Pulling herself closer to the forward console, she peered over Otho's shoulder at the forward porthole. Curt was nowhere to be seen. He was probably miles away by now and getting farther with every passing second.

"Hang in there," she said. "We're working on something."

Joan muted her headset, then closed her eyes and took a deep breath.

There was another option, probably the only one they had. However, it meant revealing something that she hadn't wanted the others to know. But with Curt's life at stake . . .

"Hey, Inspector," Otho said, "if you've got a plan, now's the time to let us in on it."

Ignoring him, Joan reached forward to the com panel. She found the frequency selector and turned its knob until she located the band reserved for official government transmissions. Then she activated her mike again and spoke:

"*Comet* Passenger Oscar One-Nine to SGS *Vigilance,* do you read? . . . SGS *Vigilance,* this is *Comet* Passenger Oscar One-Nine, Priority Alpha Alpha Alpha, please respond at once . . ."

VI

As he tumbled through star-flecked darkness, Curt fought to keep from panicking. He was barely able to do so. The same recoil from the plasmar's discharge that caused him to be thrown clear of the ship had also put him into a headfirst spin. Not enough to make him nauseous or cause him to lose consciousness, but sufficiently disorienting all the same.

He'd heard what Simon said: there was no way the *Comet* could come back to retrieve him. And aside from what the Brain had told the others, he knew that a rescue attempt would put everyone's lives in jeopardy. Even if the *Brackett*'s captain agreed to release the *Comet* from its berth, by the time his ship reached him, they'd be so far astern that catching up with the beamship would be impossible. Even in death, the saboteur would succeed. The *Comet* might eventually reach Mars, but its only surviving passengers would be Simon and Grag.

"Never mind me," Curt found himself saying, even though it had been only a minute or so since he'd last heard from the *Comet*. "Simon, just . . . I'm sorry, old man, but just let me go. I can't let you risk the others' lives for me."

A few seconds passed, then Joan's voice came over the comlink, fainter than it had been before. *"Curt, do you hear me? Speak to me if you can."*

"I'm here, Joan. I can hear you." He suddenly realized that, more than anything else, he wanted to see her again.

"Good. Have you calmed down?"

"Yeah . . . a little, I guess." He was calm because he knew that death was imminent and there was nothing he could do about it. He wasn't about to tell her that, though. If he was going to die, at least he could die bravely.

"Good. Okay . . . can you see the ship at all? The Brackett, *I mean."*

Curt peered at the stars moving around him, turning his head within his helmet first one way and then another. On his next revolution, he caught sight of a tiny cluster of lights, two of them blinking blue and red, like a miniature constellation as seen through a telescope. That would be the *Brackett,* already a hundred or more miles away and diminishing rapidly.

"I see it," he reported. "Too far for me to get to and vice versa."

"We're not going to try." Joan's signal was getting weaker; he had to strain to hear her. *"Okay, listen . . . switch your com channel to the emergency"*—a fuzzy crackle of static—*"keep talking, all right? No matter what you do, keep"*—more static—*"and don't stop."*

Then he heard Otho's voice: *"Curt, switch on"*—crackle—*"lights, so—"*

A loud rush of static drowned out the rest. "*Comet,* do you hear me?" Curt demanded, speaking loudly now. "*Comet,* this is—"

Damn it, he'd almost said "Captain Future"! Curt laughed out loud. *Well, why not? "Comet,* this is Captain Future. Simon, Otho, Grag . . . if you can hear me at all . . . um, thanks, all of you, for giving me a great life, but I guess . . . well, I think this is pretty much it. Joan, I wish we could have—"

He stopped himself. That was enough. He didn't want his last words to be embarrassing, even if no one could hear them.

Curt glanced at his helmet's translucent heads-up display. The air-reserve indicator told him that the lifepack still had a little more than four hours left at his current rate of consumption, but it might as well be four seconds, for all the chances he had of being rescued. There were no other ships nearby; beamships maintained a specific course that kept them within range of the photon railway, and the next one wouldn't be coming along for quite a while now.

For the first time, he truly realized that space is a very empty and lonely place.

There must have been a reason, though, why Joan told him to keep talking, or for Otho to tell him to turn on his suit lights. It may have been only so that the *Comet* could determine the direction he was falling, thereby giving another vessel a chance of recovering his body at a later time. But . . . perhaps there was another ship nearby? One whose course was close enough to the *Brackett*'s that there was a slim possibility it might be able to locate him. If so . . .

Curt switched on the suit rescue beacons, two red and blue lights on the back of his lifepack, and activated the emergency transponder that would send out a steady electronic dot-dash-dot on the ku-band. If there was another ship within range, they now had a better chance of spotting him.

The question was, how soon? And would that be soon enough?

Curt pushed that out of his mind. Time to get his tumbling under control. All he had to work with was the plasmar, but it would have to do. He pointed the gun above his head and waited until the bright red dot that was Mars came into view, then fired a one-second burst. It didn't seem to have much effect, so he tried again the next time he saw Mars, holding down the trigger a little longer. This seemed to retard the spin a little, so he fired again, and again, and again.

It took a dozen or so shots—he lost count after his tenth try—but finally he managed to use the plasmar to brake himself and end the tumble. Curt swore under his breath when it occurred to him that he might have used his gun to get back aboard the *Comet* while he still had a chance, but then he glanced at the gun's charge indicator. He'd all but completely drained the batteries just stopping his head-over-heels somersaults; the plasmar was never meant to be a reaction-control device, and it was unlikely he would've been able to use it to return to his ship.

Didn't matter now. He was where he was, and there was nothing he could do about it. At least the view was wonderful. He'd die surrounded by stars.

The thought passed through his mind that he could expedite things a little by adjusting his suit's atmosphere-control system so that the oxygen-nitrogen feed would gradually be replaced by carbon dioxide.

This way, instead of asphyxiation, he'd simply go to sleep, never to wake up again. He discarded that idea as soon as it occurred to him. Suicide wasn't in his temperament; one way or another, he'd see things through to the last second. He might still be rescued.

So . . . what to do? Gaze at the stars, of course, and perhaps find a way of passing the time. Unfortunately, the suit wasn't equipped with any onboard entertainment systems, so he'd have to improvise. But Curt had learned a few space chanteys from Otho over the years, and he had a fairly good memory for their lyrics.

He'd come out of his spin looking straight at Mars. This was all the inspiration he needed. Curt cleared his throat, started in on an old traditional:

> "I'm only a lonely spaceman,
> With no world to call my own.
> I've seen all the moons and planets,
> But I still just love to roam . . ."

Curt worked his way through the ballad's six stanzas, with only an occasional stumble when he couldn't quite recall all the words. When he was through, an uncomfortable silence descended, save for the muted crackle of static coming through the comlink. So he started another tune, this one from childhood, the theme song of the old *Sarge Saturn* kidvid show:

> "Freezing out by Pluto,
> Roasting near the Sun,
> Burned by the rains on Titan's plains,
> It's all a spaceman's fun . . . !"

This one took a little more effort to recall. *Sarge Saturn* had been a favorite when he was growing up under Tycho, one of the things that inspired him to create Captain Future as his fantasy alter ego, but it had been many years since he'd thought about him. In the end, Curt ended up with new lyrics, some of which caused him to laugh uproariously until he realized that he was using up oxygen. Well, so be it. He only had a little more than a couple of hours of air left; two or three minutes expended on a good belly laugh wouldn't matter all that much. At least it kept him from going crazy.

Next was a tavern song that had come from Space Guard infantrymen fighting Starry Messenger insurgents in the outer solar system:

"From Mercury to Pluto,
 From Saturn back to Mars,
 We'll fight and sail and blaze our trail,
 In crimson through the stars . . ."[1]

An odd notion stopped the song in mid-verse. What if Starry Messenger was involved somehow? Many years ago, the militant arm of the now-defunct Outer Worlds Liberation Union had sponsored terrorist attacks on Solar Coalition offices on Mars and the inhabited jovian and kronian moons in an attempt to force the coalition into ceding their colonies to offworld control. After years of Solar Guard police action that often came close to outright interplanetary war, Starry Messenger was crushed and OWLU dissolved, its more radical leaders either dead or in prison.

Yet it was rumored that Starry Messenger cells were still extant on Mars, lying low and waiting for an opportunity to return. How interesting it was that Starry Messenger went into hiding not very long before the Sons of the Two Moons appeared. Sure, the Sons were a religious cult while Starry Messenger were political extremists, but the aresian who'd attempted to kill President Carthew was performing the sort of act that Starry Messenger might have once condoned.

Not only that, but someone obviously didn't want Curt investigating the assassination attempt. Was the saboteur he'd killed also another agent of Ul Quorn, the so-called Magician of Mars who apparently had ties to both Victor Corvo and the Sons of the Two Moons? If so, did this mean there was a link between Starry Messenger and the Sons?

---

[1]All song lyrics by Edmond Hamilton.

The more Curt pondered these questions, the more tired he felt. Singing and thinking had calmed him down to the point where he was actually yawning, fighting to stay awake. Well, why bother? He could always take a nap . . . and if he never woke up, perhaps that was just the way things were meant to be.

Yawning again, he let his eyes close. Arms thrown out from his sides, legs dangling, he allowed himself to relax and let his body drift. Into the depths of space, he fell . . .

Light flashed against his eyelids, softly at first, then brighter and more urgent. Then, as if in a dream, a voice came to him:

"Comet *passenger Captain Future, this is SGS* Vigilance *launch Romeo Six Eight, do you copy?*"

It wasn't a dream. The voice was really there.

Curt opened his eyes and immediately squinted into the bright glare of a searchlight. Raising a hand to shield his eyes against the beam, he perceived, a couple of hundred feet away, the buglike form of a space vessel's skiff.

"Captain Future, this is Romeo Six Eight, please respond."

So the rescue beacon and open comlink channel hadn't been pointless. There *was* another ship out here, and it had come looking for him.

"This is Captain Future," he said, and no longer felt silly about using that name. "Thanks for coming after me."

A pause, then the voice came back. *"You're welcome, but believe me, this isn't a free ride. We know someone who wants to talk to you."*

VII

Curt had never expected to ever set foot aboard a Solar Guard patrol ship. Civilians seldom did; when the sleek cruisers weren't in space, they were in secure hangars where only their crews and others with high-level security clearances were permitted. People generally spotted Guard vessels only from a distance; it was often said that, if you were close enough to see their missile tubes, then you were too close.

So, despite the fact that he'd almost exhausted his air supply—thirty-three minutes, seventeen seconds, according to the final readout on his helmet's heads-up—Curt watched in fascination as the skiff that retrieved him closed in on the SGS *Vigilance*. A little more than two hundred feet long, with the red, white, and gold flag of the Solar Coalition painted on its armored hull, the cruiser was a streamlined wedge, its fore and aft launchers ready to take on any adversary.

The most intriguing aspect was its apparent lack of propulsion, save for maneuvering thrusters along its flanks and a magnetoplasma secondary engine at its stern. Instead, ductlike radiation shields on the port and starboard sides contained enormous generators that vaguely resembled the cyclotrons of an earlier era. These were the warp-drive engines. Like other Solar Guard vessels, the *Vigilance* contained one of the coalition's most precious secrets: the ability to harness zero-point energy to envelope itself within a bubblelike Alcubierre field that constituted a reactionless drive. When activated, this warp bubble allowed the ship to coast across the surface of spacetime like a stone skipping across the top of a pond.

Because of this, *Vigilance* and its sister ships were capable of velocities far greater than any other form of propulsion. Exactly how fast was something few people knew; this was classified information. However, it was rumored that a Guard cruiser once reached Sedna, a minor planet in the Kuiper Belt, in only one day, a journey that would have taken a ship with an ordinary fusion drive nearly a year to complete.

The lieutenant j.g. piloting the skiff noticed the look on Curt's face as the small vessel glided toward the open shuttle bay hatch in the cruiser's spine. "What's the matter, kid?" he asked, neglecting the fact that he was only a couple of years older. "Never seen a ship like this before?"

"As a matter of fact, no." Curt stared through the canopy, absorbing every detail.

"Yeah, well . . . enjoy it while you can," drawled the other crewman, the copilot who'd actually pulled Curt aboard. "If the chief isn't satisfied with the fish we've caught, he's just as liable to toss it right back out."

The two Guardsmen shared a laugh at his expense. Curt said nothing as he watched the skiff drift to a halt above the open hatch and slowly descend into the shuttle bay. It touched down behind *Vigilance*'s delta-winged shuttle; as the hatch closed above the skiff, crewmen in hardsuits moved in to attach mooring cables.

"Stand by for field activation in ten secs." The pilot reached up to snap toggle switches on the ceiling panels, and then glanced back at Curt. "Hold onto your armrests. Five . . . four . . . three . . ."

"Why, what's—?" Curt barely managed to get the words out of his mouth before he felt the abrupt sensation of falling. Until then, although he was strapped into a passenger seat in the back of the cockpit, he'd been floating about a half-inch above its cushions. Now, all at once, he was actually *in* his seat, with his hands resting upon the armrests and his feet solidly against the floor.

Gravity.

Another rumor about Guard cruisers was that the same warp bubbles that made the ships capable of reaching velocities approaching light-speed also provided them with artificial gravity. Something to do with the fields isolating the ships from the normal conditions of spacetime, but again, this was classified information that the government was unwilling to divulge. Nonetheless, Curt's mouth fell open with astonishment, causing the two crewmen to start laughing again.

"Easy there, Captain Future!" the copilot said, not bothering to hide his patronizing tone. "Welcome to the twenty-fourth century!"

Again, Curt decided it was better if he said nothing. He waited while the bay was pressurized, then a ladder was pushed against the skiff's port side and the hatch was opened. A uniformed Guard officer wearing the peaked cap and chevrons of a sergeant was waiting for him outside. He led Curt to a nearby ready-room and patiently waited while he climbed out of his EVA gear and stowed it in a locker, then escorted him out the door and down a narrow central corridor to a companionway leading up to the main deck.

The sergeant didn't speak a word to Curt as he took him down another corridor that seemed to run the length of the ship. Here, the *Vigilance* was less utilitarian than the engineering-level deck below: carpeted deck, faux-wood paneling on the bulkheads, light fixtures molded to look like small fists holding miniature torches. The ship hummed quietly. A couple of times, passing crewmen briefly darted curious looks at Curt as he was marched by, but no one said anything to him until they reached a door near the end of the corridor. The sergeant rapped on the door and swung it open without waiting for an answer.

"Here he is, Marshal," he said, and stepped aside to let Curt step into the room.

Ezra Gurney was seated on the other side of a polished oak table that took up most of the room. Somehow, Curt wasn't surprised to find him here. He knew he should have been, but ever since he and the others left the Moon, he'd had a sneaking suspicion that Gurney would never be too far away.

"Thanks, Sergeant. You may leave now." As the sergeant closed the door, Ezra rose from his seat and gestured to a leather chair across from him. "Here . . . sit. You gotta be tired. Hungry, too. Like something to eat?"

"Thanks. Maybe later." Curt was famished and he felt like he could sleep for a week but tried not to show it. He wasn't prepared for hospitality from someone who hadn't trusted him before, and he doubted that Marshal Gurney had lately changed his mind. "I appreciate your coming to the rescue. If you hadn't—"

"No need to thank me. Savin' lives is what we do." Gurney sat down again, and as Curt did the same, he reached for the water pitcher on the platter in the middle of the table. "At least drink something," he said as he poured ice water into a glass and passed it to Curt. "You can get awfully dried up when you've been in a suit for a while."

The old marshal was right. He was dehydrated. Curt drained the glass in one swallow, reached for the pitcher again. Gurney studied him as he refilled his glass, a half smile on his face. "I've gotta hand it to you, son," he said, "you got some sand in you. I once helped rescue another guy who'd been adrift the way you were, and he was sobbin' like a baby and huggin' the guy who hauled him into the airlock . . . who happened to be me. You spent twice as much time out there than he did, and all you do is have a drink of water. I am truly impressed."

"Thanks." Curt wasn't about to admit that the reason he was so calm was that he'd resigned himself to death. If Gurney wanted to interpret pragmatism as courage, then he wasn't about to argue with him. "So what brings you here, Marshal? Or did you just happen to be passing through?"

A wry smile. "I think you know better than that . . . oh, and you can call me Ezra. I think you've earned that, at least." As he spoke, Ezra sat back in his chair, propped his right leg up on his left knee, and pulled back the trouser cuff from his right calf. From inside the boot came a small silver flask engraved with the IPF seal. "I didn't think Joan should go off with you without any backup, and neither did the president. So he ordered the *Vigilance* to shadow the *Brackett*, and I came along in case Joan needed help. When you got cast away . . . well, I think you can pretty much guess the rest."

"So you didn't trust me after all, did you?"

"Until now, no." Ezra uncapped the flask, raised it to his lips, and took a long drink. "You didn't just think we'd cut someone loose like that, did you? Someone we don't know?"

"Joan trusts me . . . no thanks." Curt shook his head when Ezra offered the flask to him.

"I think Joan has a soft spot for you." Ezra screwed the cap back on and returned the flask to his boot. "Maybe she doesn't show it, and the good Lord only knows why she would, but she does. I suppose I do, too, now that I know what kind of person you are. Just don't try kissing *my* hand—"

"I'll keep that in mind. So what now? Are we going to catch up with the *Brackett* so I can transfer back aboard my ship?"

"We could do that, sure. Ol' *Vigilance* here has a warp drive, and that means we could beat even a beamship to Mars if we wanted to." Ezra paused. "But there's something else you ought to know. I'm not the only one on your tail. Senator Corvo is, too."

Hearing this, Curt sat up a little straighter. "Corvo is following us?"

Folding his arms across his chest, Ezra leaned back in his chair. "He is, indeed. The day after *Brackett* set sail, he boarded another beamship . . . a government ship, not a ferry like the one you were on. It's scheduled to arrive at Port Deimos the day after the ferry gets there."

"That's rather sudden, isn't it? Did he give a reason why he's dropping everything to head to Mars?"

"His office issued a press release stating that the senator has gone there to negotiate a trade agreement between the Lunar Republic and certain unnamed Mars-based companies. But that's just the cover story. It's a good bet that the reason why he felt it was necessary to drop everything and skedaddle off to Mars was that you shook his tree somehow and he needs to protect his interests there."

"You think he might be responsible for what happened? Someone trying to jettison the *Comet*, I mean."

"If there's a connection between him and Ul Quorn, yup, I do indeed." Ezra reached over to the table, pressed the edge of the wood top. "Here . . . let me show you something I learned just before we picked you up."

A holo screen materialized above the table. The marshal tapped a few keys to open a display. A man's face appeared, a scowling aresian whom Curt immediately recognized as the would-be saboteur he'd killed.

"The *Brackett*'s crew retrieved this gentleman's body after you blew his head off," Ezra said. "Didn't have a face left, of course, but they still managed to identify him from a bank card they found in his quarters aboard the *Brackett*. His name was Troy Reichard, and according to the IPF Mars database, he belonged to the Sons of the Two Moons."

"That figures. If Corvo wants to get rid of me and he's also linked to Ul Quorn, then he'd ask Ul Quorn to send one of his people to do the job."

"That's what I'm thinking, too, but it gets even more interesting. We've also discovered that, up until the day the other guy tried to kill the president, Reichard had been working as a servant in Corvo's household. In fact, not only had he been there for a few weeks, he'd twice visited the president's quarters on one errand or another, even delivering a meal to him."

Puzzled, Curt raised an eyebrow. "So why didn't he kill Carthew when he had the chance? If Corvo is tied to Ul Quorn and they were plotting to kill Carthew, why arrange for a sniper to shoot him when they already have someone inside the senator's mansion who could have done the job?"

"I have no idea," Ezra said, slowly shaking his head. "Whole thing is a mystery. But I'm willin' to bet the answer's on Mars . . . and this attempt on your life makes you the best man to find out."

"Why do you say that?"

"No one 'cept the people on this ship and your friends on the *Comet* know that you've been rescued. Far as the *Brackett* and the other ships are concerned, you were lost in space fightin' off someone tryin' to sabotage your ship."

"So . . . ?"

Ezra smiled. "So you're dead, Captain Future. And if we play our cards right, we can make that work to our advantage."

VIII

"Brackett *to* Comet. *Stand by for detachment in five on my mark. Mark . . . five . . . four . . . three . . . two . . . one . . .*"

A sudden jolt passed through the ship as the ferry's docking cradle released its grip on the smaller ship. From her seat in the copilot's chair, Joan watched as Otho fired the maneuvering thrusters and pulled back on the stick. The *Comet* floated free of its berth aboard the *Leigh Brackett*; through the bow window, the spar with its other empty docking cradles was visible for a moment before the ferry fell away beneath them.

"*Comet* detached and in the clear." Otho's hands—white as fine porcelain, Joan observed, yet with large tendons running across the backs—moved across the controls with unhurried ease. "Thanks for the lift, *Brackett*. Sorry for the trouble en route."

"*No need to apologize,*" the beamship's captain responded, her voice coming through Joan's headset. "*We're sorry for your loss. Hope the cops figure out who was responsible.*"

Otho cast Joan a knowing smile. This confirmed that no one except the *Comet*'s crew was aware that an IPF inspector was already aboard. "So do we," Otho replied. "Thank you for your understanding. *Comet* over and out." He tapped his mike wand and looked at Joan again. "So what are your people going to do now? About Reichard, I mean."

"Continue the investigation, of course." Joan continued to watch the *Brackett* as it receded. Its sail was visible now, still deployed but oriented in the opposite direction, catching the photon pulses from the Mars PLT array that was decelerating the ferry for orbital insertion. "They'll board the ferry and question the crew, but it's mostly for show. My people have already figured out what happened. The real follow-up is going to be on the ground."

As she spoke, Otho fired thrusters to swing the *Comet* around. The *Brackett* disappeared and was replaced by a lovely sight: Mars as seen from a distance of about twenty thousand miles, its once completely red deserts now broken by veins of blue and blotches of green, the lights of major settlements glimmering in the night that was falling across the eastern half of the western hemisphere.

In the foreground, only a few thousand miles away, was a pale, oblong rock that looked like a misplaced boulder: Deimos, the smaller and more distant of the two Martian moons. The tiny satellite was orbited by myriad spacecraft coming in and out of its commercial spaceport: hydrogen and helium-3 tankers from Jupiter and Saturn, ore freighters from the asteroid, ferries and passenger craft from Earth and Venus. Just as Mars itself was gradually becoming terraformed into a habitable world, so Deimos had been transformed over the years into an orbital spaceport. And now the *Comet* was on its way there as well, a tiny teardrop all but lost among the behemoths surrounding it.

"So what's the plan, anyway?" the Brain asked.

Joan looked over her shoulder. Simon Wright had just come up from below. He was followed by Grag, with Eek happily trailing along behind. The moonpup had no problem with adapting to zero-g; his breed were adapted for low-gravity environments and never succumbed to the vertigo that sometimes upset humans experiencing space travel for the first time. The little dog bounced from bulkhead to bulkhead, propelling himself with his long, swirling tail.

Joan didn't answer at once. A few hours ago, she'd retired to the privacy of her stateroom and had a long wireless-text conversation with Ezra Gurney aboard the *Vigilance*. She's shared little of this with Otho, Simon, and Grag, other than to let them know that they were to continue pretending Curt had lost his life defending his ship from an unknown assailant, possibly a hijacker or pirate. In just a few minutes, the *Comet* would enter the traffic pattern of ships bound for Port Deimos. The time had come to let the others in on what she'd discussed with Ezra and, indirectly, Curt.

"All right, here's what is going on." Joan swiveled her chair around to face Simon and Grag; beside her, Otho continued to pilot the ship. "As you already know, Curt is safe and sound aboard the *Vigilance*. No one is officially reporting that he was rescued, though. Both the Guard and the IPF aren't issuing any public notifications of his recovery, and in a day or so the IPF will routinely report the loss of an unidentified passenger from a private spacecraft bound for Mars. Foul play suspected but not proven, IPF officers continuing to investigate, and so forth."

"Very good." Simon purred over to the bulkhead and used a manipulator claw to anchor himself to the nearest available handrail. "With luck, Corvo will assume that Curt is dead and Ul Quorn will likewise believe that his man was successful."

"Correct." Joan was getting used to him; no longer did she shrink away when he came near. "In the meantime, we're to proceed to Port Deimos, where we'll dock just as planned. While you and Grag remain there, Otho and I will board a shuttle for Xanthe Terra, where we'll rendezvous with Curt. If we need you, we'll get in touch and have you bring down the *Comet*. Otherwise, you will remain in port with the ship."

"No." Grag had magnetized the soles of its feet and was now standing upright on the deck. Eek pushed himself to Grag's left shoulder, where the pup anchored himself by wrapping his tail around his master's neck. "I wish to accompany you and Otho when you go down to Mars."

"No way, iron butt," Otho said. "You're too conspicuous."

"I hate to say it, but he's right." Joan was surprised to find that she was talking to Grag like this. Never before had she ever felt empathy for a robot. However, she was coming to realize that Grag was special, just as Simon was and Otho, too, for that matter: perhaps not human, but worthy of human respect all the same. She often wondered why

Otho insulted the robot the way he did, or why Grag blandly tolerated it. "Folks don't often see construction 'bots following people around, and we don't want to attract attention. When Otho and I go down, we'll be posing as ordinary travelers."

"So you're not presenting yourself as an IPF officer," Simon said.

"Correct. From here on, I'm working undercover." Joan looked down at herself. "I'm going to need other clothing. This bodysuit is IPF standard issue."

"Curt has some overalls aboard he uses for maintenance work. They'll be a little baggy and you may have to roll up the cuffs and sleeves a bit, but they'll do until we can get you to a shop. There should be one in Port Deimos. We'll need to get respirators for you and Otho as well."

"Thanks." Joan smiled. "Overalls. Y'know, if I tuck my hair up in a cap, I may be able to pass as a man."

"Don't count on it," Otho said dryly.

"I'll take that as a compliment." Joan was becoming accustomed to his sense of humor.

Otho gave her a sly wink and went on. "So where do we go once we hook up with Curt? Mars is a big place. Lots of room for Ul Quorn to hide."

"We have one clue. According to intelligence reports from IPF's Section Four division on Mars, Troy Reichard belonged to a Sons of the Two Moons coven that apparently makes its home in a tolou near Mons Ascraeus in the Tharsis region. I figure that, if the three of us can get there without anyone figuring out who we are, we might be able to ask questions that will lead us to Ul Quorn."

"And if we do? What then?"

"Believe me, Ul Quorn is wanted on enough charges that, if I can pin him down, all I'd have to do is call for backup and we'd have an entire IPS tactical weapons team there in minutes."

"Uh-huh. Sounds like you've got it all worked out."

"I'm sure we'll need to improvise a bit," Joan replied, trying not to be defensive, "but . . . yes, I believe we do."

Otho turned his head to gaze down at her for a long moment. He said nothing to her, though, but simply shook his head as he returned his attention to the controls. "Deimos Traffic, this is the *Comet,* SolCol registry Delta X-Ray one-zero-nine, on primary approach. Requesting permission for rendezvous and docking . . ."

IX

A hard thump against his back, followed by the dull rumble of a big engine being fired, and Victor Corvo felt the welcome return of gravity. Despite the fact that his travels had taken him to most of the worlds of the inner solar system—Mercury was the only exception, but who the hell goes there?—he'd never enjoyed or become accustomed to zero-g. He hated to admit it, but it almost always made him ill. Sometimes he'd spend days throwing up, and wouldn't stop puking until his feet were on solid ground again.

Which was the reason why he preferred beamships. For almost half of the way, while the ship was outbound and under thrust, he had at least partial gravity, and that was enough to keep his stomach under control. And while the big ferries like the *Brackett* depended on another PLT in Mars orbit for deceleration, smaller vessels like the *Lowell*, the government passenger ship that he'd requisitioned for this trip, used nuclear fusion engines for braking maneuvers. So even though he'd have to spend the rest of his time aboard strapped into his couch in his private cabin, it was a small price to pay for not having to barf every time he saw someone or something upside down.

But gravity's pull lasted only half a minute or so, then the engine was turned off again. Once more, Corvo felt himself gently rising from the couch. Wincing, he grasped the armrests and rigidly held his body in place. His mouth tightened with exertion and he had to close his eyes for a second.

"*You seem a little pale,*" Ul Quorn said. "*Is anything wrong?*"

Corvo opened his eyes to gaze at the com panel on the bulkhead before him. Its camera was active, but the person on the other end had deliberately turned off his own video feed. A wise precaution; anyone intercepting and unscrambling this signal might recognize the individual at the Martian end of the comlink as the most wanted man on the planet. If that happened, there would be many uncomfortable questions about why a member of the Solar Coalition Senate was in contact with the Magician of Mars.

"No . . . only a little motion sickness, that's all." Corvo raised a hand to his mouth to cover a nauseous belch. "Pardon me . . . you were saying?"

There was a short delay while the radio signal traveled to Mars and a reply was received. "*I was saying that it's unwise of you to come here. We have the situation well in hand, no matter the outcome of events aboard the* Brackett."

Again, Corvo checked the readouts below the blank screen. The scrambler was still active; no one should be able to eavesdrop on this exchange between the *Lowell* and an undisclosed location somewhere on Mars. "You know how it came out. Your man knocked off the Newton kid. He may have failed to get everyone else on the ship, but at least he killed Newton." A laugh found its way up his throat. "Or Captain Future, as he called himself—can you believe it?"

"*I can believe anything except what you're telling me,*" Ul Quorn replied a few seconds later, his voice becoming noticeably colder. "*According to my sources—who are quite reliable—my associate was killed while spacewalking. Since it's unlikely that he would've lost his life to a dead man, the most reasonable explanation is that he was dispatched by this Captain Future.*"

He spoke the name without any sense of irony. Before Corvo could respond, Ul Quorn went on. "*The plan called for you to remain on the Moon while I continue my operations here. The assassination failed and this same individual was responsible, but that's not sufficient cause for you to come here. It may attract further IPF attention and therefore jeopardize everything we're trying to accomplish.*"

Corvo glowered at the blank screen. "Twice already I've trusted you to do this on your own," he said, matching Ul Quorn's frostiness with his own, "and both times you've failed. It's pretty clear to me that, if I want things done right, I have to see to it myself. The IPF suspects that I'm involved in the assassination attempt. I've given the public a legitimate reason for making this trip, but that's only a cover. I can no longer stand by and let you do things by yourself. Obviously that's not working."

A pause, longer than necessary by the time delay. Without realizing it, Corvo anxiously tapped his fingers against his armrests. He'd never liked these abrupt silences during conversations with Ul Quorn. He knew what they meant: the Magician of Mars was thinking, and seldom did his thoughts bode well for the people who heard them. It had been Corvo's idea that they go into business together, but he hadn't realized Ul Quorn would become as powerful a force in his world as the senator was in his. They needed each other in order to be successful in their mutual objectives—and besides, there was another reason—but on Mars, Ul Quorn had the upper hand.

"*Very well,*" Ul Quorn said at last. "*It means I'll have to adjust my plans somewhat, but I'm sure my people and I will be able to accommodate you. Once you've arrived on Mars and have settled in, I'll have someone collect you at your residence . . . where will you be staying?*"

"The Viking Inn in Xanthe," Corvo supplied.

"*A good choice. My representative will contact you there and surreptitiously transport you to my current whereabouts. If your staff has any questions, inform them that you're meeting with a business partner who doesn't want his identity known until an arrangement has been formalized.*"

"Sure. So what about Newton's people? And Newton himself, if he's still alive?"

"*Leave them to me. They're no doubt docking at Port Deimos. Their ship will be watched from the moment it docks, and anyone who leaves it will be followed. At some point, I'm sure they'll find a way to meet up with Newton.*"

"Okay. Then what?"

Another pause. "*They'll be deterred. If necessary, they'll be liqui-*

dated. Except for Newton." A wry chuckle. *"I think I'd very much like to meet someone who calls himself Captain Future. He may be interesting."*

"I'd rather just have him eliminated, but . . . well, it's your choice."

"Indeed it is." Another pause. *"Is this all?"*

"It is," Corvo replied. "I'll be seeing you again soon."

No response. Another moment went past, and then there was a faint beep signaling that the transmission had been terminated at its source. The Magician of Mars didn't believe in long good-byes—or indeed, any at all.

Corvo let out his breath, settled back in his chair. Even after all these years, he still felt uncomfortable speaking with Ul Quorn. Which was a strange and unsettling thing, regardless of the man's reputation as a cold-blooded gangster.

After all, a father should never be afraid to talk to his son.

PART FIVE
The Search for the Magician

1

Few people at the Wells Interplanetary Spaceport at Xanthe Terra noticed the arrival of the Solar Coalition Guard shuttle from the *Vigilance*. The coming and going of military spacecraft was a daily occurrence; one more ship mattered little. So only the ground crew watched as the delta-winged shuttle came in for a landing, its VTOL engines skipping up the red dust that had blown across the tarmac from the surrounding desert.

Once the shuttle was safely on the ground, a tractor towed it to the government side of the sprawling port, where SCG and IPF ships rested on the apron or within enormous hangars. The engines were still ticking when the spacecraft finally came to rest outside a hangar. A ladder was pushed into position, then the starboard hatch opened with a sigh of overpressurized air.

Men and women marched down the ladder. A few were in uniform, but most of them wore casual clothes and carried duffel bags, signifying that they were off-duty military personnel taking shore leave for a few days. All except a small handful of aresians wore goggles, half-face airmasks, and backpack oxygen-rebreathing units, along with parkas, gloves, and warm boots. Only Mars natives—"Martians" was considered a racial epithet—were able to breathe the planet's low-pressure oxygen-nitrogen atmosphere without assistance and tolerate the frigid cold that typified even a sunny day near the equator. Even after more than a century of terraforming, visitors from Earth still had to prepare for Mars as if they were climbing the highest peaks of the Himalayas.

While those who'd disembarked in uniform went to the nearby hangar, the rest strolled over to the open tram that pulled to a halt a short distance away. The tram waited until everyone climbed aboard, then drove off across the vast expanse of the landing field toward the glass-sided pillbox that was the civilian terminal.

One individual among the uniformed officers paused to watch the tram as it pulled away. Beneath his parka was the blue uniform of an IPF marshal, and no one could make out the pensive expression on a face hidden by an airmask.

Ezra Gurney couldn't see the red-haired young man who'd boarded the tram along with the *Vigilance* crewmen. For the sake of anonymity, the old lawman had avoided speaking to him once they'd come down the ladder from the shuttle. All the same, he wished he'd had a chance to wish him good luck.

Realizing this, Gurney quietly shook his head and turned to walk back to the shuttle for its return flight. The last thing he'd ever expected was that he'd come to trust, let alone even like, the kid who was calling himself Captain Future.

Aboard the tram, Curt watched as it moved past spacecraft of all kinds parked on the field. Most were big, turtle-backed freighters, but a few were shuttles much like the one he'd just departed, carrying passengers bound to or from interplanetary ships parked at Port Deimos. It was impossible to tell which of them was the one Otho and Joan had come down on, but he had little doubt that his friends were already here. It was just a matter of finding them.

He absently reached up to scratch an itch on his nose before he remembered that he was wearing an airmask and couldn't get at it. Catching an amused look from the ensign seated beside him, Curt self-consciously lowered his hand. When he swallowed, his ears popped again, a little less painfully this time but still enough to be unsettling. And it seemed like everything was coated with a thin layer of coarse red sand: the tram seats, the tarmac, the spacecraft hulls, the lenses of his goggles. An old joke was that the only people for whom red was a favorite color were aresians because they never saw anything else. There was probably some truth to it.

This wasn't the first time Curt had been to Mars. However, it seemed like it'd been a very long time since he was fourteen, and back then he'd had Otho at his side as surrogate brother, chaperone, and bodyguard, along with the Brain's disembodied presence in his ring as an unseen tutor. Remembering this, he decided it was time to check in with the *Comet.*

—*Simon, are you there?*

A short pause, during which Curt gazed up at the sky to see if he could spot Deimos. It wasn't visible, which meant that his signal would have to be bounced along orbital comsats until it reached his ship at Port Deimos. Then the Brain's voice came through his Anni:

—*I'm here, Curtis. Have you landed?*

—*Yes, I have. Where are Otho and Joan?*

—*Their shuttle touched down just a little while ago as well. They will find you in the terminal, as planned.*

—*Very good. I'll look for them there.*

The tram halted behind the terminal, and Curt joined the *Vigilance* crewmen heading inside. One by one, they walked through the airtight revolving doors that maintained the higher air pressure within the building, dutifully stamping their boots against floor mats on the way in. Then, pulling their goggles and masks down around their necks, they entered the customs queues, where aresians seated in low-pressure booths examined their ID tats and passport folders with the listless boredom of bureaucrats everywhere.

At Ezra's urging, Curt was posing as Rab Cain again, this time with a new tattoo and a passport issued by the *Vigilance*'s chief warrant officer. It was a persona that had served him well in the past, and anyone bothering to check would have discovered that it had some history behind it. The passport was a little too freshly printed to be completely convincing, but the aresian customs officer barely glanced at it before waving him through. No wonder Mars had become the abode of radical separatists; immigration officials apparently didn't care who came and went through the planet's largest spaceport.

Curt strolled through the customs gate into the terminal lobby. All around him, passengers from recently arrived flights were greeting friends and family who'd come out to meet them, while others waited their turn to board shuttles for Port Deimos. He noted the number of holstered guns worn by both terrans and native aresians and no longer felt quite so conspicuous about having his plasmar on his belt. The legal framework of the Libertarian Commonwealth of Mars posed a strange dichotomy: harsh penalties for criminal offenses, along with *posse comitatus* laws allowing citizens not only to carry firearms but also to act as their own legal authority. Somehow, the system worked, although accidental shootings and crime-of-passion homicides were frequent and the capital punishment rate was grotesquely high.

Putting down his bag, Curt paused amid the bustling crowd, looking about for any sign of Otho or Joan. Seeing no familiar faces, he bent down to pick up the bag again and was just about to make his way to the nearby maglev station when a hand grasped his elbow. He turned around to find Joan standing there.

"Oh . . . hello." All of a sudden, Curt was at a loss for words. "I . . . I was wondering if—"

Joan flung her arms around him and pulled him close. Curt was taller than she was, so she had to stand on her toes. Given the way she'd treated him aboard the *Comet,* this was the last thing he expected from her. Curt was still reeling when she whispered in his ear, "Kiss me . . . and make it look good."

It was only the second time in his life that he'd ever kissed a woman. Joan made it sound more like an order than a request, though, and there was no mistaking the insistence of her demand. Yet her mouth was pleasantly soft, her body firm and sensual in his arms, and he could have let this go on for quite a while longer had it not been for the hand that came down on his shoulder and the familiar voice beside him.

"Hello, Rab," Otho said. "Glad you finally made it."

As Curt turned his head to look at him, Joan gently pried herself from his arms. "We're being followed," she murmured. "Play along."

Now he understood. "Yeah, great to see you again, Vol," he replied, and Otho nodded slightly. "You, too, uh—"

"Catherine." Like Otho, Joan wore the sort of fashionable outdoor clothes one would expect of an offworlder visiting Mars: faux-fur lined parka, knee boots, gloves. Both wore rebreathers, airmasks, and goggles, and although they were carrying shoulder bags along with one for him, Curt couldn't see any weapons. He knew, however, that they probably had guns beneath their coats.

"Sorry we're a little late," Otho said aloud, dropping Curt's bag at his feet, "but y'know how it is. Our shuttle was delayed getting here." As he spoke, the Brain's voice came through Curt's Anni:

—*Someone has been trailing them ever since they arrived at Deimos Station. An aresian woman, identity unknown.*

"That's fine. No problem at all." Curt refrained from looking about. Although most of the people around them were terrans, there were quite a few aresians as well, along with a handful of jovians and aphrodites. Like most public buildings on Mars, the terminal was pressurized at a level tolerable to the air-breathing residents of Coalition worlds. "Have you seen anyone we know?"

"Just one." Joan kept a fixed smile on her face, but her dark eyes were solemn. "Haven't spotted her in the last few minutes, but I'm sure she's somewhere around."

—*She means you're probably being followed.*

Curt nodded. "So . . . where to now?"

"I've gone ahead and reserved tickets on the next maglev to Tharsis," Otho said. "We've got a sleeper cabin, two bunks."

"Two bunks?" Curt raised an eyebrow.

"Best I could get on short notice. The rest of the train is booked solid." He grinned. "Of course, if you two would care to double up—"

"We don't," Joan said coldly.

"—then I'm sure I can get someone to bring me an extra blanket and pillow so I can curl up on the floor."

"I'll take the floor," Curt said, and received a grateful nod from Joan. Obviously the hug and kiss she'd given him were as intimate as she was willing to get. "Very well, if you're ready to go . . ."

Without another word, Otho picked up his bag and headed in the direction of the overhead sign pointing the way to the maglev. Curt did the same. The bag Otho had brought him from the *Comet* was light, but sufficiently heavy to be containing that which he'd asked them to bring. Still playing the part of lover, Joan fell in beside him, even going so far as to tuck her arm around his elbow. Curt had to work hard not to smile. It might only be pretense, but he liked having her close.

However, he couldn't let her distract him. If someone had indeed followed Otho and Joan all the way here from Port Deimos, then it meant they were suspicious of their reasons for coming to Mars. And since there had already been one attempt on their lives, there was no reason to think that these individuals wouldn't try again.

It didn't seem as if anyone was trailing them as they passed beneath the sign and stepped onto the escalator leading down to the underground maglev station beneath the terminal. But Curt failed to notice the tall, dark-eyed aresian woman who watched from behind a column, then kept her distance as she followed them downstairs to the waiting train.

11

Across the southern plains of Xanthe Terra, the maglev train rushed southwest upon its elevated monorail. Six cars in length, with the bullet-nosed cab up front and the bubble-topped observation coach at the rear, the train shot down the electromagnetic track like a quicksilver serpent, a flash of metallic scarlet against the dull red landscape. Aresian sharecroppers tending their fields beneath dewtents glanced up for a moment as they heard the muted rumble of the approaching train, then returned to their tasks after it went by.

From his window seat in the forward sleeper coach, Curt quietly contemplated the scenery. The train had departed the spaceport nearly an hour ago, leaving behind the domed terran colony of Wellston and the nearby adobe barrios of the aresians, and was now traveling through rural countryside. In a little while it would turn west and enter the Lunae Planum and begin the longest part of the journey to the Tharsis region, crossing the equator to skirt past the northern chasms of the Valles Marineris.

Curt was looking forward to that part of the trip. When he'd been here six years ago, most of his time had been spent in the comparatively boring Chryse Plantia, where the Brain had insisted that he and Otho visited the old *Viking I* and *Pathfinder* landing sites from the twentieth century. All that he'd seen of the vast rift valley that gouged most of the Martian equator at the western hemisphere was a brief glimpse of the Capri Chasma from his shuttle as it was coming in for a landing. So he was hoping that it wouldn't be too dark to make out the deep badlands by the time the train reached them.

Glancing away from the window, Curt gazed at Joan. The private compartment Otho had managed to reserve was as small as he'd said it would be, with narrow fold-down bunks that doubled as seats during the day and just enough room on the floor to unroll the inflatable matt the conductor had supplied them as the third bed. Otho had gone back to see about making dinner reservations in the restaurant car while Joan opted for a nap.

Sitting across from him, arms folded across her chest and head lolling against a pillow, she seemed very much at peace, and for the moment nothing like the law officer he'd come to expect. Curt watched her sleep, remembering the way she'd kissed him in the spaceport terminal. Yes, she said that she'd done that to give the impression to anyone watching them that they were different people than they really were, but nonetheless he had to wonder. For just a second or two, he could've sworn that she was actually enjoying herself . . .

No. Joan had made it clear to him aboard the *Comet* that she was an IPF officer, first, foremost, and always. As attracted as he was to her, he couldn't expect those feelings to be reciprocated. Unless he wanted to be shot down again, he had to learn to respect her as a professional and try to put out of his mind the fact that she was a lovely young woman, however difficult that might be.

Curt looked out the window again. In the distance, at the rim of the Ophir Chasma that marked the western edge of the Xanthe Terra region, an atmosphere factory loomed against the horizon. One of eight dispersed around the Martian equator and at the poles, the factory was marked by fluted, smokestacklike towers rising high into the pink sky. Curt couldn't see the fumes drifting from the towers, but he knew what they were anyway: chloroflurocarbons, greenhouse gases derived from the carbon dioxide and flourides trapped in the Martian regolith.

Along with the introduction of gaseous nitrogen imported from Titan and hydrogen from Jupiter, the CFCs were slowly, over the course of many years, thickening and warming the Martian atmosphere. With this came the slow melting of the permafrost beneath the ground, which in turn was gradually releasing oxygen and water vapor. Already the primary atmospheric constituents of Mars were oxygen and nitrogen, not carbon dioxide, and while the pressure was still too thin yet for a terran to breathe without suffering hypoxia, for the first time in millions of years, creeks and vernal ponds were forming in the equatorial regions, furnishing just enough surface water to support small-scale agriculture like the farms the train had just passed.

All this was only the first phase of the generations-long effort to transform Mars into a habitable analogue of Earth. The Solar Coalition's terraforming operations had begun over a century ago, and while no one knew exactly how long they would last, it was certain that it would be several more centuries before Mars had green forests and blue seas instead of the vast expanses of red desert that still covered most of the planet.

In the meantime, scientists like Curt's father had succeeded in developing a supporting technology: a genetic subspecies of the human race capable of living on Mars, the aresians doing most of the hard work of ecopoiesis. The same bioengineering process was later used to create colonists for the moons of the outer planets, and later still for the Venusian sky city Stratus Venera, and all for the same reason: it would take the resources of all the planets to successfully terraform Mars, and the best and surest way of supporting human colonies in these uninhabitable places was to create *Homo cosmos* as their inhabitants.

When all was said and done, Mars was destined to become a replacement for another planet, the one whose global climate had been ruined long ago by the accidental overabundance of atmospheric chlorofluorocarbons that, ironically, were being deliberately cultivated on this world. The aresians were aware of this, of course, and also the fact that, one day not so far in the future, Mars would no longer belong to them.

And this was where Starry Messenger came in.

"Something on your mind?"

Curt looked around to find Joan gazing at him. Sometime in the last few minutes she'd woken up. There was a quiet smile on her face, yet her eyes were sharp and inquisitive. It wasn't a polite question; she really did want to know what he was thinking.

"Something occurred to me while I was adrift," Curt replied, and then he told her about how it'd occurred to him that there might be a link between Starry Messenger and the Sons of the Two Moons, and therefore an indirect connection with Ul Quorn. Joan listened patiently, nodding every now and then, and when he was done she sat up a little straighter in her seat.

"It's an interesting theory," she said. "Section Four has already looked into this and hasn't found anything." Gazing out the window, she added, "That doesn't necessarily mean nothing's there, though. The attempt on the president's life sounds more like something Starry Messenger might do than the Sons, and if there's a link between Ul Quorn and Senator Corvo—"

"Then it would mean that Corvo has ties to Starry Messenger." Curt was mildly surprised that Joan was agreeing with him. Like Gurney, perhaps she was learning to trust him.

"Uh-huh." Joan shifted a little in her seat, resting her head more comfortably against the pillow. "But it doesn't explain why someone would try to get us on the way here, unless . . ."

She closed her eyes and pounded the seat beside her in exasperation. "Damn it, unless they knew we were on our way here to find Ul Quorn. The only way they could have learned that was if—"

"Someone heard us talking about it at Corvo's house. I'd say it's pretty obvious who that must have been." Curt's eyes turned toward the window again. "Maybe it's Ul Quorn we're going after, but as far as I'm concerned, he's just a step toward taking down Victor Corvo."

Joan said nothing for a few moments. Snuggled against the pillow, she quietly studied Curt as he watched the red desert rush by. "You're really not out for justice, are you?" she said at last. "You're out for revenge."

"Same thing."

"No." She shook her head. "No, they're not. It may seem that way, but they're really two different things." She paused. "I know Corvo killed your parents, and you're right to want justice for this, but has it ever occurred to you that revenge is someone else's agenda?"

He looked at her sharply. "Whose?"

"Simon's, of course. After all, if Corvo hadn't killed the only two people who could have given him a second chance, his brain would've eventually been transplanted into an artificial body much like Otho's. His loss is nearly as great as your own, but there's no legal statute covering Corvo's offense against him. So he has to settle for revenge, and since he can't do it himself—"

"Simon's been like a father to me! He'd never, *never*—"

"Use you?" Joan raised an eyebrow.

"No!"

Joan returned her gaze to the window. For a few minutes she said nothing. "Try to believe me when I tell you this," she said at last. "Revenge will never give back what you've lost, or Simon either."

Curt didn't reply. The atmosphere factory was no longer in sight. Now all they could see were boulder fields and low hills, with the occasional arroyo showing where water had once flowed and, perhaps one day, would flow again. What Joan said had made him angry, and watching the passing scenery helped him calm down. He'd always had good control of his temper, and the last person he wanted to blow up at was Joan.

—*She's mistaken, Curtis.* The Brain had been quiet throughout all this, but his presence was there all the same. —*I'd never manipulate you. You know that.*

—*Yes, I know,* Curt replied, although he was no longer quite so certain.

After a little while, Joan spoke again. "When we find Ul Quorn, we may find Senator Corvo as well. We know he's on the way here, and if you're right, there's some tie between them. But if that happens, I want you to promise me one thing."

"What's that?" He tried to keep his voice even.

"Remember what I told you. And also that, if you'll let me help you, I can legally bring Corvo to justice. You can count on that."

"I'll—"

There was a tap at the door, then it slid open and Otho came in. "All right, we have reservations for three in the dining car at seven p.m.," he said, sitting down beside Curt. "I looked at the menu, and it seems pretty good. A bit heavy on Latino-Asian fusion, though."

"Goes with aresian culture," Joan said. "Is that what took you so long? Checking out the menu?"

"No, not entirely. I was also watching the lady who's watching us." Otho nodded as Joan's eyes widened. "Yeah, she's here—the same woman we spotted on Deimos and again on the shuttle. She was in the dining car when I started to leave, so I made a detour to the observation car before I came back here, and she stayed behind me all the way."

"Then Corvo has someone else on our trail," Curt said. "Or Ul Quorn."

"Or both." Otho pensively played with his cap. "Funny thing is, she didn't make any real attempt to hide from me. It was almost as if she wanted me to spot her. If that's so, maybe she wants to talk to us."

"No . . . not us." Joan looked over at Curt. "You."

III

The woman approached Curt when and where he expected, in the observation car shortly after dinner. Otho caught a glimpse of her while they were eating, and the fact that she immediately disappeared only confirmed Joan's suspicion that she was waiting for a chance to speak with Curt alone. So once dinner was over, Curt went back to the observation coach while the others returned to their sleeper, and that was when the woman came to him.

By then, the train was traveling along the northern rim of the Mariner Valley, the setting sun casting amber twilight upon canyons vast enough to hold entire cities. The observation car was divided into two decks: the lower one heated and pressurized for the comfort of terran passengers, the upper level cooler and unpressurized in deference to aresian passengers. Curt decided to head upstairs, so he put on his airmask again before cycling through the revolving-door airlock and climbing up a short flight of spiral stairs. Here, the windows were replaced by a transparent dome running the length of the car, with padded benches facing outward along either side of a central aisle. The arrangement gave the illusion that one was riding on the train's roof; it was an excellent way to see Mars, and Curt was surprised that the deck was vacant when he arrived.

He wasn't alone for very long. The first stars were appearing in a sky slowly turning dark when someone walked down the aisle and stopped beside his seat. Looking around, Curt found an aresian woman of exceptional beauty. Mars natives were usually taller than most terrans, but even among her kind her height was unusual: six-six as a guess, perhaps more. The hooded traveler's cape she wore couldn't conceal a statuesque, full-breasted figure, and voluminous black hair that curled down around her shoulders and back framed a fine-boned, almost elfin face.

"Good evening," she said, her voice deep and pleasantly smoky. "Care for a little company?"

"Certainly." Curt did his best not to stammer as he waved a hand to the empty seat beside him. "I was even hoping that someone might share the view."

"Thank you." The woman gracefully alighted upon the bench, crossing her ankles and wrists together while arching her back. "It is a spectacular sight, isn't it? I've seen this many times, and I never get used to it."

The canyons were quickly vanishing. All that was left was a craggy horizon, with a few buttes still illuminated by the last rays of the sun. "Then you must travel this way quite a bit," Curt said. "Do you live around here, Señorita . . . ?"

"N'Rala . . . just N'Rala. And yes, I do. My home is Tharsis, at the Ascraeus tolou. Have you ever been to Mars before, Señor . . . ?"

"Newton. Curt Newton." Spontaneously, he made the decision to use his real name, not Rab Cain. If she was following him, she must already know who he was; there was no point in hiding behind a false identity. "Yes, once before. But never here."

"Ah." N'Rala nodded, smiling a bit as she looked straight ahead. "So what brings you back to Mars? Are you sightseeing, or . . . ?"

She let her question trail off. Curt had the impression that she was playing with him, as if she already knew the truth and was daring him to tell her a lie. "The sights are beautiful," he replied, never looking away from her, "but besides that, I have business here as well. I'm searching for someone."

"I see." Accepting the compliment as her due, N'Rala favored him with a sidelong look beneath a delicately arched eyebrow. "And who may this gentleman be?"

"Ul Quorn."

"Ah . . . I see." Her gaze darkened, her face becoming solemn. "Ul Quorn is well known. The Magician of Mars, he's sometimes called. Do you know why?"

"I've been told it's because he can make people disappear."

"That's correct, but it's also a measure of the respect my people feel for him. You would do well to avoid having anything to do with him, Señor Newton." She nodded toward the Valles Marineris, now completely darkened by the coming of night. "The Martian deserts are vast, and it's said that those who've annoyed the Magician have disappeared into them."

"Still, I'd like to find him, as would my companions." No sense in trying to hide what she already knew, that he wasn't traveling by himself. "Do you think you could tell us how we might find him?"

N'Rala idly gazed up through the transparent dome, watching Phobos as it came into view. "Why do you wish to meet Ul Quorn?"

"I want to bring to justice the man who killed my parents. I'm hoping he will help me." It wasn't the entire truth, but he'd have to gamble that she wouldn't already know the rest.

N'Rala didn't answer immediately. Gazing upon her, Curt had the impression of a regal and enigmatic figure, a Martian princess from one of the old Edgar Rice Burroughs novels he'd absorbed when he was a child. Unlike Joan, there was a sense of mystery about her. Only once before had he ever met a female as enigmatically alluring, and that was the aphrodite girl Simon had forbidden him from ever seeing again . . .

"I believe I can help you," N'Rala said at last. "Are you planning to get off the train when we reach the Ascraeus tolou?"

"Yes."

"Very well. Find the tavern called the King and Queen of the Desert. I'll be there tomorrow evening, and I'll introduce you to someone I know. If he likes you and your friends, he'll tell you how you may be able to find Ul Quorn."

"The King and Queen of the Desert, tomorrow night." Curt nodded. "We'll be there."

N'Rala started to rise, then stopped herself. Seemingly on impulse, she leaned over and kissed him on the cheek, just above his airmask.

"You should think twice about wanting to meet Ul Quorn," she said softly. "You're too young to end your life here."

And then she stood up and, amid the swirl of her cape, glided out of the observation car.

IV

There was a game called catch that dogs liked. Even moonpups.

Grag found out about this when it did a quick Anni search for ways to keep dogs entertained. The long hours the robot was spending with Simon aboard the *Comet* as they waited to hear from Curt, Otho, and Joan were plainly driving Eek crazy with boredom, but there was an easy solution to this: a rubber replica of Mars purchased from a souvenir kiosk in the Port Deimos arcade. Once Eek learned to bring it back to Grag after retrieving it, both robot and dog discovered the sublime pleasures of such a simple pastime.

Deimos's low gravity made catch a particularly challenging game, and Grag had just found that Eek could perform a midair catch of a ball ricocheted from the floor off the ready-room bulkhead when there was a knocking sound against the airlock's inner hatch. Apparently someone had just entered the airlock through the unsealed outer hatch and now wanted to come the rest of the way in. Leaving the ball with Eek, Grag rose from its knees and turned to the inner hatch. The robot touched the intercom button and asked, "Who is there, please?"

"*This is Marshal Ezra Gurney, IPF. Who's this, the 'bot?*"

"Yes, I am a robot."

A long pause. Grag made no move to open the door. Eek whined impatiently, his tail thrashing back and forth as he held the ball in his mouth. Finally, Marshal Gurney spoke again. "*Would you open the door, please? I'd like to come in.*"

"Just a moment, Marshal." Grag tapped the intercom button. "Marshal Ezra Gurney is here to visit us. He would like to come in."

"*Please let him in, Grag,*" the Brain said from elsewhere in the ship. "*Escort him up to the middeck.*"

"Affirmative." Grag twisted the lock lever to unseal the inner hatch and pulled it open, and Ezra stepped in.

Like all humans visiting Port Deimos, Ezra wore ankle weights while walking through the spaceport's subsurface tunnels. He came in from the gangway that had been pushed against the *Comet*'s hull in the silolike hangar where the ship was currently berthed. He scowled as he looked up at Grag's emotionless round eyes.

"Don't you know what this badge means?" he demanded, pointing to the silver-plated shield on the chest of his uniform jacket.

"Yes, I do know. It identifies you as a senior officer with the Interplanetary Police Force."

"Then why the hell didn't you open up when I told you to?"

"First, I did not see the badge. Second, you did not give a specific reason why you wished to come in. Therefore, I was under no obligation to do so. I opened the hatch only after consulting with Dr. Wright, who is—"

"I know who he is. Take me to him."

In the time it took Gurney to say these words, Grag accessed the legal database for the Libertarian Commonwealth of Mars Department of Justice and performed a search of the conditions under which a law officer like Ezra Gurney could enter a vessel docked at an orbital spaceport operated by the Solar Coalition. As it turned out, the officer could enter the ship only so long as he'd been invited aboard, which Simon had just done. However, unless Marshal Gurney was investigating a possible offense and had a warrant giving him specific authorization to do so, Grag could remove him at any time. Which it was inclined to do; the marshal was being unnecessarily rude. But Simon had told Grag to bring Marshal Gurney to see him, so Grag put the Brain's instructions above its own desires.

"Very well, then. Follow me, please." Grag turned to walk across the compartment, only to find Eek blocking its way. The moonpup clearly wanted to continue the game. The robot paused to bend down and lower its right hand, and when the little dog placed the ball in its palm, Grag lightly tossed the ball against the bulkhead farthest from him and Marshal Gurney.

Ezra Gurney watched in amazement as the moonpup went scampering off in pursuit of the ball. He recognized the dog as being the same one President Carthew had given away after being bitten by the little mutt. The last thing he'd ever expected was to see him playing catch with Curt Newton's robot. It wasn't the dog that astonished him, though, but the 'bot.

"Who programmed you to do that?" he asked. "Play catch, I mean."

"No one did." Grag paused at the foot of the ladder. "I needed to entertain Eek, so I learned the game myself, and then I taught Eek."

"And this is something you figured out on your own?"

"Yes, it is."

"Why?"

"Because it's fun." Grag regarded him with an unblinking red gaze. "*Fun?*"

"Yes. Why, is that against the law?"

Ezra felt his mouth fall open. He couldn't tell for the life of him whether the 'bot was being sarcastic or not. Which was a hell of a thing. Since when did robots become capable of sarcasm . . . or have fun playing catch with a puppy?

"Never mind." Ezra closed his eyes and shook his head. "Just forget I asked, okay? Take me to see Dr. Wright." He stopped, and then added, "Please."

Grag responded by silently continuing up the ladder. Ezra climbed up behind it, and found himself in the *Comet*'s middeck wardroom. And there he met the Brain.

During the first conversation he had with Joan after she'd come aboard the *Comet*, she'd warned him what to expect from Simon Wright. It was one thing to learn that the scientist, once renowned in the bioengineering field but officially declared dead many years ago, had become a disembodied brain suspended within a modified drone. It was quite another to see the cyborg itself gliding toward him, its eyestalks moving until they were level with his own eyes.

"Hello, Marshal Gurney." The gentle voice that came from the speaker on the front of the saucerlike carapace was that of an old man. "A pleasure to meet you at last. Joan—Inspector Randall, that is—has told me so much about you. I'm Simon Wright."

Even the robot wasn't nearly as weird as this. "Ah . . . yeah, same here," Ezra said. Out of habit, he started to raise his hand. Realizing that a handshake was probably futile, he dropped it. "I just . . . I mean, I wanted to stop by and . . . well, see if I could coordinate things with you, now that I've heard from Joan about . . . that is, since she—"

The sound that came from the speaker was nothing more than a polite laugh; nonetheless, it took Ezra a moment to recognize it as such. "No need to be flustered, Marshal—or may I call you Ezra? I long since discarded my mortal coil, but in some ways I'm still a man. In fact, in biological terms, you and I are just a few years apart in age. Or at least we were, before my former body had the misfortune of meeting a premature end."

"I'm—" Ezra took a deep breath, tried again. "Look, I'm sorry. It's just . . . first Newton, then the android, then the 'bot, and now you. It's a lot to take, y'know what I mean?"

"I suppose you're right. The four of us have been together for so long, perhaps we've forgotten what it's like to be around those whom most people regard as 'normal.'" Another laugh. "On the other hand, even when I had a human form, I considered normalcy to be rather overrated."

"That's an appropriate outlook, I guess."

"Yes, I rather think so." The Brain purred across the compartment to settle upon the wardroom table. "What brings us the pleasure of your company, Ezra? I trust your earlier suspicions of Curt have been alleviated."

Ezra ignored the last as he took a seat across the table. "I've just been in touch with Joan. She, Otho, and Curt are aboard a maglev to the Tharsis region, and according to her, Curt has made contact with someone who may connect him with Ul Quorn."

"I received much the same message just a little while ago," Simon said. "From Curt."

"You're in touch with him?"

"I can always reach him. He has a neural implant like everyone else, but he doesn't necessarily require a public Anni node to use it. He has another means of communicating with me."

"That ring he wears?" Ezra asked, and was secretly pleased to see Simon's eyestalks visibly twitch. "Ain't hard to guess. When it looks like he's linkin', you can sometimes see him looking at his ring."

"Very observant. Yes, his ring serves as an independent Anni node. He inherited it from his late father, and through it he can access virtually any communication system. What's more, as long as he keeps it on his finger, it serves as a convenient means of tracking his movements as well. So we're not dependent on local nodes to keep in touch with each other."

"That's good to know," Ezra said, "and I appreciate your sharing it with me, 'cause I'd give odds that this is some sort of trap. Joan says this same lady followed her and Otho all the way from here, and that she waited till Curt was on his own before she sidled up to him." He gave Simon a sly wink. "Apparently she's a looker, too. That always helps."

"Curt isn't affected by feminine beauty," Simon said coldly.

"Uh-huh. I'll let Joan know. I'm sure she'll be surprised." Ezra leaned back in his chair and folded his arms together. "In any case, if this is indeed a trap, it may lead them straight to Ul Quorn. In that case, it'll be to our advantage if we're able to pinpoint your boy's location and communicate directly with him."

"I agree," the Brain said. "I'm able to interface directly with the *Comet*'s navigation and communications equipment, so this should increase our range. And once this is done, I can interface directly with *Vigilance*'s mission intelligence systems. I assume this is what you want, yes?"

"Bull's-eye." Ezra cocked a forefinger at him and fired it like a gun. "And I assure you, if it appears that he and the others may be in trouble, the IPF and Solar Guard have authority under President Carthew to move in at once."

"I appreciate that, Marshal. If there's any reason to get in touch with you—"

"Don't be afraid to ask."

"I shan't." Simon's impellors whirred again, and he rose from the table. "Well, if that's all you'd like to talk to me about—"

"Ah, yeah, there is just one thing." Ezra leaned forward in his seat and, clasping his hands together on the tabletop, stared directly at the Brain. "Senator Corvo's ship from Earth is scheduled to arrive here within the next hour or so, and shortly after that he's scheduled to shuttle down to the surface. His official itinerary calls for him to spend his time in Xanthe Terra, but if there's a tie between him and Ul Quorn, I have little doubt that they'll find a way to meet up. If they do, that's sufficient cause for us to move in for an arrest."

"Yes, I suppose that's possible." There was just a touch of reticence in Simon's voice.

"In that case, I hope Curt remembers that he's been deputized as a special operative for the IPF, and that apprehending Ul Quorn and placing him and Senator Corvo under arrest takes precedence over any notions of revenge." As he spoke, Ezra let his smile fade and replaced it with a meaningful stare. "He may call himself Captain Future, but I don't want no heroics."

"You'll have our utmost cooperation, Marshal Gurney."

"Call me Ezra." A grin and another wink, just to take the edge off what he'd just said.

"We'll be in touch." The Brain continued floating his way toward the manhole leading to the flight deck. "Grag, will you show our guest to the airlock, please?"

The moonpup was waiting for them when Grag led Ezra back down to the ready-room. The marshal paused to give Eek—what a name!—a scratch behind the ears, then he stepped through the airlock hatches and out onto the gangway. He'd nearly reached the hangar door when a sudden thought gave him reason to pause and turn back around again.

The *Comet* rested on its landing gear within the hangar, its blunt nose pointed upward at the closed ceiling hatch. It would not be able to lift off without anyone knowing about it . . . or at least it couldn't if it was a normal vessel. But Joan had already informed him that the little racing yacht possessed some sort of invisibility device, and if that was so . . .

He'd better keep an eye on the hangar. Just to be safe.

Straddling the equator west of the Valles Marineris are the Tharsis Montes, three volcanoes that came into being above a tectonic hot spot during Mars's early history. With Olympus Mons, the largest volcano in the solar system, towering above the Amazonis Planitia, farther away to the northwest, the three smaller yet no less significant volcanoes forming a chain known as the Tharsis Ridge are Arsia Mons, southwest of the equator; Pavonis Mons, at zero degrees longitude; and Ascraeus Mons to the northeast.

Like a row of fire-breathing dragons who'd long ago gone to sleep, the Tharsis Ridge is a reminder that Mars was once an active, living planet. This is underscored by the presence of lava tubes. The lowlands are riddled with enormous, rimless pits resembling sinkholes except much larger, each plunging deep underground as openings to broad tunnels through which lava once flowed. The nearby volcanoes have gone extinct, but in ancient times the tubes allowed molten rock to escape beneath the surface during eruptions, exploding into the open many miles away.

Back then, lava tubes functioned much like relief valves for volcanoes. Many millions of years later, terrans and aresians found a new purpose for them.

The maglev made only a brief, ten-minute stop at Tharsis Station before proceeding on its westward course toward Amazonis Planitia. About twenty passengers disembarked from the train; Curt, Otho, and

Joan were among them. They lingered on the elevated platform just long enough for their goggles and masks to get blasted by a faceful of red sand kicked up by the maglev's rushed departure, then Curt turned to look around.

Several miles away, Ascraeus Mons loomed to the north, a massive rock wall rising thirty thousand feet above the surrounding terrain. From this direction it didn't resemble a traditional volcano so much as it did a low, eroded mountain; its caldera was invisible from where Curt stood. But that wasn't what drew his attention.

A little less than a mile from the station, a dirt road led to what appeared to be a giant anthill, a conical structure seventy feet tall and nearly six hundred feet wide, with several rows of slotlike windows along its rammed-dirt walls. Fat-wheeled cars and trucks traveled along the road leading to it, surrounded by windmills, solar and antenna farms, greenhouses, a landfill, and a small aircraft landing field. Several miles to the west, they could see stacks of another atmosphere plant upon the horizon, rising between Ascraeus Mons and Pavonis Mons.

When the first aresians moved out of the enclosed cities inhabited by terrans to start their own settlements, they borrowed a form of architecture from their Chinese ancestors: the tolou, a doughnut-shaped building in the countryside built by peasant collectives who then lived there as clans. The aresians discovered that tolous were particularly suitable for living on a desert world, especially since they could be built above lava tubes and therefore provide not only windbreaks and additional living space, but also access to underground aquifers from which potable water could be distilled.

As the terraforming project began picking up speed and atmosphere plants began to spread out along the equator, tolous were built by aresians working to tame the Martian wilderness. Now there were a dozen or more, connected to one another by a network of roads and maglev lines.

The Ascraeus tolou was their destination, the place from which the aresian who'd tried to sabotage the *Comet,* and presumably President

Carthew's would-be assassin, had come. If all worked well, this was also the place where Curt and the others would find someone who'd lead them to Ul Quorn.

Stairs led down from the station platform to a small parking area. Their fellow passengers were already there, climbing into cars that would carry them the rest of the way to the tolou. Curt caught a brief glimpse of N'Rala climbing into the back of what appeared to be a three-wheeled rickshaw peddled by a young aresian. She glanced up at the platform and for an instant their eyes met, then N'Rala gave Curt a sly smile before turning away to say something to the driver. He nodded and stood up on his pedals, and the cab began to pull away from the station.

"Your new girlfriend is hot," Otho said.

"She's not—" Curt began, then noticed the laugh lines around his friend's eyes and the amused way with which Joan was regarding him. "Aw, shut up," he said, and bent over to pick up his bag. "Let's hurry and get another cab before they're all taken."

Curt had dressed in layers when he'd woken up earlier this morning, putting on the gear Otho had brought him from the *Comet* and covering it with a sweater and his parka, and that meant he was able to abandon the smaller of the two bags he'd carried aboard the maglev. Together with Otho and Joan, the three of them looked like what they were pretending to be: young adventure travelers from Earth, using the maglev to see the sights of the red planet without resorting to package tours and the like.

—*Simon, are you there?* Curt asked.

—*I'm here, Curtis.* The Brain's voice sounded a little faint; he was apparently reaching him through a weak Anni node. —*I'm tracking you, Otho, and Joan.*

—*Good. Try to keep a fix on us—and if we move from this location or I give you the signal, you know what to do.*

There was a pause. He and the Brain had discussed their options last night, in private, without Otho or Joan tapping into their Anni link. Simon didn't like what Curt had come up with, but they'd agreed it was only to be used as a last, desperate measure.

—*I understand,* Simon said at last, *and I'll await your signal. But . . . think twice before you do this, all right?*

—*I will,* Curt replied, and let it go at that.

Ten minutes later, a cab dropped them at the tolou's main entrance, a keyhole door with mandarin ideograms inscribed in the red sandstone wall above it. There was no airlock, only a bamboo door that pushed aside on well-oiled hinges. Curt led the others through a short, dimly lit passageway that cut through the structure's thick outer walls, and suddenly they found themselves within the tolou's interior.

From the inside, the habitat resembled an immense drum that had been laid to rest above a deep hole and had its skins removed. The tolou was about six hundred feet in diameter, the same width as the lava tube entrance above which it had been erected, and had three tiers of covered balconies around its circumference. Beneath this lay a shaft approximately eight hundred feet deep, separated from the tolou by a natural stone ledge that ran around the edge of the pit. More tiers had been carved out of the rock walls along the sides of the pit, while narrow suspension bridges arranged every other tier provided easy access from one side to the other. At the bottom of the pit, a broad courtyard surrounded what appeared to be a groundwater pool fed by runoff from gutters spiraling down the surrounding walls; in this way, morning dew forming on the balcony eaves was collected as drinking water.

Everywhere he looked, Curt saw aresians. Mars natives dressed in handwoven serapes and hooded capes strolled along the walkways and relaxed on balconies, while their children chased each other from one tier to the next. The tolou walls reverberated with the echoes of their voices. There were nearly no terrans to be seen. In fact, Curt began to notice the curious glances being cast in their direction, along with a few hostile glares.

"Perhaps we ought to find the inn where we're staying." Joan had noticed the same thing; her voice was low and wary.

"I agree." Otho looked around, saw a young aresian walking in their direction. "Pardon me, sir, but would you—?"

The aresian muttered something obscene and stalked past them. The next resident to walk by was only slightly more welcoming; at least she didn't say anything nasty. It wasn't until Otho and Curt both stepped in front of a local and politely but firmly demanded directions to the inn that they were grudgingly told where it was located, on the opposite side of the tolou, up on the third tier.

"Not very hospitable, are they?" Curt remarked.

"No," Joan said quietly, "and there's a reason for that." She pointed to the wall beside them. "Look."

Painted in bright orange on the sandstone wall beside the entrance was a symbol Curt hadn't noticed until then: a circle with a small pair of horns at its top and an equally small cruciform at its bottom. He recognized it immediately as the ancient Greek symbol for the planet Mercury . . . otherwise known as the Starry Messenger.

Curt raised his left hand and removed his glove, allowing his ring to be exposed. He held it up to the wall. —*Are you seeing this, Simon?* he asked softly.

—*I am indeed. It's obviously there to serve notice that this tolou is under Starry Messenger protection.*

"Oh, nice." Otho rolled his eyes as he caught sight of the symbol. "So much for a warm welcome."

"I don't care if they like us or not. All I want is Ul Quorn." Curt dropped his hand and turned away from the wall. "C'mon . . . the day's getting late. Let's go to the inn and park our bags, and then find the King and Queen of the Desert."

VI

The Ascraeus Oasis, the inn where they were staying, was located on the tolou's highest tier, nearly nine hundred feet above the pit floor. Their rooms were pressurized to Earth-normal and warmer than the ambient temperature of most aresian domiciles; the inn was one of the few places in the tolou built to accommodate offworld visitors. Curt, Joan, and Otho enjoyed the luxury of being able to remove their masks and respirators for a little while. After ordering food and drink, they took turns napping and using the shower, with Joan given the privacy of a separate room.

By evening the three of them were fed, rested, changed into fresh clothes, and ready to find the King and Queen of the Desert. The innkeeper—another terran, a short and rotund gent with a Santa Claus beard—seemed surprised that anyone would want to go there. When Curt asked for directions at the front desk, he shook his head. "Not a place you want to visit, son. I've got a nice bar here. If you and your friends stay, the first round is on the house." But he reluctantly gave directions to the nearest elevator, with the parting advice to have a quick drink and leave before the regulars noticed them.

The tavern was located on the tolou floor, at the bottom of the pit above which the settlement had been built. The elevator that carried them there was open-sided, little more than a wooden stall that traveled up and down the shaft on nanofilament cables. Night had fallen, and as they made the ride down, lanterns were coming to life along the balconies and crosswalks, turning the tolou into a barrel lined with multicolored lights.

The King and Queen of the Desert could have been a beer joint any-where, except that it had been excavated from the pit's rock walls with a wooden façade out front. As Curt and the others stepped off the ele-vator and walked toward the tavern, he noticed a tunnel in the wall on the other side of the pit. It was a good guess that this was the entrance to the lava tube. The entrance was barred by a gate, but what appeared to be light fixtures suspended from the tunnel's rock ceiling led away into an unknown distance.

—*Simon, is there any indication how far back the lava tube goes?* he asked.

The pause that followed was unexpectedly long, and when he finally heard the Brain, his voice was faint. —*I'm sorry, Curtis, but I'm having trouble receiving you. The node you're using is—*

Abruptly, there was nothing but silence.

Curt stopped, looked at Otho. "I've just lost Simon," he said quietly. "Try your Anni, see if you can reach him."

Otho nodded. While Curt and Joan waited, he lowered his face and closed his eyes. A few moments passed, then he looked up again. "Not getting through. Not a peep from Anni, either."

"Same here," Joan said. "Something's interfering with our uplink."

Beneath his airmask, Curt frowned. This could simply be a natural consequence of being so far underground, but the fact that he'd heard the Brain at all, even for only a couple of seconds, made him suspect that their neural-net interfaces were being deliberately jammed. Some-one didn't want them to have contact with the outside world.

"We're on our own," he said quietly. The others nodded, yet there was little they could do about it except find out what awaited them inside the tavern.

On the other side of a solid-looking door was a large, dimly lit room with battered furniture, a couple of billiards tables, and a bar running the length of the far wall. There was no airlock or any other conces-sions to offworlders. As soon as Curt, Otho, and Joan walked in, every eye in the place turned toward them, and save for the shrill sound of aresian music—flutes, drums, and sitars played serpentine harmony by a group squatting on rugs in the corner—for an instant it seemed as if the entire room paused to take a deep breath.

"You ever get the feeling you're not welcome?" Otho said softly.

"No . . . do you?" Joan gave him a sidelong glance, and then crooked her arm through Curt's elbow. "C'mon . . . buy a lady a drink."

Curt said nothing. He wasn't about to admit to her that this was only the second time he'd been in a bar. He very seldom drank, and in most places he was underage anyway. He caught a slight nod from Otho giving him tacit permission to do so, though, and he'd just started to walk Joan to the bar when someone moved to block their way.

"Guns," he growled.

"Pardon me?" Curt asked.

The figure standing before them was a jovian, not quite as tall as the average aresian but more than twice as wide, with arms as thick as his legs and a black beard falling to the middle of his massive chest. He glared at Curt with smoldering dark eyes that suggested there was little he'd like to do more than break his neck and throw his body out into the desert.

"Your guns . . . check 'em here." He cocked his head toward a booth the three of them hadn't noticed when they'd walked in; an aresian within it sat before a row of cubbyholes containing firearms of all kinds. "Not allowed in the bar."

Curt hesitated, then nodded and turned toward the booth. "Actually, it's kind of a relief," Otho said quietly as he removed the particle-beam pistol he'd purchased at Port Deimos and handed it over. "If no one is allowed to carry guns in here, the less likely we'll have any serious trouble."

"So you're saying we're safe?" Curt asked.

"No. I'm just saying that no one will be able to shoot us. We can still get in a fight."

"Don't listen to him. He doesn't know what he's talking about." As she surrendered her IPF-issue pistol, Joan nodded toward the ceiling.

"See those? Motion-activated stunners. They're controlled from the bar. First sign of a brawl, the bartender flips a switch and anyone who isn't perfectly still gets knocked down."

Curt looked up. Every few yards along the ceiling were small, trackball-mounted barrels resembling the business ends of stun guns. "I've seen vids where bar brawls—"

"Don't believe what you see in vids. In real life, the management wants everyone to drink and be happy. Nothing's going to happen here."

"No . . . they'll wait until we leave," Otho quietly added. "Then they'll come after us."

The man at the gun-check booth raised an inquisitive eyebrow when Curt unholstered his plasmar and placed it on the counter. Like everyone else, he'd never seen a weapon like it before. As he placed it in the cubbyhole behind him, Curt coiled up the gun's power line, and without disconnecting it from the battery pack on his belt, surreptitiously slipped it beneath his parka. He then accepted the claim ticket and let Joan lead him away. The jovian grunted and stepped aside, and the three of them sauntered the rest of the way in.

They were not the only offworlders here—Curt spotted several aphrodites gathered around a billiards table, while another jovian was huddled with a pair of aresians—but they were the only terrans. The reason why was obvious. A black tapestry hanging from a rock wall was embroidered with the Starry Messenger symbol, an indication that there was little love for Earth or the Solar Coalition to be found in the King and Queen of the Desert.

Curt did his best to ignore this as they approached the bar. There were quite a few aresians on this side of the room; they grudgingly parted to make way for them. The bartender gave Curt an inquisitive look, and for the moment Curt was stymied. He'd never ordered a drink in a bar before, and didn't know what to ask for.

Otho moved closer to Curt. "Order a beer," he murmured. "You don't have to drink it, but it'll look strange if you don't get anything."

"A session ale is the best if you don't drink much," Joan quietly added. "I recommend a Lost Planet Lager."

He followed her recommendation, and the bartender silently nodded and walked over to the taps to fill a ceramic mug with an amber liquid. Curt felt as if every eye in the room was on his back as the mug was placed before him. "How do you drink with these on?" he whispered to Joan, pointing to his mask. His familiarity with aresian respirators didn't extend to wearing one under social circumstances, particularly while visiting a drinking establishment.

"There's a little valve in the middle, see?" She tapped her mask with her finger. "The bartender will bring you a straw—or at least he should—and you can sip your drink through it." She paused. "Or you can try pulling down your mask and drinking while holding your breath, but I wouldn't recommend it. If you do it wrong, you could get the hiccups, and then you'll pass out. I don't think that would go down well in here."

"I'll take the straw."

"Beer isn't good when you drink it that way," a woman's voice said from behind him.

Curt turned to find N'Rala materializing from the crowd around them. With her hood raised, it wasn't surprising that he hadn't spotted her earlier. She'd probably been there the whole time, quietly observing him and the others as they entered the tavern. Now she emerged from the aresians surrounding them, pushing back her hood to give Curt a smile that managed to be both warm and predatory at the same time.

"Perhaps it's just as well." Curt tried not to seem surprised by her sudden appearance. "I've never had much of a taste for alcohol."

"Pity. I'm sure there's any number of people here who'd like to show you an old aresian drinking game." N'Rala's eyes moved to take in the local men standing about, all of whom were taking an interest in the tall, darkly beautiful woman in their midst. Or perhaps they knew her already.

"Maybe some other time." Curt gestured to Otho and Joan standing beside him. "Let me introduce you to my friends. This is—"

"I already know who they are." N'Rala's smile widened as she turned to his companions. "Vol . . . or should I call you Otho? . . . I have a friend who'd very much like to meet you. Perhaps you shall before long." Otho stared back at her, not saying anything. "And you"—she stepped a little closer to Joan—"I think it would be better if I didn't let on who you really are, don't you?"

Joan's face colored above her mask. "Do whatever you want," she retorted, staring back at her. "I'm not afraid of you."

Some of N'Rala's self-assured arrogance disappeared, to be replaced by anger barely under restraint. Her hand started to rise from her side, and she seemed ready to strike the IPF inspector before her. Seeing this, Curt stepped between her and Joan.

"You said that if I came here, you'd introduce me to someone who could lead me to Ul Quorn," he said, speaking so that only she could hear him.

N'Rala stopped. The smile reappeared and she relaxed again. "Why, yes . . . yes, I did, didn't I? And in fact, they're here now."

" 'They?' "

"Surprise." As she said this, her gaze traveled past Curt's shoulder to the aresian men standing behind him. "Take him," she said. "Take them all."

VII

"Duck!" Otho shouted.

Curt didn't need the warning. Even before N'Rala finished speaking, he was in motion, collapsing his legs at his knees to drop his head and shoulders beneath the blow he'd anticipated would come from behind.

The beer mug an aresian attempted to bring down on his head barely missed its target before smashing to pieces against the bar. Still crouching, Curt whirled about and kicked sideways; his assailant's breath woofed from his lungs as Curt's boot slammed into his stomach.

Even as the aresian doubled over, though, another Mars native was taking his place, rushing forward to hurl a wild roundhouse blow at Curt. He easily dodged the fist and stuck out his right ankle to trip his opponent as he blundered past. Sharp punches to the liver and kidneys sent the second man crashing into N'Rala, who'd by then turned on Joan.

From the corner of his eye, Curt caught a glimpse of Joan sidestepping the taller woman only to fall into the outstretched arms of the aresian behind her. Caught in a bear hug, Joan threw her elbows back into his ribs, then whirled about and smacked the heel of her hand against his nose. Blood spurted from his nostrils and he lurched back as N'Rala moved to attack her again.

Curt darted forward to protect Joan, only to be blocked by an aphrodite who made a grab for his face mask. Curt swatted aside his hand, and since turnabout is fair play, he snatched off the aphrodite's airmask and the tube leading to his pack. The Martian atmosphere was too thin for Venus natives as well as terrans; gasping and clawing at his breathing gear, the aphrodite was desperately trying to put everything back where it should be when a hard punch to the solar plexus knocked the air from his lungs. He folded in upon himself and toppled to the floor.

Curt was about to turn again to the first aresian to attack him, who'd by then regained his feet and was rushing him again, but Otho saved him the trouble with a jujitsu blow to the native's lower back. As the aresian collapsed, Otho ducked a haymaker thrown by another patron, then delivered a sidekick that sent him flying against a nearby billiards table. A pool cue clattered to the floor; Otho snatched it up and, holding it sideways with both hands, assumed a staff-fighting pose even as other opponents threw themselves at him.

Hearing a scream, Curt looked around to see Joan locked in combat with N'Rala. The aresian woman had grabbed a handful of Joan's hair and was using it to wrench her head back, but Joan threw a fist straight into the other woman's face. With a harsh curse, N'Rala let her go and staggered backward, eyes blazing as she clutched her mouth with her hands. Another aresian took up the attack, but N'Rala instead shoved a couple of people aside and, placing her hands on the bar, made an agile leap over the counter, pushing the bartender out of her way.

Curt had no time to wonder what she was doing. He, Otho, and Joan were holding their own, but the entire bar was against them; for every person they knocked down, two or three were ready to take their place. Joan had been wrong, and so was Otho. N'Rala had never intended to lure them out of the bar and into a trap; the trap was here, in this very room. And while it was evident that Joan was as well trained in hand-to-hand combat as he was, and Otho was nearly tireless in a fight, the numbers were against them.

He'd barely realized this when he heard an enraged roar, and turned to see the huge jovian bouncer rushing at him from the front of the room. The crowd parted for the jovian, and Curt waited until the giant was close enough before jumping on top of the nearest table. The bouncer had no time to react before Curt grabbed a ceiling lamp with both hands and used it to swing himself feet-first at his foe.

His heels caught the jovian within his dense black beard. The bouncer's chin snapped back as he lost his balance and fell, but he wasn't out of it yet. Curt let go of the lamp and landed neatly on the floor before him, and was about to take on the behemoth before he could fully recover when an agonizing pulse swept through his entire body.

His nerves on fire, every muscle paralyzed, Curt gasped as he collapsed to the floor. All around, everyone else was doing the same. In a moment of clarity, Curt realized what N'Rala was doing when she went over the bar: she'd been going for the ceiling stunners.

Then cold darkness closed upon him.

VIII

Consciousness returned to him as a slow awakening to intermittent flashes of light and a gentle but persistent swaying.

His body ached and the inside of his skull throbbed with a headache that seemed to reach all the way to his eyes. The air he breathed still had the faint chemical aftertaste of a rebreather, though, and when he exhaled there was the familiar sensation of being inhibited by an airmask. Whatever else may have happened, at least he knew he was still on Mars.

Curt slowly opened his eyes. The light flashes were coming from luminescent panels rigged in sections along a rock ceiling; the motion he felt was from the vehicle he was in passing beneath them. He was being carried down a tunnel, apparently a long one at that.

He tried to move and discovered that his wrists had been tied together behind his back. His legs hadn't been similarly secured, though, so he was able to push his heels against the padded cushion upon which he lay and sit up a little. He discovered that he lay across the backseat of a small, open-top rover, the sort of utility vehicle used on farms and construction sites. And, yes, it appeared to be traveling down a lava tube; it was safe to presume it was the same one he'd spotted earlier at the bottom of the Ascraeus tolou.

Two aresians were sitting up front: one of the men he'd fought in the bar, who was driving the vehicle, and N'Rala. Neither appeared to have noticed that Curt had regained consciousness; they gazed straight ahead, not glancing behind them. Curt decided to play possum for a little while longer, if only to give himself a chance to get his bearings.

The lava tube looked like the inside of an immense blood vessel, an artery deep beneath the rocky Martian skin. But it was not empty. Along the sides of the central passageway, boxes, cartons, and containers of all sizes had been carefully stacked. White labels identified their contents, but the rover was moving too fast for him to read any of them. It was obvious, though, that someone considered them worth guarding. Every once in a while, the vehicle passed an aresian standing watch amid the stacks, a particle-beam rifle cradled in his or her arms.

Curt raised his head in an effort to identify one of the boxes. When he did, there was a sharp beep from somewhere close behind. Too late, he realized that his rover was being followed by another. Its driver had seen him move and was alerting the people in the front seats that their passenger was awake.

N'Rala looked around, then smiled a little when she saw him. "Oh good, you're awake. How are you feeling?"

He decided not to tell her. "Where are we?" he asked, even though he'd already figured it out.

"About halfway to where we're going. Don't worry, this is the longest part of the trip." She gave him a concerned look. "Come on, Captain . . . your head must be hurting. Stunners will do that to you. Your people have used them enough on mine for me to know how painful a good shot can be, and you caught one at point-blank range. I have some painkillers on me . . . all you have to do is ask."

Curt hesitated, then nodded. There was no point in suffering if he didn't have to, and he'd need a clear head if he was going to attempt to escape and rescue the others. And come to think of it . . . "Where are my friends?"

"Behind us, in the other rover." N'Rala pulled aside her cape to reach for a pouch on her belt. "They're probably waking up right about now," she went on as she opened a flap and dug into the pouch; her hand came out a second later with an analgesic patch. "Don't worry, they haven't been harmed. Probably just sore the same way you are."

"I don't know why you're bothering." The driver eyed the patch as N'Rala tore open its foil envelope. "The master will—"

"There's no reason to let a prisoner suffer unnecessarily. We're not barbarians." N'Rala unpeeled the patch back, then turned in her seat toward Curt. "Please hold still. My companion is armed, and I'm sure he wouldn't appreciate any stupid moves on your part any more than I would."

There was little Curt could have done even if he weren't surrounded by armed aresians, so he turned his head and let her fix the patch to the side of his neck. There was a cool rush as the drugs entered his bloodstream, and almost immediately the headache and body soreness began to subside. "Thanks. You're very kind."

"And you're very handsome." N'Rala favored him with a coy smile as she settled back in her seat. "So sad that we can't be friends . . . but maybe that can change."

"Maybe." Curt shrugged noncommittally. "So where are you taking us?"

"You'll see, Captain." She turned away. "You'll see."

This was the second time she'd called him that. She knew his real name; why was she doing this, other than to show that she was aware that Captain Future was his nom de guerre? He wondered how she'd learned that until he then remembered again that his private meeting with President Carthew in Corvo's home hadn't been quite so private after all. So if she was in league with Ul Quorn, this was more proof that there was a link between the Magician and Corvo.

Curt just had to hope that he'd live long enough to use that knowledge.

Because Curt had no idea how long he'd been unconscious, he also had no idea how far he'd already traveled. Nonetheless, the rovers continued onward for what seemed like a couple of more miles. They left most of the crates and boxes behind, and after a while even the light panels became intermittent; the driver turned on his headlights, as did the rover behind them. Looking back, Curt caught a glimpse of Otho and Joan in the rear rover. They were both awake and sitting up, but he had no way of communicating with them. Although his ring contained its own Anni node, the neural implants they wore were dependent upon external nodes; this far underground, there was no way for them to link with one. Curt also had little doubt that their arms were probably bound just as his were, so getting free was out of the question.

All they could do was wait until they reached their final destination. As N'Rala promised, it wasn't long before they did just that.

IX

The tunnel gradually began to rise, its floor sloping upward toward some unseen point. There were no ceiling panels now, only a pair of battery lamps affixed to the walls some distance ahead. The lava tube abruptly came to an end just in front of those torches, where an accordion gate had been rigged across the tunnel. Nothing could be seen beyond this point except darkness.

The rovers slowed to a halt in front of the gate. The driver climbed out, picked up a rifle from where it had been lying on the floorboards between his feet, and turned to point it at Curt. N'Rala got out and offered Curt an outstretched hand.

"Be good," she said. "I won't hurt you, but my friends will if you misbehave."

Curt ignored her as he squirmed out of the backseat. The headache was gone, and the only pain he felt now was that of humiliation. The driver and guard in the other rover helped Otho and Joan get out; they led them over to where Curt and N'Rala were standing. Curt gave his companions a silent nod. Otho responded in kind, but Joan was busy studying their surroundings.

"What is this place?" she demanded. "Where have you taken us?" Then she walked closer to the gate, saw what was on the other side, and gasped as she instinctively shrank back in fear. Wondering what she'd just seen, Curt stepped past her. No one tried to stop him as he approached the gate. There was no need to do so, for on the side was . . . nothing.

The lamps revealed an open, vertical shaft, so wide that their rays barely reached the far walls, so deep that it appeared to be bottomless. Curt peered upward; it was difficult to tell for certain how high the shaft was, but it seemed to rise thousands of feet. So far as he could tell, there was no ceiling; the shaft was a red chimney, rising to an opening far above.

"Do you know where we are?" N'Rala had come up beside him.

There was only one possible explanation. "We're inside Mons Ascraeus," Curt replied, awestruck by what lay before him.

"Very good." She nodded in approval. "Yes, we're deep within the volcano. Many millions of years ago, while Ascraeus was still active, lava tubes were formed during its eruptions, and they in turn were connected to the central vent. The volcano is extinct, of course, but its tubes and vents remain as sort of an underground tunnel network." She pointed to the shaft yawning before them. "This leads through the planet's crust to the mantle . . . perhaps even to the core."

"It could be interesting to find out." The fledgling scientist in Curt was intrigued. "Perhaps a probe or a drone—"

"Some have already discovered what's down there," N'Rala said quietly. "But they'll never report back."

One of the aresians laughed when she said this. Joan gaped at him, the fear evident on her face. Otho glared at N'Rala. "Is that why you've brought us here? To see how your boss makes his enemies disappear?" He made a flatulent sound with his lips. "Some magician. Kind of a charlatan, if you ask me."

Another aresian grabbed his wrists and yanked them upward, twisting Otho's arms just enough to make him wince. "Careful how you speak of Ul Quorn!" he hissed, pushing his face next to Otho's. "The Sons of the Two Moons have little tolerance for those who disrespect our leader."

"Yeah, okay, okay," Otho muttered. "Ul Quorn . . . nicest guy on Mars. Real peach of a fella."

"Your fate is something only you can decide," N'Rala said. "Your actions in the next few minutes will decide whether you'll see this place again. Choose them wisely."

Curt chose not to respond. A couple of minutes passed, then a new sound entered the volcano shaft: the roar of jet engines, as if something was coming down from above. Peering upward through the gate, Curt spotted a dark object outlined by small running lights arrayed about its circular rim. As it came closer, the object resolved itself into an air raft, the kind often used to clean the windows of high-rise buildings on Earth, piloted by a single individual at its control pedestal and kept aloft by rotary jets.

The pilot brought the raft to hover beside the entrance to the lava tube. One of the aresians unlatched the gate and pushed both sides open, then the pilot nudged the raft close enough to the ledge for those waiting for it to come aboard. The aresian who'd opened the gate stepped onto the raft, then helped N'Rala, her driver, and their three prisoners aboard. He then stepped back off the raft into the tunnel, and was already closing the gate as the raft began its ascent back the way it had come.

The trip up the shaft was gradual and easy, with barely any vibration. Curt was mildly surprised to find that he was able to stay on his feet. He thought briefly about attempting to overcome N'Rala and the two Sons of the Two Moons but decided against it. His hands were tied, as were Otho's and Joan's. Even if they overcame N'Rala and her driver, all the raft pilot would have to do was roll the craft just a few degrees port or starboard to cause everyone aboard to lose their balance. And falling off the raft would be a hideous way to die. It would take a very long time for someone to reach whatever lay at the bottom of the vent, and they'd be conscious all the way down.

Glancing up, Curt saw something new: a dark purple sky, tinged pink and gleaming with starlight. They'd nearly reached the top of the volcano; above them lay the Martian surface, touched by the first light of day.

He'd just realized this when the raft cleared the vent. As the vehicle veered to the right, Curt saw that they were on a broad plain encompassed on all sides by a circle of ragged peaks and hills. This was the caldera of Mons Ascraeus: an immense, irregularly formed rock bowl at the volcano's summit. Where there had once been a lake of molten lava was now a bare, flat expanse so large that the northern wall disappeared over the horizon while the southern cliffs loomed above them like an immense wall.

Next to the pit from which they'd emerged was a settlement.

Tents and open-sided tarps had been set up in a wide semicircle, an inflated airdome at one end. A radio mast stood nearby, and tripod-mounted floodlights were positioned within the row of tents, their beams focused upon a large space where it seemed as if work was being done to excavate something from the rocky ground. As strange as it may seem, it appeared as if an archaeological dig was taking place here, in a place where no ancient civilization had ever flourished, where no man had even set foot until modern times.

The raft set down on a landing pad behind the tents where a small, broad-winged aircraft was already parked. While the driver stood guard, the pilot helped N'Rala assist Curt, Joan, and Otho down from the platform. Then, without a word, the two aresians marched Joan and Otho away, while N'Rala and an aresian who'd been waiting for them took custody of Curt.

"Where are they taking them?" Curt asked, although he'd already noticed that Otho and Joan were being led toward the airdome.

"Somewhere they'll be comfortable," N'Rala said. "They must be hungry. After all, you haven't eaten since last night, and we've been traveling ever since then. So they'll get a meal, too, if they'll accept it."

Curt eyed the aresian who was covering him with a rifle. "Is that where we're going? Breakfast?"

"Not quite yet. Someone would like to meet you first." She started to gently take hold of one of his bound arms, then shook her head in dismay. "He's not going to need to be restrained anymore," she said to the guard. "Release him."

The guard didn't argue, but instead withdrew a large knife from a scabbard beneath his robe. Handing his rifle to N'Rala, he used the serrated blade to saw through the cords binding Curt's wrists. Curt could see why N'Rala was so confident that he would cause them no trouble if he were cut loose. The sound of the returning raft had awakened the camp; as they walked past the tents, dozens of aresians were stepping out to see them. Most were armed.

As they walked through the camp, Curt thrust his hands inside the pockets of his parka. A casual gesture, perfectly normal considering that he wasn't wearing gloves and the early-morning air within the volcano summit was as frigid as it was thin, but it also hid what he was doing with his left hand: twisting the ring about until its crown was inside his palm, then tapping against it with his thumb.

Curt had taken note of the radio mast as soon as the raft had touched down. That meant there was a transmitter somewhere in the camp. If there was, then his ring's Anni node should be able to access it. It was still possible that normal Anni transmissions might be jammed, though, so now he was using an old, seldom-used code to send a brief, silent message . . . and hope that it got through.

He, N'Rala, and the guard reached the largest tent, the one at the opposite end of the semicircle from the airdome where Otho and Joan had been taken. The guard unzipped its fabric door and walked in. A couple of moments passed, then he reappeared and motioned for N'Rala to bring Curt in.

The tent was spacious and warm, with embroidered rugs laid across its floor and tapestries suspended from the walls. Shaded lanterns hung from the ceiling beams; they revealed a tall, robed figure seated in an armchair at the other end of the room. As N'Rala led Curt into the tent, the figure rose from his seat.

"Good morning, *Señor* Newton . . . or should I say, Captain Future?" Smiling, the man before him spoke without a trace of condescension. "Allow me to introduce myself. I am Ul Quorn."

PART SIX
Fire on the Mountain

1

The being who stood before Curt was nearly his own height, making him a little shorter than the average aresian. His skin was darker, too, lacking the distinct reddish hue of a Mars native. His hair was very long and as ivory white as that of an aphrodite, swept straight back from a high forehead and braided down his neck and past his shoulders. Dark eyes blazed within the deep sockets of a face lean and fine-boned, resembling a bas-relief sculpted from dark brown porcelain by a skilled artist.

It was apparent that Ul Quorn was multiracial, a synthesis of terran, aresian, and aphrodite bloodlines. Yet it was his face that caught Curt's attention. Somehow, he felt as if he'd seen it before, even though he knew this couldn't be. The man was a stranger, and yet he was oddly familiar. And while it was also clear that Ul Quorn was perhaps as young as Curt himself, there was something about him that seemed aged, as if his body was a vessel for an old and corrupt soul.

"The Magician of Mars, I presume." It was the best Curt could manage at the moment. "I've heard much about you."

"Really?" Ul Quorn arched a whisker-thin eyebrow. "I'm flattered my reputation extends all the way to the Moon. Time was when no one beyond the Tharsis Ridge knew that name." He gazed past Curt at N'Rala. "Appears I've become famous. Or infamous, at least."

"Is that all you have to say to me?" she asked.

"Oh, no, of course not." Ul Quorn extended an arm, and N'Rala crossed the room to let him drape it around her shoulders. "Thank you, m'lady," he said as he pulled her close for a kiss on the cheek. "You've done well to bring him here, and unharmed as well."

"I've also brought his companions. The IPF officer and the albino." She had to lean over a little for the buss; she was taller than her . . . master? Lover? Both? "I know you said they are expendable, but—"

"Only if it was unavoidable, and I'm glad you didn't. Having an IPF officer in custody may be useful, and as for the other fellow . . ." He smiled as he let her go, and gave Curt what was obviously intended to be a meaningful look. "Well, he's more than merely an albino, isn't he? I know someone who's going to be interested in meeting him."

"Why be coy?" Curt tried to appear more relaxed than he actually was. "It's Senator Corvo you're talking about—Victor Corvo, who murdered my parents. Your silent partner in . . . well, whatever it is you're trying to do."

Still smiling, Ul Quorn slowly nodded. "Very good. You've made that association. Yes, the senator and I are partners, although our relationship is a bit more"—he shared a glance with N'Rala—"complicated than that."

N'Rala laughed softly as she stepped away from Ul Quorn and headed for an antique Earth-made sideboard upon which a crystal decanter of dark wine rested. Ul Quorn gestured to the glass she was pouring and cocked an eye, asking Curt a silent question. Curt shook his head and he went on. "Actually, you and I have something in common so far as the honorable senator is concerned. He killed your father and mother . . . and he's also the man who helped my mother conceive me."

Curt stared at him. "Corvo is your father?"

Ul Quorn gravely nodded. "He is, indeed."

Curt did his best to hide his emotions, but nothing Ul Quorn could have said would have surprised him more. Now he realized why Ul Quorn seemed familiar. In his face, he saw Victor Corvo. There weren't many offspring of Earth and Mars inhabitants, let alone those who'd intermarried with Venus natives as well. The three races were genetically compatible, of course, but social and cultural differences made such pairings uncommon. At once, he knew why Corvo had never claimed to have either wife or child. For a politician, this might have been too politically risky to reveal to voters, many of whom might harbor secret prejudices about mixed marriages.

"I take it he never wanted anyone to know that he'd fathered a child with someone from Mars," Curt said.

"If it had only been that simple. If he'd just slept with an aresian, that might have been tolerable. But that he'd had an affair with a half-Martian, half-Venusian woman and knocked her up?" Ul Quorn shook his head, an angry scowl on his face. "Oh no . . . very bad for business. Especially since, even then, he was harboring certain political ambitions. So I was born not very long after you were, and while he was here making sure that my mother and I would be . . . taken care of, your parents and Simon Wright went into hiding on the Moon. You know the rest."

"Only so much as I'm concerned. But I think I can make a good guess."

"Oh, by all means, do so." Ul Quorn accepted a glass of wine from N'Rala and strolled back to his chair, the hem of his robe brushing softly against the carpeted floor. "In fact, let's make a little game of it. You make your guesses, and if you're right, I'll tell you everything you don't know. And believe me, there's quite a lot."

N'Rala cast him a sharp look. "Are you sure you want to do that?"

"Indulge me." Ul Quorn silenced her with a casual wave of his hand. "I'm bored."

"And if I guess wrong?" Curt asked.

"Well, I'll probably tell you anyway . . . but then you won't get the special prize that's waiting for you if you succeed." The Magician of Mars languorously stretched out his legs and crossed his feet as he nestled the wineglass in his hands. "So, please. Let's find out just how smart Captain Future really is."

He was trying to needle him by using that name. Somehow, he'd figured out that it was something he wasn't quite comfortable wearing. Curt swallowed his irritation and folded his arms together. From the corner of his eye, he could see the aresian who'd escorted him and N'Rala from the landing pad shift. He was still holding a gun on him, but perhaps if he became just a little careless . . .

"So there's the two of you, secretly working with each other," Curt began. "Victor Corvo, former venture capital entrepreneur who killed my parents because they wouldn't go along with his plans for creating an android slave race." He paused to look over at N'Rala. "That's my friend Otho, if you didn't know that before." Her eyes widened, telling him that she didn't, and he returned his attention to Ul Quorn. "And when that didn't pan out the way he'd hoped, he went into politics and eventually became the senator for the Lunar Republic."

"Not bad." Ul Quorn's expression was unreadable. "Go on."

"He never became completely legit, though, and he still had big plans, so once you reached a certain age, he came to you and brought you in as his quiet partner—Ul Quorn, the Magician of Mars, leader of the Sons of the Two Moons." Curt paused. "But the Sons have never been more than a front for what remained of Starry Messenger, have they? They're not actually worshipping the Denebians. They're just cover for what you're really doing."

An angry hiss from the aresian guard. He took a step toward Curt, but stopped himself when Ul Quorn held up a hand. "There, my dear captain, you're not entirely correct. Quite a few members of the Sons do indeed believe in the Old Ones." He nodded toward his guard. "I'd be careful what you say about the Denebians. It's a rather touchy subject for them."

"So that's why the senator sponsored the Straight Wall monument?" Curt forgot for the moment the game he was supposed to be playing. "He wanted to preserve the Dancing Denebians because they're worshipped by the Sons?"

"There's quite a bit more to it than that, but since you can't possibly know what it is, I'll let it pass, at least for now." Ul Quorn took a sip of wine. "Please, continue . . . oh, and N'Rala? Would you please invite our other guest to join us?"

She nodded and left, making sure that she didn't walk between Curt and the guard on her way out. Curt briefly considered taking advantage of her departure to attack Ul Quorn, but decided against it; the guard was much too alert for that. "I know you're behind the attempt on Carthew's life," he went on. "What I don't understand is why you want to do that. How would the president's death benefit you in any way?"

Ul Quorn didn't answer. He seemed to be awaiting N'Rala's return. When it appeared to be taking longer than he expected, he let out his breath as an annoyed sigh. "You've done very well, Captain Future—"

"Don't call me that." Curt was becoming irritated by the way Ul Quorn kept saying his name. His *other* name.

"—so I'm willing to cede the game even though you haven't completely guessed my motives. You've demonstrated what I'd hoped to find in you—an intelligent and resourceful man who might be an asset to my operations."

"Don't count on it."

"I'm not. However, you may change your mind once I show you what you've won."

Before Curt could answer, he heard the tent flap open behind him. As he began to turn, Ul Quorn rose from his chair. "Thank you for fetching our other guest, N'Rala," he said, a smile stretching across his face. "Captain, I believe you two have met before."

N'Rala and another Son of the Two Moons had entered the tent. Braced between them, wrists lashed together behind his back, was Victor Corvo.

Curt couldn't make out the senator's expression behind his airmask, but his eyes were infuriated. Ul Quorn glided toward them, arms outstretched in a grand gesture. "Curt Newton, I give you my father, Victor Corvo—the man who killed your parents."

11

The ensign posted outside *Vigilance*'s control room snapped to attention the moment he saw Ezra Gurney come up the companionway. Gurney paid no attention to the salute he was given, though, but instead marched straight into the cruiser's bridge.

"Where's the CO?" he demanded. The control room was a long, dark compartment built on two levels. The blue-white glow of comp screens and instrument panels provided most of the illumination, and his eyes hadn't yet adjusted to the gloom.

"Here, Marshal." A feminine voice spoke from the far end of the room. "Come this way, please."

Squinting a little, Ezra made his way down the narrow aisle between the duty stations, passing senior crew members seated at luminescent consoles on either side, until he finally reached *Vigilance*'s commanding officer. Captain Elizabeth Jane Henniker sat in a high-backed chair overlooking the pit where the helm and navigation officers were seated before a massive, wraparound viewscreen. There were no windows in this part of the vessel; the only thing on the screen was a virtual-periscope image of the underground hangar in which the ship presently lay.

"Thanks for the heads-up, E.J." Ezra didn't bother to salute even though it was officially expected. He and E.J.—not even her closest friends called her by her full name—were old acquaintances, and Ezra was very pleased when his superior, Halk Anders, managed to have the *Vigilance* placed at his disposal. E.J. was nearly the same age, an attractive woman in late middle-age; she'd been commanding Solar Guard cruisers for half her career, and would probably become fleet admiral one day. "What's happening?"

Without looking away from him, E.J. called down into the pit, "Mr. Sturdivent, throw us the view you caught just a few minutes ago."

The navigator tapped his fingers against his console, and a window opened in the center of the main screen: the outside surface of Port Deimos, from an angle adjacent to the docking silos reserved for small private vessels. One of the silos was open, and hovering above it was a familiar teardrop-shaped spacecraft: the *Comet,* apparently having just left port.

"Son of a—" Ezra bit off the rest. He'd asked E.J. to have her crew place the *Comet* under round-the-clock watch, just to make sure nothing like this happened without his knowledge. "When did it take off?"

"Not five minutes ago. I called you as soon as I found out, and Deimos Traffic notified me the second it was cleared for departure." E.J. looked down into the pit again. "Status, Mr. Sturdivent?"

"It's moving away from port but still in visual range, ma'am. Distance twenty-six kilometers, on course for Mars."

"Dammit!" Ezra clenched his fists. "Gimme a line to it!"

The captain swiveled about in her seat and calmly asked her communications officer to hail the *Comet.* A few moments passed, then the com officer reported that he'd made contact with the other ship. Ezra angrily snatched the headset the officer offered him; he didn't put it on, but instead held it to his face.

"*Comet,* this is Marshal Gurney." He was through trying to make friends with that freak show; time to remind them who was in charge here. "Where are you going and what are your intentions?"

Almost immediately, Simon Wright's voice came through his headset. "*Marshal Gurney, please forgive the abrupt departure. We received a signal from Curt—Captain Future—just a little while ago after losing contact with him for several hours, and we have reason to believe that he and his companions are in considerable danger.*"

At once, Ezra's attitude changed. He might care less about this so-called Captain Future, but Joan was with him and that made matters different. "Talk to me. What did he tell you?"

"*He wasn't able to say much. The signal I received was in Morse code—*"

"What code?"

"*A system of dots and dashes designating individual letters of the alphabet. It's rarely used anymore, but I taught it to Curt for when an Anni node isn't available. Apparently he has managed to piggyback his message to the carrier wave of a high-frequency radio transmitter at his location. It's a rather cumbersome means of communication, though, so it can't carry a lot of information.*"

The com officer caught Ezra's eye, nodded agreement. Apparently what the Brain had said was credible enough for him to vouch for it. "All right, go on," Ezra said. "What did his message say?"

"*He said, 'Captured by uq at tolou now in a mons summit need comet stop.'*"

It took Ezra a moment to figure out what all that meant. He'd already known that Joan was on her way to the Ascraeus tolou in an effort to track down Ul Quorn. Apparently she and the others had been captured there by his people, and for some reason they'd been taken to the summit of the nearby volcano. "So you're coming to the rescue?"

"*The* Comet *is on the way, yes. I'm going to move the ship into equatorial orbit above the Tharsis Ridge and stand by for further orders.*"

E.J. prodded her headset. "*Comet*, this is *Vigilance* actual. Do you need assistance?"

Another pause, a little longer now. "*Affirmative*, Vigilance," the Brain responded. "*I recommend that you launch and bring your ship into the same orbit as the* Comet. *If and when Captain Future sends another signal, I'll inform you at once.*"

"Understood, *Comet*. We'll take that under advisement. *Vigilance* out." E.J. clicked off and looked up at Ezra. "Your call. Do you trust 'em?"

Ezra thought it over a moment before reluctantly nodding his head. "So far, that boy hasn't told me anything untruthful. And as weird as he is, neither has Dr. Wright. Yeah, I think we oughta do as he says."

"I agree." E.J. swiveled about in her chair until she faced forward and tapped her headset again. "Attention, all stations. Prepare for launch. Repeat, prepare for immediate launch. Combat units, stand by for action. This is not a drill."

If anything, Corvo was even more nonplussed than Curt. "What the hell are you trying to prove?" he snarled, ignoring him for the moment as his furious glare locked on Ul Quorn. "Let me go!"

Curling a forefinger around his chin as he gazed up at the ceiling, Ul Quorn mockingly made a show of considering his demand. "Hmmm . . . no. No, my father, I think not. You have much to answer for, from both our friend *Señor* Newton and myself. And in both cases, it has to do with our respective mothers."

Even though an airmask covered the lower half of his face, Curt could tell that Corvo's expression had changed. "I have no idea what you're talking about," he said, anger subsiding to a plea for understanding. "I loved your mother. You know that. I—"

"*Liar!*"

The rage that surged forth from the Magician of Mars caught everyone by surprise. Even the aresian guards stepped back a little, while N'Rala stared at her lover in shock and Curt found himself stunned by the vehemence of Ul Quorn's response. Before Corvo could react, his son struck him across the face in a backhand blow that knocked his airmask askew and sent him sprawling across the floor.

"Don't think for a moment that I don't know what you did to my mother!" Ul Quorn yelled as his father crawled on his hands and knees, gasping for breath. "Her death was no accident! You had her killed as soon as I was born, so you wouldn't have the embarrassment of having the world know that you'd sired a child with a Martian whore! *You did this and I know it!*"

One of the Sons who'd escorted Corvo into the tent hauled the senator to his feet and held him upright while the other one put his airmask back in place. As they did, Ul Quorn recovered some of his earlier poise. Taking a deep breath, he turned to Curt. "My father—you have no idea how much I hate calling him that—my *dear* father took me from my mother's arms and brought me to the tolou you visited yesterday, where I was placed in the care of N'Rala's family."

N'Rala nodded. "He told my parents that my master's mother perished in a sandstorm," she said to Curt, "but they suspected even then that this wasn't true. No aresian woman would ever allow herself to be caught out in the open during a sirocco. It took many years, but eventually my people learned what had actually happened." She gave Corvo a significant look. "One of your people talked. The Sons can be quite persuasive."

"He didn't want my mother," Ul Quorn continued, "but nonetheless he desired to have a son as heir apparent, so he reached out to me again some years ago and brought me into the criminal enterprise he'd built. By then he'd established himself as a respectable politician, and he needed someone to run the shadier side of his operations. Someone loyal who'd nonetheless keep his distance."

"I see," Curt said. "There's Victor Corvo, senator of the Lunar Republic and one of the most powerful men in the Coalition government . . . and then there's Ul Quorn, the Magician of Mars, underworld figure and leader of the Sons of the Two Moons. And because no one knows that they're father and son, each are able to support the other and therefore collaborate with inpunity."

"Correct. Very good." The smile with which Ul Quorn rewarded him, though, lasted only a moment. "But while he believed that I was doing his bidding, what he didn't know was that I was making plans of my own. N'Rala and her people needed a new leader, and they found it in me."

"A half-terran child?"

"A half-terran child who learned a secret no one else ever had. Starry Messenger may have been crushed by the Coalition, but the desire for an independent Mars has never died. It's always been there, like smoldering coals just waiting for something to reignite the blaze. And I found it."

"I helped you," Corvo said, in a wounded tone that was both accusative and pleading. "I helped you discover this, and this is how you repay me?"

Ul Quorn regarded him as a wise man would regard a fool. "You had no idea, did you? I think that's the best part . . . you didn't have a clue what I was up to. When you asked me to provide an assassin who'd take out President Carthew and open the way for you to take control of the Coalition government, you didn't know that same man was instructed to shoot you as well. And then, to make sure that he'd never tell anyone who was behind the killings, I planted yet another killer in your household who would then liquidate him. He let in the assassin, then it was his job to dispose of him before he could be captured and interrogated."

Corvo's mouth fell open. "You . . . you meant to kill me even then? How could you? You're my—"

"Please don't refer to me as your son. The very thought nauseates me." Ul Quorn turned to Curt again. "Unfortunately, you interfered with that part of my plans, which would have sent the Coalition government into disarray and thus given the Sons of the Two Moons an opportunity to stage a civil insurrection here on Mars."

Curt now understood what he'd seen in the lava tube beneath Ascraeus Mons: crates of guns and other weapons, smuggled to Mars and intended for an uprising. The nearby tolou was more than just a hotbed of anti-SolCol sentiment. It was the epicenter of a Martian revolution that Ul Quorn intended to lead.

"Sorry," he said dryly, shrugging a little. "Guess I messed up." Then he frowned. "But what's this you have going on outside? Why put a base camp up here, when you've got the tolou and lava tubes to hide in?"

"Something insane," Corvo muttered. "I've indulged him with this, but . . . Newton, you gotta believe me, he's out of his mind."

Ul Quorn ignored his father as he strolled past both him and Curt to the tent entrance. "Please, both of you, come this way," he said, letting one of his guards pull back the tent flap. "I have something wonderful to show you. And then, Curt Newton, I'll let you have your gift."

Curt nodded and followed him to the door. And as he did, he casually put his hands in the parka's pockets and began tapping at his ring again.

IV

Through the enormous underground hangar in which the *Vigilance* rested, men and machines hurried to prepare for liftoff.

Until the moment Captain Henniker made her announcement, the hangar had been filled with crewmen, ground techs, and robots performing the routine tasks that awaited an interplanetary vessel whenever it made port: loading fresh food and water, conducting an inventory of other supplies and restocking what was necessary, checking the hull for metal fatigue, inspecting the engines, making minor repairs, and so forth. All this activity came to an abrupt halt when the CO came over the speakers and told everyone to prepare for immediate liftoff. Now, as ramps were being withdrawn and service carts were driven out of the hangar, crewmen and 'bots disappeared through ports and hatches, which were then closed and sealed behind them.

Within minutes, the cruiser was ready for liftoff. While its main engines were warming up, the hangar was gradually decompressed, its air bled away until there was only hard vacuum in the vast chamber. Then, as red beacons along the rock walls silently rotated, the ceiling hatch parted at the centerline and opened outward. With a mute, fiery blast of its keel thrusters *Vigilance* slowly rose from its docking cradle.

In the control room, everything was quiet efficiency. The flight officers carried out their roles with a minimum of drama, murmuring to one another through their headsets, their hands darting across their consoles. The ship's artificial gravity generator hadn't yet been activated, so everyone was buckled into his or her chair. In the pit, the helm and navigation officers worked as a single unit, one piloting the ship while the other plotted its course.

Captain Henniker sat calmly in her chair, saying little as she watched the actions of her people. So intent was everyone on their respective jobs, they barely glanced at the immense screen before them, which now displayed the cratered surface of Deimos quickly falling away beneath them.

"Rig for field gravity," she said, and a moment later a horn blared three times, warning everyone aboard that the ship's internal gravitational field was about to be activated. A minute later, the crew felt themselves settling into their seats as weight returned.

From a small seat that had been folded down from the bulkhead near the command station, Ezra Gurney eyed a window that had been opened on the screen. It displayed a navigational plot depicting the respective positions of both the *Vigilance* and the *Comet*. The latter was farther away from Deimos and falling toward Mars. The smaller ship had a head start, but that would soon change; the patrol cruiser would be able to quickly catch up with the yacht and follow it wherever it was heading . . . presumably the summit caldera of Ascraeus Mons, the place were Curt's signal had originated.

At least, that's what everyone believed was happening.

"There's something wrong here," Ezra said.

At first, he didn't think E.J. heard him. She was focused on launch operations, making sure that *Vigilance* had safely left port. He must have gotten her attention, though, because she turned her head to peer at him.

"Pardon me?" she asked. "What do you mean?"

"This doesn't make sense, the *Comet* coming to the rescue." Ezra didn't look away from the plotting board. "E.J.—Cap'n, I mean—I've been aboard that ship. It ain't got armor and it ain't got guns. Hell, even the sidearms are gone. Newton, Joan, and Otho took everything they had with 'em. It's got just one hatch that they need a ladder to use when it sets down. And once it lands, it won't be able to take off again. It's a yacht, not a warship, meant for racing and nothing more."

"He's right, ma'am." This from Sturdivent, who had overheard the conversation from his station in the pit. "I've played around with racing vessels like that back home. They're pretty fast when they're out in space, but they're useless for landing anywhere but the Moon or Deimos. Their engines can't build sufficient thrust to achieve planetary escape velocity. So once that baby sets down on Mars, it's stuck there."

E.J. quietly pondered what he said, her fingers absently drumming the armrests of her seat. "And you say there's just two passengers aboard? The robot and the cyborg?"

"A 'bot, a drone with a brain inside, and a dog. That's it. Not exactly what I'd call a fighting force."

"You're right. They're poorly equipped for any sort of rescue mission, which is why we're coming with them."

"Yes, but E.J., they didn't *ask* for help. They launched without telling us, and it wasn't until you offered assistance that they agreed to it." Ezra jabbed a finger at the screen. "Wright ain't stupid. He's got something else in mind."

Captain Henniker was quiet for another moment, then turned to the com officer. "Hail the *Comet*," she said, and once the officer told her that he'd reestablished contact with the other ship, she prodded her headset. "*Comet*, this is *Vigilance* actual. Dr. Wright, would you please explain your intentions?"

A brief delay, then the Brain's voice came through. "Vigilance, *the* Comet *is on its way to Ascraeus Mons, where Captain Future had indicated that he and his party have been taken prisoner by Ul Quorn.*"

"I understand that," E.J. replied. "What I don't understand is what you're planning to do about this. Your ship is not equipped for either combat or rescue operations. It has no armaments or armor plating, and I've been reliably informed that it won't be able to safely lift off again once it's on the ground. So again . . . what are your intentions?"

No answer.

"*Comet*, this is *Vigilance*." E.J. leaned forward slightly in her seat. "Please respond."

Silence. Then the Brain's voice returned. "*Please continue on course,*

*Captain, and assume parking orbit above the northeast Tharsis Ridge.
Have your people prepare for possible ground assault. But don't do anything until I contact you again.* Comet *out."*

"Wright!" Ezra started to rise before he remembered that he was
buckled into his seat. "Wright, what in blue hell are you tryin' to—?"

"Captain!" Sturdivent snapped. "The *Comet* has disappeared!"

"*What?*" E.J. and Ezra both yelled at the same time.

"It's not there anymore, ma'am." He gestured helplessly at the long-
range telemetry displays. "It's vanished from radar. Same for visual
contact. I can't tell you how, but—"

"I know. It's gone." Ezra sighed and shook his head, then gave E.J.
an apologetic look. "Sorry, but there's one thing I forgot to tell you."

V

Ul Quorn escorted Curt toward the middle of the camp where he'd earlier caught a glimpse of ground excavations. By then, the sun had fully risen above the caldera walls; at this altitude, there was no morning haze as there was in the lowlands. Although Victor Corvo was still being led with his hands tied behind his back, no effort had been made to do the same to Curt. Were it not for the Sons walking alongside them, each with a gun trained on him, he might have been the honored guest Ul Quorn claimed him as.

Then he saw Otho and Joan approaching from the other direction, and he was reminded that they were all prisoners no matter how they were treated. Their bonds had been removed, but four armed Sons accompanied them from the pressurized dome where they'd been held. No one was taking chances with Captain Future and his companions.

Curt had little doubt that Ul Quorn intended to eliminate all four of them. There seemed to be little they could do about that; they were unarmed and outnumbered. The only chance they had was the ring on his left hand.

As he walked, Curt casually kept his hands in his parka pockets, using the concealment to laboriously tap out a new message in Morse code. He had no way of knowing whether it was getting through; all he could do was hope that the carrier-wave signal he'd secretly accessed from the nearby radio tower had sufficient strength to be picked up by the *Comet*.

He glanced up at the sky above the volcano's eastern walls, rapidly fading from deep purple to pink with the coming of the new day. If help was on the way, it would come from that direction. And when it arrived, he and the others would have to move *fast*.

A tarp had been set up above a folding table near the excavation. Otho and Joan got there a couple of seconds before Curt did. "How are you doing?" he asked quietly once he'd joined them. "Are they treating you well?"

"Actually, not too badly, " Otho replied. "We got a chance to take our masks off and rest a bit, and they even offered us some breakfast." He shrugged. "Could be worse, I suppose."

Joan gave a disgusted sigh. Curt couldn't see her expression through her mask, but apparently she was unimpressed by Ul Quorn's courtesy. "Don't expect lunch," she murmured. "And I doubt you'll get a souvenir to take with you."

"That's not entirely true." UI Quorn was smiling as he ducked to step beneath the tarp. Walking over to the table, he laid a hand on a small metal box. "I may be inclined to give you a small gift, too, just as I have one for Curt." Looking at Corvo, he added, "Something else we found wandering into camp uninvited."

Observing Corvo's presence, Otho raised a querying eyebrow. Curt didn't notice; he was surreptitiously studying their immediate surroundings. They weren't far from the gaping mouth of the volcanic vent through which they'd emerged a little while earlier, and the landing pad was about the same distance away in the opposite direction. Details worth remembering; they might make a difference in the next few minutes.

"I came to help you, son," Corvo growled, causing Joan to stare at him in amazement. "I knew these three were after you, and I was doing my best to stop them before—"

"Yes, yes, I know," Ul Quorn said impatiently. "It cost me the life of one of my best men, and that's just one more thing I owe you. But that's not what I wish to talk about, so would you kindly be quiet and let me speak?"

Turning his back to the table, he faced Curt. "Now, then . . . as I understand matters, the first time you took an interest in the senator, it was at the Straight Wall. So I take it that you're interested in the Denebian Petroglyphs?"

Puzzled, Curt nodded. "Yes, I am. I've been studying the carvings most of my life."

"Really? What a coincidence. So have I." A brief smile that faded just as quickly. "But then again, we seem to share a few things in common, don't we? We both had loved ones killed by the same man, we both were raised in hiding by a surrogate family, and now it seems we both grew up wondering who the Old Ones were and what they were doing here." Folding his arms across his chest, Ul Quorn cupped his chin in his right hand. "So tell . . . have you ever figured out the meaning of the Dancing Denebians?"

"No, I haven't. No one has."

"Wrong," the Magician of Mars said. "I have."

He picked up from the table a photo and held it up for Curt to see. It was a shot of the lunar carvings as taken from inside the new dome. "For years, the assumption that everyone's been working under is that the Dancing Denebians are petroglyphs in the same sense as those left by ancient cultures on Earth—that is, a hieroglyphic or pictorial form of language. But a few years ago, I began to ask a different question. What if it's not language the Dancing Denebians are supposed to represent, but rather something more universal—say, mathematics?"

"You think the carvings are numerical?"

"Why not?" Ul Quorn placed the photo back on the table. "We're pretty certain that Denebians passed through our solar system approximately a million years ago—the mid-Calabrian era of the Pleistocene, to be a little more specific. Mars was already biologically dead, having long since lost its atmosphere and surface water, but it was still exhibiting some geological activity, particularly deep beneath the Tharsis Ridge. In the meantime, on Earth, the glaciers had receded for a little while and humankind was in the last transitive stages between hominids and *Homo sapiens*. No longer beast, not entirely civilized either, but showing great potential nonetheless. That's what the visitors found when they came here."

"Why?" Despite himself, Curt was becoming drawn into the conversation. "Why did the Denebians come all this way?"

"Who knows? Perhaps they were explorers and their purposes were entirely scientific. Or maybe they were conquerors who'd discovered that this system was unsuitable for them. In any case, the Old Ones were here for only a short time. Before they left, though, they put in place a couple of markers meant to be found by the indigenous race they knew would eventually come along behind them—namely, us. And since they knew that we'd never learn their language, they decided instead to rely upon a common frame of reference."

"Math," Otho said.

"Why, yes, that's correct. Math." Ul Quorn seemed surprised that Otho would come up with the answer; apparently he underestimated the android's intelligence. "They decided to use numbers instead of letters or words as the means of communication with the descendants of the primitive species they'd observed on Earth. To accomplish this, the Denebians carved a series of bipedal figures resembling themselves, with ten major poses representing the digits of a base-ten numerical system. Next to each of these hieroglyphic representations are the actual figures of their numerical system."

"I think I see," Curt said. "We've been looking for a Rosetta stone that would enable us to interpret their message, not realizing that the message provided its own translation key."

"Precisely!" Ul Quorn folded his arms across his chest. "All those who preceded me in studying the lunar petroglyphs overlooked the obvious. The Old Ones had deliberately passed along a message meant to be read countless years later by those who'd never understand their native tongue, and therefore resorted to mathematics, not language, as the medium."

Whenever Ul Quorn referred to the Denebians as the Old Ones, Curt noticed that the Sons standing around them briefly lowered their eyes and touched their foreheads with their fingertips. Apparently it was a ritualistic gesture of respect. Worth remembering. He stole another glance at the sky, as if idly observing the morning sun. "So why leave the message on the Straight Wall? And what's the connection between there and here?"

"The Straight Wall should be obvious. It's a natural feature on the lunar surface visible from Earth. The Denebians correctly figured that once the human species evolved sufficiently to be able to venture out into space, one of the first places we'd inevitably visit was our planet's own satellite, and so we'd eventually explore one of its most prominent landforms. And since there's practically no erosion on the Moon, the Dancing Denebians would remain undisturbed for hundreds of thousands of millennia."

"And as for Mars . . . ?"

"Ah!" Ul Quorn raised a finger. "Now there's the *really* interesting part!"

He reached around behind him again to pick up a second sheet of paper lying on the table. Passing it to Curt, he quietly waited while Curt studied it.

The page was divided into three horizontal bars: Dancing Denebians on the top row, Denebian geometric figures in the middle, and Arabic numerals on the bottom. The last was divided into two sets that resembled . . .

"These are coordinates," Curt said, his voice little more than an awestruck whisper. "Latitude and longitude, just like we ourselves use."

"Yes, precisely!" Ul Quorn was both delighted and impressed. "And since the topmost image of the Straight Wall petroglyphs is a diagram of our solar system, with a line connecting Earth and Mars, it didn't take a lot of imagination to deduce that the coordinates were somewhere on Mars. All that remained was figuring the meridian and the degrees of separation, and the rest was easy."

Joan spoke up. "And the coordinates were for . . . ?"

"The very spot on which we now stand." Ul Quorn spread his arms apart to encompass the site. "The Old Ones wanted us to come to this place, a location they judged would experience the least amount of surface erosion over a long period of time: the caldera of an extinct volcano, nearly thirty thousand feet above the surrounding terrain. And here is where we found the final piece of the puzzle . . . the Denebian main base in our solar system. "

"A Denebian settlement here?" Otho asked. "In a volcano?"

Ul Quorn gave him a patronizing look. "Oh, come now . . . don't be so thick. Scientists have been searching Mars for alien artifacts for years, trying to find another trace of the Old Ones." He looked at Corvo, who stood silently glaring at him. "For this, at least, I'm grateful to you, my father. In return for my running your criminal enterprises while you sought public legitimacy, you honored my request by funding archaeological studies of the Straight Wall and establishing the site as a protected reserve. What you didn't know was that this wasn't merely a whim. Behind the scenes, I secretly directed the work being done there by Dr. Winters and Dr. Norton. They didn't know it, but they were working for me the entire time."

"Your gratitude is overwhelming." Corvo wasn't amused.

"Nothing you've done will ever atone for my mother's death. Try to remember that." Ul Quorn turned to Curt again. "It's my belief that the other reason why the Denebians established a base here was that Ascraeus Mons wasn't entirely extinct, that there was still some geothermal activity occurring deep beneath the planetary crust. The Old Ones were able to tap into this energy for their own purpose, which was . . . well, perhaps it's best if I showed you."

He reached over to the small box that lay on the table and carried it over to them. "At every archaeological site, there's always an unexpected discovery, an object that no one thought they'd find." He held the box out to Curt, Otho, and Joan and slowly lifted the cover. "Here's what we found."

Nestled within the box was a soft, almost rubbery object, off-white and oval in shape, about sixteen inches in length. At first glance it appeared to be an oversize larva, and indeed, as Ul Quorn opened the lid, a shudder ran down its segmented flanks. The Magician gently pulled it out of the box and it made a quiet, almost contented sound— "*Oooog*"—as it wrapped itself around his hands, and now they could see that it had six small pseudopods for legs and a pair of small, black eyes above a puckered round mouth.

"What is it?" Otho asked as Joan shrank back in revulsion.

"That is a very good question. Like to hold it?" Ul Quorn offered it to him. Otho hesitated for a moment, then carefully took it from his hands. "We found it wandering around camp shortly after we arrived, and while it's obviously not an indigenous life form, we're not certain what purpose it may have served for the Denebians. Perhaps it was a pet who was left behind." He smiled. "We call it Oog, for the only sound it seems to be able to make."

"A pet?" Otho was incredulous. Oog was warm and soft, and seemed to be making itself at home in his hands. "But if the Denebians left it behind, that would mean that it's . . ."

His voice trailed off in astonishment. "Nearly a million years old," Ul Quorn finished. "It seems to be a bit like yourself, neither completely organic nor completely mechanical, and appears to subsist on nothing except sunlight and the Martian regolith. Oh, and it has an interesting talent. Close your eyes and concentrate on thinking of something about its same size and mass."

Wondering what this was about, Otho did as Ul Quorn asked. A few seconds passed, then he felt Oog begin to shift about in his hands. Joan cried out in astonishment, and that caused him to open his eyes again . . . to find himself holding not the amorphous creature he'd previously had in his grasp, but rather Grag's moonpup Eek.

"I'll be damned," he murmured. "Did it just do what I think it did?"

"Yes, it did. It read your mind and changed shape to match whatever you'd imagined." Ul Quorn seemed amused. "You adopted my father's gift to the president, I take it. Just as well. I always thought it was a stupid idea."

Otho didn't reply, but instead gently stroked the mimic. It gazed at him in the same loving way Eek did with Grag, and even its fur felt real. Joan overcame her disgust to come closer and pet Oog as well.

Forgotten for the moment, Curt quietly stood off to the side. No one noticed that his hands were back in his pockets, or that his gaze had briefly returned to the sky again.

VI

"Captain, the *Comet* is entering the atmosphere."

Ezra wondered how Mr. Sturdivent could tell. Then the navigator opened a window on the main screen, and within it appeared a telescopic view of Mars as seen from low orbit. A fireball was beginning to form in the upper atmosphere, leaving behind a thin white tail that grew longer with each passing second.

The *Comet* itself couldn't be seen, but the plasma shell created by its passage revealed its whereabouts. Ezra smiled at the irony. The little teardrop-shaped craft had truly come to resemble a comet.

"Position?" E.J. asked.

"Altitude 32.4 kilometers, 10 degrees north by 85.6 west, bearing 5.2 degrees west by northwest. It's coming in over the Lunae Planum just north of the Valles Marineris and making a beeline for Ascraeus Mons." Sturdivent looked up and over his shoulder at her. "We're maintaining line-of-sight contact with her, ma'am. Orders?"

Captain Henniker didn't respond at once. Absently rubbing a forefinger against her lips, she swiveled her chair about to look at Gurney. "How about it, Ezra?" she asked. "What do you think they're up to?"

"I'm not sure," he said slowly. "Maybe they expect us to send down an assault team after them, but if that's the case, why land the *Comet* at all? It'll never get off the—"

He was interrupted by a commotion at the control room door. From the direction of the corridor, he heard a voice: "Hey, stop . . . *stop!* You can't come in here without—!"

Then a dog barked, immediately followed by the sound of padded feet running across the deck. Ezra barely had time to recognize the noises for what they were when a small brown-and-white form dashed out of the semidarkness and vaulted into his lap.

Startled, Ezra nearly dropped the dog to the floor, but the little mutt had already wrapped its forepaws around his neck and was slopping his mustache with wet, happy doggie kisses.

"Eek?" The marshal couldn't have been more astonished. "What are you doing here?"

There was no answer, of course, but in the same instant that Ezra realized what the moonpup's presence implied, he heard another sound: heavy, stamping footfalls, followed an instant later by the purr of rotary impellors.

He looked around and saw Grag and the Brain walking through the control room, followed by the ensign who'd failed to stop them at the door. The bridge personnel stopped what they were doing to watch. "You," Ezra muttered, swatting Eek from his lap as he rose from his seat. "How the hell did you—?"

"Ezra, what are these things?" E.J. also stood up. More angry than confused, she was plainly outraged by the intrusion. "Is this Newton's crew?"

"Captain Henniker, I cannot help but be offended." The Brain floated to within a few feet of her, his eyestalks moving until they were level with her face. "I may no longer have a human form, but appearances notwithstanding, I still consider myself a human being. As for my companion, he is much more than the mere automaton he appears to be. Therefore, we are not *things*."

"Hello, Captain." Grag stopped beside the Brain and raised its right hand. "I'm Grag, companion to Curt Newton, sometimes also known as Captain Future. It is a pleasure to meet you." Eek was running in circles around the robot's legs, yapping excitedly, and Grag turned its large red eyes toward the little dog. "Be quiet, Eek," it said quietly. "Sit."

Obediently, Eek squatted on his hind legs beside Grag, his tongue lolling from his mouth. Apparently the 'bot had been spending quite a bit of time lately training its new pet. Ezra was in no mood to compliment him, though. "Captain, this is Simon Wright and . . . um, Grag, as it prefers to be known. And, yes, they're the crew of the *Comet*"—he glanced at them again—"although it's now obvious they're not aboard their ship."

"Please forgive the unauthorized intrusion, ma'am." The Brain continued to float before her, but his eyestalks twisted away to inspect the forward wallscreen. "Grag and I disembarked from our vessel shortly before it launched. We then proceeded through service tunnels to your ship's hangars, where we posed as maintenance 'bots in order to stow away. We've been in the cargo hold until just a few minutes ago, waiting until the proper moment to reveal ourselves."

"The proper—?" E.J. stared at him. "You still haven't told me why you're here. You're supposed to be aboard the *Comet* . . . that's where you said you were!"

"No, ma'am, that's not true. I said that the *Comet* had launched and was on its way down to Mars, but I didn't explicitly state that either Grag or I was aboard."

"Then if you're not on the *Comet*," Ezra asked, "who's flying the ship?"

"I am," the Brain replied. "Even as we speak, I'm using *Vigilance*'s telemetry to interface directly with the *Comet*'s command and control network. This is one of the reasons why I asked you to launch this vessel and follow us. So long as the *Vigilance* remains within communications range of the *Comet*, I can operate the ship just as if it was on a fly-by-wire system . . . my presence aboard isn't necessary." He paused. "Or desirable, as the case may be."

"What do you mean by that?"

"Marshal Gurney, as you may have surmised by now, the *Comet* is unsuitable for a rescue effort. It has no armaments, nor can it lift off from the Martian surface and achieve escape velocity."

"We can send in an assault force," E.J. said. "After all, that's what you requested."

"Yes, but not for the camp Curt has located in the Ascraeus Mons caldera. I believe he wants you to send troops to the tolou instead, to shut down the Starry Messenger stronghold he, Otho, and Joan have discovered. An attack on the volcano, though, would be futile. Ul Quorn has them prisoner, and would probably execute them the instant he saw a Solar Guard or IPF craft."

"Then the *Comet*? What's it doing?"

"The one thing it *can* do—crash into the camp where they have been taken prisoner and destroy it entirely. I've just received another Morse code signal from Curt, confirming that those are his instructions."

Ezra stared at the Brain. He knew what he wanted to say, but suddenly found that he was unable to speak; it was as if his throat had closed up. Yet E.J. seemed to know what he was thinking, for she voiced the thoughts he was unable to express. "You know, of course, what that means. Everyone down there will be killed."

"I'm aware of that," Simon Wright said, "and I'm certain Curt is, too. But I'm confident that he'll figure a way out of their predicament."

"Or so you hope," Ezra quietly added.

VII

"So what were the Old Ones doing here, you ask?" Ul Quorn left Oog in Otho's hands as he stepped out from beneath the tarp. "Well, I'll show you. Come."

He beckoned for the others to follow him over to where the excavations lay. When they got closer, Curt saw where it appeared that the sand and stones had been painstakingly shoveled aside, exposing what lay just beneath the surface. And it was here that he saw what countless archaeologists had dreamt of finding: evidence of a second Denebian presence in the solar system.

What appeared to be a half-dozen arches lay upon their sides, partially buried by the red silt beneath which they'd rested for countless millennia. Looking closer, Curt realized that they were actually rings that had broken apart, perhaps as they were toppling over from the vertical position they'd once occupied. Each was about ten feet in diameter, the outer surface smooth and rounded, the inner surface flat and grooved. Irregular markings upon the sides showed where something once had been etched, but had long since been rubbed clean by wind, sand, and time.

Ul Quorn said nothing, but only smiled and waited patiently while Curt knelt beside one of the broken rings and lightly ran his hand over it. Some compound of metal and stone, as improbable as it may seem; he wondered if it was the same metallic ore found in class-M asteroids. He looked about, noting the placement of the rings. Whatever they were, the rings had once stood in a row, much as if they were a tunnel or . . .

"A portal," he said quietly.

"Very good, Captain. An excellent deduction." Ul Quorn softly clapped his hands. "Yes, this was once a portal. A wormhole generator, or perhaps a matter transmitter. In any case, a conduit between worlds, maybe even the Denebian system itself."

"How can you be so sure?" Standing up, Curt made a show of brushing the sand off his hands. In the second that his back was turned to Ul Quorn, he raised his hand to the front of his parka and unzipped it. "It could be anything. A sculpture. A religious artifact. A broken laundry machine."

Joan laughed at this, but their captors weren't amused. "Blasphemer," one of the Sons of the Two Moons hissed angrily as he took a couple of steps toward Curt.

"Stop." The Magician of Mars raised his hand. "Forgive our guest. He will be only but the first to learn the error of his beliefs, when he's told the truth of the Old Ones."

Once again, the Sons briefly bowed their heads at the mention of the Old Ones. This was the distraction for which Curt had been waiting. In the second that he'd turned his back to Ul Quorn, and the Sons were looking down, he slipped his hand inside his parka and under the sweater he wore beneath it. His fingers found the disconnected power cord for his plasmar. A quick snap, and it was connected to the object he wore under his sweater.

Now he was ready. Another glance up at the sky. No sign of the *Comet* yet. He slid his hand out of his parka before anyone noticed.

"Deneb is almost three thousand light-years away," Curt said. "Even if they could build some sort of gateway to their homeworld, why would they want to do so? They didn't travel all this distance just to provide themselves with the means of getting home."

"They would if they were building an interstellar empire." Ul Quorn looked at him again; apparently he didn't notice that Curt's parka was unzipped. "And if that was their intent, and they were accustomed to strategic planning in terms of hundreds of millennia, why not provide the means for other races to do this for them? Visit a system, place a portal in a stable place on an inhabited world, provide clues as to where it can be found by a race that they estimate will eventually develop spacefaring capabilities, and then move on. That way, you don't have to build and maintain an empire—the empire builds itself and comes to you."

"That's the craziest thing I've ever—" Otho began, and shut up when he caught a threatening shove from the Son behind him.

"It's an intriguing idea," Curt said. "There's just one problem." He pointed to the ruins. "This isn't a functional portal. It hasn't been in many, many years."

"That's correct," Ul Quorn said, "but this isn't the only thing we found here." He pointed to another excavation, this one on the other side of the rings. "There's nothing there now but a hole," he continued, "but even before we discovered the portal, we discovered something even more important—another tablet of Denebian petroglyphs, this one more sophisticated than the ones left on the Moon. Once I finish translating it, I believe that it will provide me with all the information I need to build a second portal. And when this is accomplished—"

As he spoke, Ul Quorn turned away from Curt to address the Sons of the Two Moons gathered around them. "—We will meet our true masters, the Old Ones who came to these worlds when the human race was still in its infancy. We will request their aid in driving the men of Earth from the rest of the solar system, and in return we'll allow them to replace the Solar Coalition with the Denebian empire. We will become part of a galactic union older than recorded history, and thus achieve the destiny ordained by the Old Ones."

All around them, the Sons of the Two Moons touched fingers to foreheads and bowed in reverence. As they did, Curt happened to glance at Victor Corvo. The senator was staring at his son with horror and disbelief. At last, he'd come to realize what Curt already had: Ul Quorn, the Magician of Mars, was raving mad.

"You're out of your mind," Corvo said.

Hearing this, Ul Quorn turned to regard him silently for several long seconds before beckoning N'Rala to come closer. He whispered something in her ear, and she smiled, nodded, and walked away. Ul Quorn watched her go, then turned to Curt again.

"So, Curt . . . or Captain Future, as you may prefer—"

"My friends call me Curt. You can call me Captain Future."

"Perhaps that will change." Clasping his hands together behind his back, Ul Quorn walked closer until the two men were eye to eye. "I've told you everything you wished to know and then some, but I didn't do this out of braggadocio. I meant it earlier when I said that I've come to respect you. I'm also sympathetic to the fact that you desire revenge." He cocked his head toward Corvo. "He took from you even more than he took from me. I can't give that back to you, but I can give you something else—a place at my side, and a role in the empire that's soon to come."

"Curt—" Joan began.

"Be quiet," Ul Quorn said without looking at her, and the Son guarding Joan grabbed her arm hard enough to make her yelp. "I'll also spare the lives of your companions . . . or dispose of them, if that's what you prefer. Your choice."

"I see." Curt slowly nodded. "And if I choose not to accept your offer?"

"Then you'll find out how I make my foes disappear."

A meaningful glance in the direction of the nearby volcano vent was unnecessary but chilling nonetheless. Curt didn't reply but instead looked away, as if contemplating the choice that had been laid before him. He didn't dare look upward again. Ul Quorn might be out of his mind, but nonetheless he was quite intelligent, and he might begin to seriously wonder why Curt kept checking the sky. So Curt had to hope that the Brain had received his signals and he and Grag had followed his orders, and assume that the *Comet* was closing in. For if not . . .

"Ah . . . thank you, N'Rala," Ul Quorn said. "This will do nicely."

Curt looked back at Ul Quorn again, and discovered that N'Rala had just handed him a familiar object: the plasmar.

"Such an interesting weapon." Ul Quorn turned Curt's gun over in his hands, speculatively examining it. "It was brought to me from the King and Queen, and obviously it's not your usual firearm. On the other hand, my people have been unable to use it." He looked at Curt questioningly. "Can you tell me why?"

"It's a plasma toroid gun," Curt said. "Simon Wright and I invented it. It can't be fired because it needs to be plugged into an outside energy source, like the battery pack on my belt."

"Oh, so that's how it works." Ul Quorn juggled the gun for another moment or two, and then extended it to Curt. "Why don't you show me? Shoot my father."

"No!" Corvo went pale. "Son, you don't—!"

He tried to bolt, but the Sons stopped him before he could take more than a few steps. One of them threw his fist into the senator's stomach hard enough to sink him to his knees, then both aresians stepped aside, leaving Corvo on his own.

"This is my gift to you," Ul Quorn said, speaking as if Corvo's escape attempt was nothing more than a minor distraction. "My father's life, yours to take." He continued to offer Curt's gun to him. "Kill him. With my compliments."

Curt gazed at the plasmar for a moment, and then took it from Ul Quorn. Folding his arms together, the Magician of Mars stepped back. He seemed confident that Curt wouldn't turn his weapon on him, and he was right; Curt knew that if he so much as twitched in Ul Quorn's direction, the Sons would shoot him dead.

"Curt . . . don't do it," Joan said, her voice all but entirely muffled by her airmask.

He ignored her, and reached to his belt and uncoiled the spare power cord attached to it. He plugged the cord in the gun's butt; it made a soft whine, then a light on the stock flashed on, signaling that the plasmar was fully charged and ready to be fired.

Satisfied, Curt turned toward Corvo. He stared at the man who'd ordered the death of his father and mother for a long time, savoring the fear in his face. High above the craggy walls of the volcano's summit, a thin white streak was beginning to form in the sky, but he didn't notice this as he slid his left hand within his parka again while, at the same moment, he raised the gun in his right hand and leveled it at his target.

"Good-bye, Senator," Curt said.

And then he disappeared.

VIII

When Otho and Joan had taken the shuttle down from Port Deimos to meet him in Xanthe Terra, Curt had Otho bring an important piece of equipment: the portable fantome generator. Joan didn't know he had it with him, but Otho passed it to Curt in the duffel bag he'd carried through Martian customs. Curt had waited until they reached the Ascraeus tolou to strap the generator's halter beneath his sweater and parka. He'd delayed using it since then, intuitively knowing that the moment would come when he'd need it the most.

When he saw that moment coming, he'd surreptitiously plugged the power cable into the battery pack on his belt. Curt wouldn't be able to use both it and the plasmar at the same time—the power drain was too high—but he knew that he wouldn't need to *if* he timed everything just right. So when he pressed the button beneath his parka and pitch-black darkness suddenly closed upon him, he was already in motion.

He couldn't see anything, but he wasn't deaf to the bewildered and angry shouts from the aresians surrounding them. By then, he'd already ducked low and taken two steps to the left, away from the spot where he'd been standing when he'd become invisible and toward the place where Otho and Joan were being held.

"Fire!" Ul Quorn shouted. Curt could hear him just off to his right. "Shoot him!"

"Shoot where?" This from an aresian to his left. "We can't see—"

"Shoot the place where he was!"

Crouching low, Curt raised his gun and pointed it in the direction of the second voice, judging it to belong to one of the Sons who were guarding Joan and Otho. Sure enough, a moment later he heard the static *fzzt!* of a particle-beam rifle being fired, followed almost instantly by another shot from what he presumed was the second guard. The fact that he was still alive was enough evidence that they'd both missed.

Curt was ready. Still aiming the gun in that direction, he used his free hand to switch off the fantome generator. The darkness vanished the instant he squeezed the trigger. Neither of the Sons had time to re-act to his sudden reappearance several feet from where he'd last been seen before first one, then the other, were knocked off their feet by translucent rings of plasma energy.

"Grab their guns!" Curt yelled. "Get Corvo!"

Joan didn't hesitate; she dove for one of the rifles dropped by the guards and, snatching it up, whipped around to open fire on the other aresians. Somehow, Otho had already managed to get his hands on another rifle. He didn't fire it, though, but instead held Corvo at bay. Still on his hands and knees, the senator was bewildered by everything that had just happened, not making an effort to flee even when he had the chance.

For the moment, Corvo was the least of Curt's concerns. The Sons had recovered from their surprise, and several were already rushing to put themselves between him and Ul Quorn. "Kill them all!" the Magician shouted, pointing at him, Otho, and Joan. "I want them dead!"

Curt dropped two aresians aiming at him, and Joan was protecting herself and Otho. For some reason, Otho still hadn't fired his weapon; still keeping it pointed at Corvo, he was blindly groping for the rifle dropped by the Son who'd been guarding him. Curt didn't have time to wonder why. More cultists were charging from the camp, and as fast as he and Joan could shoot them down, their brethren were taking their places.

Curt was about to go invisible again when something caught his eye: a white streak forming in the sky above the caldera. He didn't need to wonder what was causing this; it could only be one thing. And it was only a matter of minutes, and precious few at that, before it would come down on top of them.

No time for any more tricks. They had to get out at once.

"Joan, head for the plane!" Still firing, Curt backpedaled toward the aircraft he'd spotted earlier, parked on the landing pad on the outskirts of the camp. "Otho, grab Corvo!"

Otho gave up trying to retrieve the abandoned weapon. He took hold of the back of Corvo's parka and yanked him to his feet. "You're coming with us, Senator!" he snarled as he shoved the barrel of the rifle in his hands against the back of Corvo's neck. Frightened out of his wits, Corvo did as he was told.

"What about Ul Quorn?" Joan was running sideways toward the aircraft, still firing at any aresian who presented himself or herself as a target.

Curt couldn't see Ul Quorn or N'Rala either. Then he looked around and spotted them both. They were running from the camp . . . but strangely, in opposite directions. While N'Rala sprinted in the direction of the landing pad, UI Quorn was heading for the vent.

Had they seen the approaching vapor trail and, figuring out what was about to happen, lost faith in each other and run wherever their legs could carry them? N'Rala meant little to him, but as much as Curt wanted to capture Ul Quorn—after all, it wasn't Victor Corvo who was the true nemesis here, but rather his son—there was no time to do so. For a few seconds, there was a lull in combat as the remaining cult members sought cover behind anything big enough to hide them. Curt took advantage of the break to make a dash for the aircraft, with Joan right behind him and still firing at the Sons.

Otho and Corvo reached the aircraft before either of them. Otho twisted open the canopy hatch and stood aside. "Okay, Senator, into the plane!" he snapped, prodding him with his gun to encourage him. "Move it!"

Corvo numbly obeyed and clambered into the rear seat. "We could've used your help," Joan said to Otho when she and Curt caught up with them a few seconds later. "Why didn't you fire?"

In response, Otho smiled and closed his eyes. A second passed, then Curt watched in astonishment as the rifle in Otho's hands melted, reshaping itself into the small Denebian mimic Ul Quorn had given him.

"Better than nothing," Otho said as Oog nestled within his arms. "And it fooled nimrod here, didn't it?" Seeing this, Corvo groaned.

"That's cute, but we need to get out of here." Joan looked back toward the camp. The remaining Sons had regained their courage and were coming out from under cover; no doubt they'd make another attempt to swarm their former prisoners. "I'm flying," she said as she handed her gun to Otho and scrambled for the pilot's seat.

Curt didn't argue. The white streak in the sky was nearly directly above the volcano and was now showing a reddish-orange head. The *Comet* itself was still invisible, but its engine exhaust was not. He fired a couple of last shots, taking down the two closest cultists in the mob running toward them, then ran around to the other side of the aircraft and threw himself into the front passenger seat, slamming the hatch shut after him.

In seconds, the broad-winged aircraft was airborne, its vertical ascent engines kicking up dust as it lifted off from the caldera. "Get us out of here!" Curt snapped. "We need altitude, fast!"

"What are you—?" Joan began

"*Punch it!*" Curt wasn't strapped in. He held his seat frame as tightly as he could and prayed that he wouldn't get thrown from the aircraft. As it stood on its tail and clawed for the sky, he turned his head to gaze out the window beside him.

In the final seconds before impact, the *Comet* became visible, a teardrop-shaped missile hurtling toward the ground below. The Sons of the Two Moons had finally spotted what was coming their way. In panic, they ran in all directions, a futile attempt to escape the inevitable. At the last instant, Curt caught a glimpse of a tall, robed figure poised at the lip of the vent and staring up at the sky: Ul Quorn, watching the *Comet* coming down on top of him and his followers . . .

And then he turned and threw himself headlong into the dark and bottomless pit.

Curt was still staring at what the Magician of Mars had just done when the *Comet* plunged into Ascraeus Mons.

The gaseous argon of its fuel mixture, an ion plasma one million degrees Kelvin, was normally contained only by the superconducting magnetosphere of its engine core. When the little racing yacht slammed into the center of Ul Quorn's hidden camp, the engine ruptured and everything that had been within it detonated like a miniature sun.

In that instant, for the first time in millions of years, there was fire on the mountain.

IX

The raid on the Ascraeus tolou was over.

On the screens lining the walls of *Vigilance*'s combat information center, Solar Guard forces stood upon the balconies and catwalks, assault rifles cradled in their arms. Behind them, nylon cords dangled like vines, the ziplines by which the raiders had rappelled into the pit. At the bottom of the pit, soldiers stood guard over prisoners kneeling outside the King and Queen of the Desert, while more soldiers and IPF inspectors ventured into the lava tube in search of the arms caches. Outside the tolou, IPF shuttles waited to take aboard the prisoners deemed worth further interrogation.

There had been casualties on both sides, but not as many as might have been expected. As fortuitous happenstance would have it, the raid had commenced the same minute the *Comet* crashed into Mons Ascraeus. The inhabitants, most of whom either belonged to Starry Messenger or were sympathizers, were still wondering why the ground was shaking when armed soldiers began dropping into their midst. Only a handful managed to grab their guns, and most of them didn't do so fast enough. Their bodies lay where they'd fallen, hastily covered with blankets by family and friends.

"We've shut down a major Starry Messenger nest." Captain Henniker stood in the center of the CIC, observing the mop-up operations being supervised by the officers seated around her. "From what your people tell us, they've found enough weapons down there to supply a full-fledged revolution. If Ul Quorn hadn't been stopped—"

"It would've been bloody as hell, that's for sure." Ezra Gurney slowly nodded, then looked over at Curt. "You're responsible for this . . . you know that, right?"

Curt managed an offhand shrug. "I just wish we'd been able to shut them down entirely, the way we did in the caldera."

"You mean, the way *you* shut them down." A wry smile appeared beneath Ezra's mustache. "The blast wiped out every damn thing in the volcano . . . there was nothin' left standing when we sent another plane down there. Maybe we ain't done with Starry Messenger, much as we'd like to think so, but the Sons of the Two Moons are toast."

"No pun intended," E.J. quietly added.

Ezra chuckled at his own unintentional and rather macabre joke, but Curt wasn't smiling. It had been only a few hours ago that he'd landed the plane outside the Tharsis Ridge atmosphere plant, where a shuttle was waiting to transport him and the others up to the *Vigilance*. Since then, he hadn't gotten a chance to rest. Otho, Grag, and the Brain were waiting for him in the cruiser's passenger quarters, and he hadn't seen Joan again since she'd gone away to be debriefed. His own interrogation had occurred here in this room, where he'd told Captain Henniker's officers to send the raiding party into the lava tube once they succeeded in taking control of the tolou.

He was tired, yes, but that wasn't all. He was also disappointed.

"Still no sign of Ul Quorn?" he asked.

E.J. gave him a curious look. "Why do you think there would be? You told us he took a swan dive into the vent. He's probably still falling. I mean, he wasn't kidding when he said it probably leads to the planet's core."

"Yes, I know, but . . ." Curt shook his head. "He didn't strike me as the suicidal type. And I don't know what happened to N'Rala. The last I saw her, she was running toward the landing pad."

"You think she managed to escape? Or even help her master?"

Curt didn't answer E.J. at once. Instead, he stepped a little closer to the bank of screens displaying images from the volcano caldera and looked closer. As Ezra said, the blast had obliterated just about everything in the camp: tents, equipment, and people. Apparently the

Denebian artifacts had been lost along with his father's ship, and he knew that both sacrifices would haunt him for years to come.

Bringing down the *Comet*, though, was the only way he could've saved his life and the lives of his friends. Even if he'd agreed to join Ul Quorn, he had little doubt that the Magician of Mars would have murdered Otho and Joan . . . and inevitably Curt himself, once he'd outlived whatever useful purpose Ul Quorn had in mind for him. A person who'd betray his own father could never be trusted by anyone.

Everything in the camp had apparently been destroyed. Yet amid all those twisted and incinerated remains, there was nothing that even vaguely resembled the air raft that had been used to transport him and the others up the vent from the lava tube.

"I think it's possible," he quietly replied.

He was exhausted and his body craved rest, but there was still one thing he had to do. He needed to pay a visit to the brig.

Captain Henniker had issued firm orders that no one was to speak with Victor Corvo before the *Vigilance* reached Earth. She didn't want to risk having anyone in the ship's crew who might be loyal to the senator being swayed by him. She made an exception for Curt, though, so Ezra escorted him two decks down to the brig, where a soldier had been posted outside.

The Solar Guard ensign snapped to attention at Curt's approach and gave him a brisk salute. Curt fumbled to respond in kind. This was the third or fourth time he'd been saluted since returning to the *Vigilance*. Not only that, but on a couple of occasions he'd overheard crewmen referring to him as Captain Future. Curt didn't know if he was ready to be treated as a hero yet, but he had to admit that it was better than being regarded as a suspect or a castaway.

Ezra hesitated a moment before unlocking the door. "Should I take that away from you?" He cast a meaningful glance at Curt's plasmar, which rested in its holster on his belt.

"No." Curt shook his head. "That's nothing you need to worry about. And I'd prefer to keep it with me, if you don't mind."

Ezra's mouth tightened. "Well, all right, then . . . would you like for me to stay?"

"No, I'll be fine—but I'd like to see him alone, please."

The marshal nodded, then pushed his thumb against the lockplate.

There was a click; he grasped the handle, twisted it, and pushed the door open. "Okay, here you be . . . but for just a minute, okay?" Curt nodded in agreement, and Ezra moved aside to let him go in.

Victor Corvo sat on a fold-down bunk in a tiny room with no other amenities save for a seatless toilet and a small metal sink. He was unshaven and hollow-cheeked, with dark circles beneath his eyes, and didn't look as if he'd had any more sleep than Curt had. The clothes he'd been wearing were gone; all he wore now were disposable orange overalls and paper slippers. Corvo had risen to his feet when the door was unlocked, but when he'd seen who was visiting him his legs had given way beneath him and he'd collapsed back upon the bunk.

"You," Corvo said, his voice little more than a dull murmur. "I thought it might be—" He looked down at the floor and shook his head. "But of course, it would be you."

"Hello, Senator." It was all Curt could manage. Everything he thought he'd like to say to this man was forgotten in that instant. Despite the promise he'd made to Ezra, though, his right hand involuntarily twitched beside his holster.

Corvo apparently noticed this, because a humorless smirk appeared upon his face. "Is that why you're here?" he asked, cocking his head toward Curt's gun. "To take care of unfinished business? You had one chance already . . . why not give yourself another?"

He almost seemed to welcome the possibility of death. Curt was glad Corvo had made that remark, though. It reminded him of what he'd meant to say.

"No," he said, "that's not why I've come."

Hands at his sides, he regarded Corvo with eyes as cold and gray as a sea just before a storm. "When we first met, when I first came to find you, it was to put an end to your life. That was what I wanted—revenge, pure and simple. But even though I grew up hating those who'd killed my father and mother, a friend of mine has taught me something I'd never learned. Revenge and justice are not one and the same, and given a choice between the two, one should choose justice." He almost said *always*, but checked himself. He still wasn't sure of that.

"So you're not going to kill me?" Corvo was surprised, perhaps even disappointed.

"No. Your life is not mine to take. Instead, you're going back to Earth, where I've been told that you'll be incarcerated for a good long time before you finally stand trial. And when you do, it will be not only for conspiring in the attempt on President Carthew's life and the planned insurrection on Mars, but also for the murder of my parents."

"I'll get lawyers—"

"I'm sure you will, for all the good they'll do you. I have little doubt that you'll be convicted. And when it's all over and done, you'll no longer be a senator and you'll no longer be rich. You'll just be another guy in orange pajamas with a number on the back, living the rest of your life in a miserable little cell on Pluto, as far away from everything that once mattered to you as you can get."

Curt paused. "And when someone asks you how you got there," he quietly finished, "I hope you'll tell them about me, and give them my name."

Without another word, Curt turned, opened the door, and walked out of the room.

XI

Much to Curt's surprise, Ezra had left. Instead, Joan was waiting for him in the corridor.

"Did you say to him what you needed to say?" She'd cleaned up quite a bit since he'd last seen her. The civilian clothes were gone, and instead she wore the dark blue uniform of an IPF officer.

"Yeah . . . yeah, I did." Curt slowly let out his breath. All of a sudden, it felt as if a weight had been lifted from him. One that had been on his shoulders his entire life. "I told him . . . well, pretty much what you'd said to me." He looked into her dark eyes and smiled. "Thank you. That was something I didn't know I needed to learn."

Joan didn't reply at once, but instead fell in step beside him as he started walking down the corridor. "Life is all about learning," she said after a moment. "But some things are easier to learn than others."

It sounded a little like she was leading up to something. "Such as . . . ?"

"Nothing." She slowly shook her head. "Nothing that you need to worry about just now." Then, unexpectedly, she rose on her toes to give him a kiss on the cheek. "Maybe you've got a lot to learn," she finished, taking advantage of his surprise to take his hand and link her arm with his, "but I think you've got promise."

EPILOGUE
The Coming of the Futuremen

Government Tower rose above the canals of Manhattan as a sleek glass pylon that dwarfed New York's other skyscrapers. Built on the site of the old United Nations Plaza, the immense, 250-story edifice had served as the center of government for the Solar Coalition for nearly a century. When the representatives of the different worlds of the solar system convened to discuss matters of state, it was here that they came.

As the IPF shuttle descended upon the rooftop landing pad, the squad of Solar Guard soldiers in dress blacks came to attention. Heels together, ceremonial rifles presented, they stood stiffly on either side of a red carpet running across the roof from the painted circle where the spacecraft touched down. The soldiers never blinked, but instead continued to stare straight ahead, as the passenger hatch opened and Curt stepped out onto the landing stairs. He paused to take in the sight of the honor guard standing at attention, then slowly let out his breath.

"I don't think I could get used to this," he murmured.

"I could." Behind him, Otho was grinning broadly. "Last week, we were bums. Now we're heroes. I think I like being a hero better."

Perched on his shoulder, the Denebian mime he'd adopted squirmed and purred its name—the only sound it ever made—with what could only be interpreted as contentment. "Are you sure you should be carrying that?" Simon asked, his eyestalks studying Oog as he floated through the hatch behind them. "If it assumes the wrong shape while we're here, like a gun . . ."

"Relax. It only did that once, back on Mars, and that was when I needed him to look like a weapon. Oog won't turn into something else until I tell him . . . isn't that right, Bolts-for-Brains?"

"That wasn't a good joke." Grag lowered its head and shoulders as it came through the hatch. "Poor Eek was confused."

As if in agreement, the little moonpup trotting alongside his master peered up at Oog and gave a soft but menacing growl. In response, the mime's amorphous form shifted shape, size, and color, once again becoming Eek's identical twin. The little dog's growl became a ferocious bark even as he sought cover behind the boots of the nearest soldier, who continued to stolidly stare straight ahead.

"Maybe we should have left them both on the Moon," the Brain said.

"You idiots!" Curt hissed as he looked over his shoulder at Otho and Grag. "Get 'em under control or I'll call the nearest humane society!"

" 'You idiots' . . . oh, really?" Otho scowled at him in a half-mocking way as they marched down the red carpet. "Getting a little full of yourself, aren't you, Captain Future?"

Curt didn't have a chance to answer. As they reached the end of the carpet, a dark-skinned young man in a collarless morning coat and pinstriped ascot appeared. "Captain Future?" he asked, holding out a white-gloved hand. "I'm North Bonnell, the president's personal assistant. I trust you had a good flight, yes?" He didn't wait for a reply, but only briefly grasped Curt's hand before turning to the elevator behind them. "Very well, if you'll follow me . . ."

The elevator ride was short. Just one level down was Government Tower's top floor, the offices of the president of the Solar Coalition. Plainclothes IPF security agents were waiting for them, but they didn't catch Curt's attention. In that moment, the only person who mattered to him was the dark-haired young woman in the full dress uniform who smiled as the elevator doors slid open.

"Hello, Curt," Joan said. "Good to see you again."

"Yeah. You, too." From the corner of his eye, Curt saw Otho silently regarding him and Joan with an unfathomable expression. He'd noticed, of course, that the two of them had spent a lot of time together on the way back from Mars. While Otho hadn't voiced any objections, Curt had a feeling that he was jealous as only a lifelong friend can become, while the Brain was plainly concerned that a woman might distract him from . . .

Well, what exactly? Victor Corvo had been brought to justice. The task for which Simon, Otho, and Grag had spent a lifetime training him was complete. What was he going to do now? If only the Denebian tablet Ul Quorn had discovered at Mons Ascraeus could be found. Now that the significance of the Dancing Denebians had been revealed, Curt and Simon might be able to figure out how the portal of the Old Ones worked.

"President Carthew will see you now." Unnoticed, Bonnell had disappeared into an inner office. Holding open the oak-paneled door, he bowed formally as he invited his guests into the president's chambers.

Curt took a deep breath. Much to his own surprise, he realized that he was nervous. Then a soft hand briefly touched his own, and he looked around to find Joan gazing at him with what seemed to be barely concealed amusement.

"Don't be nervous," she said quietly. "You're going to like this . . . I promise."

On the other side of an enormous office, President Carthew stood up from behind his desk, the top surface of which, as legend had it, was fashioned from the lower stage of the Apollo 17 lunar lander from the twentieth century. "Curt Newton . . . a pleasure to see you again, sir," he said, walking around the desk to extend a hand. "And thank you for bringing your—what in God's name is that?"

"A Denebian mime, Mr. President." Otho grinned proudly, evidently enjoying Carthew's reaction to the creature curled around his shoulders. "Something we got on Mars. A parting gift from Ul Quorn."

"Yes . . . so I see." Carthew was visibly repelled. Curt tried not to smile. At least Oog wasn't growling at him the way Eek was. The moonpup recognized the president at once, and clearly hadn't forgotten Corvo's training. Perhaps they *should* have left the pets behind after they'd made a brief stop at Tycho Base on the way to Earth.

"Looks like your crew is getting bigger all the time, Cap." The voice that spoke up from behind him was both familiar and expected. Turning around, Curt found Ezra Gurney seated in an armchair. Apparently he'd arrived earlier with Joan; Curt guessed that they'd already briefed the president about what had happened on Mars.

"If that's the case, then perhaps you'll need them." President Carthew shook Curt's hand, then nodded to other seats facing his desk, behind which the gleaming New York skyline extended all the way out to Battery Pier and the harbor beyond. "Please be seated, all of you," he added, with an uncertain glance in Simon's direction. "I have a proposition for you."

When everyone except Grag and the Brain had taken seats, Carthew returned to his chair. "Curt, when we met a couple of weeks ago, you identified yourself to me as sort of a troubleshooter. I know now, of course, that this wasn't entirely true."

"Yes, sir, Mr. President," Curt replied. "I apologize to you for lying, but I—"

"Don't apologize. I understand completely." Carthew made a casual flip of his hand. "I'm very glad I placed my trust in you. Not only did you verify the truth behind Senator Corvo's scheme, but you also unearthed a far more dangerous plot that could have put the entire Coalition in danger, perhaps even sparked a war. For this, you have not only my own gratitude, but also that of every Solar Coalition citizen."

Curt started to speak, but Carthew raised his hand again. "Let me finish, please. I've discussed this matter in detail with Marshal Gurney and Inspector Randall, and also with their superiors, and we've agreed that the IPF's association with you and your crew shouldn't end here. Perhaps there's a role for a troubleshooter after all, Curt . . . or better, Captain Future."

Curt felt his face growing warm. "To be honest, Mr. President, I've never been entirely comfortable with that name. It's a long story how I got it, but . . . well, I'd just as soon that people didn't use it."

Carthew nodded sympathetically. "I understand. To be candid, I've never been comfortable with people always calling me Mr. President. If I thought I could get away with it, I'd have people address me as Jim." He shook his head. "But names like this aren't for our benefit, Curt. They're for the benefit of others. People need a leader to look up to, and they show that respect by addressing him or her as Mr. President. And even in these times—*especially* in these times—they need a hero. Someone they can call Captain Future."

Otho pointedly cleared his throat, and Carthew glanced in his direction. "I was thinking that the 'Futuremen' might be suitable for your companions," he added, and Otho responded with a thumbs-up.

"Captain Future and his Futuremen." Repeating this, Curt couldn't help but smile at the absurdity of the name. He hoped it wouldn't be used often, although he had a sneaking suspicion that it would. "And you say you'd want us to be—"

"Troubleshooters." Ezra steepled his fingers together. "Sort of an unofficial independent unit for the IPF, taking on cases where we can't get involved without someone investigating them first. Or maybe just a good, hard fist when the Coalition needs it."

"We'll supply you with a new ship," Carthew continued. "In fact, we can build one with the same warp-drive capability that Solar Guard ships now have. You'll have a budget to draw upon, and you can continue working out of your base of operations in Tycho, which will become a classified installation. When you're not working for us, you're free to pursue your own interests."

"And who would we report to?" Simon asked.

"I'm gonna be your IPF liaison," Ezra said. "As for Inspector Randall here, she's being promoted to captain and permanently reassigned as your case officer."

He was grinning as he said this, and a sly wink told Curt that the old lawman knew more than he'd thought he did. Curt glanced at Joan, and although she was carefully maintaining a neutral expression, the brightness in her eyes told him that she was looking forward to her new role.

And as for himself?

Curt gazed out the window for a moment, thinking about all that laid behind, all that possibly lay ahead. He considered what the president had said about how people needed a hero. He'd never set out to become one, but perhaps this was what he was meant to do.

"Very well, then," he said. "If this is what you want, then this is what I'll do my best to be." He took a deep breath, slowly let it out. "I'm Captain Future."

Afterword

When I was eleven years old, I met Captain Future in a drugstore in Franklin, Tennessee.

Franklin was my father's hometown, where my grandmother still lived. Every couple of weeks or so, we'd go see her. On one of these visits, we went to a drugstore on Main Street to get a few things for her, and while Papa did his business at the prescription counter I combed through the paperback spinner rack in search of something interesting to read—which, for me, was usually a science fiction book.

On this particular Sunday afternoon in 1969, that turned out to be a Popular Library paperback whose cover featured a menacing robot lying prone on a lunar surface, firing a laser rifle straight at the reader. This was *Outlaws of the Moon* by Edmond Hamilton, and who could resist? Not me. I begged Papa for sixty cents to buy the thing, and despite his better judgment—why couldn't his son be interested in football instead?—my father relented, and the rest of my visit to Gran's house was spent with my nose in that book.

Outlaws of the Moon wasn't the greatest science fiction novel I'd ever read (and by the time I'd reached the sixth grade, I'd already read a lot of SF and fantasy). With the Apollo 11 only a few months away from achieving the first lunar landing, I could tell at once that the story was very dated; a 1942 publication date on the copyright page confirmed that the novel was twenty-seven years old. It was clearly written long before the Space Age, when it was still possible for a writer to portray the moon as being secretly inhabited by underground denizens.

But it didn't matter, really. This was one of those swashbuckling space adventure stories I couldn't get enough of (really, I couldn't . . .

space opera wasn't in vogue at that time), and it was also my introduction to Curt Newton and his odd band, the Futuremen. Over the next several years, even while I discovered the paperback reprints of other Depression-era heroes—Doc Savage, Conan, the Shadow, the Spider, the Avenger, G-8 and his Battle Aces—I kept coming back to Captain Future, the most science-fictional of all those pulp adventurers of a period that was gone long before I was born.

I grew out of pulp fiction, as most young readers eventually do, and moved on to more adult fare. But I never completely lost interest in the pulps. Over the years, I'd continue to occasionally dip into a Shadow or Doc Savage paperback, on the theory that you can't read serious literature all the time without becoming jaded, but mainly because this stuff is just plain fun. And once I became an SF writer myself, it wasn't long before I wrote a satirical homage to one of my favorites, a novella titled "The Death of Captain Future."

This story was very well received when it came out; it won the Hugo and Seiun Awards and was nominated for the Nebula, and since then has been reprinted and translated numerous times. It wasn't really about Curt Newton and the Futuremen, though, but instead the way a fan's devotion can be carried to an extreme. A couple of years later, I wrote a sequel, "The Exile of Evening Star," that was an attempt to produce a space adventure that was more representative of the pulp era. However, readers didn't take to it as well as they did to the first story, and after a while it occurred to me that the only way to truly write something like a Captain Future story was . . . well, to write a Captain Future story.

Avengers of the Moon is the first new, authorized Captain Future story since "Birthplace of Creation" appeared in the May 1951 issue of *Startling Stories* (along with an editorial sidebar, "Well Done and Farewell," announcing that the series was taking "an indefinite leave of absence"). It is neither an homage to the Hamilton novels nor a parody, but rather an effort to bring Captain Future into the twenty-first century for a new generation of readers.

In order to do this, it was necessary to completely revise and update the characters and situations created by Hamilton. If one relies on the internal chronology of the original series, the first novel, *Captain Future and the Space Emperor* (published in the inaugural Winter 1940 issue of *Captain Future*), takes place in the far-distant year of 2015. When those novels were written over seventy years ago, nearly everything we knew about the solar system was what could be observed through the lens of a telescope, and the most advanced rockets were the V-2 missiles being built by the German army. Much has changed since then, and although some purists may object, I decided that it was more important to bring the series in line with the science and technology of our century than to be consistent with the 1940s version.

At the same time, though, I've sought to maintain the spirit of the original. So, while developing this novel, I re-read the Hamilton novels and stories (whenever possible, in their first magazine publication in *Captain Future* and *Startling Stories*) and took extensive notes. As a result, the springboard for this novel is the "origin story" related in Chapter II of *The Space Emperor* and also the unpublished chapters of the same reprinted in *The Captain Future Handbook* by Chuck Juzek (a useful reference for everything about this character). Added to this revised and greatly expanded backstory is Curt Newton's archnemesis Ul Quorn, who was introduced in *Captain Future and the Seven Space Stones* (*Captain Future*, Winter 1941) and reappeared in *The Magician of Mars* (*Captain Future*, Summer 1941) and *The Solar Invasion* (*Startling Stories*, Fall 1946), the last written by Manly Wade Wellman and one of three canonical Captain Future stories not authored by Hamilton.

The one place where I directly quoted Hamilton are the three songs quoted in Part Four, which appeared in various stories over the course of the series. In most places, I took Hamilton's creations, revised and updated them, and combined them with those of my own, much the same way Ian Fleming's James Bond and Sir Arthur Conan Doyle's Sherlock Holmes have been revised and updated by later writers. And while I'm aware of the 1970s Japanese anime version, I deliberately avoided any reference to this and instead took my inspiration entirely from the pulp stories. Therefore, Otho is not a comic relief sidekick renamed Otto, the Brain is not a robot, Grag is not stupid, Joan is not a helpless blonde, and kid sidekick Ken Scott doesn't exist.

There are many people who need to be thanked for helping me make this novel possible:

David Hartwell, my late editor at Tor, for expressing interest in a new Captain Future novel and encouraging me to write it, and my new editor, Jennifer Gunnels, for a fine and insightful critique of the novel's original draft.

Eleanor Wood of the Spectrum Literary Agency, Edmond Hamilton's literary executor, and my own agent, Martha Millard, for negotiating a formal arrangement with the Huntington National Bank, the Trustee for the Estate of Edmond Hamilton, for allowing me to use the characters and situations of the original Captain Future novels in this authorized continuation.

Stephen Haffner of Haffner Press, publisher of *The Collected Captain Future*, for helping me trace the copyright ownership.

Rob Caswell for reading the novel while it was being written and offering valuable criticism, and also updating the *Comet* while sticking close to the original hull design.

Ron Miller for information about the Straight Wall and sending me a copy of his painting of the same.

Dr. Young K. Bae for an intriguing conversation several years ago at the 100 Year Starship Conference about his concept of a photon railroad.

Doug Beason, Wil McCarthy, Geoffrey Landis, Jeffrey Kooistra, Larry Niven, G. David Nordley, and Arlan Andrews, my colleagues at the Sigma group, for brainstorming the plasma-toroid gun (aka "plasmar") I gave Curt Newton in homage to the "smoke-gun" ray gun depicted on the covers of the original Captain Future pulps.

The staff at Gary Dolgoff Comics in Easthampton, Massachusetts, for allowing me to search their extensive magazine collection for copies of *Captain Future* and *Startling Stories*.

And finally, as always, my wife, Linda, who has supported my writing for so many years, even mad projects such as this.

—*Allen Steele*
Whately, Massachusetts,
December 2014–November 2015